SHAKESPEARE AND
HIS CRITICS

The Workes of William Shakespeare,

containing all his Comedies, Histories, and Tragedies: Truely set forth, according to their first
ORIGINALL.

The Names of the Principall Actors
in all these Playes.

William Shakespeare.

Richard Burbadge.

John Hemmings.

Augustine Phillips

William Kempt.

Thomas Poope.

George Bryan.

Henry Condell.

William Slye.

Richard Cowly.

John Lowine.

Samuell Crosse.

Alexander Cooke.

Samuel Gilburne.

Robert Armin.

William Ostler.

Nathan Field.

John Underwood.

Nicholas Tooley.

William Ecclestone.

Joseph Taylor.

Robert Benfield.

Robert Goughe.

Richard Robinson.

Iohn Shancke.

Iohn Rice.

ACTORS' LIST FROM THE FIRST FOLIO

SHAKESPEARE AND HIS CRITICS

F. E. HALLIDAY

When a poet is a great poet as Shakespeare is,
we cannot judge of his greatness unaided; we
need both the opinions of other poets, and the
diverse views of critics who were not poets, in
order to help us to understand.

T. S. ELIOT

SCHOCKEN BOOKS · NEW YORK

First Schocken Paperback edition, 1963

Library of Congress Catalog Card Number: 63-11039
This edition published by arrangement with
Gerald Duckworth & Co., Ltd., London.
Manufactured in the United States of America

CONTENTS

LIST OF ILLUSTRATIONS

PREFACE

THOUSANDS and thousands of books have been written about Shakespeare, and most of them are mad', wrote Logan Pearsall Smith. But whatever the faults of the present work I do not think that it can fairly be charged with a lack of sanity. I have no particular axe to grind, unless a defence of the few articles in a simple and orthodox creed can be interpreted as such. I believe that Shakespeare was the author of the works attributed to him by his friends Heminge and Condell, and that with the exception of relatively few passages and scenes he wrote everything in the thirty-six plays of the First Folio; and I believe that Shakespeare is the greatest poet and dramatist who has ever written, certainly in English, probably in any language.

A creed, however, will not justify a book, least of all will it justify another book on Shakespeare. The justification of this work lies not so much in the originality of the matter itself—though even here, perhaps, some originality may be allowed—as in its arrangement, in the assembly of material that, so far as I know, has never before been brought together in one volume. There are books devoted to Shakespearean scholarship and to æsthetic appreciation, there are numerous anthologies of Shakespeare's poetry, and some of Shakespearean criticism, but none that draws all these elements together within a comparatively small compass. Nor, I think, is there any other book that illuminates as it were in the round each play and poem by the criticism that falls on it from the various angles of three centuries. For, in the words of Mr. T. S. Eliot, 'when a poet is a great poet as Shakespeare is, we cannot judge of his greatness unaided; we need both the opinions of other poets, and the diverse views of critics who were not poets, in order to help us to understand'.

F. E. H.

1947

PREFACE TO THE REVISED EDITION

IT should be stated at once that this edition of *Shakespeare and his Critics* is a reprint of Part Two only of the original book, though it is, as Shakespeare's publishers would have put it, a Part Two 'newly corrected, amended, and (considerably) augmented'.

Two impressions having been exhausted and the type broken up, there were two alternatives: either to reprint the book approximately in its original form, or to reprint a revised version of the second part. The latter alternative has been adopted for a number of reasons. The expense of resetting the whole would have been virtually prohibitive. Then, in the last ten years I have covered more fully in a number of books most of the matter in Part One. Finally, Part Two remains, as far as I know, unique in scope: a history of Shakespeare criticism, an anthology of general Shakespeare criticism from Elizabethan to neo-Elizabethan times, and an anthology of representative criticism of each play from the Restoration to the present day.

Although the original book was published in 1949, it was begun in the last year of the war and finished in 1947—which is one reason why my essay on Shakespearean Critics and the sequent critical anthologies ended round about 1935. When I wrote, Shakespeare criticism as well as the world as a whole was in a state of flux, and the developing pattern was far from clear. Moreover, the book ran to more than five hundred closely printed pages, and the cost of copyright material was already sufficiently heavy.

Now, however, by jettisoning the first half it has been possible to add about a hundred pages of recent criticism and bring out the other half at a reasonable price. The second part of my introductory essay has also been expanded, brought up to date, and completely rewritten, and the rest of the material carefully revised.

For various reasons it has been thought best to retain the title *Shakespeare and his Critics*, and if anybody buys the book under the impression that it is the original one I hope he will be agreeably surprised, finding the additions far more valuable, as I believe they are, than the omissions.

F. E. H.

St. Ives
Cornwall
13 July 1957

ACKNOWLEDGMENTS

I AM grateful to the following authors and publishers for their permission to quote extracts from copyright work: the Clarendon Press (*William Shakespeare: A Study of Facts and Problems* by Sir Edmund Chambers; *The Approach to Shakespeare* by J. W. Mackail); the Oxford University Press ('Tolstoy's *Shakespeare and the Drama; Landmarks in French Literature* by Lytton Strachey); Mr. John Masefield and the Oxford University Press (*William Shakespeare*); Professor G. Wilson Knight and the Oxford University Press (*The Wheel of Fire* and *The Crown of Life*); Professor O. J. Campbell and the Oxford University Press (*Shakespeare's Satire*); Professor Dover Wilson and the Cambridge University Press (*Introduction to Much Ado About Nothing; What Happens in Hamlet*); Professor E. E. Stoll and the Cambridge University Press (*Art and Artifice in Shakespeare*); the Cambridge University Press (*Shakespeare's Imagery* by Caroline Spurgeon); Professor H. B. Charlton and the Cambridge University Press (*Shakespearian Tragedy*); Messrs. Ernest Benn Ltd. (*Shakespeare's Workmanship* by Sir Arthur Quiller-Couch); Messrs. Constable and Co. Ltd. (*On Reading Shakespeare* by Logan Pearsall Smith); The Public Trustee and the Society of Authors (*Cymbeline Refinished* by Bernard Shaw); Professor L. L. Schücking and Messrs. G. G. Harrap and Co. Ltd. (*Character Problems in Shakespeare's Plays*); Messrs. G. G. Harrap and Co. Ltd. (*The Contemporary Theatre* by James Agate); Dame Edith Sitwell and Messrs. Macmillan and Co. Ltd. (*A Notebook on William Shakespeare*); Messrs. Macmillan and Co. Ltd. (*Shakespearean Tragedy* by A. C. Bradley; *Shakespeare* by Sir Walter Raleigh); Mr. T. S. Eliot and Messrs. Faber and Faber Ltd. (*Selected Essays*); Messrs. William Heinemann Ltd. (*A Study of Shakespeare* by A. C. Swinburne; *William Shakespeare* by Georg Brandes); Mr. Mark van Doren and Messrs. George Allen and Unwin Ltd. (*Shakespeare*); Messrs. George Allen and Unwin Ltd. (*Ariosto, Shakespeare and Corneille* by Benedetto Croce); Messrs. Wm. Collins, Sons and Co. Ltd. (*Countries of the Mind* by Middleton Murry); Messrs. Sidgwick and Jackson Ltd. (*Shakespeare: A Survey* by Sir Edmund Chambers; *Prefaces to Shakespeare* by Harley Granville-Barker); Messrs. Routledge and Kegan Paul Ltd. (*Shakspere: His Mind and Art* by Edward Dowden); Miss M. C. Bradbrook and Messrs. Chatto and Windus Ltd. (*Shakespeare and Elizabethan Poetry*); Dr. F. R. Leavis and Messrs. Chatto and Windus Ltd. (*The Common Pursuit*); Dr. E. M. W. Tillyard and Messrs. Chatto and Windus Ltd. (*Shakespeare's History Plays*); Messrs. P. S. King and Staples Ltd. (*Shakespeare and the Popular Dramatic Tradition* by S. L. Bethell); Professor Henri Fluchère and Messrs. Longmans, Green and Co. Ltd. (*Shakespeare*); Mr. J. I. M. Stewart and Messrs. Longmans, Green and Co. Ltd. (*Character and Motive in Shakespeare*); Professor L. C. Knights and Penguin Books Ltd. (*King Lear and the Great Tragedies*, from *The Age of Shakespeare*); Mr. J. C. Maxwell and Penguin Books Ltd. (*Shake-*

speare: *The Middle Plays,* from *The Age of Shakespeare*); Professor G. I.
Duthie and Messrs. Hutchinson and Co. Ltd.(*Shakespeare*); Dr. Leslie Hotson
and the Nonesuch Press (*Shakespeare versus Shallow*); Professor W. H.
Clemen and Messrs. Methuen and Co. Ltd.(*The Development of Shakespeare's
Imagery*); Professor W. W. Lawrence (*Shakespeare's Problem Comedies*);
Miss Lily B. Campbell and the Huntington Library, San Marino, California,
U.S.A. (*Shakespeare's 'Histories'*).

In addition to the above, grateful acknowledgment is due the following
authors and publishers for permission accorded by them for this edition:
Holt, Rinehart & Winston, Inc. (*Shakespeare* by Mr. Mark van Doren;
Landmarks in French Literature by Lytton Strachey; *Shakespeare's Workmanship* by Sir Arthur Quiller-Couch; *Ariosto, Shakespeare and Corneille*
by Benedetto Croce); Little, Brown & Co. (*A Notebook on William Shakespeare* by Dame Edith Sitwell); Harcourt, Brace & World, Inc. (*On Reading Shakespeare* by Logan Pearsall Smith; *Selected Essays* by Mr. T. S.
Eliot); Princeton University Press (*Prefaces to Shakespeare* by Harley Gran-
ville-Barker); Harvard University Press (*The Development of Shakespeare's
Imagery* by Professor W. H. Clemen); Cambridge University Press (*Much
Ado About Nothing; What Happens in Hamlet* by Professor Dover Wilson;
Shakespeare's Imagery by Caroline Spurgeon; *Art and Artifice in Shake-
speare* by Professor E. E. Stoll); St. Martin's Press, Inc., and Macmillan &
Co., Ltd. (*Shakespearean Tragedy* by A. C. Bradley; *Shakespeare* by Sir
Walter Raleigh); Dr. Leslie Hotson (*Shakspeare Versus Shallow*); the
Estate of Professor W. W. Lawrence (*Shakespeare's Problem Comedies*).

SHAKESPEARE AND
HIS CRITICS

CHAPTER I

SHAKESPEAREAN CRITICS

IT was almost exactly two hundred years after Shakespeare's death that Coleridge, in 1818, delivered his Lectures on Shakespeare. In the course of those two centuries, before Shakespearean criticism had become almost an international industry,[1] five great critics, each of whom may be said to have represented the educated opinion of his age, an opinion for whose education he was himself no doubt largely responsible, pronounced their judgments at fairly regular intervals of fifty years. Ben Jonson wrote his verses 'to the memory of my beloved the author Mr. William Shakespeare' for the Folio of 1623; Dryden's *Essay of Dramatic Poesy* was published in 1668; Pope's *Preface to Shakespeare's Works* appeared in 1725; Johnson's *Preface* in 1765; and Coleridge's *Lectures* were delivered in 1818. We have, therefore, a representative of Shakespeare's contemporaries, of the Restoration, of the Augustan Age, of the later Age of Reason, and of the Romantic Movement—and all were poets as well as critics, and some were dramatists as well—to explain to us the peculiar impact of Shakespeare on their own age.

When Shakespeare died there were no daily or even weekly newspapers to publish the fact and to supply an obituary, and even if there had been it is more than probable that the death in the provinces of a retired actor and writer of plays which could scarcely be considered as serious literature would have passed unnoticed. It remained for Heminge and Condell, Shakespeare's fellow-actors and friends, to collect and publish in one volume, the Folio of 1623, all Shakespeare's plays, and to recommend them to 'the great variety of *readers*', that is as literature to be studied, plays with a claim to something more than the ephemeral notoriety of a stage performance. 'Read him, therefore; and again, and again. And if then you do not like him, surely you are in some manifest danger, not to understand him.'

No doubt Heminge and Condell, being financially involved in the venture, were not entirely disinterested, and perhaps even the sturdily independent and forthright Ben Jonson was sufficiently prejudiced by his friendship and a possible payment for his services just a little to

---

[1] In Mr. Augustus Ralli's *History of Shakespeare Criticism*, 158 pages suffice for the period between the First Folio and Coleridge. The succeeding century, 1818–1925, needs almost 1,000 more.

suspend his critical faculties when he wrote his verses 'to his beloved the author and what he hath left us' and claimed that Shakespeare was not of an age, but for all time, that not only was he the wonder of our stage but, in spite of his small Latin and less Greek, was the equal of all that insolent Greece and haughty Rome sent forth. Certainly he was more severe when in his *Discoveries* he wrote, after protesting that he loved the man and honoured his memory this side idolatry, that 'his wit was in his own power; would the rule of it had been so too'. He also told Drummond of Hawthornden that 'Shakespeare wanted art', and whatever he may have meant by that, through the criticism of the next two hundred years there runs, with varying degrees of emphasis, the theme that Shakespeare with his small Latin and less Greek was a wild and irregular genius for whose faults and excesses it was necessary to apologise, and whose plays needed polishing, refining, and trimming before they could be produced upon the stage. It was not until the beginning of the nineteenth century that Schlegel and Coleridge independently refuted this nonsense and maintained that 'the judgment of Shakespeare is commensurate with his genius'. Ben Jonson and the rest of Shakespeare's contemporaries were inevitably too close to their subject to see it in perspective and correct focus, but there is no doubt that they recognised Shakespeare's genius, and they bore generous witness to his popularity, though until the end of the seventeenth century Shakespeare had to share the laurels with Beaumont and Fletcher.[1]

Restoration Critics

Dryden was sufficiently far removed in time to take a wider view of Shakespeare's works, but a view not yet obscured by the mists and fogs of former criticism; he was near enough to be in a simple and unperplexed relationship with his subject, not only through the text of the Folios but also through the stage performances of the King's and the Duke's companies, the former of which, composed of older men, must have carried into the Restoration theatre, with its innovations of scenery and women actors, much of the Shakespearean tradition. Dryden was a very great critic, and generous in his judgments: 'Shakespeare was the man who of all modern, and perhaps ancient poets, had the largest and most comprehensive soul.' For Dryden he was the 'divine Shakespeare, the father of our dramatic poets', and yet, as was only to be expected of one 'untaught, unpractis'd in a barbarous Age', he had his faults, and 'the fury of his fancy often transported him beyond the bounds of judgment'. It was the

[1] The Duchess of Newcastle had no doubts. See her remarkable panegyric on p. 55.

dramatist and the philosopher in Shakespeare that so captivated Dryden, and he was deaf to much of the poetry. Living 'in an age which is more refined'[1] he mistook sublimity for extravagance, vehemence for roaring madness, and sense for a sound of words; and he honestly believed that just as Chaucer was a rough diamond that must first be polished ere he shines,[2] so Shakespeare's characters would be improved by speaking the elegant language of the Restoration, his thoughts would be given their true lustre by adding somewhat of his own where his author was deficient, and a slight readjustment of the plays, the omission of a scene here to get rid of the barbarisms, the addition of a character there—Caliban must have a sister and Ariel 'a gentle spirit for his love'—to improve the symmetry, was all in the true interests of Shakespeare who wanted words in the beginning of our language.

It may be as well here to digress for a moment and consider the *Poetics* of Aristotle and the Neo-Classicism based upon it, without a knowledge of which much of the criticism of the seventeenth and eighteenth centuries is scarcely intelligible.

The *Poetics* is the incomplete notes of a student who attended a course of lectures given by Aristotle at Athens some time before his death in 322 B.C. It is a discourse 'of Poetry in itself and of its various kinds', but it treats most fully of Tragedy; and here it is important to remember that Aristotle's induction was inevitably based on Greek tragedy alone, the only model he had, and there is no reason to doubt that 'if he had seen ours he might have changed his mind'.

His famous definition of tragedy runs as follows:

Tragedy is an imitation of an action that is serious, complete, and of a certain magnitude; in language embellished with each kind of artistic ornament, the several kinds being found in separate parts of the play; in the form of action, not of narrative; through pity and fear effecting the proper purgation of these emotions.[3]

---

[1] Lamb thought differently: 'Much has been said, and deservedly, in reprobation of the vile mixture which Dryden has thrown into the Tempest. Doubtless without some such vicious alloy, the impure ears of that age would never have sate out to hear so much innocence of love as is contained in the sweet courtship of Ferdinand and Miranda.'

[2] Compare Chaucer, 'The smyler with the knyf under the cloke', with Dryden's 'translation':

> Next stood Hypocrisy, with holy leer,
> Soft smiling, and demurely looking down,
> But hid the dagger underneath the gown.

[3] Trans. S. H. Butcher.

He then goes on to elaborate his definition, the following points for our purpose being the most important:

> The Plot is the first principle, and, as it were, the soul of a tragedy: Character holds the second place.
> Third in order is Thought.
> Fourth among the elements enumerated comes Diction.
> Of the remaining elements Song holds the chief place among the embellishments.
> The Spectacle has, indeed, an emotional attraction of its own, but, of all the parts, it is the least artistic, and connected least with the art of poetry.

Having established these principles he goes on to discuss the proper structure of the Plot, 'since this is the first and most important thing in Tragedy':

> According to our definition, Tragedy is an imitation of an action that is complete, and whole, and of a certain magnitude; for there may be a whole that is wanting in magnitude. . . . And to define the matter roughly, we may say that the proper magnitude is comprised within such limits, that the sequence of events, according to the law of probability or necessity, will admit of a change from bad fortune to good, or from good fortune to bad. . . . (This suggestion is Aristotle's only reference to the so-called 'Unity of Time'.)
> As therefore, in the other imitative arts, the imitation is one when the object imitated is one, so the plot, being an imitation of an action, must imitate one action and that a whole, the structural union of the parts being such that, if any one of them is displaced or removed, the whole will be disjointed and disturbed. For a thing whose presence or absence makes no visible difference, is not an organic part of the whole. ('Unity of Action.')

After discussing the Simple and Complex Plot: the first when a change of fortune takes place without, the second with, Reversal of the Situation or Recognition or both, he turns to consider the Tragic Hero, 'a man who is not eminently good and just, yet whose misfortune is brought about not by vice or depravity, but by some error or frailty, and he must be one who is highly renowned and prosperous', and then he sums up the position as far as he has gone:

> A well constructed plot should, therefore, be single in its issue, rather than double as some maintain. The change of fortune should be not from bad to good, but, reversely, from good to bad. It should come about as the result not of vice, but of some great error or frailty, in a character either such as we have described, or better rather than worse.

The first thing to be noticed is his emphasis on the primary importance of the plot, and the subordinate position of character. Then it will be observed that the only Unity that Aristotle insists on, if 'insist' be not too strong a word, is that of Action. By this 'rule' *King Lear* would be condemned for its double plot, and so presumably would *Hamlet* for its irrelevant comedy. All that he says with reference to the Unity of Time is to suggest that 'roughly' the time supposed to elapse in the play should allow of a change of fortune from good to bad: not too long and not too short, but of 'a proper magnitude'. Of the Unity of Place—that there should be no change of scene—he says nothing.

The *Poetics* was unknown in Europe during the Dark and Middle Ages, and was only rediscovered at the time of the Renaissance, about 1500, but it was not long before Italian scholars with their worship and imitation of 'the ancients' seized on it and transformed it into rules, much as, at the same period, Palladio reduced architecture to prescribed forms based on those of Vitruvius. So we find Castelvetro writing in 1570—and this was the orthodox doctrine:

> But it is evident that, in tragedy and comedy, the plot contains one action only, or two that by their interdependence can be considered one . . . not because the fable itself is unsuited to contain more actions than one, but because the space of time, of twelve hours at most, in which the action is represented, and the strait limits of the place in which it is represented likewise, do not permit a multitude of actions.

Twelve hours at most! And the strait limits of the place! Wherever he got that, it was certainly not from Aristotle. And then it will be noticed that instead of emphasising Aristotle's one Unity—of Action —he makes it dependent on the newfangled Unities of Time and Place, the former of which Aristotle had scarcely mentioned, and the latter not at all.

In the seventeenth century this 'Neo-Classic' creed passed into France where Boileau, Rapin, and Le Bossu codified it into its most preposterously rigid form, the cult of Rules and Reason. 'Love Reason', wrote Boileau in *L'Art Poétique* in 1669. 'Too many, carried away by insensate excitement, fetch their thoughts far from plain sense: they would think themselves degraded if, in their monstrous verses, they gave a thought which another had given before them.' And Rapin:

> I make no pretence of justifying the necessity, justice, and truth of these rules of Aristotle. I take all that for granted. I only say that, if you consider them all, you will find that they are merely made to methodise Nature, to follow her step by step. If there is not unity of place, time, and action, in poems, there is no verisimilitude. The Poetics of Horace, which is merely an

interpretation of that of Aristotle, sufficiently shows the necessity of subjecting oneself to rules.

It was according to these rules that French Classical drama was constructed, and so the opinion of Voltaire and the other French critics that Shakespeare was a barbarian becomes comprehensible.

In England Neo-Classicism had its effect, but it never established itself comfortably among a people given to commonsense and compromise. Yet Sir Philip Sidney, of all men, in his *Apology for Poetry* (1581) felt compelled to write:

Our Tragedies, and Comedies (not without cause cried out against), observing rules neither of honest civility nor of skilful Poetry, excepting *Gorboduc* (again, I say, of those that I have seen), which notwithstanding, as it is full of stately speeches and well sounding Phrases, climbing to the height of *Seneca* his style, and as full of notable morality, which it doth most delightfully teach, and so obtain the very end of Poesy; yet in truth it is very defectious in the circumstances: which grieveth me, because it might not remain as an exact model of all Tragedies. For it is faulty both in Place and Time, the two necessary companions of all corporal actions. For where the stage should always represent but one place, and the uttermost time presupposed in it should be, both by *Aristotle's* precept and common reason, but one day: there is both many days, and many places, inartificially imagined.

Sir Philip Sidney had been reading his Scaliger and Castelvetro. And presumably the learned Ben Jonson when he complained that Shakespeare 'wanted art' meant that he had neglected, either through ignorance or perversity, the 'rules' of Aristotle who 'was the first accurate critic and truest judge the world ever had'.

Thomas Rymer, at the end of the seventeenth century, when Neo-Classicism had been remade by the French 'into a kind of critical shoddy', was the most hide-bound of the English school; he ridicules the way in which 'Fancy leaps and frisks, and away she's gone; while Reason rattles the chain, and follows after', and not only the English 'Stage-quacks and Empirics in poetry', but also the 'eternal triflings of French Grammaticasters' themselves.

Dryden, Pope, and Johnson respected the Ancients, Reason, and the Rules, though they interpreted them much more liberally than the French, and it was against this Classical restraint that the Romantic writers—and painters and musicians—so violently revolted at the beginning of the nineteenth century.

Dryden had little sympathy with the pedants who condemned Shakespeare because he was either ignorant of or ignored the *Poetics* of Aristotle, and who thought the English drama should imitate the classical drama of the French, of Corneille, Molière, and Racine: 'By their servile observations of the unities of time and place, and the integrity of scenes, they have brought on themselves that dearth of plot, and narrowness of imagination, which may be observed in all their plays. How many beautiful accidents might naturally happen in two or three days, which cannot arrive within any probability in the compass of twenty-four hours.'

Still less could he agree with Rymer, according to Macaulay 'the worst critic who ever lived', and certainly one of the most reactionary. In 1678 Rymer published a small volume called *The Tragedies of the last Age Consider'd and Examin'd by the Practice of the Ancients, and by the Common Sense of all Ages*, in which he maintained that 'had our Authors begun with Tragedy, as Sophocles and Euripides left it; had they either built on the same foundation, or after their model; we might ere this day have seen Poetry in greater perfection, and boasted such Monuments of wit as Greece or Rome never knew in all their glory'. In 1693 he followed this up with his *Short View of Tragedy* in which he ridiculed *Othello*, 'The Tragedy of the Handkerchief', a play in which there is 'some burlesk, some humour, and ramble of Comical Wit, some shew, and some Mimickry to divert the spectators: but the tragical part is plainly none other than a Bloody Farce, without salt or savour'. It is a characteristic of the English that, like the climate and the scenery of their country, they rarely run to extremes, whether in religion or politics or art or in anything else: we are not a violent people, our religious settlement was a compromise, our Revolution a bloodless one, and we have avoided on the one hand the excesses of Sturm und Drang and the over-exuberance of Baroque, on the other the sterile formulas of Vignola and of the Senecan tradition. Rymer, therefore, was a lonely figure, and Dryden with his good sense dismissed him with: 'It is not enough that Aristotle has said so, for Aristotle drew his models of tragedy from Sophocles and Euripides: and, if he had seen ours, might have changed his mind.'

It would not be true, however, to suggest that Dryden was altogether uninfluenced by French models. He was inconsistent, at one time favouring blank verse, at another rhyme; now conforming to the French 'rules', then ignoring them altogether. So it was that he and Davenant and others forced Shakespeare's plays—*Measure for Measure, Macbeth, Troilus and Cressida, The Tempest*, and many more—into the severe and symmetrical moulds of classical drama; and incidentally they added a spicier love-interest than that contained in Shakespeare's plays, the heroines of which were originally acted by boys, an interest essential to success at the Court of Charles II.

For it must be remembered that the audience of Restoration times was very small and confined almost entirely to Court circles, to which Betterton and other famous actors might almost be said to belong, the Puritan middle classes shunning the theatre as something dangerously licentious, as indeed it often was. Until 1682 there were only two theatres in London, one of them Drury Lane, while from 1682 to 1695 the second Drury Lane, built by Wren, was the only theatre in the town.[1] These theatres were modifications of the Elizabethan 'private' theatre such as the Blackfriars, the winter quarters of Shakespeare's company, roofed in, artificially lit, with painted side wings, and shutters or flats that could be run together to give a change of scene. The inner stage had been enlarged and withdrawn inside a proscenium arch, and though there was still an apron stage on which the actor could be seen in the round, and could audibly declaim the poetry of Shakespeare and the verse of Dryden, by the beginning of the nineteenth century the apron stage was little more than vestigial, having inevitably for financial reasons been sacrificed to make more room for the pit, while the inner stage was becoming a framed and glamorous cavern into the recesses of which the actors could with impunity retire and mutter inaudibly, and often invisibly, the poetry of Shakespeare or the verse of Dryden, it scarcely mattered which.

Eighteenth-Century Critics

Dryden was a dramatist as well as a critic, so that his Shakespearean criticism was in a special sense dramatic; but with the eighteenth century—Dryden died in 1700—came a change, and criticism became literary rather than dramatic. The adaptations of Dryden, Davenant, Ravenscroft, Otway, Tate, and Cibber held the stage, but the criticism was of the plays as written by Shakespeare and printed in the Folios—the Fourth and last Folio was published in 1685.

[1] In 1660 Charles II issued patents to Davenant and Thomas Killigrew, which officially established two major theatres until 1843 when the monopolies lapsed. Davenant asked for and was given the exclusive right to produce, 'reform', and 'make fit' certain of Shakespeare's plays, including *Hamlet* and *The Tempest*, and Killigrew's company were later granted twenty of the plays.

Davenant formed the Duke of York's Company which acted first at Lincoln's Inn Fields, then in 1672 at Dorset Garden. In 1663 Killigrew with the King's Company moved from their theatre in Vere Street to the First Dury Lane, which was burned down in 1672 and rebuilt by Wren in 1674. From 1682 to 1695 the two companies amalgamated and acted at Drury Lane, Betterton seceding to Lincoln's Inn Fields in the latter year.

When Covent Garden theatre was built in 1732 it and Drury Lane were the two patent theatres. By the Licensing Act of 1737 all other theatres should have been closed, but they managed to evade the law. The Queen's Theatre in the Haymarket, built by Vanbrugh in 1705, became the centre for opera. Both Covent Garden and Drury Lane were burned down in the winter of 1808-9 and rebuilt to hold about 3,000 spectators. In 1843 they lost their monopoly.

This was partly the result of the new interest in textual criticism and Shakespearean scholarship. In 1709 Nicholas Rowe, another dramatist, published his octavo edition of Shakespeare's plays, based mainly on the 1685 Folio but with an immensely improved text, and prefixed by the first formal life of Shakespeare. After this came the editions of Pope (1725), Theobald (1733), Hanmer (1744), Warburton (1747), and Johnson (1765). Then came the epoch-making editions of Capell in 1768 and of Steevens in 1773: epoch-making because their texts were based no longer mainly on the Folios, but only after careful collation with the Quartos, the serious study of which they inaugurated.

It was in this atmosphere of scholarship that Pope produced his edition of Shakespeare in 1725; the text was printed from Rowe's but so arbitrarily altered according to Pope's personal preferences that Theobald, the first really serious Shakespearean scholar, had little difficulty in exposing its shortcomings in his *Shakespeare Restored, or a Specimen of the many Errors as well committed as unamended by Mr. Pope in his late Edition of this Poet*. There is nothing very original in Pope's *Preface*, which is interesting partly because it was written by Pope, partly because it so ably embodies the accepted opinion of Shakespeare's plays during the greater part of the eighteenth century. His method is conventional: 'I cannot however but mention some of his principal and characteristic excellencies, for which (notwithstanding his defects) he is justly and universally elevated above all other dramatic writers.' Then comes a tribute to his originality, to his characters which 'are so much Nature herself, that 'tis a sort of injury to call them by so distant a name as copies of her', to his power over our passions, and to his sentiments, followed by an apology for his defects, 'for as he has certainly written better, so he has perhaps written worse than any other'. Some of these defects, 'a wrong choice of the subject, a wrong conduct of the incidents, false thoughts, forc'd expressions, &c.', were not entirely his own, but rather those of the illiterate audience for whom he had to write, while others might more properly be called 'Superfœtations: and arise not from want of learning or reading, but from want of thinking or judging'. There is no attempt at detailed criticism, no analysis of the poetry, of character, or of a single play; it is all very general, and a variation on the theme of, and an apology for, the wild irregular genius who with his small Latin and less Greek wanted art and judgment.

This theme was developed in its most emphatic form by the French critics of the eighteenth century, notably by Voltaire, La Harpe, and Diderot. Racine, always fine, was their man, while Shakespeare's genius flashed fitfully like lightning in a weary night. It is the wild,

irregular genius once more: a barbarian, sometimes even a drunken
barbarian, savagely splendid in spite of his vulgarity and want of art,
his extravagances and wild improbabilities. 'Il avait un génie plein
de force et de fécondité, de naturel et de sublime, sans la moindre
étincelle de bon goût et sans la moindre connaissance des règles.' And
as for *Hamlet*, 'c'est une pièce grossière et barbare, qui ne serait pas
supportée par la plus vile populace de la France et de l'Italie. On
croirait que cet ouvrage est le fruit de l'imagination d'un sauvage
ivre'. It is difficult for the Englishman not brought up and steeped
in the tradition of classical French tragedy, its simplicity, restraint,
and formal symmetry, to understand these French critics who preferred Addison's *Cato* to Shakespeare's *Hamlet* and *Othello*.[1]

Voltaire was given the English answer by Johnson in the *Preface*
to his edition of Shakespeare, 1765. 'Voltaire expresses his wonder,
that our author's extravagances are endured by a nation, which has
seen the tragedy of *Cato*. Let him be answered, that Addison speaks
the language of poets, and Shakespeare of men. We find in *Cato*
innumerable beauties which enamour us of its author, but we see
nothing that acquaints us with human sentiments or human actions;
we place it with the fairest and the noblest progeny which judgment
propagates by conjunction with learning, but *Othello* is the vigorous
and vivacious offspring of observation impregnated by genius. *Cato*
affords a splendid exhibition of artificial and fictitious manners, and
delivers just and noble sentiments, in diction easy, elevated and
harmonious, but its hopes and fears communicate no vibration to the
heart; the composition refers us only to the writer; we pronounce
the name of Cato, but we think on Addison.' Such words, his simple
and generous preference for genius and humanity to judgment,
learning, and abstractions more than redeem his occasional insensibility to Shakespeare's poetry. We can always be sure of Johnson in
this sense: that he meant what he said, and said what he meant, and
it has been given to few men to say it so forcibly. Though he may
often be wrong, he is always sincere, and there is never anything
perfunctory about his judgments.

With sturdy common sense Johnson defends Shakespeare's practice,
censured by Voltaire, of mixing comic and tragic secnes: 'That this
is a practice contrary to the rules of criticism will be readily allowed;
but there is always an appeal open from criticism to nature. The end
of writing is to instruct; the end of poetry is to instruct by pleasing.
That the mingled drama may convey all the instruction of tragedy or
comedy cannot be denied, because it includes both in its alternations of

[1] But see Lytton Strachey's admirable defence of the French point of view on
p. 106.

exhibition, and approaches nearer than either to the appearance of life.'

It may be admitted that Johnson, like Pope, has nothing very original to say in his *Preface*: Shakespeare was a genius, but not so wild and irregular as he is often made out to be—certainly not so wild and irregular as those Frenchmen would like to think him; but he has his faults: he sacrifices virtue to convenience, his plots are often loosely formed, in comedy he is often gross, in tragedy tumid, in narrative tedious, while 'a quibble was to him the fatal Cleopatra for which he lost the world, and was content to lose it', and so on. He seems almost unaware that Shakespeare was a poet, and sometimes he is so perplexingly wrong as to appear almost wrong-headed—though that, when he writes, he never is: 'In tragedy Shakespeare often writes, with great appearance of toil and study, what is written at last with little felicity; but, in his comic scenes, he seems to produce, without labour, what no labour can improve. . . . In his tragic scenes there is always something wanting, but his comedy often surpasses expectation or desire.'

Johnson's *Preface* is remarkable not so much for what it says as for what it is, the judicial summing up of the opinion of a century; it is the impartial estimate of Shakespeare's virtues and defects by a powerful mind anxious not to let his prejudices prevent the defects as he saw them from weighing too lightly in the balance. It is the final verdict of an epoch.

It was this judicial attitude that Hazlitt interpreted as indifference and which so infuriated him: 'We may sometimes, in order "to do a great right, do a little wrong". An overstrained enthusiasm is more pardonable with respect to Shakespeare than the want of it; for our admiration cannot easily surpass his genius. . . . Dr. Johnson's Preface looks like a laborious attempt to bury the characteristic merits of his author under a load of cumbrous phraseology, and to weigh his excellences and defects in equal scales, stuffed full of "swelling figures and sonorous epithets".' And yet we cannot help thinking Mr. T. S. Eliot nearer the truth when he says, quoting the fifth paragraph of the *Preface*: 'One would willingly resign the honour of an Abbey burial for the greater honour of words like the following from a man of the greatness of their author. . . . What a valedictory and obituary for any man to receive! My point is that if you assume that the classical criticism of England was grudging in its praise of Shakespeare, I say that no poet can ask more of posterity than to be greatly honoured by the great; and Johnson's words about Shakespeare are great honour.' (*Cf.* p. 65.)

Johnson's unimpassioned estimate is the final summing up of the classical Shakespearean criticism of the hundred years that lie between the Restoration and the accession of George III—Dryden's *Essay of Dramatic Poesy* was published in 1668, Johnson's *Preface* in 1765. It is the verdict of the Age of Reason, of an age that willingly accepted the restrictions of 'rules' lest too great a freedom should lead to those mysterious and incomprehensible regions

> Of calling shapes, and beck'ning shadows dire,
> And airy tongues that syllable men's names
> On sands, and shores, and desert wildernesses.

Enthusiasm and curiosity were in chains, and minute discrimination was rejected in favour of the broader and safer generalisation. 'The business of the poet', said Imlac, 'is to examine, not the individual but the species; to remark general properties and large appearances. He does not number the streaks of the tulip.'[1] We do not look to Johnson, therefore, for any analysis of Shakespeare's characters— though he has a good note on Polonius and draws a moral from Falstaff. 'Nothing can please many, and please long, but just representations of general nature', and he claims it for the first of Shakespeare's virtues that his characters, unlike those of other writers, are not invididuals but representatives of a species.[2] Nor do we look to Johnson for an appreciation of Shakespeare's poetry, the music and *mystery* of which lay beyond the reach of his common sense. But even in English criticism of the period there are signs of the impending change, an Ariel-like impatience of the imagination to be free, a mild symptom of the mighty forces that were soon to find expression in the Sturm and Drang of Germany and the Revolution in France.

Thus, as early as 1742, the poet Gray wrote to Richard West:

In truth, Shakespear's language is one of his principal beauties; and he has no less advantage over your Addisons and Rowes in this, than in those other great excellencies you mention. Every word in him is a picture. Pray put me the following lines into the tongue of our modern Dramatics:

> But I, that am not shaped for sportive tricks,
> Nor made to court an amorous looking-glass:
> I, that am rudely stampt, and want love's majesty
> To strut before a wanton ambling nymph:
> I, that am curtail'd of this fair proportion,
> Cheated of feature by dissembling nature,
> Deform'd, unfinish'd, sent before my time
> Into this breathing world, scarce half made up—

And what follows. To me they appear untranslatable; and if this be the case, our language is greatly degenerated.

[1] *Rasselas.*

[2] Hazlitt is impatient with Johnson: 'He in fact found the general species or *didactic* form in Shakespear's characters, which was all he sought or cared for.'

And ten years later Joseph Warton wrote a series of critical papers on *The Tempest* and *King Lear* in which he protested that 'general criticism is on all subjects useless and unentertaining, but is more than commonly absurd with respect to Shakespeare, who must be accompanied step by step, and scene by scene, in his gradual developments of characters and passions, and whose finer features must be singly pointed out, if we would do complete justice to his genuine beauties'.

When Thomas Whately died in 1772 he was engaged on a book devoted to the analysis of Shakespeare's characters, but all that we have is the essay, published after his death, comparing Richard III and Macbeth. It is an interesting piece of critical writing and important as being a fragment from what would have been the first *book* dealing exclusively with Shakespeare's characters.[1]

William Richardson's *Philosophical Analysis and Illustration of some of Shakespeare's Remarkable Characters*, 1774, is important mainly as an example of the new trend in criticism and as being the first book, as opposed to essays, to be published on Shakespeare. Intrinsically it is not very valuable, being an attempt to attach Shakespeare to philosophy, but he makes the acute remark that Hamlet's actions were the result of his mother's conduct rather than of his father's murder.

But the most remarkable essay of this transitional phase between the Classical and Romantic periods is that of Maurice Morgann *On the Dramatic Character of Sir John Falstaff*, published in 1777. In this essay he draws attention for the first time to the fact that there is something essentially different between Shakespeare's characters and those of other writers: 'There is a certain roundness and integrity in the forms of Shakespeare, which give them an independence as well as a relation, insomuch that we often meet with passages, which tho' perfectly felt, cannot be sufficiently explained in words, without unfolding the whole character of the speaker.' He lifts Falstaff out of his dramatic environment and considers him as an historical person,

---

[1] It was to Whately that Hazlitt—who was infuriatingly careless about verifying his facts and quotations—referred in the Preface to his own *Characters of Shakespear's Plays* (1817): 'A gentleman of the name of Mason, the author of a Treatise on Ornamental Gardening (not Mason the poet), began a work of a similar kind about forty years ago, but he only lived to finish a parallel between the characters of Macbeth and Richard III, which is an exceedingly ingenious piece of analytical criticism.' He adds: 'Richardson's Essays include but a few of Shakespeare's principal characters. The only work which seemed to supersede the necessity of an attempt like the present was Schlegel's very admirable Lectures on the Drama.' It was a matter of some importance to the critics concerned as to who had the honour of introducing the new criticism. Coleridge claimed it for himself.

and speculates as to how he would act under other circumstances.[1] But in the middle of his essay he can restrain himself no longer, and after attacking with gusto the 'wild, uncultivated barbarian' conception of Shakespeare, he allows himself to be carried away by his admiration for the sheer beauties of Shakespeare, and, forgetting Falstaff, writes a panegyric that might have come from the pen of Coleridge or Hazlitt, and pauses only when 'his observations have brought him near to the regions of poetic magic'—but not before he has made the significant remark that 'Poesy is *magic*, not *nature*'.

The critics of the classical school had viewed Shakespeare's work as a whole, but as it were from a distance, as though it were a building to be judged by Palladian and measurable standards of construction, and though they were bound to admit its power, and seen in certain lights indeed its sublimity, they were appalled by its lack of plan, its sprawling irrelevancies, its extravagant and barbaric mixture of styles. But the pre-Romantic critics, in particular Morgann, recognised within the bewildering diversity the unifying force of Shakespeare's creative power as exemplified in his characters, and on these they principally concentrated their attention.

This interest in the characters may have been stimulated by Garrick, with whose productions of Shakespeare—he produced twenty-four of the plays at Drury Lane between 1747 and 1776—the period coincided. Not only did he bring to the stage a new naturalism in place of the old declamatory style of acting,[2] but he abandoned many of the Restoration versions of the plays and restored much of the original text, though he was guilty of an egotistic adaptation of *Hamlet* with rather more of the prince and none of the 'grossièretés abominables' of the grave-diggers, and he made new and pretty adaptations of three or four of the comedies. He did much to popularise Shakespeare, and it would not perhaps be very far wrong to say that the popular conception of Shakespeare even today is that projected by

---

[1] This is the earliest example of what Croce calls *objectivistic* criticism, legitimate up to a point, but 'what is known as the *Hamlet-Litteratur* is the most appalling of all these manifestations and it is daily on the increase. Historians, psychologists, lovers of amorous adventures, gossips, police-spies, criminologists investigate the character, the intentions, the thoughts, the affections, the temperament, the previous life, the tricks they played, the secrets they hid, their family and social relations, and so on, and crowd, without any real claim to do so, round the "characters of Shakespeare", detaching them from the creative centre of the play and transferring them into a pretended objective field, as though they were made of flesh and blood.' —*Ariosto, Shakespeare, and Corneille*.

[2] 'Garrick was no declaimer; there was not one of his own scene-shifters who could not have spoken *To be, or not to be* better than he did; yet he was the only actor I ever saw whom I could call a master both in tragedy and comedy.'—*Johnson*.

Garrick in the statue that Roubiliac made to his order, a peculiarly composite and histrionic figure.[1]

Garrick retired in 1776, Maurice Morgann's essay was published in 1777, and between then and 1811, when Lamb wrote his essay *On the Tragedies of Shakespeare*, there was no English Shakespearean criticism of importance, though Coleridge gave a course of lectures as early as 1802. In the theatre it was the age of Mrs. Siddons and John Philip Kemble,[2] the manager first of Drury Lane and then from 1803 to 1817 of the rival house of Covent Garden. Both these theatres had been burned down within six months of one another in 1808-9 and were rebuilt on a considerably larger scale to cope with the swelling audience; this increase in size necessitated a slower and more simplified form of acting than Garrick's, something very different from the intimate productions of Shakespeare's time.

However, though the last quarter of the eighteenth century produced little English criticism it marks a new era in scholarship. In 1778 appeared Steevens's revised edition of the plays, containing in the introduction a mass of new material, including extracts from the Stationers' Register, a drawing of the Globe Theatre, a reproduction of Shakespeare's will, and a catalogue of the quartos then known.

---

[1] It was the statue of Garrick in Westminster Abbey that inspired Lamb to write his essay *On the Tragedies of Shakespeare*:
'Taking a turn the other day in the Abbey, I was struck with the affected attitude of a figure, which I do not remember to have seen before, and which upon examination proved to be a whole-length of the celebrated Mr. Garrick. Though I would not go so far with some good catholics abroad as to shut players altogether out of consecrated ground, yet I own I was not a little scandalised at the introduction of theatrical airs and gestures into a place set apart to remind us of the saddest realities. Going nearer, I found inscribed under this harlequin figure the following lines:

> To paint fair nature by divine command,
> Her magic pencil in his glowing hand,
> A Shakespeare rose: then, to expand his fame,
> Wide o'er this breathing world, a Garrick came.
> Though sunk in death the forms the Poet drew,
> The actor's genius bade them breathe anew;
> Though, like the bard himself, in night they lay
> Immortal Garrick call'd them back to day
> And till Eternity with pow'r sublime
> Shall mark the mortal hour of hoary Time,
> Shakespeare and Garrick like twin-stars shall shine,
> And earth irradiate with a beam divine.

'It would be an insult to my readers' understandings to attempt anything like a criticism on this farrago of false thoughts and nonsense.'

[2] 'It is difficult for a frequent playgoer to disembarrass the idea of Hamlet from the person and voice of Mr. K. We speak of Lady Macbeth, while we are in reality thinking of Mrs. S.'—*Lamb*.

Capell's *Notes and Various Readings* and *The School of Shakespeare*
were published in 1783, with an essay on the chronology of the plays
based partly on internal evidence, partly on the external evidence of
Meres's *Palladis Tamia* and of the Stationers' Register. In 1778 the
industrious Malone had published his *Attempt to ascertain the order in
which the plays attributed to Shakespeare were written*, in which he
explains how 'all the ancient copies of Shakespeare's plays, hitherto
discovered, have been collated with the most scrupulous accuracy. . . .
Almost every circumstance that tradition or history has preserved
relative to him or his works has been investigated, and laid before the
public.' He followed this up in 1780 with an edition of the *Poems* and
the seven doubtful plays of the Third Folio; in 1790 he produced his
own ten-volume edition of Shakespeare's works, and his labours were
crowned in 1821 with the publication in twenty-one volumes of
'Boswell's Malone', the Third Variorum edition which embodies the
results of eighteenth-century research, not only into the text, authenticity, and chronology of the plays, but also into Shakespeare's life,
verse, grammar, even punctuation, and into contemporary literature
and records such as Henslowe's *Diary*.

Romantic Critics

It was, however, from Germany that came in this period the criticism that revolutionised the conception of Shakespeare, the dramatist.
Until the eighteenth century, Germany, whose polite society spoke
French, had no great native literature, and taking their lead from
Frederick the Great, her writers were content to imitate the Neo-
Classical French who derided the barbarous Shakespeare; but in the
second half of the century there appeared a school of writers who
reacted violently against both political and literary despotism, against
tyranny in any form, and therefore against the rules and restrictions
of classicism, and who instead of Racine chose Shakespeare as their
model. The very characteristics that Voltaire condemned, his law-
lessness and irregularity, were seized upon as virtues by these apostles
of Sturm und Drang, and Shakespeare was hailed as a 'pure virgin
genius, ignorant of rules and limits, a force as irresistible as those of
nature'. In 1767-8 Lessing wrote a series of articles in connection
with the newly established but short-lived German National Theatre
in Hamburg; these are known as the *Hamburgische Dramaturgie*, and
in them he discusses the true meaning of Aristotle's *Poetics*, and
maintains the inferiority of French tragedy to that of Shakespeare.
'But is it always Shakespeare, always and eternally Shakespeare who
understood everything better than the French?' he asks rhetorically.
And the answer implied is 'Yes'.

But the Sturm und Drang movement may be said to have begun in Strasburg in the winter of 1770-1, when Herder, a warmer and even more enthusiastic supporter of Shakespeare than Lessing, opened the young Goethe's imagination to the beauties of Shakespeare. Goethe tells how the first page of Shakespeare that he read made him a life-long admirer, and how he was overwhelmed by the colossal scale of the characters and his elemental power. With Goethe as champion the position of Shakespeare in Germany was assured, and A. W. Schlegel's brilliant translation of the plays, 1797-1810, besides being perhaps the most significant achievement of the Romantic School, made Shakespeare into a national poet of the German people.[1] German criticism is more philosophic than that of England and France: for Schlegel Shakespeare is 'in strength a demi-god, in profundity of view a prophet, in all-seeing wisdom a protecting spirit of a higher order', and the German critics as a whole saw in his plays a deeper and more mysterious significance than had hitherto been perceived, but a significance that was appreciated by the English Romantics and was powerfully to influence the work of Coleridge.

It was this discovery of Shakespeare by the Germans, almost their identification of Shakespeare with themselves, and particularly Schlegel's *Lectures on Dramatic Art* in 1808, that was partly respons-ible for Hazlitt's book on *The Characters of Shakespear's Plays* (1817), the first English *book* of Romantic Shakespearean criticism. 'We will at the same time confess', he writes, 'that some little jealousy of the character of the national understanding was not without its share in producing the following undertaking, for "we were piqued" that it should be reserved for a foreign critic to give "reasons for the faith which we English have in Shakespear".'

Hazlitt's book had a conventional enough title, reminiscent of the critics of forty years before, of Whately and Morgann, but there is little that is conventional in the text; it is something new in the criticism of Shakespeare, not a judicial balancing of virtues against defects, not Shakespeare at a distance but Shakespeare at close quarters, an intimate revelation of the beauties of the plays. Ostensibly the theme is 'the characters', but, like Morgann, Hazlitt is carried away by the magic of poetry which, in his 'happy intoxication', he cannot refrain from quoting—and often misquoting—at length, and the book becomes the first interpretation of Shakespeare in English. 'The book', wrote Francis Jeffrey, 'is written less to tell the reader what

[1] Croce, the Italian, writes ironically: 'Shakespeare stands, either beside Dürer and Rembrandt, or on a spur of Parnassus, facing Homer and Aeschylus on another spur, sometimes permitting Dante to stand at his side—Dante was of German origin—while the impotent crowd of poets of the Latin race seethes at his feet.'

Mr. H. *knows* about Shakespeare or his writings, than to explain to him what he *feels* about them—and *why* he feels so—and thinks that all who profess to love poetry should feel so likewise. . . . When we have said that his observations are generally right, we have said, in substance, that they are not generally original.' But the observations were original in this sense: that whatever other people might have thought, nobody before had written in such detail and at such length, with such understanding and with such gusto on the *poetry* of Shakespeare. It is all the more remarkable that his idolatry of Shakespeare (not to say his admiration) ceased with his plays, that *Venus and Adonis* and *Lucrece* appeared to him 'like a couple of ice-boxes', and that he did not well know what to say about the *Sonnets*, for it seemed to him that 'in expressing the thoughts of others, Shakespeare was inspired; in expressing his own, he was a mechanic'.

Lamb wrote little Shakespearean criticism, but the little he wrote is more the precious for its scarcity. In 1808 he had produced his *Specimens of English Dramatic Poets who lived about the time of Shakespeare*, the notes to which reveal a new and sensitive appreciation of the Elizabethans,[1] and the startling gap that separates him and the Romantics from Johnson and the Classicists. Then in 1811 came his essay *On the Tragedies of Shakespeare, considered with reference to their fitness for Stage Representation*, with its passionate and typically Romantic plea for the liberty of the imagination and its emancipation from the tyranny of the stage. 'The Lear of Shakespeare cannot be acted', he roundly declared, and though Granville-Barker has given him an answer[2] the fact remains that many of those who care most for Shakespeare are infrequent attenders at the performances of his plays, or at least of his great tragedies,[3] preferring the 'fine abstraction' of reading to seeing them on the stage.

[1] See, for example, his comparison of Fletcher with Shakespeare:
'Fletcher's ideas moved slow; his versification, though sweet, is tedious, it stops at every turn; he lays line upon line, making up one after the other, adding image to image so deliberately, that we see their junctures. Shakespeare mingles everything, runs line into line, embarrasses sentences and metaphors; before one idea has burst its shell, another is hatched and clamorous for disclosure.'
[2] See p. 256.
[3] 'How, I ask you, are stage-enthusiasts—I ask you, Granville-Barker, and you, too, Desmond MacCarthy, and you, Maurice Baring—going to answer Robertson, Charles Lamb, Hazlitt, Coleridge, Goethe and me? It is really up to you to make a reply; and such a reply to be valid should, I suggest, enumerate first of all the scenes in Shakespeare's plays which are only effective upon the stage, and secondly a record of concrete esthetic experiences, of the rendering of Shakespearean rôles by great actors and actresses by which the imaginative impression of these rôles has been deepened and enriched.'—*Logan Pearsall Smith: On Reading Shakespeare.*
But Hazlitt was not a very certain supporter of Lamb: 'Perhaps one of the finest

But it is Coleridge above all others who is the interpreter of Shakespeare, the inspired critic who revealed for the first time the immense range of Shakepeare's genius, and pointed out the innumerable and previously undiscovered approaches to an appreciation of it. He was jealous of his claim to be the founder of the new criticism and resented the implication in Wordsworth's essay that he might owe something to the Germans. The passage in Wordsworth's *Essay, Supplementary to the Preface* (1815) is worth quoting at length:

At this day the French Critics have abated nothing of their aversion to this darling of our Nation: 'the English, with their bouffon de Shakspeare', is as familiar an expression among them as in the time of Voltaire. Baron Grimm is the only French writer who seems to have perceived his infinite superiority to the first names of the French Theatre: an advantage which the Parisian Critic owed to his German blood and German education. The most enlightened Italians, though well acquainted with our language, are wholly incompetent to measure the proportions of Shakspeare. The Germans only, of foreign nations, are approaching towards a knowledge and feeling of what he is. In some respects they have acquired a superiority over the fellow-countrymen of the Poet: for among us it is current, I might say, an established opinion, that Shakspeare is justly praised when he is pronounced to be 'a wild irregular genius, in whom great faults are compensated by great beauties'. How long may it be before this misconception passes away, and it becomes universally acknowledged that the judgment of Shakspeare in the selection of his materials, and in the manner in which he has made them, heterogeneous as they often are, constitute a unity of their own, and contribute all to one great end, is not less admirable than his imagination, his invention, and his intuitive knowledge of human Nature?

To this Coleridge replied in a letter dated February 1818 'to a gentleman who attended the course of Lectures given in the spring of that year':

My next Friday's lecture will, if I do not grossly flatter-blind myself, be · interesting, and the points of view not only original, but new to the audience. I make this distinction, because sixteen or rather seventeen years ago, I delivered eighteen lectures on Shakspeare, at the Royal Institution: three-fourths of which appeared at that time startling paradoxes, although they

pieces of acting that ever was witnessed on the stage, is Mr. Kean's manner of doing this scene and his repetition of the word *Banished*. He treads close indeed upon the genius of his author. A passage which this celebrated actor and able commentator on Shakespear (actors are the best commentators on the poets) did not give with equal truth,' etc.

On the other hand:

Boswell: 'But has Garrick not brought Shakespeare into notice?'

Johnson: 'Sir, to allow that, would be to lampoon the age. Many of Shakespeare's plays are the worse for being acted: Macbeth, for instance.'

have since been adopted even by men, who then made use of them as proofs
of my flighty and paradoxical turn of mind; all to prove that Shakspeare's
judgment was, if possible, still more wonderful than his genius; or rather,
that the contradistinction itself between judgment and genius rested on an
utterly false theory. This, and its proofs and grounds have been—I should
not have said adopted, but produced as their own legitimate children by some,
and by others the merit of them attributed to a foreign writer, whose lectures
were not given orally till two years after mine, rather than to their country-
man; though I dare appeal to the most adequate judges . . . whether there is
one single principle in Schlegel's work (which is not an admitted drawback
from its merits), that was not established and applied in detail by me.

Whether Coleridge owed anything to Schlegel, or Schlegel to
Coleridge, or whether they worked independently, as seems most
probable, is perhaps not very important; but it is almost impossible to
over-estimate the importance of Coleridge's criticism itself. It is true
that Coleridge can be intolerably tedious, that he rarely seems able to
resist a philosophical détour—'I have a smack of Hamlet myself, if I
may say so', he ingenuously remarks—and that occasionally, like a
conjurer bringing rabbits out of a hat, he professes to have discovered treasure in some neglected and dusty corner of his subject. Sir
Walter Raleigh in his *Six Essays on Johnson* (1907), writing of the
Romantic critics in general but with particular reference to Coleridge,
remarks:

The romantic attitude begins to be fatiguing. The great romantic critics,
when they are writing at their best, do succeed in communicating to the
reader those thrills of wonder and exaltation which they have felt in contact
with Shakespeare's imaginative work. This is not a little thing to do; but it
cannot be done continuously, and it has furnished the workaday critic with a
vicious model. There is a taint of insincerity about romantic criticism, from
which not even the great romantics are free. They are never in danger from
the pitfalls that waylay the plodding critic; but they are always falling upward,
as it were, into vacuity. They love to lose themselves in *O altitudo*. From the
most worthless material they will fashion a new hasty altar to the unknown
God. When they are inspired by their divinity they say wonderful things;
when the inspiration fails them their language is maintained at the same
height, and they say more than they feel. You can never be sure of them.

This is excellently said, and all this may be admitted, but the solid
achievement of Coleridge remains, and it is worth more than that of
any other Shakespearean critic before or since.

The critics of the classical school, particularly the French, judged
Shakespeare as a dramatist whose worth must depend on the structure
of his plays and the conduct of his actions; the one they found too
irregular, the other too extravagant. In England about the middle

of the eighteenth century came a transitional phase, when a few amateur critics seized on the characters as the most significant feature of the plays, while in Germany a few years later the characters were alternately defined by the light and obscured by the mists of metaphysics and mysticism. Coleridge modified and developed the criticism of all these aspects of Shakespeare's work, added his own inspired contribution, and swept them into a great critical synthesis.

His first object was to overthrow the pernicious classical doctrine that Shakespeare's plays are remarkable only because the splendour of the parts compensates for the barbarous shapelessness and irregularity of the whole: 'In all the successive courses of lectures delivered by me, since my first attempt at the Royal Institution, it has been, and it still remains, my object, to prove that in all points from the most important to the most minute, the judgment of Shakespeare is commensurate with his genius—nay, that his genius reveals itself in his judgment, as in its most exalted form.' This he does once and for all when he explains how 'the true ground of the mistake lies in the confounding mechanical regularity with organic form'; that Shakespeare's form is not mechanically impressed from without, but like natural forms is organic, shaping itself as it develops, from within.

Coleridge's second great contribution to the critical study of Shakespeare was to proclaim and demonstrate to the world that not only was Shakespeare a great dramatist but also the greatest poet that England, certainly, possibly the world, had produced. It is remarkable that, apart from contemporaries and near-contemporaries like Ben Jonson and Milton, no critic before Coleridge seems to have been aware that Shakespeare was before all else a poet.[1] Indeed, this is still not widely appreciated, and the divinest aspect of Shakespeare's genius, his poetry, is the one that has been most neglected. Thousands of books have been written about Shakespeare and every subject remotely connected with him, from botany to Bacon, but only in recent years has the primary importance of his poetry been recognised. Shakespeare was a poet before he was a dramatist, and it is possible that he turned playwright only, or at least mainly, from economic motives. 'Clothed in radiant armour', says Coleridge, 'Shakespeare came forward to demand the throne of fame, as the dramatic poet of England. . . . But he had shown himself a poet, previously to his appearance as a dramatic poet', and in the ensuing analysis of *Venus and Adonis* he shows that the young Shakespeare had 'the chief, if not every, requisite of a poet'.

[1] The *Biographia Literaria* was published in 1817, *Notes and Lectures upon Shakespeare* posthumously in 1849, but some of the notes were compiled and some of the lectures delivered as early as 1802.

It is by the means of these two new conceptions of Shakespeare, as a great artist and a great poet, that Coleridge achieves what is after all the end of his criticism, the 'communicating to the reader those thrills of wonder and exaltation which he has felt in contact with Shakespeare's imaginative work'. 'Not a little thing to do', indeed! Without in the least wishing to belittle the achievements of Johnson, I suggest that the reader look at Coleridge's notes on, say, *Romeo and Juliet* or *The Tempest*, and then consider who has added most to his understanding and appreciation of Shakespeare, Johnson or Coleridge. He may be an uncertain guide, and his followers need to be on their guard against his aberrations, but if, as Mr. Eliot says, 'it is impossible to understand Shakespeare criticism to this day, without a familiar acquaintance with Coleridge's lectures and notes', it might almost as truly be said that without such an acquaintance it is impossible to understand—so far as it is possible to understand at all—Shakespeare himself.

The fourth of the great Romantic critics was De Quincey, who wrote the famous essay *On the Knocking at the Gate in Macbeth* (1823). Perhaps it is not altogether irrelevant here to observe that in *Crime and Punishment* Dostoevski adopts the same device as Shakespeare does. It will be remembered that when Raskolnikov, with whom we are in sympathy—in De Quincey's sense of the word—has murdered the two women in the garret there comes a ring at the bell and cheerful talk on the stairs outside which, like the knocking at the gate and the porter's ribaldry in *Macbeth*, 'makes known audibly that the reaction has commenced; the human has made its reflex upon the fiendish; the pulses of life are beginning to beat again; and the re-establishment of the goings-on of the world in which we live, first makes us profoundly sensible of the awful parenthesis that had suspended them'.

When Wordsworth wrote in 1815 that French critics had abated nothing of their aversion to Shakespeare and that Baron Grimm was the only French writer really to understand him, he was not being strictly accurate. There were two writers, at least, of the epoch of the Revolutionary and Napoleonic Wars, the uneasy period that lies between French Classicism and Romanticism, who did not think of Shakespeare as a *bouffon*. Madame de Staël, although her roots were in the eighteenth century, recognised that the age of Voltaire was over, and in her *De la Littérature* (1800) admitted that England and Germany, Shakespeare and Schiller were the models for France. Although she could not condone all the extravagances of Shakespeare, and incidentally ranked *Henry VI* with *King Lear*, her appreciation is far less qualified than Voltaire's; Shakespeare has his faults, but he is certainly not a buffoon. Chateaubriand, too, in his *Mélanges Littéraires* (1801), though not without regret for the glories of the past, turns to Shakespeare as a source of the Romantic beauty which he preached.

But it was the youthful Victor Hugo who trumpeted the full Romantic faith and scattered the rearguard of Classicism.[1] 'Art', he maintained, 'has nothing to do with leading-strings, with hand-cuffs, with gags: it says "Go your ways" and lets you loose in the great garden of poetry, where there is no forbidden fruit. Space and time are the domain of the poet. Let him go where he will and do what he pleases: this is the Law.' And again: 'Is the work good or bad? This is the whole extent of the critical province.' In his *Preface to Cromwell* he vigorously attacks the unities, defends Shakespeare's combination of the sublime with the grotesque, and proclaims him a god of the theatre who unites in himself the genius of Corneille, Molière, and Beaumarchais. A Frenchman could scarcely make a greater claim than this, and though other French critics could not go all the way with him, there was in nineteenth-century France a generous appreciation of Shakespeare and a wide recognition that he is perhaps the greatest of them all.

In France, in Russia too, but above all in Germany, Shakespeare was one of the main sources of inspiration of the Romantic Movement that swept through Europe in the early years of the nineteenth century, and since then he has been firmly established as the most influential and international of modern poets, although the Germans have from time to time attempted to adopt him. According to Gervinus, writing in 1850, 'the man who first valued Shakespeare according to his full desert was indisputably Lessing. One single passage, where, in his *Dramaturgie*, he speaks of *Romeo and Juliet*, shows plainly that he apprehended his plays in their innermost nature'. Then a few years later: 'in *Wilhelm Meister*, Goethe produced that characteristic of Hamlet, which is like a key to all works of the poet'. So it is small wonder that 'through industry and love, just as England did with our Handel, we have won the great poet for ourselves, and Shakespeare, from his diffusion and influence, has become a German poet almost more than any of our native writers'. He complains, however, that

---

[1] How powerful these forces still were may be judged by the violence of the attack on Hugo when at the opening of *Hernani* he was so vulgar as to mention a back-staircase, *un escalier dérobé*, and so revolutionary as to place *escalier* at the end of one line and *dérobé* at the beginning of the next. Words had come to be divided into those that were 'noble' and those that were 'bas', and only the noble were permissible in poetry. This explains why, at about the time Hugo was writing his *Preface to Cromwell*, there was a riot in the theatre during a performance of *Othello* when the word 'mouchoir' was mentioned.

'England has not suffered herself to be robbed of the poet in the same manner as we have been of the musician'.

In England the impact of the great Romantic critics was twofold, both good and bad; on the one hand they succeeded in communicating to others something of the ecstasy they experienced themselves in their discovery of Shakespeare, on the other they supplied later critics with a vicious model, and the nineteenth century resounds with what Croce calls *exclamatory* criticism, 'which instead of understanding a poet in his particularity, his finite-infinity, drowns him beneath a flood of superlatives'. Few poeple, not even Voltaire, had ever questioned Shakespeare's genius; on the other hand, until about 1770 few people had admitted his art; but when Coleridge had demonstrated that his art was as great as, if not greater than, his genius, what could there be left to find fault with? 'Others abide our question', Arnold sang, but Shakespeare was beyond criticism, and there was nothing left for the critics but to adore and see who could shout his adulation the loudest.

The high Romantic period, the thirty-seven years of the nineteenth century before the accession of Queen Victoria, was that of John Philip Kemble and Edmund Kean, Hazlitt's favourite and first of the fiery star-actors about whom revolved the pallid satellites who made up the rest of the company. Although it was not until 1843 that the two patent theatres lost their monopoly, when the increase in numbers checked increase in size, Drury Lane and Covent Garden were already so big that a large proportion of their audience could not hear and could scarcely see the actors. This led naturally to exaggerated gestures and declamation and to a dependence on music and spectacle for effect, a development that was intensified by the disappearance of the apron stage and by a growing demand for realism. This movement towards realism may be said to have begun with J. P. Kemble's brother, Charles, who in 1823, with the aid of the antiquarian J. R. Planché, produced *King John* 'in the precise Habit of the Period'. Romanticism was becoming as rigid and exacting in its conventions as the classicism that it had superseded.

Victorian Critics, 1837-1873

This romantic realism, or spectacular antiquarianism, was inherited by Macready and Charles Kean. Although Macready retired in 1851, Kean was only just beginning his triumphant series of sumptuous and pedantic revivals of Shakespeare at the Princess's theatre. Perhaps his greatest achievement was *The Winter's Tale*, when he ingeniously resolved Shakespeare's intolerable chronological and topographical blunders by changing Bohemia to Bithynia, introduced *tableaux vivants* of the private and public life of the ancient Greeks and ravished the spectators—he did not call them an audience—with a Dionysiac Festival of three hundred revellers instead of a paltry dance of twelve rustics, which was all that Shakespeare had demanded. Song, dance, *tableau vivant*, and elaborate scenery elaborately removed left little time for Shakespeare's text, and what was left after cutting had to be rearranged so that scenes could be run together. Although the Victorians were beginning to present what Shakespeare really had written, instead of what Davenant, Dryden, Cibber, Tate, even Garrick, and the rest had made of the plays, it was Shakespeare reduced and transposed. The improved version had given place to the acting version.

The end of the Drury Lane–Covent Garden monopoly was the beginning of better times for Shakespeare. As most of the new theatres could not compete with the lavish spectacles offered by the two old ones, they concentrated more on the words and less on the apparatus. Thus, at the Haymarket in 1844 Benjamin Webster staged *The Taming of the Shrew*, not Garrick's version nor Lacy's perversion, but the whole of the original play, with curtains and locality boards instead of scenery. In the same year Samuel Phelps became manager of Sadler's Wells, where in the course of some twenty years he produced all but seven of the plays, for the most part the original text, with scenery and spectacle reduced to more modest proportions. Sadler's Wells, however, was a cheap and popular playhouse, and the sumptuous 'realism' of the Kemble-Kean tradition went from triumph to triumph in the fashionable London theatres.

The year 1840 is memorable as that in which the first Shakespeare Society was founded. This was the work of John Payne Collier, the greatest Elizabethan scholar of the age, author of the important *History of English Dramatic Poetry*, and instead of the bitter rivalry of the eighteenth century a new era of harmonious co-operation was hopefully inaugurated. In addition to their official *Papers* the Society published a mass of new material, including Dyce's edition of *Sir Thomas More*, Peter Cunningham's *Extracts from the Accounts of the Revels at Court*, and Collier's *Diary of Philip Henslowe*. One of the leading members was J. O. Halliwell (later Halliwell-Phillipps) whose main interest was biographical, and in 1848 he published his *Life of Shakespeare*. Unfortunately he gave undue weight to the testimony of John Jordan, a self-educated Stratford antiquary of the late eighteenth century, who wrote of the descendants of the poet's sister Joan Hart, still living at the Birthplace, 'The Hart family is very illiterate, so totally ignorant that they cannot give any account of their illustrious predecessor beyond their own memory'. Then in 1847 Halliwell was present at the sale of the Birthplace, which by that time was in such a deplorable condition that it was described as a 'filthy remnant of a butcher's shamble'. It was not altogether surprising, therefore, that he wrote, 'Removed prematurely from school, residing with illiterate relatives in a bookless neighbourhood, thrown into the midst of occupations adverse to scholastic progress, it is difficult to believe that when Shakespeare first left Stratford, he was not all but destitute of polished accomplishments'. This exaggeration of the poverty and illiteracy of Shakespeare's Stratford environment was to lead to confusion.

The Shakespeare Society came to a disastrous end in 1853 owing to the forgeries of Collier, and the controversy dragged wretchedly and inconclusively along until the Stratford celebration of the tercentenary of Shakespeare's birth in 1864. Although this was scarcely an unqualified success, owing to the inexperience and muddling of the Committee, at least they presented a number of the plays, unlike Garrick, who had contented himself with reciting his own poetry at the Jubilee that he organised in 1769.

The tercentenary produced more permanent memorials than the Stratford celebrations. The *Cambridge Shakespeare*, the nine volumes of which were completed in 1866, superseded Malone's *Variorum* as the most important edition of the century, and for a long time remained the standard text. The Germans celebrated the occasion by forming their own society, the Shakespeare-Gesellschaft, and the four volumes of the Heidelberg professor, G. G. Gervinus, were translated into English as *Shakespeare Commentaries*.

It had been a bleak period for Shakespeare commentary. Carlyle was the first of the Victorian school of exclamatory critics. In 1840 he delivered a course of lectures in which he claimed that 'Shakespeare is the chief of all Poets hitherto; the greatest intellect who has left record of himself in the way of literature . . . All the intellect you will find in Bacon is poor in comparison with this.' And he added, 'There rises a kind of universal Psalm out of this Shakespeare, not unfit to make itself heard among the still more sacred Psalms'. Carlyle had been concerned with Heroes and Hero-Worship, and Mrs. Cowden Clarke followed up his success on the parallel theme of Heroines and Heroine-Worship, the three volumes of her *Girlhood of Shakespeare's Heroines* appearing in the early fifties. It was the Victorian plunge into sentimental bardolatry and the beginning of the emotional treatment of the characters as though they were real people who could be abstracted from the plays with an existence outside the brief traffic of the scene. David Masson abstracted and sentimentalised Shakespeare himself, and at the same time claimed even more for him than did Carlyle: 'In Shakespeare's plays we have Thought, History, Exposition, Philosophy, all within the round of the poet. It is as if into a mind poetical in form there had been poured all the matter which existed in the mind of his contemporary Bacon.'

The Victorians had failed to develop the creative criticism of Coleridge in the direction that he had indicated. Instead of integrating the man and his work they were divorcing them and taking them to pieces; instead of pursuing the secret of the organic growth of the plays they were bandying conventional and uncritical hyperbole. Gervinus with his German metaphysics attempted to change the course. Following up the work of the 'aesthetic philosophers', Goethe and Schlegel, he professed to see Shakespeare as a whole, each play as a whole, unified by one ruling idea that linked every character and every episode, a fundamentally moral idea that justified much that seemed to him needlessly offensive and even immoral. Yet even Gervinus failed to keep the oneness of Shakespeare always in mind; too often he forgot the dramatist, and scarcely remembered the poet in his preoccupation with the philosopher and in his humility before the 'severe moral austerity' that justified the deaths of Desdemona and Othello. It was this kind of interpretation that moved his compatriot, Gustav Rümelin, to protest that such dramatic justice is like Draco's sanguinary code, which decreed a single penalty for all misdeeds—death.

Rümelin's book appeared in the year after Gervinus's *Commentaries*, and was a healthy attack on the over-philosophic approach as well as on mid-Victorian adulatory criticism. It is a strange book, at once obscurantist and enlightened; it reverts to the eighteenth-century viewpoint that Shakespeare's plots are ill-constructed and unworthy of his genius, anticipates Tolstoy in the assertion that there is little truth of dialogue because all the characters speak like Shakespeare, but it also anticipates twentieth-century critics in attempting to re-instate Shakespeare in his Elizabethan environment. Its title was significant: *Shakespeare Studies by a Realist*. But 'realist' criticism was half a century away; for the Victorians Shakespeare was a Victorian.

It was a confused and confusing picture of Shakespeare that had emerged by the middle of the reign. On the one hand there was the virtually uneducated son of illiterate parents, the 'Warwickshire peasant' of Carlyle and Halliwell, on the other there was the consummate dramatist who, according to the critics, was scholar and philosopher as well, a universal genius of whom it was possible to speak only in superlatives. And superlatives were not yet exhausted.

Victorian Critics, 1873-1901

In the theatre the second half of Queen Victoria's reign was dominated by Henry Irving. Charles Kean died in 1868, and when

Phelps followed ten years later Irving was left without a rival on the professional London stage. At the Lyceum he produced Shakespeare's plays on a scale that would have staggered even the Kembles and Keans, and, in order to make time for his scenic splendours, cut and shuffled the text with increasing abandon. It was magnificent, but it was scarcely Shakespeare, for not only was it Shakespeare truncated, transposed, and transformed into visual entertainment, it was Shakespeare sentimentalised as well; *Hamlet*, for example, being elevated from a tragedy of revenge into a tragedy of love. There were those, however, who remembered the pioneering work of Webster and Phelps, and in 1883 F. R. Benson formed his famous touring company which produced all Shakespeare's plays, many of them at Stratford, with a minimum of scenery and cuts. For a time his stage manager was William Poel, who in 1881 produced the first quarto version of *Hamlet* under approximately Elizabethan conditions, and in 1895 founded the Elizabethan Stage Society for the production of the plays of Shakespeare and his contemporaries without scenery and without intervals.

The advent of Irving coincided with the formation of the New Shakspere Society in 1873. The founder was F. J. Furnivall, a breezy director of literary studies with an impregnable faith in progress and science. Moreover, he was a disciple of the Germans. Their criticism was on the right lines. It was a disgrace that there was no book by an Englishman dealing with Shakespeare as a whole, for 'Shakspere *must* be studied chronologically and as a whole', and the *Commentaries* of Gervinus was the only book that could be put into the hands of the student who wanted to know the mind of Shakespeare. The first thing, then, was to establish the order in which the plays were written, when it would be found that they fell naturally into groups, corresponding to distinct periods in Shakespeare's life. Gernivus had found three periods, but Furnivall suspected that he had overlooked one. The key, of course, to Shakespeare's secret was science. The verse of each play must be analysed, its metrical devices counted and tabulated, and from these figures, on the reasonable assumption that the subtler the versification the later the play, the correct chronological order would be revealed.

Furnivall collected his team and put F. G. Fleay in charge of the department of metrical tests. 'We must adopt', wrote Fleay, 'every scientific method from other sciences', from geology, chemistry, botany, and biology. Ignoring, therefore, outcrops of other men's work, he analysed, tabulated, and classified the genuine Shakespearean strata, and found that there were four epochs, as Furnivall had anticipated, that 'Shakespeare's course is shown to have run from the amorousness and fun of youth, through the strong patriotism of early manhood, to the wrestling with the dark problems that beset the man of middle age, till at last, in his Stratford home again, peace came to him, with sheep-shearings to be talkt of, and Perdita with the Spring flowers to be lovd, and everything else serenely enjoyd; and so he ends his life.'

It was the province of Professor Dowden to expand and elaborate the portrait revealed by Fleay's scientific metrical tests, and in 1875 he published his *Shakspere: A Critical Study of his Mind and Art.* England's honour was redeemed; it was the first book by an Englishman, or rather an Irishman, to treat Shakespeare as a whole, but, although it was sensitively and sympathetically written, with flashes of penetrating insight and acute criticism, it imposed on the Carlyle-Halliwell portrait of the ill-educated Warwickshire peasant a sentimental mid-Victorian Shakespeare babbling of green fields, spring flowers, and sheep-shearings to loyal and tender English maidens. It remained the standard critical work until well after the end of the century.

Fleay was so carried away by the momentum of his new scientific method that he was unable to stop, and by applying his metrical tests to the verse of the other Elizabethans he found astonishing quantities of their work embedded in genuine Shakespeare. This process of disintegration, from which Furnivall vigorously dissociated himself, was carried still further by J. M. Robertson who, with the aid of a sensitive ear alone, discovered that *A Midsummer Night's Dream* was Shakespeare's only complete play.

However, in spite of their abuse, metrical tests did help to establish the chronology of the plays, and the New Shakspere Society did an immense amount of valuable work by publishing, in addition to their *Transactions,* a number of Shakespeare's sources and allusion books, and it was owing to Furnivall that a new and cheaper 'Englisht *Gervinus'* was published, as well as a translation of *Shakespeares Dramatische Kunst* by Hermann Ulrici, who had worked along similar lines.

Swinburne, however, was not interested in the Germans and the new scientific criticism; his model was Victor Hugo, and his voice the shrillest of all those who honoured Shakespeare the other side idolatry. In his *Study of Shakespeare,* 1880, he claimed that *Henry IV* and *Henry V* alone established him as the greatest playwright of the world, and that, although Cymbeline was the human father of Imogen, Shakespeare was the divine. Swinburne's hysterical excesses may be defended on the ground that he always soared into hyperbole when talking about the Elizabethans, and it is only fair to add that this inspired and errant critic, a poet interpreting a poet, like Coleridge gave immense insights into the processes of artistic creation.

In his *Shakespeare as a Dramatic Artist* (1885) R. G. Moulton did something to check sentimental and exclamatory criticism by a heavy insistence on Shakespeare's moral and didactic purpose, but Sidney Lee's *Life* did even more. The New Shakspere Society had come to an end in 1894, soon after the death of Halliwell-Phillipps, whose *Outlines of the Life of Shakespeare*, an outline of a thousand pages first published in 1881, had gone through six revised editions in as many years. Lee now took over his rôle of official biographer and in 1898 published his *Life of William Shakespeare*. It is a dull and desiccated figure that emerges. Shakespeare 'inherited his father's love of litigation', the maturity of his genius coincided with a series of 'astute business transactions', and 'his literary attainments and successes were chiefly valued as serving the prosaic end of providing permanently for himself and his daughters'. Lee would have nothing to do with the Furnivall-Dowden theory of four periods, for that ignores 'the objectivity of Shakespeare's dramatic work'. The *Sonnets* are equally objective, and 'one more proof of his punctilious regard for the demands of public taste'. Shakespeare, in short, was an ambitious and successful man of business with a flair for giving the public what it wanted, without betraying his own opinions and emotions.

Success appealed to the late Victorians as much as sentiment had appealed to those of the preceding generation, but Lee's portrait was very different from that of the Dane, Georg Brandes, whose massive *William Shakespeare* was translated into English in the same year. Lee dismissed it as 'an elaborately critical but somewhat fanciful study'. Fanciful it was, and far-fetched, but at least it was a more credible and human portrait than Lee's. So far from never giving himself away, Brandes maintained, Shakespeare revealed himself in everything he wrote; not only did he unpack his heart in the *Sonnets*, but he himself was Brutus, Henry V, Coriolanus, King Lear, and even Richard III. A few years later, infuriated by Lee and inspired by Brandes, Frank Harris wrote *The Man Shakespeare and his Tragic Life Story*, a romantic biography inflated with imaginary evidence from the plays and poems, depicting Shakespeare as a neurotic sensualist, broken by his love for the faithless Dark Lady of the Sonnets, Mary Fitton.

Apart from a few essays by Walter Pater, the Victorians had produced curiously little Shakespeare criticism of the first order, yet right at the end of the era came one of the best books of all, A. C. Bradley's *Shakespearean Tragedy*, published in 1904, but based on lectures delivered some years earlier. Bradley's one object was dramatic appreciation, to increase the understanding and enjoyment of the four principal tragedies as dramas. His criticism was handicapped by the static spectacular method of producing the plays at this period, and this accounts for his complaint that too often Shakespeare strings together a number of short scenes, as also for his appeal to the reader rather than the playgoer. The right way to read a play, he argues, is as if we were actors who had to study all the parts, and most of his book is devoted to analysis of the characters. Sometimes, it is true, he forgets his object, *dramatic* appreciation, in his enthusiasm for psychological understanding, speculates on the early histories of his heroes and, like so many of his predecessors, treats them as though they were once real people. But, despite its over-emphasis on character, the book has done as much for the appreciation and understanding of Shakespearean tragedy as any other that has ever been written, and it brought Victorian criticism to an unexpectedly brilliant conclusion.

Twentieth-century Critics

When Irving died in 1905 Beerbohm Tree was already established at His Majesty's theatre, where he carried the opulently 'realistic' presentation of Shakespeare as far as ingenuity and money could take it. But it was the end. Tree died in 1917, but even before the beginning of the war there were signs that the old order was crumbling. Between 1912 and 1914 Harley Granville-Barker produced *The Winter's Tale, Twelfth Night*, and *A Midsummer Night's Dream* on an apron stage, with formalised scenery and only one interval; and this was at a West End theatre, the Savoy. Then, during the war Ben Greet joined forces with Lilian Baylis at the Old Vic, which rapidly became Shakespeare's London home where his plays were staged after the manner of Granville-Barker. Meanwhile Barry Jackson had founded the Birmingham Repertory Theatre, in 1921 Nugent Monck built the 'Elizabethan' Maddermarket Theatre in Norwich, and in 1932 the new Shakespeare Memorial Theatre was opened at Stratford.

This revolution was partly the result of research that followed the discovery of the drawing of the Swan theatre, the only contemporary illustration of the inside of an Elizabethan playhouse that we possess. Before the end of the war W. J. Lawrence and the Americans G. F. Reynolds, A. H. Thorndike and J. Q. Adams had all published books on the Elizabethan theatre, and in 1923 came the four volumes of E. K. Chambers's *Elizabethan Stage*.

Granville-Barker was in a position to give an authoritative answer to Charles Lamb. 'The plays of Shakespeare,' Lamb had written, 'are less calculated for performance on a stage than those of almost any other dramatist whatever.' 'Not so', replied Granville-Barker; Lamb was merely disgusted with the theatre of Kemble's day, and based his arguments on 'the stage of spectacle, not upon Shakespeare's'. The

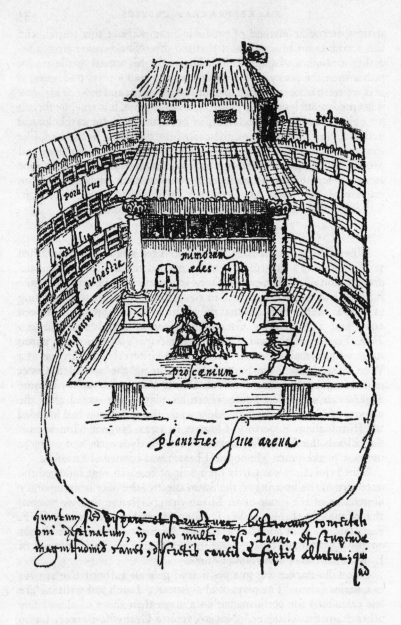

THE SWAN THEATRE

From the drawing of J. de Witt, c. 1596

first of Granville-Barker's *Prefaces to Shakespeare* appeared in 1927, and four more volumes followed before his death twenty years later. His object was to describe how Shakespeare might have produced the plays to-day with the aid of modern apparatus, and both as producer and writer he has perhaps done more for the staging of Shakespeare than any other man.

There were other reactions and revolts at the beginning of the century. In 1906 came Lytton Strachey's essay on *Shakespeare's Final Period*, in which he attacked the cosy idealism of Furnivall and Dowden and their conception of a quiet and serene last period, and, remembering Caliban and Leontes, discovered a Shakespeare 'half bored to death', a singer of ethereal songs who, 'urged by a general disgust, burst occasionally through his torpor into bitter and violent speech'. Strachey's realism was no more helpful than Dowden's idealism as a means to the understanding of the last plays. Tolstoy's remarkable outburst in the same year was equally unhelpful. This, however, was ethical rather than literary criticism: Shakespeare's art is bad because it is disruptive and fails to transmit the highest religious feeling. Walter Raleigh published his *Shakespeare* in 1907, an admirably balanced approach to the subject, in which he turned away not only from Dowden's sentiment but also from the excesses of Coleridge to the 'cool and manly utterances of Dryden, Johnson, and Pope with a heightened sense of moderation and candour'.

In 1910 came the first application of the new science to the study of Shakespeare's characters with Dr. Ernest Jones's *The Oedipus-Complex as an Explanation of Hamlet's Mystery*. According to this theory, Claudius succeeded in doing the two things that Hamlet had unconsciously wished to do as a child, murdered his father and married his mother, but, though Hamlet wanted to kill his uncle, his power to act was paralysed by his repressed desire and consequent feeling of guilt. In the light of modern knowledge this is an attractively simple explanation, though it is difficult to square with all the facts, and it seems unlikely to have been Shakespeare's. Even more thoroughly than Bradley, Dr. Jones was treating Hamlet as though he were a real person, a patient in his consulting-room. But a reaction against this psychological naturalism had already set in.

Ever since the Restoration it had been held that Shakespeare wrote for an audience barely emerged from barbarism. Thus Carlyle had complained that 'Shakespeare had to write for the Globe Playhouse; his great soul had to crush itself, as it could, into that and no other mould'. And as late as 1906 the fastidious Robert Bridges could write: 'Shakespeare should not be put into the hands of the young without the warning that the foolish things in his plays were written to please the foolish, the filthy for the filthy, and the brutal for the brutal,' for an audience, that is, of 'wretched beings who can never be forgiven their share in preventing the greatest poet and dramatist of the world from being the best artist.'

Levin Schücking, the German professor, took a similar view of the Elizabethan audience, but whereas Bridges believed that Shakespeare was compelled to write down to it Schücking maintained that he deliberately gave it what it wanted, not so much filth as exciting and popular drama. Schücking was the leader of a new school of criticism, a 'realist' school parallel to the new scholarship of the theatre and the comparative study of the Elizabethan dramatists, its object being to relate Shakespeare to his real dramatic environment. In 1919 he published his *Charakterprobleme bei Shakespeare,* translated in 1922 as *Character Problems in Shakespeare's Plays,* a book that owed much to the 'realism' of Rümelin. Shakespeare, argues Schücking, wrote for an unsophisticated audience to whom he made all sorts of concessions, his art being essentially popular and naïve, and full of conventions from the old drama. For example, he used the old convention of 'direct self-explanation'. making his characters tell us in soliloquy what would more properly be told us by a Chorus. Thus, when Prince Hal explains to the audience that he will throw off his loose behaviour when it suits him, we are not to take his words as the self-revelation of a princely hypocrite, but merely as an assurance by the author that all will be well, that his hero is fundamentally sound. Again, Shakespeare's method was one of 'episodic intensification'; his plays were written to be effective on the stage, not for critical reading in the study, and to secure a series of effective episodes he readily sacrificed both the structure of the play and consistency of character. It is useless, therefore, Schücking concludes, to search like Bradley for psychological naturalism in the plays when the characters frequently behave according to these primitive conventions. Shakespeare can only be understood by recognising the primitiveness of his technique and taking these conventions into account.

More recent research into the nature of the Elizabethan audience has invalidated much of what Bridges had to say, and undermined some of Schücking's assumptions and conclusions, for the studies of A. C. Sprague, Alfred Harbage, and H. S. Bennett have revealed an audience made up for the most part of eager and attentive listeners, appreciative of fine language and, though noisy, by no means altogether filthy and foolish, or even unsophisticated. In his later criticism Schücking finds Shakespeare rather less naïve than he had originally thought, and Muriel Bradbrook has shown in her *Elizabethan Stage Conditions* (1932) and *Themes and Conventions of Elizabethan Tragedy*

(1935) that Shakespeare and his great contemporaries transformed the limitations of convention into positive virtues.

In America Professor E. E. Stoll had long been working along realist lines, clearing away the accumulation of Romantic and Victorian idealism and the mists of German metaphysics, and relating Shakespeare to the theatre for which he wrote. As early as 1907 in *The Ghosts* he showed that Shakespeare's ghosts were real and visible apparitions, revivified corpses, and not the abstractions of nineteenth-century philosophy. This he followed with a series of books in which he maintained that we háve sentimentalised Shylock, who was for Shakespeare and his audience an object of derision, and over-subtilised his criminals, who were actuated by fear and not by such emasculated emotions as conscience and remorse; that Falstaff, in spite of Morgann, was a coward, and that Hamlet is a straightforward hero in an Elizabethan revenge play who needs neither Goethe nor Freud to explain his mystery, for there is no mystery to be explained.

Then in *Art and Artifice in Shakespeare* (1933) Stoll advanced a more ingenious argument than Schücking's as an explanation of the character problems in the plays. He agreed that neither Shakespeare's situations nor his characters and their actions are true to life, but full of inconsistencies and impossibilities which, in the rapid traffic of the stage would pass unnoticed, and that to analyse them as if they were true is to run into all sorts of inexplicable absurdities. But Shakespeare was concerned less with the psychology of his characters than with the psychology of his audience; indeed, many of his finest effects come from the deliberate contradiction between nobility of character and viciousness of action, which by his art he makes acceptable. Shakespeare, in short, was not concerned with an image of life but with an illusion, and real life is not to be confused with dramatic art. He often resorts to artifice, 'he evades and hedges, manœuvres and manipulates, suppresses or obscures', but it is his supreme art, his poetry, that makes him the greatest of dramatists, 'because the illusion he offers is the widest and highest, the emotions he arouses the most irresistible and overwhelming'.

Two more Americans pursued a similar realist, or historical, line. In *Shakespeare's Problem Comedies* (1931) W. W. Lawrence analysed the medieval elements surviving in *All's Well*, *Measure for Measure*, and *Troilus and Cressida*, and argued that many of the problems of Shakespeare's characters are the result of his acceptance of the medieval code of conduct and conventions of chivalry. On the other hand, in *Comical Satire* (1938) O. J. Campbell sought to show that in *Troilus and Cressida* Shakespeare 'made a highly original contribution to the new genre of dramatic satire' that had been developed by Jonson and

Marston, and in *Shakespeare's Satire* (1943) expanded his thesis to include *Measure for Measure* and other plays.

Logan Pearsall Smith was unimpressed by the realist arguments and sufficiently old-fashioned to write his urbane *On Reading Shakespeare* (1933) and to twit Professor Stoll with being 'the leader of the American and hardest-boiled of all the hard-boiled schools of Shakespeare criticism'. But in *How Many Children had Lady Macbeth?* he was rebuked by L. C. Knights, not for making fun of the realists, but for praising Shakespeare 'because he provides "the illusion of reality", because he puts "living people" upon the stage, because he creates characters who are "independent of the work in which they appear".' Bradleyism was discredited, almost a term of derision, and another school of criticism had appeared giving another reason why we should not look in the plays for psychological naturalism.

In 1930 Wilson Knight published *The Wheel of Fire*. Rejecting criticism that compares and judges in favour of an 'interpretation' that tends to merge into the work it analyses, he argued that it is wrong to select what is easy to understand and neglect the superlogical. A Shakespeare play is not true to life but a vision only roughly corresponding to actuality; it is the development of a central idea to which everything else, incident, thought, imagery, and poetic symbol is immediately related. Thus, it must be considered not only temporally but spatially, not only as a sequence of events but as a pattern composed of the elements related to the central idea; for example, the pattern in *Macbeth* is the conflict of life and death, in *Troilus and Cressida* 'the Trojan party stands for human beauty and worth, the Greek party for the bestial and stupid elements of man'. The emphasis was shifted from character and 'prolix attention to any one element' to the play as a whole. T. S. Eliot wrote an appreciative introduction to the book, and most of the all too little Shakespeare criticism that he has written dates from this period. In accordance with the principles thus laid down, Knight continued his interpretation of the plays in *The Imperial Theme* (1931) and *The Shakespearean Tempest* (1932).

The year 1930 was a turning-point: scholarship was summarised by E. K. Chambers in his two monumental volumes, *William Shakespeare: A Study of Facts and Problems,* Lascelles Abercrombie made his *Plea for the Liberty of Interpreting Shakespeare,* and the first important books on the imagery of the plays were published, not only *The Wheel of Fire* but William Empson's *Seven Types of Ambiguity* and Caroline Spurgeon's *Leading Motives in the Imagery of Shakespeare's Tragedies.* Empson was not primarily concerned with Shakespeare, but as he was a pupil of I. A. Richards and F. R. Leavis, who were much occupied with problems similar to Wilson Knight's, the new method of interpretation became associated with the new Cambridge school of criticism. More immediately important was the work of Miss Spurgeon who, after years of research, published her *Shakespeare's Imagery and What It Tells Us* in 1935.

As long ago as 1794 William Whiter had written *A Specimen of a Commentary on Shakespeare,* based on 'a new principle of criticism derived from Mr. Locke's Doctrine of the Association of Ideas', showing that certain ideas were always associated in Shakespeare's mind; flatterers, for example, suggested dogs, and dogs suggested sweetmeats, as in 1 *Henry IV* (I. iii).

> Why, what a candy deal of courtesy
> This fawning greyhound then did proffer me!

Bradley had noted how the animal imagery in *King Lear* intensifies the atmosphere of bestiality, and the new science of psycho-analysis encouraged a more exhaustive study of imagery. Dr. Spurgeon's method was the reverse of Knight's, objective and scientific instead of subjective and mystical, and not unlike Fleay's analysis of verse. By counting and classifying she was able to show that in most of the plays there is a symbolic imagery that gives atmosphere and background, and 'image-clusters' like those discovered by Whiter, while throughout each tragedy runs a peculiar and dominating image, sustaining and emphasising the emotion and interpreting the thought: in *Hamlet*, for example, this 'iterative imagery' is one of disease, symbolising the rottenness in the state of Denmark. Unlike Knight, Dr. Spurgeon tended to examine the imagery in isolation, without relating it to the other elements in the play, and again like Fleay she pressed her system too far. Thus, she found in the imagery not only Shakespeare's unconscious revelation of his mind but of his physical characteristics and appearance as well.

In the following year, 1936, came Wolfgang Clemen's *Shakespeare Bilder,* translated in 1951 as *The Development of Shakespeare's Imagery.* More subjective than Miss Spurgeon in his analysis, Clemen traces the increasing dramatic function of the imagery and its relation to character. Middleton Murry, whose early work influenced Wilson Knight, was much concerned at this period with the integrating effect of imagery, and 1936 saw the publication of his *Shakespeare.*

Two more important books were published in the same year, opening up another critical approach to Shakespeare, an historical method that related him to the political philosophy of his age much as the realists related him to his theatre. These books were Hardin Craig's *The Enchanted Glass: the Elizabethan Mind in Literature* and

A. O. Lovejoy's *Great Chain of Being*, certain aspects of which were elaborated in 1943 by Theodore Spencer in *Shakespeare and the Nature of Man* and by E. M. W. Tillyard in *The Elizabethan World Picture*. The essence of these books is a picture of the world as Shakespeare and his contemporaries saw it. Under God, all is arranged in a majestic hierarchy: angels, men, animals, plants and minerals; and within each category are minor hierarchies, the king in the category of men corresponding to God. Everything therefore has its duly appointed place and, though there is scope for evolution, forcibly to usurp a higher position is to upset the natural, the divine, order. In the light of this philosophy we can understand why Hamlet hesitated to kill a king, and appreciate the problem that Shakespeare had to face in writing *Richard II*.

Dr. Tillyard develops this last theme in *Shakespeare's History Plays* (1944). Treating *Richard II*, the two parts of *Henry IV*, and *Henry V* as a tetralogy, he shows how Shakespeare insisted on the disorder that followed the murder of Richard and then traced the gradual re-emergence of order and evolution of the ideal king in Henry V. Shakespeare's acceptance of this reading of history, which he may have derived from a study of Hall's *Chronicles*, affords another explanation of apparent inconsistencies in characterisation, particularly in the Histories. For example, without an appreciation of this fundamental belief in a divine order Falstaff, Hotspur, and Prince Henry may be quite misunderstood, as they were, according to Tillyard, by older critics like Quiller-Couch and Masefield.

In America, Lily B. Campbell was pursuing a similar course, and in *Shakespeare's 'Histories': Mirrors of Elizabethan Policy* (1947) traced in the plays 'a dominant political pattern characteristic of the political philosophy of his age', at the same time, though more doubtfully, finding in them Shakespeare's comments on contemporary events, a correspondence, for example, between the death of Arthur in *King John* and the execution of Mary Queen of Scots.

In his *Shakespeare* (1951) Professor G. I. Duthie carries the 'order-disorder antithesis' into the realm of comedy, for 'it is essential to a right understanding of Shakespeare to realize that the fundamental antithesis between order and disorder is ubiquitous in his work'. It is inadequate, for example, to consider *The Taming of the Shrew* simply as a rather brutal farce; for Shakespeare the relationship of husband to wife corresponds to that of king to subject, and in this play he emphasises the foolishness, not as in the tragedies the horror, of trying to upset the natural order.

Another solution of character problems was offered in 1944 by S. L. Bethell in *Shakespeare and the Popular Dramatic Tradition*. Bethell is a realist who, while rejecting the psychological naturalism of Bradley, is not wholly satisfied with the conventions discovered by Schücking and Stoll and advanced as explanations of the characters' actions: that the villain is always conscious of his villainy, the hero of his virtue, that slander is always believed, and so on. Such an explanation is too rigid; Shakespeare worked according to no system of conventions but constantly varied his position, even in the same play, between conventionalism and naturalism. This was possible because for the popular audience at the Globe, as for a cinema audience today, the illusion was rarely complete; they were conscious that the play was a play and not real life, and were able therefore to respond on more than one plane of attention at the same time. This 'principle of multi-consciousness' also accounts for Shakespeare's anachronisms, topical allusions, his ability to use without incongruity all the riches of his contemporary experience when writing of the past, and for the element of allegory and symbolism in his plots and characters. More important perhaps, it accounts for the dual nature of many of the characters. To the audience Falstaff would be both amusing and morally reprehensible as a corrupter of the young prince, while Touchstone is at the same time a 'natural' and a sophisticated wit.

In his introduction to Bethell's book T. S. Eliot wrote: 'A verse play is not a play done into verse, but a different kind of play: in a way more realistic than "naturalistic drama", because, instead of clothing nature in poetry, it should remove the surface of things, expose the underneath, or the inside, of the natural surface appearance. It may allow the characters to behave inconsistently, but only with respect to a deeper consistency. It may use any device to show their real feelings and volitions, instead of just what, in actual life, they would normally profess or be conscious of; it must reveal, underneath the vacillating or infirm character, the indomitable unconscious will; and underneath the resolute purpose of the planning animal, the victim of circumstance, and the doomed or sanctified being.'

This was the principal theme elaborated by J. I. M. Stewart in *Character and Motive in Shakespeare* (1949). Stewart believes that Bradley's, the classical, approach by way of character is fundamentally sound, though it must be modified by the findings of the realists, or rather by some of their findings, and much of his book is devoted to a witty exposure of the excesses of Schücking and Stoll. Then, invoking the aid of psycho-analysis and anthropology, he suggests that many inconsistencies of character are only superficial, because Shakespeare 'clears away obvious motives for much the same reason as the psychologist: to give us some awareness of motives lying deeper down'. And only in poetic drama, because of the nature of poetry, can this deeper reality be fully explored and revealed. In a sense, therefore, there is more psychological naturalism in Shakespeare than Bradley suspected.

Stewart's book was partly a protest against the extreme anti-Bradleyism of 'the New Bowdlers . . . who would give us not merely *Hamlet* without the Prince but the Complete Works without their several *dramatis personae*', and at the same time an attempt to reconcile Bradleyism with 'the best Shakespearean theatre recently erected, that of Dr. Wilson Knight', which, however, 'shows occasionally as bleak and empty as a hall hired for poetry-readings by some philosophical society in a provincial town'.

There had been a slight though significant change in the wind of criticism, and Stewart was not alone in his attempt to repeople the Shakespearean scene. Three years earlier H. B. Charlton, a devout and unrepentant Bradleyite, had carried the cause into Cambridge itself, where he delivered the Clark Lectures with the provocative title of *Shakespearian Tragedy* and with Bradley's 'conviction of the place of characterisation in Shakespearian drama'.

However, support for the interpretative school came from a new quarter when in 1948 Henri Fluchère published his *Shakespeare: Dramaturge Élisabéthain*. But although he ridicules critics from Dryden to Bradley and John Palmer for their over-emphasis on character, and dismisses the Romantics, apart from Coleridge, as of largely negligible critical importance, his book is an admirable statement of the new criticism, and concludes with an illuminating analysis of the plays.

It was fitting that the first half of the century should close with a review of its achievement, and in 1948 appeared the first volume of *Shakespeare Survey*, edited by Allardyce Nicoll, an annual publication devoted to current work and an appreciation of what the last fifty years have contributed to some selected field of investigation.

Scholarship as well as criticism and stage production has been revolutionised, principally by the bibliographical studies of A. W. Pollard, R. B. McKerrow, and W. W. Greg. It used to be thought that the 'copy' from which the first quartos and the Folio were set up was at many removes from Shakespeare's original papers, and therefore hopelessly corrupt. But Pollard has shown that the first editions were often set up from Shakespeare's originals, and that Heminge and Condell fulfilled their claim to have used them for the good Folio texts that replaced those of the 'bad' quartos. Thus, it is often only the compositor who stands between us and Shakespeare's manuscript, and emendation is not guesswork on a corrupt text, but a scientific correction based on the kind of error made by Elizabethan printers. Hence the importance of McKerrow's research into Elizabethan methods of book-production and of the study of manuscript plays by Greg, whose *Editorial Problem in Shakespeare* (1942 and 1951) summarises the position today. It is on the basis of this new 'critical bibliography' that J. Dover Wilson is editing the new *Cambridge Shakespeare*, the first volume of which appeared as far back as 1921.

Dover Wilson's criticism might almost be said to be a by-product of his editorial labours, *What Happens in Hamlet* (1935) and *The Fortunes of Falstaff* (1943) both being inspired by his editions of the plays. He, too, is a Bradleyite and, in the field of biography a romantic, in his *Essential Shakespeare* (1932) freely interpreting Shakespeare's thought and spiritual experiences as reflected in his plays and poems. So does Ivor Brown in his *Shakespeare* (1949), though C. J. Sisson in *The Mythical Sorrows of Shakespeare* (1932) demonstrated the dangers that beset such biographical adventures.

The most original work in biography has been that of Leslie Hotson, a sort of literary detective who has among other things discovered who killed Kit Marlowe, the relations of Shakespeare with Francis Langley, Justice Gardiner, Thomas Russell, Leonard Digges, and others, thrown new light on the writing of the *Sonnets* and *Troilus and Cressida*, and on the first production of *Twelfth Night*. Although he is apt to be carried away by his enthusiasm and to reach conclusions not entirely justified by his exciting discoveries, his books are among the most readable of any ever written on the subject of Shakespeare.

All through this revolutionary half-century valuable books have been produced unaffected by the contention between the old and the new criticism, from Masefield's *William Shakespeare* (1911) and Quiller-Couch's *Shakespeare's Workmanship* (1918) to Mark van Doren's *Shakespeare* (1939) and Edith Sitwell's *Notebook on William Shakespeare* (1948), but yet the contention remains. How then do we stand now that we have passed the middle of the century and are approaching the quatercentenary of Shakespeare's birth?

There has been, as we have remarked, some return in the direction of Bradley and the classical criticism that concentrates on character. This is partly owing to the discomfiture of one of the opposing schools, the realists, at the hands of the other. Two attacks on the realist position have come from Italy, one delivered by Croce in the early twenties, the other in 1946 by N. Orsini, who in *La Critica Shakespeariana* objects to a Shakespeare who is merely the product of his age and not of his own genius. The essential element is the poetry.

Of course the poetry is the essential element, and the new interpretative school of criticism is so important because it has focussed attention on the poetry and on the play as a work of art. A Shakespeare play is not a slice of life, and to consider it as such is to mistake the meaning of art; it is like judging a painting by the standards of photography. Art must not be confused with nature; it is a representation, not a reproduction, of life. Unfortunately, however, in their revolutionary ardour the critics of the new school have been so much concerned with demonstrating that a Shakespeare play is a work of art ,integrated by various elements in the poetry that they have neglected the most obvious and popular element of all. They have tended to forget that Shakespeare was a playwright as well as a poet, treated the plays as dramatic poems and not as poetic drama, and reduced the characters to little more than symbols. Their interest has been in certain aspects of the poetry, not so much in the sheer beauty of the words as in the underlying pattern of imagery, allegory, and symbolism. Aware, as no critics before them have ever been aware, of the two levels of our lives, the conscious and the unconscious, they have sought for double and multiple meanings, ambivalence, ambiguities and remote correspondences, all of which admittedly may be potent properties shaping the work of art, yet it is a pity that criticism should be so preoccupied with subterranean exploration that it neglects what lies on the surface, which is as important as, some would say more important than, what lies below.

Imagery, allegory, and symbolism are all of secondary importance in the poetry of Shakespeare's plays. The essential element is the words that the characters speak, for after all they are nothing but words; they *are* the poetry. Here, for example, is Macbeth:

> To-morrow, and to-morrow, and to-morrow,
> Creeps in this petty pace from day to day
> To the last syllable of recorded time,
> And all our yesterdays have lighted fools
> The way to dusty death.

And all the critics in the world will not persuade us that the character of Macbeth as revealed in his poetry is not a major interest in the play, as well as an integral element in the work of art. As a dramatist, Shakespeare was trying to represent (not to reproduce) real people in the various predicaments of life, but because all poetry is ambiguous, meaning so much more than it says, and because Shakespeare was so great a poet, he was able to create the illusion of life and make of words forms more real than living man. Shakespeare did not write morality plays, nor was he concerned with abstractions; his characters are not symbols of this and that, but representations of real people created out of poetry, and to neglect this aspect of his poetry is to fail to see the work of art as a whole, the very thing for which the new critics blame Bradley and the classical school.

Fortunately there are signs that they are beginning to realise this, and we have only to compare L. C. Knights's satirical essay on *How Many Children had Lady Macbeth?*, written in 1933, with that on *King Lear and the Great Tragedies*, written in 1955, to see that this is so. In the first essay, after tilting at Bradley, Knights wrote: 'the only profitable approach to Shakespeare is a consideration of his plays as dramatic poems, of his use of language to obtain a total complex emotional response'. When, however, it was reprinted in *Explorations* in 1946, he admitted that 'throughout the first half of the essay I detect a slight headiness springing from the exhilaration of attacking what was still the orthodox academic view of Shakespeare'. And he added, 'If I were writing *How Many Children had Lady Macbeth?* to-day I should make far more allowance for the extraordinary variety of Shakespeare's tragedies . . . and I should not, I hope, write as though there were only one "right" approach to all of them'. Even in 1946 the essay was something of a period-piece, and in 1955 he writes, 'Of course no single mode of appreciation was ever completely dominant', and he warns the reader against the danger of regarding 'the meaning of a play as residing exclusively or even predominantly in the imagery'. 'Character', however, is still printed in inverted commas, and the verse, we are told, 'works in conjunction with the dramatic action and our sense of *what the different persons in the drama stand for* as each play develops'. The italics are mine; the characters, apparently, are still to be treated primarily as symbols.

For F. R. Leavis, however, Bradley is still the arch-mischiefmaker, and he cannot understand how the author of *How Many Children had Lady Macbeth?* could write such traditional criticism about *Measure for Measure,* and even quote Hazlitt and Coleridge, when the 'unsatisfactoriness' of the play 'has to be explained in terms of that incapacity for dealing with poetic drama, that innocence about the nature of convention and the conventional possibilities of Shakespearean dramatic method and form, which we associate classically with the name of Bradley'. However, even Dr. Leavis admits that relevant discussion of the tragic significance of *Othello* is mainly a matter of character-analysis.

Wilson Knight rejects the term 'character' altogether, 'since it is so constantly entwined with a false and unduly ethical criticism' (but is this really so?). He prefers 'person', but his interpretation is so apocalyptic that we often lose sight of human beings altogether. For example, 'Macbeth and Lear are created in a soul-dimension of primal feeling', and Timon is 'a principle of the human soul, a possibility, a symbol of mankind's aspiration'. As a result there is not only a dearth of flesh and blood, of men and women, in his interpretation of Shakespeare, but a certain lack of proportion, or humour, as well.

We shall never return to an unqualified Bradleyism, but what is needed now is a criticism that is a synthesis of all that is valuable in old and new. It must take into account the discoveries and revelations of the last thirty years: the medieval element in Shakespeare's plots, Elizabethan cosmology and political philosophy, the conventions of the Elizabethan theatre, and the underlying pattern of the poetry, formed not only by the imagery but also by the recurrence and variation of rhythms, phrases, words, and even syllables. But it must also recognise that the primary object of Shakespeare was to write a play, to represent men and women (not abstractions) in the perplexities of life, that poetry was the means whereby he developed the action, the stuff out of which he created his characters, and that being a supreme artist, incidentally almost and not altogether consciously, he created a work of art, an 'organic form', as Coleridge put it, 'that shapes, as it develops, from within'. And this organic form, this work of art, is more, much more, than a harmony of image, allegory, and symbol; it is the product of the poetry as a whole.

CHAPTER II

SHAKESPEAREAN CRITICISM
CONTEMPORARY CRITICISM

ROBERT GREENE *Groats-worth of Wit.* Sept., 1592. (The reference is to
3 *Henry VI*, and Greene parodies the line in that play,
'Oh Tiger's heart wrapt in a woman's hide'.)

There is an vpstart Crow, beautified with our feathers, that with his
Tygers hart wrapt in a Players hyde, supposes he is as well able to bombast
out a blanke verse as the best of you: and beeing an absolute *Iohannes fac
totum,* is in his owne conceit the onely Shake-scene in a countrey.

HENRY CHETTLE *Epistle* to *Kind-Harts Dreame.* Dec. 1592. (Chettle apolo-
gises, apparently to Shakespeare, for the part he had taken
in preparing Greene's *Groatsworth of Wit* for the press.)

I am as sory as if the originall fault had beene my fault, because my selfe
haue seene his demeanor no lesse ciuill than he exelent in the qualitie he
professes: Besides, diuers of worship haue reported his uprightnes of dealing,
which argues his honesty, and his facetious grace in writing, that aprooues
his Art.

FRANCIS MERES *Palladis Tamia*: *Wits Treasury.* Sept. 1598. (Meres was
a Cambridge man; he was in London 1597–8, and later
rector and schoolmaster at Wing, Rutland.)

As the soule of *Euphorbus* was thought to liue in *Pythagoras*: so the sweete
wittie soule of *Ouid* liues in mellifluous & hony-tongued *Shakespeare*, witnes
his *Venus* and *Adonis*, his *Lucrece*, his sugred Sonnets among his priuate
friends, &c.

As *Plautus* and *Seneca* are accounted the best for Comedy and Tragedy
among the Latines: so *Shakespeare* among the English is the most excellent
in both kinds for the stage; for Comedy, witnes his *Gentlemen of Verona*, his
Errors, his *Loue labors lost*, his *Loue labours wonne*[1], his *Midsummers night
dreame*, & his *Merchant of Venice*; for Tragedy his *Richard the 2*, *Richard the
3*, *Henry the 4*, *King Iohn*, *Titus Andronicus* and his *Romeo* and *Iuliet*.

As *Epius Stolo* said, that the Muses would speake with *Plautus* tongue,

[1] This was the only reference to *Love's Labour's Won* until the recent discovery of a bookseller's list of 1603 in which the play is given as an item of stock.
It seems, therefore, that there was a quarto edition, no copies of which have sur-
vived. Either it is a lost play by Shakespeare, or the title is an alternative one for
another early comedy printed in the Folio, as had previously been assumed. Professor T. W. Baldwin has written a monograph on the subject.

if they would speak Latin: so I say that the Muses would speak with *Shake-speares* fine filed phrase, if they would speake English.

RICHARD BARNFIELD *Poems in Divers Humors*. 1598.

> And *Shakespeare* thou, whose hony-flowing Vaine,
> (Pleasing the World) thy Praises doth obtaine,
> Whose *Venus*, and whose *Lucrece* (sweete, and chaste)
> Thy Name in fames immortall Booke haue plac't.
>> Liue euer you, at least in Fame liue euer:
>> Well may the Bodye dye, but Fame dies neuer.

JOHN WEEVER *Epigrammes in the oldest Cut, and newest Fashion*. 1599.

> Honie-tong'd *Shakespeare* when I saw thine issue
> I swore *Apollo* got them and none other,
> Their rosie-tainted features cloth'd in tissue,
> Some heauen born goddesse said to be their mother:
> Rose-checkt *Adonis* with his amber tresses,
> Faire fire-hot *Venus* charming him to loue her,
> Chaste *Lucretia* virgine-like her dresses,
> Prowd lust-stung *Tarquine* seeking still to proue her:
> *Romea Richard*; more whose names I know not,
> Their sugred tongues, and power attractiue beuty
> Say they are Saints althogh that Sts they shew not
> For thousands vowes to them subiectiue dutie:
> They burn in loue thy children *Shakespear* het them,
> Go, wo thy Muse more Nymphish brood beget them.

ANON *Parnassus*. (A series of three plays performed at Cambridge, probably at Christmas 1598, 1599, 1601. *a.* from 2 *Parnassus*; *b.* from 3.)

a.   *Gull.* Not in a vaine veine (prettie, i' faith!): make mee them in two or three divers vayns, in Chaucer's, Gower's and Spencer's and Mr. Shakspeare's. Marry, I thinke I shall entertaine those verses which run like these;

>> Even as the sunn with purple coloured face
>> Had tane his last leave on the weeping morne, &c.

O sweet Mr. Shakspeare! I'le have his picture in my study at the courte. . . .

Let this duncified worlde esteem of Spencer and Chaucer, I'le worshipp sweet Mr. Shakspeare, and to honour him will lay his Venus and Adonis under my pillowe, as we reade of one . . . slept with Homer under his bed's heade.

b.   *Kempe.* Few of the vniuersity men pen plaies well, they smell too much of that writer *Ouid*, and that writer *Metamorphosis*, and talke too much of *Proserpina* & *Iuppiter*. Why heres our fellow *Shakespeare* puts them all downe, I and *Ben Ionson* too. O that *Ben Ionson* is a pestilent fellow, he brought vp *Horace* giuing the Poets a pill, but our fellow *Shakespeare* hath giuen him a purge that made him beray his credit: *Burbage.* Its a shrewd fellow indeed.

GABRIEL HARVEY *Marginalia.* 1601?

The younger sort takes much delight in Shakespeares Venus, & Adonis: but his Lucrece, & his tragedie of Hamlet, Prince of Denmarke, haue it in them, to please the wiser sort.

ANTHONY SCOLOKER *Epistle* to *Daiphantus.* 1604.

It should be like the *Neuer-too-well read Arcadia,* where the *Prose* and *Verce* (*Matter* and *Words*) are like his *Mistresses* eyes, one still excelling another and without Coriuall: or to come home to the vulgars *Element,* like *Friendly Shakespeare's Tragedies,* where the *Commedian* rides, when the *Tragedian* stands on Tip-toe: Faith it should please all, like Prince *Hamlet.*

JOHN WEBSTER *Epistle* to *The White Devil.* 1612.

And lastly (without wrong last to be named), the right happy and copious industry of M. *Shake-speare,* M. *Decker,* & M. *Heywood,* wishing what I write may be read by their light: Protesting, that, in the strength of mine owne iudgement, I know them so worthy, that though I rest silent in my owne worke, yet to most of theirs I dare (without flattery) fix that of *Martiall, Non norunt, Haec monumenta mori.*

THOMAS FREEMAN *Runne and a Great Cast.* 1614.

> *Shakespeare,* that nimble *Mercury* thy braine,
> Lulls many hundred *Argus*-eyes asleepe,
> So fit, for all thou fashionest thy vaine,
> At th' *horse-foote* fountaine thou hast drunk full deepe,
> Vertues or vices theame to thee all one is:
> Who loues chaste life, there's *Lucrece* for a Teacher:
> Who list read lust there's *Venus* and *Adonis,*
> True modell of a most lasciuious leatcher.
> Besides in plaies thy wit windes like *Meander*:
> Whence needy new-composers borrow more
> Than *Terence* doth from *Plautus* or *Menander.*
> But to praise thee aright I want thy store:
>   Then let thine owne works thine owne worth upraise,
>   And help t' adorne thee with deserued Baies.

WILLIAM BASSE c. 1620.

> *On Mr. Wm. Shakespeare*
> *he dyed in Aprill* 1616.

Renowned Spencer, lye a thought more nye
To learned Chaucer, and rare Beaumont lye

A little neerer Spenser to make roome
For Shakespeare in your threefold fowerfold Tombe.
To lodge all fowre in one bed make a shift
Vntill Doomesdaye, for hardly will a fift
Betwixt this day and that by Fate be slayne
For whom your Curtaines may be drawn againe.
If your precedency in death doth barre
A fourth place in your sacred sepulcher,
Vnder this carued marble of thine owne
Sleepe rare Tragœdian Shakespeare, sleep alone,
Thy vnmolested peace, vnshared Caue,
Possesse as Lord not Tenant of thy Graue,
That vnto us and others it may be
Honor hereafter to be layde by thee.

BEN JONSON *a*. From *Conversations with William Drummond*. 1618–19.
(These are notes by Drummond on his talks with Jonson, who
set out to see him at Hawthornden in the summer of 1618.)

b. *Verses* on the fifth preliminary leaf to F1, 1623. Jonson is one of the
'Friends and guides' referred to by Heminge and Condell.

c. From *Timber: or Discoveries*. Probably written after 1630 when Jonson
was 'prest by extremities', and struggling with want and disease 'for breath'.

a. His Censure of the English Poets was this . . .
That Shaksperr wanted Arte.

b.
To the memory of my beloued
The Avthor
Mr. William Shakespeare:
And
what he hath left vs.

To draw no enuy (Shakespeare) *on thy name,*
Am I thus ample to thy Booke, and Fame:
While I confesse thy writings to be such,
As neither Man, *nor* Muse, *can praise too much.*
'Tis true, and all mens suffrage. But these wayes
Were not the paths I meant vnto thy praise:
For seeliest Ignorance on these may light,
Which, when it sounds at best, but eccho's right;
Or blinde Affection, which doth ne're aduance
The truth, but gropes, and vrgeth all by chance;
Or crafty Malice, might pretend this praise,
And thinke to ruine, where it seem'd to raise.
These are, as some infamous Baud, or Whore,
Should praise a Matron. What could hurt her more?
But thou art proofe against them, and indeed

Aboue th'ill fortune of them, or the need.
 I, therefore will begin. Soule of the Age!
  The applause! delight! the wonder of our Stage!
My Shakespeare, *rise; I will not lodge thee by*
 Chaucer, *or* Spenser, *or bid* Beaumont *lye*
A little further, to make thee a roome:
 Thou art a Moniment, without a tombe,
And art aliue still, while thy Booke doth liue,
 And we haue wits to read, and praise to giue.
That I not mixe thee so, ny braine excuses;
 I meane with great, but disproportion'd Muses:
For, if I thought my iudgement were of yeeres,
 I should commit thee surely with thy peeres,
And tell, how farre thou didst our Lily *out-shine,*
 Or sporting Kid, *or* Marlowes *mighty line.*
And though thou hadst small Latine, *and less* Greeke,
 From thence to honour thee, I would not seeke
For names; but call forth thund'ring Æschilus,
 Euripides, *and* Sophocles *to us,*
Paccuuius, Accius, *him of* Cordoua *dead,*
 To life againe, to heare thy Buskin tread,
And shake a Stage: Or, when thy Sockes were on,
 Leaue thee alone, for the comparison
Of all, that insolent Greece, *or haughtie* Rome
 Sent forth, or since did from their ashes come.
Triumph, my Britaine, *thou hast one to showe,*
 To whom all scenes of Europe *homage owe.*
He was not of an age, but for all time!
 And all the Muses *still were in their prime,*
When like Apollo *he came forth to warme*
 Our eares, or like a Mercury *to charme!*
Nature her selfe was proud of his designes,
 And ioy'd to weare the dressing of his lines!
Which were so richly spun, and wouen so fit,
 As, since, she will vouchsafe no other Wit.
The merry Greeke, *tart* Aristophanes,
 Neat Terence, *witty* Plautus, *now not please;*
But antiquated, and deserted lye
 As they were not of Natures family.
Yet must I not giue Nature all: Thy Art,
 My gentle Shakespeare, *must enioy a part.*
For though the Poets *matter, Nature be,*
 His Art doth giue the fashion. And, that he,
Who casts to write a liuing line, must sweat,
 (Such as thine are) and strike the second heat
Vpon the Muses anuile: turne the same,
 (And himselfe with it) that he thinkes to frame;

Or for the lawrell, he may gaine a scorne,
*   For a good* Poet's *made, as well as borne.*
And such wert thou. Looke how the fathers face
*   Liues in his issue, euen so, the race*
Of Shakespeares *minde, and manners brightly shines*
*   In his well torned, and true-filed lines:*
In each of which, he seemes to shake a Lance,
*   As brandish't at the eyes of Ignorance.*
Sweet Swan of Auon! *what a sight it were*
*   To see thee in our waters yet appeare,*
And make those flights vpon the bankes of Thames,
*   That so did take* Eliza *and our* Iames!
But stay, I see thee in the Hemisphere
*   Aduanc'd, and made a Constellation there!*
Shine forth, thou Starre of Poets, *and with rage,*
*   Or influence, chide, or cheere the drooping Stage;*
Which, since thy flight from hence, hath mourn'd like night,
*   And despaires day, but for thy Volumes light.*

c. I *remember*, the Players have often mentioned it as an honour to *Shake-speare*, that in his writing, (whatsoever he penn'd) hee never blotted out line. My answer hath beene, would he had blotted a thousand. Which they thought a malevolent speech. I had not told posterity this, but for their ignorance, who choose that circumstance to commend their friend by, wherein he most faulted. And to justifie mine own candor, (for I lov'd the man, and doe honour his memory (on this side Idolatry) as much as any.) Hee was (indeed) honest, and of an open, and free nature: had an excellent *Phantsie*; brave notions, and gentle expressions: wherein hee flow'd with that facility, that sometime it was necessary he should be stop'd: *Sufflaminandus erat*: as *Augustus* said of *Haterius*. His wit was in his owne power; would the rule of it had beene so too. Many times hee fell into those things, could not escape laughter: As when hee said in the person of *Cæsar*, one speaking to him: *Cæsar thou dost me wrong*. He replyed: *Cæsar did never wrong, but with just cause* and such like: which were ridiculous. But hee redeemed his vices with his vertues. There was ever more in him to be praysed, then to be pardoned.

JOHN HEMINGE AND HENRY CONDELL (The editors of the First Folio, 1623.)

To the great Variety of Readers

It had bene a thing, we confesse, worthie to haue been wished, that the Author himselfe had liu'd to haue set forth, and ouerseen his owne writings; But since it hath bin ordain'd otherwise, and he by death departed from that right, we pray you do not envie his Friends, the office of their care, and paine, to haue collected & publish'd them; and so to haue publish'd them, as where (before) you were abus'd with diuerse stolne, and surreptitious copies, maimed, and deformed by the frauds and stealthes of iniurious impostors that expos'd them: euen those, are now offer'd to your view cur'd, and perfect of their limbes; and all the rest, absolute in their numbers, as he conceiued them. Who, as he was a happie imitator of Nature, was a most gentle expresser of it. His mind and hand went together: And what he thought, he vttered with that easinesse, that wee haue scarce receiued from him a blot in his papers. But it is not our prouince, who onely gather his works, and giue them you, to praise him. It is yours that reade him. And there we hope, to your diuers capacities, you will finde enough, both to draw, and hold you: for his wit can no more lie hid, then it could be lost. Reade him, therefore; and againe, and againe: And if then you doe not like him, surely you are in some manifest danger, not to vnderstand him. And so we leaue you to other of his Friends, whom if you need, can bee your guides: if you neede them not, you can leade your selues, and others. And such Readers we wish him.

HUGH HOLLAND From sixth preliminary leaf to F 1, 1623.

Vpon the Lines and Life of the Famous
Scenicke Poet, Master William Shakespeare.

Those hands, which you so clapt, go now, and wring
You *Britaines* braue; for done are *Shakespeares* dayes:
His dayes are done, that made the dainty Playes,
Which made the Globe of heau'n and earth to ring.
Dry'de is that veine, dry'd is the *Thespian* Spring,
Turn'd all to teares, and *Phœbus* clouds his rayes:
That corp's, that coffin now besticke those bayes,
Which crown'd him *Poet* first, then *Poets* King,
If *Tragedies* might any *Prologue* haue,
All those he made, would scarse make one to this:
Where *Fame*, now that he gone is to the graue
(Deaths publique tyring-house) the *Nuncius* is.
  For though his line of life went soone about,
  The life yet of his lines shall neuer out.

LEONARD DIGGES From eighth preliminary leaf to F 1, 1623.

To the Memorie
of the deceased Author Maister
W. Shakespeare.

Shake-speare, at length thy pious fellowes giue
The world thy Workes: thy Workes, by which, out-liue
Thy Tombe, thy name must: when that stone is rent,
And Time dissolues thy Stratford Moniment,
Here we aliue shall view thee still. This Booke,
When Brasse and Marble fade, shall make thee looke

Fresh to all Ages: when Posteritie
Shall loath what's new, thinke all is prodegie
That is not *Shake-speares*; eu'ry Line, each Verse,
Here shall reuiue, redeeme thee from thy Herse.
Nor Fire, nor cankring Age, as *Naso* said,
Of his, thy wit-fraught Booke shall once inuade.
Nor shall I e're beleeue, or thinke thee dead
(Though mist) untill our bankrout Stage be sped
(Impossible) with some new strain t' out-do
Passions of *Iuliet*, and her *Romeo*;
Or till I heare a Scene more nobly take,
Then when thy half-Sword parlying *Romans* spake,
Till these, till any of thy Volumes rest
Shall with more fire, more feeling be exprest,
Be sure, our *Shake-speare*, thou canst neuer dye,
But crown'd with Lawrell, liue eternally.

MICHAEL DRAYTON From *Elegy to Henry Reynolds*. 1627.

And be it said of thee,
Shakespeare, thou hadst as smooth a Comicke vaine,
Fitting the socke, and in thy naturall braine,
As strong conception, and as Cleere a rage,
As any one that trafiqu'd with the stage.

JOHN MILTON Published in prefatory matter to the Second Folio, 1632.
(This was the first of Milton's poems to be published.)

On *Shakespear*, 1630.

What needs my *Shakespear* for his honour'd Bones,
The labour of an age in piled Stones,
Or that his hallow'd reliques should be hid
Under a Star-ypointing *Pyramid*?
Dear son of memory, great heir of Fame,
What need'st thou such weak witness of thy name?
Thou in our wonder and astonishment
Hast built thy self a live-long Monument.
For whilst toth' shame of slow-endeavouring art,
Thy easie numbers flow, and that each heart
Hath from the leaves of thy unvalu'd Book,
Those Delphick lines with deep impression took,
Then thou our fancy of it self bereaving,
Dost make us Marble with too much conceaving;
And so Sepulcher'd in such pomp dost lie,
That Kings for such a Tomb would wish to die.

THOMAS HEYWOOD From *The Hierarchie of the Blessed Angels*. 1635.

> Our moderne Poets to that passe are driuen,
> Those names are curtal'd which they first had giuen;
> And, as we wisht to haue their memories drown'd,
> We scarcely can afford them halfe their sound. . . .
> Mellifluous *Shake-speare*, whose inchanting Quill
> Commanded Mirth or Passion, was but *Will*.

LEONARD DIGGES From John Benson's edition of Shakespeare's *Poems*, 1640.

> Poets are borne not made, when I would prove
> This truth, the glad rememberance I must love
> Of never dying *Shakespeare*, who alone,
> Is argument enough to make that one.
> First, that he was a Poet none would doubt,
> That heard th'applause of what he sees set out
> Imprinted; where thou hast (I will not say)
> Reader his Workes (for to contrive a Play
> To him twas none) the patterne of all wit,
> Art without Art unparaleld as yet.
> Next Nature onely helpt him, for looke thorow
> This whole Booke, thou shalt find he doth not borrow,
> One phrase from Greekes, nor Latines imitate,
> Nor once from vulgar Languages Translate,
> Nor Plagiari-like from others gleane,
> Nor begs he from each witty friend a Scene
> To peece his Acts with, all that he doth write,
> Is pure his owne, plot, language exquisite,
> But oh! what praise more powerfull can we give
> The dead, than that by him the Kings men live,
> His Players, which should they but have shar'd the Fate,
> All else expir'd within the short Termes date;
> How could the Globe have prospered, since through want
> Of change, the Plaies and Poems had growne scant.
> But happy Verse thou shalt be sung and heard,
> When hungry quills shall be such honour bard.
> Then vanish upstart Writers to each Stage,
> You needy Poetasters of this Age,
> Where *Shakespeare* liv'd or spake, Vermine forbeare,
> Least with your froth you spot them, come not neere;
> But if you needs must write, if poverty
> So pinch, that otherwise you starve and die,
> On Gods name may the Bull or Cockpit have
> Your lame blancke Verse, to keepe you from the grave:
> Or let new Fortunes younger brethren see,
> What they can picke from your leane industry.

I doe not wonder when you offer at
Blacke-Friers, that you suffer: tis the fate
Of richer veines, prime judgments that have far'd
The worse, with this deceased man compar'd.
So have I seene, when Cesar would appeare,
And on the Stage at halfe-sword parley were,
Brutus and *Cassius*: oh how the Audience,
Were ravish'd, with what wonder they went thence,
When some new day they would not brooke a line,
Of tedious (though well laboured) *Catiline*;
Sejanus too was irkesome, they priz'de more
Honest *Iago*, or the jealous Moore.
And though the Fox and subtill Alchimist,
Long intermitted could not quite be mist,
Though these have sham'd all the Ancients, and might raise,
Their Authors merit with a crowne of Bayes.
Yet these sometimes, even at a friend's desire
Acted, have scarce defraid the Seacoale fire
And doore-keepers: when let but *Falstaffe* come,
Hall, Poines, the rest you scarce shall have a roome
All is so pester'd: let but *Beatrice*
And *Benedicke* be seene, loe in a trice
The Cockpit Galleries, Boxes, all are full
To heare *Maluoglio* that crosse garter'd Gull.
Briefe, there is nothing in his wit fraught Booke,
Whose sound we would not heare, on whose worth looke
Like old coynd gold, whose lines in every page,
Shall pass true currant to succeeding age.
But why doe I dead *Sheakspeares* praise recite,
Some second *Shakespeare* must of *Shakespeare* write;
For me tis needlesse, since an host of men,
Will pay to clap his praise, to free my Pen.

RESTORATION CRITICISM

THOMAS FULLER From *Worthies, Warwickshire*. 1662. (Fuller [1608–1661]
            began collecting materials for his *Worthies*, possibly as early
as 1643.)

William Shakespeare was born at *Stratford* on *Avon* in this County, in
whom three eminent Poets may seem in some sort to be compounded.

1. *Martial* in the *Warlike* sound of his Sur-name (whence some may
conjecture him of a *Military extraction*), *Hasti-vibrans*, or *Shake-speare*.

2. *Ovid*, the most *naturall* and *witty* of all Poets, and hence it was that
Queen *Elizabeth*, coming into a Grammar-School, made this extemporary
verse,

> 'Persius a Crab-staffe, Bawdy *Martial*,
> *Ovid* a fine Wag.'

3. *Plautus*, who was an exact Comædian, yet never any Scholar, as our *Shake-speare* (if alive) would confess himself. Adde to all these, that though his genius generally was *jocular*, and inclining him to *festivity*, yet he could (when so disposed) be *solemn* and *serious*, as appears by his Tragedies, so that *Heraclitus* himself (I mean if secret and unseen) might afford to smile at his Comedies, they were so *merry*, and *Democritus* scarce forbear to sigh at his Tragedies they were so *mournfull*.

He was an eminent instance of the truth of that Rule, *Poeta non fit, sed nascitur*, one is not *made*, but *born* a Poet. Indeed his Learning was very little, so that as *Cornish diamonds* are not polished by any Lapidary, but are pointed and smoothed even as they are taken out of the Earth, so *nature* it self was all the *art* which was used upon him.

Many were the *wit-combates* betwixt him and *Ben Johnson*, which two I behold like a *Spanish great Gallion* and an *English man of War*; Master *Johnson* (like the former) was built far higher in Learning; *Solid*, but *Slow* in his performances. *Shake-spear*, with the *English-man of War*, lesser in *bulk*, but lighter in *sailing*, could turn with all tides, tack about and take advantage of all winds, by the quickness of his Wit and Invention.

MARGARET CAVENDISH, Duchess of Newcastle *Letter CXXIII*, 1664.

MADAM,

I Wonder how that Person you mention in your Letter, could either have the Conscience, or Confidence to Dispraise *Shakespear's* Playes, as to say they were made up onely with Clowns, Fools, Watchmen, and the like; . . .

Shakespear did not want Wit, to Express to the Life all Sorts of Persons, of what Quality, Profession, Degree, Breeding, or Birth soever; nor did he want Wit to Express the Divers, and Different Humours, or Natures, or Several Passions in Mankind; and so Well he hath Express'd in his Playes all Sorts of Persons, as one would think he had been Transformed into every one of those Persons he hath Described; and as sometimes one would think he was really himself the Clown or Jester he Feigns, so one would think, he was also the King, and Privy Counsellor; also as one would think he were Really the Coward he Feigns, so one would think he were the most Valiant, and Experienced Souldier; Who would not think he had been such a man as his Sir *John Falstaff*? and who would not think he had been *Harry* the Fifth? & certainly *Julius Cæsar*, *Augustus Cæsar*, and *Antonius*, did never Really Act their parts Better, if so Well, as he hath Described them, and I believe that *Antonius* and *Brutus* did not Speak Better to the People, than he hath Feign'd them; nay, one would think that he had been Metamorphosed from a Man to a Woman, for who could Describe *Cleopatra* Better than he hath done, and many other Females of his own Creating, as *Nan Page*, Mrs. *Page*, Mrs. *Ford*, the Doctors Maid, *Bettrice*, Mrs. *Quickly*, *Doll Tearsheet*, and others, too many to Relate? and in his Tragick Vein, he Presents Passions so Naturally, and Misfortunes so Probably, as he Peirces the Souls of his Readers with such a true Sense and Feeling thereof, that it Forces Tears through their Eyes, and almost Perswades them, they are Really Actors, or at least Present at those Tragedies. Who would not Swear he had been a

Noble Lover, that could Woo so well? and there is not any person he hath Described in his Book, but his Readers might think they were Well acquainted with them; indeed *Shakespear* had a Clear Judgment, a Quick Wit, a Spreading Fancy, a Subtil Observation, a Deep Apprehension, and a most Eloquent Elocution; truly, he was a Natural Orator, as well as a Natural Poet, and he was not an Orator to Speak Well only on some Subjects, as Lawyers, who can make Eloquent Orations at the Bar, and Plead Subtilly and Wittily in Law-Cases, or Divines, that can Preach Eloquent Sermons, or Dispute Subtilly and Wittily in Theology, but take them from that, and put them to other Subjects, and they will be to seek; but *Shakespear*'s Wit and Eloquence was General, for, and upon all Subjects, he rather wanted Subjects for his Wit and Eloquence to Work on, for which he was Forced to take some of his Plots out of History, where he only took the Bare Designs, the Wit and Language being all his Own; and so much he had above others, that those, who Writ after him, were Forced to Borrow of him, or rather to Steal from him.

DRYDEN a. *An Essay of Dramatick Poesie,* 1668. b. *Essay on the Dramatique Poetry of the Last Age,* 1672. c. *Preface to Troilus and Cressida, or Truth found too late,* 1679.

a. To begin, then, with Shakespeare. He was the man who of all modern, and perhaps ancient poets, had the largest and most comprehensive soul. All the images of Nature were still present to him, and he drew them, not laboriously, but luckily; when he describes any thing, you more than see it, you feel it too. Those who accuse him to have wanted learning, give him the greater commendation: he was naturally learned; he needed not the spectacles of books to read Nature; he looked inwards, and found her there. I cannot say he is every where alike; were he so, I should do him injury to compare him with the greatest of mankind. He is many times flat, insipid; his comic wit degenerating into clenches, his serious swelling into bombast. But he is always great, when some occasion is presented to him; no man can say he ever had a fit subject for his wit, and did not then raise himself as high above the rest of poets,

Quantum lenta solent inter viburna cupressi.

The consideration of this made Mr. Hales of Eaton say, that there was no subject of which any poet ever writ, but he would produce it much better treated of in Shakespeare; and however others are now generally preferred before him, yet the age wherein he lived, which had contemporaries with him Fletcher and Jonson, never equalled them to him in their esteem: and in the last King's court, when Ben's reputation was at highest, Sir John Suckling, and with him the greater part of the courtiers, set our Shakespeare far above him. . . .

If I would compare Jonson with Shakespeare, I must acknowledge him the more correct poet, but Shakespeare the greater wit. Shakespeare was the Homer, or father of our dramatic poets; Jonson was the Virgil, the pattern of elaborate writing; I admire him, but I love Shakespeare.

b. But, malice and partiality set apart, let any man, who understands English, read diligently the works of Shakespeare and Fletcher, and I dare undertake, that he will find in every page either some solecism of speech, or some notorious flaw in sense; and yet these men are reverenced, when we are not forgiven. That their wit is great, and many times their expressions noble, envy itself cannot deny. But the times were ignorant in which they lived. Poetry was then, if not in its infancy among us, at least not arrived to its vigour and maturity: witness the lameness of their plots; many of which, especially those which they writ first (for even that age refined itself in some measure), were made up of some ridiculous incoherent story, which in one play many times took up the business of an age. I suppose I need not name *Pericles, Prince of Tyre,* nor the historical plays of Shakespeare: besides many of the rest, as the *Winter's Tale, Love's Labour Lost, Measure for Measure,* which were either grounded on impossibilities, or at least so meanly written, that the comedy neither caused your mirth, nor the serious part your concernment. . . .

Shakespeare, who many times has written better than any poet, in any language, is yet so far from writing wit always, or expressing that wit according to the dignity of the subject, that he writes, in many places, below the dullest writer of ours, or any precedent age. Never did any author precipitate himself from such height of thought to so low expressions, as he often does. He is the very Janus of poets; he wears almost everywhere two faces; and you have scarce begun to admire the one, ere you despise the other.

c. If Shakespeare be allowed, as I think he must, to have made his characters distinct, it will easily be inferred that he understood the nature of the passions: because it has been proved already that confused passions make undistinguishable characters: yet I cannot deny that he' has his failings; but they are not so much in the passions themselves, as in his manner of expression: he often obscures his meaning by his words, and sometimes makes it unintelligible. I will not say of so great a poet, that he distinguished not the blown puffy style from true sublimity; but I may venture to maintain, that the fury of his fancy often transported him beyond the bounds of judgment, either in coining of new words and phrases, or racking words which were in use, into the violence of a catachresis. It is not that I would explode the use of metaphors from passions, for Longinus thinks 'em necessary to raise it: but to use 'em at every word, to say nothing without a metaphor, a simile, an image, or description, is, I doubt, to smell a little too strongly of the buskin. I must be forced to give an example of expressing passion figuratively; but that I may do it with respect to Shakespeare, it shall not be taken from anything of his: 'tis an exclamation against Fortune, quoted in his *Hamlet* but written by some other poet[1]—

---

[1] Dryden was probably wrong here. As far as we know Shakespeare wrote the passage, but in the earlier rhetorical style of Marlowe as a contrast to his own verse in *Hamlet.*

> Out, out, thou strumpet, Fortune! all you gods,
> In general synod, take away her power;
> Break all the spokes and felleys from her wheel,
> And bowl the round nave down the hill of Heav'n,
> As low as to the fiends.

And immediately after, speaking of Hecuba, when Priam was killed before her eyes—

> The mobbled queen
> Threatening the flame, ran up and down
> With bisson rheum; a clout upon that head
> Where late the diadem stood; and for a robe,
> About her lank and all o'er-teemed loins,
> A blanket in th'alarm of fear caught up.
> Who this had seen, with tongue in venom steep'd
> 'Gainst Fortune's state would treason have pronounced.
> But if the gods themselves did see her then,
> When she saw Pyrrhus make malicious sport
> In mincing with his sword her husband's limbs,
> The instant burst of clamour that she made
> (Unless things mortal move them not at all)
> Would have made milch the burning eyes of heaven,
> And passion in the gods.

What a pudder is here kept in raising the expression of trifling thoughts! Would not a man have thought that the poet had been bound prentice to a wheelwright, for his first rant? and had followed a ragman, for the clout and blanket in the second? Fortune is painted on a wheel, and therefore the writer, in a rage, will have poetical justice done upon every member of that engine: after this execution, he bowls the nave down-hill, from Heaven, to the fiends (an unreasonable long mark, a man would think); 'tis well there are no solid orbs to stop it in the way, or no element of fire to consume it: but when it came to the earth, it must be monstrous heavy, to break ground as low as the centre. His making milch the burning eyes of heaven was a pretty tolerable flight too: and I think no man ever drew milk out of eyes before him: yet, to make the wonder greater, these eyes were burning. Such a sight indeed were enough to have raised passion in the gods; but to excuse the effects of it, he tells you, perhaps they did not see it. Wise men would be glad to find a little sense couched under all these pompous words; for bombast is commonly the delight of that audience which loves Poetry, but understands it not: and as commonly has been the practice of those writers, who, not being able to infuse a natural passion into the mind, have made it their business to ply the ears, and to stun their judges by the noise.

But Shakespeare does not often thus; for the passions in his scene between Brutus and Cassius are extremely natural, the thoughts are such as arise from the matter, the expression of 'em not viciously figurative. I cannot leave this subject, before I do justice to that divine poet, by giving you one of his passionate descriptions: 'tis of Richard the Second when he was deposed, and led in triumph through the streets of London by Henry of Bullingbrook: the painting of it is so lively, and the words so moving, that I have scarce read anything comparable to it in any other language. Suppose you have seen already the fortunate usurper passing through the crowd, and followed by the shouts and acclamations of the people; and now behold King Richard entering upon the scene: consider the wretchedness of his condition, and his carriage in it; and refrain from pity if you can—

> As in a theatre, the eyes of men,
> After a well-graced actor leaves the stage,
> Are idly bent on him that enters next,
> Thinking his prattle to be tedious:
> Even so, or with much more contempt, men's eyes
> Did scowl on Richard: no man cried, God save him:
> No joyful tongue gave him his welcome home.
> But dust was thrown upon his sacred head,
> Which with such gentle sorrow he shook off,
> His face still combating with tears and smiles
> (The badges of his grief and patience),
> That had not God (for some strong purpose) steel'd
> The hearts of men, they must perforce have melted,
> And barbarism itself have pitied him.

To speak justly of this whole matter: 'tis neither height of thought that is discommended, nor pathetic vehemence, nor any nobleness of expression in its proper place; but 'tis a false measure of all these, something which is like them; 'tis the Bristol-stone, which appears like a diamond; 'tis an extravagant thought, instead of a sublime one; 'tis roaring madness, instead of vehemence; and a sound of words instead of sense. If Shakespeare were stripped of all the bombasts in his passions, and dressed in the most vulgar words, we should find the beauties of his thoughts remaining; if his embroideries were burnt down, there would still be silver at the bottom of the melting-pot: but I fear (at least let me fear it for myself) that we, who ape his sounding words, have nothing of his thought, but are all outside; there is not so much as a dwarf within our giant's clothes. Therefore, let not Shakespeare suffer for our sakes; 'tis our fault, who succeed him in an age which is more refined, if we imitate him so ill, that we copy his failings only, and make a virtue of that in our writings which in him was an imperfection.

For what remains, the excellency of that poet was, as I have said, in the more manly passions; Fletcher's in the softer: Shakespeare writ better betwixt man and man; Fletcher betwixt man and woman: consequently, the one described friendship better; the other love: yet Shakespeare taught Fletcher to write love: and Juliet and Desdemona are originals. 'Tis true, the scholar had the softer soul; but the master had the kinder. Friendship is both a virtue and a passion essentially; love is a passion only in its nature, and is not a virtue but by accident: good nature makes friendship; but effeminacy love. Shakespeare had an universal mind, which comprehended all characters and passions; Fletcher a more confined and limited: for though he treated love in perfection, yet honour, ambition, revenge, and generally all the stronger passions, he either touched not, or not masterly. To conclude all, he was a limb of Shakespeare.

EDWARD PHILLIPS *Theatrum Poetarum*. 1675. (Phillips was Milton's
    nephew.)

Shakespear, in spite of all his unfiled expressions, his rambling and indigested
Fancys, the laughter of the *Critical*, yet must be confess't a *Poet* above many
that go beyond him in Literature some degrees. . . .

William Shakespear, the Glory of the English Stage; whose nativity at
Stratford upon *Avon*, is the highest honour that Town can boast of: from an
Actor of Tragedies and Comedies, he became a *Maker*; and such a Maker,
that though some others may perhaps pretend to a more exact *Decorum* and
œconomie, especially in Tragedy, never any express't a more lofty and Tragic
heighth; never any represented nature more purely to the life, and where the
polishments of Art are most wanting, as probably his Learning was not extraordinary, he pleaseth with a certain wild and native Elegance; and in all his
Writings hath an unvulgar style, as well in his *Venus and Adonis*, his *Rape of
Lucrece* and other various Poems, as in his Dramatics.

THOMAS RYMER *A Short View of Tragedy*. 1693.

What Reformation may not we expect now, that in *France* they see the
necessity of a *Chorus* to their Tragedies? *Boyer*, and *Racine*, both of the Royal
Academy, have led the Dance; they have tried the success in the last Plays
that were Presented by them.

The *Chorus* was the root and original, and is certainly always the most
necessary part of Tragedy.

The *Spectators* thereby are secured, that their Poet shall not juggle, or put
upon them in the matter of *Place*, and *Time*, other than is just and reasonable
for the representation.

And the *Poet* has this benefit; the *Chorus* is a goodly *Show*, so that he need
not ramble from his Subject out of his Wits for some foreign Toy or Hobby-
horse, to humor the multitude. . . .

Gorboduck is a fable, doubtless, better turn'd for Tragedy, than any on this
side the *Alps* in his time; and might have been a better direction to *Shakespear*
and *Ben. Johnson* than any guide they have had the luck to follow.

It is objected by our Neighbours against the English, that we delight in
bloody spectacles. Our Poets who have not imitated *Gorboduck* in the regularity and roundness of the design, have not failed on the Theatre to give us
the *atrocité* and blood enough in all Conscience. From this time Dramatick
Poetry began to thrive with us, and flourish wonderfully. The French
confess they had nothing in this kind considerable till 1635, that the Academy
Royal was founded. Long before which time we had from *Shakespear*,
Fletcher, and *Ben. Johnson* whole Volumes; at this day in possession of the
Stage, and acted with greater applause than ever. Yet after all, I fear what
Quintilian pronounced concerning the Roman Comedy, may as justly be said
of English Tragedy: In Tragedy we come short extreamly; hardly have we a
slender shadow of it. . . .

Shakespears genius lay for Comedy and Humour. In Tragedy he appears quite out of his Element; his Brains are turn'd, he raves and rambles, without any coherence, any spark of reason, or any rule to controul him, or set bounds to his phrenzy. His imagination was still running after his Masters, the Coblers, and Parish Clerks, and *Old Testament Stroulers*. So he might make bold with *Portia*, as they had done with the Virgin Mary. Who, in a Church Acting their Play call'd *The Incarnation*, had usually the *Ave Mary* mumbl'd over to a stradling wench (for the blessed Virgin) straw-hatted, blew-apron'd, big-bellied, with her Immaculate Conception up to her chin.

EIGHTEENTH-CENTURY CRITICISM

NICHOLAS ROWE *Preface* to his edition of Shakespeare. 1709.

His plays are properly to be distinguished only into Comedies and Tragedies. Those which are called Histories, and even some of his Comedies, are really Tragedies, with a run or Mixture of Comedy amongst 'em. The way of Tragi-Comedy was the common mistake of that age, and is indeed become so agreeable to the English taste, that tho' the severer critics among us cannot bear it, yet the generality of our audiences seem to be better pleased with it than with an exact Tragedy. . . .

The style of his Comedy is, in general, natural to the characters, and easy in itself; and the wit most commonly sprightly and pleasing, except in those places where he runs into dogrel rhymes, as in the *Comedy of Errors*, and a passage or two in some other plays. As for his jingling sometimes, and playing upon words, it was the common vice of the age he lived in: and if we find it in the pulpit, perhaps it may not be thought too light for the stage.

But certainly the greatness of this author's Genius does no where so much appear, as where he gives his imagination an entire loose, and raises his fancy to a flight above mankind and the limits of the visible world. Such are his attempts in *The Tempest, Midsummer Night's Dream, Macbeth* and *Hamlet*. . . .

If one undertook to examine the greatest part of these (the Tragedies) by those rules which are established by Aristotle, and taken from the model of the Grecian stage, it would be no very hard task to find a great many faults: but as Shakespeare lived under a kind of mere Light of Nature, and had never been made acquainted with the regularity of those written precepts, so it would be hard to judge him by a law he knew nothing of. We are to consider him as a man that lived in a state of almost universal license and ignorance: there was no established judge, but everyone took the liberty to write according to the dictates of his own fancy. When one considers, that there is not one play before him of a reputation good enough to entitle it to an appearance on the present stage, it cannot but be a matter of great wonder that he should advance dramatic poetry as far as he did.

ADDISON *The Spectator*, 592. 1714.

Our critics do not seem sensible that there is more beauty in the works of a great genius who is ignorant of the rules of art, than in those of a little genius who knows and observes them. . . . Our inimitable Shakespear is a stumbling-block to the whole tribe of these rigid critics. Who would not rather read one of his plays, where there is not a single rule of the stage observed, than any production of a modern critic, where there is not one of them violated? Shakespear was indeed born with all the seeds of poetry, and may be compared to the stone in Pyrrhus's ring, which, as Pliny tells us, had the figure of Apollo and the Nine Muses in the veins of it, produced by the spontaneous hand of Nature, without any help from Art.

POPE a. *Preface* to his edition of Shakespeare, 1725. b. *Epistle to Augustus*, 1737.

a. If ever any author deserved the name of an *Original*, it was Shakespear. . . . The poetry of Shakespear was inspiration indeed: he is not so much an imitator, as an instrument, of Nature; and 'tis not so just to say that he speaks from her, as that she speaks thro' him.

His *Characters* are so much Nature her self, that 'tis a sort of injury to call them by so distant a name as copies of her. Those of other poets have a constant resemblance, which shews that they received them from one another, and were but multipliers of the same image: each picture like a mock-rainbow is but the reflexion of a reflexion. But every single character in Shakespear is as much an individual, as those in life itself; it is as impossible to find any two alike; and such as from their relation or affinity in any respect appear most to be twins, will upon comparison be found remarkably distinct. To this life and variety of character, we must add the wonderful preservation of it; which is such throughout his plays, that had all the speeches been printed without the very names of the persons, I believe one might have applied them with certainty to every speaker.

The *Power* over our *Passions* was never possessed in a more eminent degree, or displayed in so different instances. Yet all along, there is seen no labour, no pains to raise them; no preparation to guide our guess to the effect, or be perceived to lead towards it: but the heart swells, and the tears burst out, just at the proper places: we are surprised, the moment we weep; and yet upon reflection find the passion so just, that we should be surprised if we had not wept, and wept at that very moment.

How astonishing is it again, that the passions directly opposite to these, Laughter and Spleen, are no less at his command! that he is not more a master of the *Great*, than of the *Ridiculous* in human nature; of our noblest tendernesses, than of our vainest foibles; of our strongest emotions, than of our idlest sensations!

Nor does he only excel in the Passions: in the coolness of Reflection and Reasoning he is full as admirable. His *Sentiments* are not only in general the most pertinent and judicious upon every subject; but by a talent very peculiar, something between Penetration and Felicity, he hits upon that particular point on which the bent of each argument turns, or the force of each motive depends. This is perfectly amazing, from a man of no education or experience in those great and public scenes of life which are usually the subject of his thoughts: so that he seems to have known the world by intuition, to have looked through human nature at one glance, and to be the only author that gives ground for a very new opinion, that the Philosopher and even the Man of the world, may be *Born*, as well as the Poet.

It must be owned that with all these great excellencies, he has almost as great defects; and that as he has certainly written better, so he has perhaps written worse, than any other. But I think I can in some measure account for these defects, from several causes and accidents; without which it is hard to imagine that so large and so enlightened a mind could ever have been susceptible of them. . . .

Not only the common audience had no notion of the rules of writing, but few even of the better sort piqued themselves upon any great degree of knowledge or nicety that way. . . . To judge therefore of Shakespear by Aristotle's rules, is like trying a man by the laws of one country, who acted under those of another. He writ to the *People*; and writ at first without patronage from the better sort, and therefore without aims of pleasing them: without assistance or advice from the learned, as without the advantage of education or acquaintance among them; without that knowledge of the best models, the Ancients, to inspire him with an emulation of them; in a word, without any views of reputation, and of what poets are pleased to call immortality.

Yet it must be observed, that when his performances had merited the protection of his Prince, and when the encouragement of the Court had succeeded to that of the Town; the works of his riper years are manifestly raised above those of his former. The dates of his plays sufficiently evidence that his productions improved, in proportion to the respect he had for his auditors. . . .

Another cause (and no less strong than the former) may be deduced from our author's being a player, and forming himself first upon the judgments of that body of men whereof he was a member. They have ever had a standard to themselves, upon other principles than those of Aristotle. As they live by the majority, they know no rule but that of pleasing the present humour, and complying with the wit in fashion; a consideration which brings all their judgment to a short point. Players are just such judges of what is *right*, as taylors are of what is *graceful*. And in this view it will be but fair to allow, that most of our author's faults are less to be ascribed to his wrong judgment as a Poet, than to his right judgment as a Player. . . .

As to a wrong choice of the subject, a wrong conduct of the incidents, false thoughts, forced expressions, &c. if these are not to be ascribed to the foresaid accidental reasons, they must be charged upon the poet himself, and there is no help for it. But I think the two disadvantages which I have mentioned (to be obliged to please the lowest of people, and to keep the worst of company) if the consideration be extended as far as it reasonably may, will appear sufficient to mis-lead and depress the greatest genius upon earth.

But as to his *Want of Learning*, it may be necessary to say something more: there is certainly a vast difference between *Learning* and *Languages*. How far he was ignorant of the latter, I cannot determine; but 'tis plain he had much Reading at least, if they wiH not call it Learning. Nor is it any great matter, if a man has Knowledge, whether he has it from one language or from another. . . .

I am inclined to think this opinion proceeded originally from the zeal of the partisans of our author and Ben Jonson; as they endeavoured to exalt the one at the expense of the other. It is ever the nature of parties to be in extremes; and nothing is so probable, as that because Ben Jonson had much the most learning, it was said on the one hand that Shakespear had none at all; and because Shakespear had much the most wit and fancy, it was retorted on the other, that Jonson wanted both. . . .

I will conclude by saying of Shakespear, that with all his faults, and with all the irregularity of his *Drama,* one may look upon his works, in comparison of those that are more finished and regular, as upon an ancient majestic piece of *Gothic* architecture, compared with a neat modern building: the latter is more elegant and glaring, but the former is more strong and more solemn. It must be allowed, that in one of these there are materials enough to make many of the other. It has much the greater variety, and much the nobler apartments; tho' we are often conducted to them by dark, odd, and uncouth passages. Nor does the Whole fail to strike us with greater reverence, tho' many of the Parts are childish, ill-placed, and unequal to its grandeur.

b.   Shakespear, (whom you and ev'ry Play-house bill
             Style the divine, the matchless, what you will)
             For gain, not glory, wing'd his roving flight
             And grew Immortal in his own despight . . .

             Late, very late, correctness grew our care
             When the tir'd nation breath'd from civil war.
             Exact Racine, and Corneille's noble fire
             Show'd us that France had something to admire.
             Not but the Tragic spirit was our own,
             And full in Shakespear, fair in Otway shone:
             But Otway fail'd to polish or refine,
             And fluent Shakespear scarce effac'd a line.
             Ev'n copious Dryden wanted, or forgot,
             The last and greatest Art, the Art to blot.

JOHNSON *Preface to Shakespeare.* 1765.

The poet, of whose works I have undertaken the revision, may now begin to assume the dignity of an ancient, and claim the privilege of established fame and prescriptive veneration. He has long outlived his century, the term commonly fixed as the test of literary merit. Whatever advantages he might once derive from personal allusions, local customs, or temporary opinions, have for many years been lost; and every topic of merriment, or motive of sorrow, which the modes of artificial life afforded him, now only obscure the scenes which they once illuminated. The effects of favour and competition are at an end; the tradition of his friendships and his enmities has perished; his works support no opinion with arguments, nor supply any faction with invectives; they can neither indulge vanity, nor gratify malignity; but are read without any other reason than the desire of pleasure, and are, therefore, praised only as pleasure is obtained; yet, thus unassisted by interest or passion, they have passed through variations of taste and changes of manners, and, as they devolved from one generation to another, have received new honours at every transmission. . . . [The fifth paragraph referred to on p. 11.]

Shakespeare is, above all writers, at least above all modern writers, the poet of nature; the poet that holds up to his readers a faithful mirror of manners and of life. His characters are not modified by the customs of particular places, unpractised by the rest of the world; by the peculiarities of studies or professions, which can operate but upon small numbers; or by the accidents of transient fashions or temporary opinions: they are the genuine progeny of common humanity, such as the world will always supply, and observation will always find. His persons act and speak by the influence of those general passions and principles by which all minds are agitated, and the whole system of life is continued in motion. In the writings of other poets a character is too often an individual: in those of Shakespeare it is commonly a species.

It is from this wide extension of design that so much instruction is derived. It is this which fills the plays of Shakespeare with practical axioms and domestic wisdom. It was said of Euripides, that every verse was a precept; and it may be said of Shakespeare, that from his works may be collected a system of civil and economical prudence. Yet his real power is not shown in the splendour of particular passages, but by the progress of his fable, and the tenour of his dialogue; and he that tries to recommend him by select quotations, will succeed like the pedant in Hierocles, who, when he offered his house to sale, carried a brick in his pocket as a specimen. . . .

Other dramatists can only gain attention by hyperbolical or aggravated characters, by fabulous and unexplained excellence or depravity, as the writers of barbarous romances invigorated the reader by a giant and a dwarf; and he that should form his expectations of human affairs from the play, or from the tale, would be equally deceived. Shakespeare has no heroes; his scenes are occupied only by men, who act and speak as the reader thinks that he should himself have spoken or acted on the same occasion: even where the agency is supernatural, the dialogue is level with life. Other writers disguise the most natural passions and most frequent incidents; so that he who contemplates them in the book will not know them in the world; Shakespeare approximates the remote, and familiarizes the wonderful; the event which he represents will not happen, but, if it were possible, its effects would, probably, be such as he has assigned; and it may be said, that he has not only shown nature as it acts in real exigencies, but as it would be found in trials, to which it cannot be exposed.

This, therefore, is the praise of Shakespeare, that his drama is the mirror of life; that he who has mazed his imagination, in following the phantoms which other writers raise up before him, may here be cured of his delirious ecstasies, by reading human sentiments in human language, by scenes from which a hermit may estimate the transactions of the world, and a confessor predict the progress of the passions. . . .

The censure which he has incurred by mixing comic and tragic scenes, as it extends to all his works, deserves more consideration. . . . That this is a practice contrary to the rules of criticism will be readily allowed: but there is always an appeal open from criticism to nature. The end of writing is to instruct; the end of poetry is to instruct by pleasing. That the mingled drama may convey all the instruction of tragedy or comedy cannot be denied, because it includes both in its alternations of exhibition, and approaches nearer than either to the appearance of life, by showing how great machinations and slender designs may promote or obviate one another, and the high and the low co-operate in the general system by unavoidable concatenation. . . .

Shakespeare engaged in dramatic poetry with the world open before him; the rules of the ancients were yet known to few; the public judgment was unformed; he had no example of such fame as might force him upon imitation, nor critics of such authority as might restrain his extravagance: he, therefore, indulged his natural disposition, and his disposition, as Rymer has remarked, led him to comedy. In tragedy he often writes, with great appearance of toil and study, what is written at last with little felicity; but, in his comic scenes, he seems to produce, without labour, what no labour can improve. In tragedy he is always struggling after some occasion to be comic; but in comedy he seems to repose, or to luxuriate, as in a mode of thinking congenial to his nature. In his tragic scenes there is always something wanting, but his comedy often surpasses expectation or desire. His comedy pleases by the thoughts and the language, and his tragedy, for the greater part, by incident and action. His tragedy seems to be skill, his comedy to be instinct.

The force of his comic scenes has suffered little diminution from the changes made by a century and a half, in manners or in words. As his personages act upon principles arising from genuine passion, very little modified by particular forms, their pleasures and vexations are communicable to all times and to all places; they are natural, and, therefore, durable; the adventitious peculiarities of personal habits are only superficial dyes, bright and pleasing for a little while, yet soon fading to a dim tinct, without any remains of a former lustre; but the discriminations of true passion are the colours of nature; they pervade the whole mass, and can only perish with the body that exhibits them. The accidental compositions of heterogeneous modes are dissolved by the chance that combined them; but the uniform simplicity of primitive qualities neither admits increase, nor suffers decay. The sand heaped by one flood is scattered by another, but the rock always continues in its place. The stream of time, which is continually washing the dissoluble fabrics of other poets, passes, without injury, by the adamant of Shakespeare. . . .

Shakespeare with his excellencies has likewise faults, and faults sufficient to obscure and overwhelm any other merit. I shall show them in the proportion in which they appear to me, without envious malignity or superstitious veneration. No question can be more innocently discussed than a dead poet's pretensions to renown; and little regard is due to that bigotry which sets candour higher than truth.

His first defect is that to which may be imputed most of the evil in books or in men. He sacrifices virtue to convenience, and is so much more careful to please than to instruct, that he seems to write without any moral purpose. From his writings, indeed, a system of social duty may be selected, for he that thinks reasonably must think morally; but his precepts and axioms drop casually from him; he makes no just distribution of good or evil, nor is always careful to show in the virtuous a disapprobation of the wicked; he carries his persons indifferently through right and wrong, and, at the close, dismisses them without further care, and leaves their examples to operate by chance. This fault the barbarity of his age cannot extenuate; for it is always a writer's duty to make the world better, and justice is a virtue independent on time or place.

The plots are often so loosely formed, that a very slight consideration may improve them, and so carelessly pursued, that he seems not always fully to comprehend his own design. He omits opportunities of instructing or delighting, which the train of his story seems to force upon him, and apparently rejects those exhibitions which would be more affecting, for the sake of those which are more easy.

It may be observed, that in many of his plays the latter part is evidently neglected. When he found himself near the end of his work, and in view of his reward, he shortened the labour to snatch the profit. He, therefore, remits his efforts where he should most vigorously exert them, and his catastrophe is improbably produced or imperfectly represented.

He had no regard to distinction of time or place, but gives to one age or nation, without scruple, the customs, institutions, and opinions of another, at the expense not only of likelihood, but of possibility. . . .

In his comic scenes he is seldom successful, when he engages his characters in reciprocations of smartness and contests of sarcasm; their jests are commonly gross, and their pleasantry licentious; neither his gentlemen nor his ladies have much delicacy, nor are sufficiently distinguished from his clowns by any appearance of refined manners. . . .

In tragedy his performance seems constantly to be worse, as his labour is more. The effusions of passion, which exigence forces out, are, for the most part, striking and energetic; but whenever he solicits his invention, or strains his faculties, the offspring of his throes is tumour, meanness, tediousness, and obscurity.

In narration he affects a disproportionate pomp of diction, and a wearisome train of circumlocution, and tells the incident imperfectly in many words, which might have been more plainly delivered in few. Narration in dramatic poetry is naturally tedious, as it is unanimated and inactive, and obstructs the progress of the action; it should, therefore, always be rapid, and enlivened by frequent interruption. Shakespeare found it an incumbrance, and instead of lightening it by brevity, endeavoured to recommend it by dignity and splendour.

His declamations or set speeches are commonly cold and weak, for his power was the power of nature; when he endeavoured, like other tragic writers, to catch opportunities of amplification, and instead of inquiring what the occasion demanded, to show how much his stores of knowledge could supply, he seldom escapes without the pity or resentment of his reader.

It is incident to him to be now and then entangled with an unwieldy sentiment, which he cannot well express, and will not reject; he struggles with it a while, and, if it continues stubborn, comprises it in words such as occur, and leaves it to be disentangled and evolved by those who have more leisure to bestow upon it.

Not that always where the language is intricate, the thought is subtile, or the image always great where the line is bulky; the equality of words to things is very often neglected, and trivial sentiments and vulgar ideas disappoint the attention, to which they are recommended by sonorous epithets and swelling figures.

But the admirers of this great poet have most reason to complain when he approaches nearest to his highest excellence, and seems fully resolved to sink them in dejection, and mollify them with tender emotions, by the fall of greatness, the danger of innocence, or the crosses of love. What he does best, he soon ceases to do. He is not long soft and pathetic without some idle conceit, or contemptible equivocation. He no sooner begins to move, than he counteracts himself; and terror and pity, as they are rising in the mind, are checked and blasted by sudden frigidity.

A quibble is to Shakespeare, what luminous vapours are to the traveller; he follows it at all adventures; it is sure to lead him out of his way, and sure to ingulf him in the mire. It has some malignant power over his mind, and its fascinations are irresistible. Whatever be the dignity or profundity of his disquisitions, whether he be enlarging knowledge or exalting affection, whether he be amusing attention with incidents, or enchanting it in suspense, let but a quibble spring up before him, and he leaves his work unfinished. A quibble is the golden apple for which he will always turn aside from his career, or stoop from his elevation. A quibble, poor and barren as it is, gave him such delight, that he was content to purchase it, by the sacrifice of reason, propriety and truth. A quibble was to him the fatal Cleopatra for which he lost the world, and was content to lose it.

It will be thought strange, that, in enumerating the defects of this writer, I have not yet mentioned his neglect of the unities; his violation of those laws which have been instituted and established by the joint authority of poets and of critics. . . .

His histories, being neither tragedies nor comedies, are not subject to any of their laws; nothing more is necessary to all the praise which they expect, than that the changes of action be so prepared as to be understood; that the incidents be various and affecting, and the characters consistent, natural and distinct. No other unity is intended, and, therefore, none is to be sought.

In his other works he has well enough preserved the unity of action. . . .

To the unities of time and place he has shown no regard; and, perhaps, a nearer view of the principles on which they stand will diminish their value, and withdraw from them the veneration which, from the time of Corneille, they have generally received, by discovering that they have given more trouble to the poet, than pleasure to the auditor. . . .

Whether Shakespeare knew the unities, and rejected them by design, or deviated from them by happy ignorance, it is, I think, impossible to decide, and useless to inquire. We may reasonably suppose, that, when he rose to notice, he did not want the counsels and admonitions of scholars and critics, and that he, at last, deliberately persisted in a practice, which he might have begun by chance. As nothing is essential to the fable but unity of action, and as the unities of time and place arise evidently from false assumptions, and, by circumscribing the extent of the drama, lessen its variety, I cannot think it much to be lamented, that they were not known by him, or not observed: nor, if such another poet could arise, should I very vehemently reproach him, that his first act passed at Venice, and his next in Cyprus. Such violation of rules merely positive, become the comprehensive genius of Shakespeare, and such censures are suitable to the minute and slender criticism of Voltaire. . . .

His plots, whether historical or fabulous, are always crowded with incidents, by which the attention of a rude people was more easily caught than by sentiment and argumentation; and such is the power of the marvellous, even over those who despise it, that every man finds his mind more strongly seized by the tragedies of Shakespeare than of any other writer: others please us by particular speeches; but he always makes us anxious for the event, and has, perhaps, excelled all but Homer in securing the first purpose of a writer, by exciting restless and unquenchable curiosity, and compelling him that reads his work to read it through. . . .

The work of a correct and regular writer is a garden accurately formed and diligently planted, varied with shades, and scented with flowers; the composition of Shakespeare is a forest, in which oaks extend their branches, and pines tower in the air, interspersed sometimes with weeds and brambles, and sometimes giving shelter to myrtles and to roses; filling the eye with awful pomp, and gratifying the mind with endless diversity. Other poets display cabinets of precious rarities, minutely finished, wrought into shape, and polished into brightness. Shakespeare opens a mine which contains gold and diamonds in unexhaustible plenty, though clouded by incrustations, debased by impurities, and mingled with a mass of meaner minerals. . . .

Perhaps it would not be easy to find any author, except Homer, who invented so much as Shakespeare, who so much advanced the studies which he cultivated, or effused so much novelty upon his age or country. The form, the characters, the language, and the shows of the English drama are his. . . .

Yet it must be at last confessed, that as we owe every thing to him, he owes something to us; that, if much of his praise is paid by perception and judgment, much is, likewise, given by custom and veneration. We fix our eyes upon his graces, and turn them from his deformities, and endure in him what we should in another loathe or despise. If we endured without praising, respect for the father of our drama might excuse us; but I have seen, in the book of some modern critics, a collection of anomalies, which show that he has corrupted language by every mode of depravation, but which his admirer has accumulated as a monument of honour.

He has scenes of undoubted and perpetual excellence; but, perhaps, not one play, which, if it were now exhibited as the work of a contemporary writer, would be heard to the conclusion. I am, indeed, far from thinking that his works were wrought to his own ideas of perfection; when they were such as would satisfy the audience, they satisfied the writer.

VOLTAIRE a. *Lettres Philosophiques*, 1734. b. *Letter to Horace Walpole*, 1768.

a. Les Anglais avaient déjà un Théâtre, aussi bien que les Espagnols, quand les Français n'avaient que des Tréteaux. Shakespeare, qui passait pour le Corneille des Anglais, fleurissait à peu près dans le temps de Lope de Véga. Il créa le théâtre. Il avait un génie plein de force et de fécondité, de naturel et de sublime, sans la moindre étincelle de bon goût et sans la moindre connaissance des règles. Je vais vous dire une chose hasardée, mais vraie: c'est que le mérite de cet Auteur a perdu le théâtre anglais; il y a de si belles scènes, des morceaux si grands et si terribles répandus dans ses Farces monstrueuses qu'on appelle Tragédies, que ces pièces ont toujours été jouées avec un grand succès. Le temps, qui seul fait la réputation des hommes, rend à la fin leurs défauts respectables. La plupart des idées bizarres et gigantesques de cet auteur ont acquis au bout de deux cents ans le droit de passer pour sublimes; les auteurs modernes l'ont presque tous copié; mais ce qui réussissait chez Shakespeare est sifflé chez eux, et vous croyez bien que la vénération qu'on a pour cet ancien augmente à mesure que l'on méprise les modernes. On ne fait pas réflexion qu'il ne faudrait pas l'imiter, et le mauvais succès de ses copistes fait seulement qu'on le croit inimitable.

Vous savez que dans la tragédie du *More de Venise*, pièce très touchante, un mari étrangle sa femme sur le théâtre, et quand la pauvre femme est étranglée, elle s'écrie qu'elle meurt très injustement. Vous n'ignorez pas que dans Hamlet des fossoyeurs creusent une fosse en buvant, en chantant des vaudevilles, et en faisant sur les têtes des morts qu'ils rencontrent des plaisanteries convenables à gens de leur métier. Mais ce qui vous surprendra, c'est qu'on a imité ces sottises sous le règne de Charles Second, qui était celui de la politesse et l'âge d'or des beaux-arts.

Otway, dans sa *Venise sauvée*, introduit le Sénateur Antonio et la courtisane Naki au milieu des horreurs de la conspiration du Marquis de Bedmar. Le vieux Sénateur Antonio fait auprès de sa courtisane toutes les songeries d'un vieux débauché impuissant et hors du bon sens; il contrefait le taureau et le chien, il mord les jambes de sa maîtresse, qui lui donne des coups de pied et des coups de fouet. On a retranché de la pièce d'Otway ces bouffonneries, faites pour la plus vile canaille; mais on a laissé dans le *Jules César* de Shakespeare les plaisanteries des cordonniers et des savetiers romains introduits sur la scène avec Brutus et Cassius. C'est que la sottise d'Otway est moderne, et que celle de Shakespeare est ancienne. . . .

C'est dans ces morceaux détachés que les tragiques Anglais ont jusqu'ici excellé; leurs pièces, presque toutes barbares, dépourvues de bienséance, d'ordre, de vraisemblance, ont des lueurs étonnantes au milieu de cette nuit. Le style est trop ampoulé, trop hors de la nature, trop copié des écrivains hébreux si remplis de l'enflure asiatique; mais aussi il faut avouer que les échasses du style figuré, sur lesquelles la langue anglaise est guindée, élèvent aussi l'esprit bien haut, quoique par une marche irrégulière.

Le premier Anglais qui ait fait une pièce raisonnable et écrite d'un bout à l'autre avec élégance est l'illustre M. Addison. Son *Caton d' Utique* est un chef-d'œuvre pour la diction et pour la beauté des vers. Le rôle de Caton est à mon gré fort au-dessus de celui de Cornélie dans le *Pompée* de Corneille; car Caton est grand sans enflure, et Cornélie, qui d'ailleurs n'est pas un personnage nécessaire, vise quelquefois au galimatias. Le Caton de M. Addison me paraît le plus beau personnage qui soit sur aucun théâtre, mais les autres rôles de la pièce n'y répondent pas, et cet ouvrage si bien écrit est défiguré par une intrigue froide d'amour, qui répand sur la pièce une langueur qui la tue.

La coutume d'introduire de l'amour à tort et à travers dans les ouvrages dramatiques passa de Paris à Londres vers l'an 1660 avec nos rubans at nos perruques. Les femmes, qui parent les spectacles, comme ici, ne veulent plus souffrir qu'on leur parle d'autre chose que d'amour. Le sage Addison eut la molle complaisance de plier la sévérité de son caractère aux mœurs de son temps, et gâta un chef d'œuvre pour avoir voulu plaire.

Depuis lui, les pièces sont devenues plus régulières, le peuple plus difficile, les auteurs plus corrects et moins hardis. J'ai vu des pièces nouvelles fort sages, mais froides. Il semble que les Anglais n'aient été faits jusqu'ici que pour produire des beautés irrégulières. Les monstres brillants de Shakespeare plaisent mille fois plus que la sagesse moderne. Le génie poétique des Anglais ressemble jusqu'à présent à un arbre touffu planté par la nature, jetant au hasard mille rameaux, et croissant inégalement et avec force; il meurt, si vous voulez forcer sa nature et le tailler en arbre des jardins de Marly.

b. Vous avez presque fait accroire à votre nation que je méprise Shakespeare. . . . J'avais dit que son génie était à lui, et que ses fautes étaient à son siècle. C'est une belle nature, mais bien sauvage; nulle régularité, nulle bienséance, nul art, de la bassesse avec de la grandeur, de la bouffonnerie avec du terrible; c'est le chaos de la tragédie, dans lequel il y a cent traits de lumière.

MAURICE MORGANN *On the Dramatic Character of Sir John Falstaff.* 1777.

Yet whatever may be the neglect of some, or the censure of others, there are those, who firmly believe that this wild, this uncultivated Barbarian, has not yet obtained one half of his fame; and who trust that some new Stagyrite will arise, who instead of pecking at the surface of things will enter into the inward soul of his compositions, and expel by the force of congenial feelings, those foreign impurities which have stained and disgraced his page. And as to those *spots* which will still remain, they may perhaps become invisible to those who shall seek them through the medium of his beauties, instead of looking for those beauties, as is too frequently done, through the smoke of some real or imputed obscurity. When the hand of time shall have brushed off his present Editors and Commentators, and when the very name of *Voltaire*, and even the memory of the language in which he has written, shall be no more, the *Apalachian* mountains, the banks of the *Ohio*, and the plains of *Sciota* shall resound with the accents of this Barbarian: in his native tongue he shall roll the genuine passions of nature; nor shall the griefs of *Lear* be alleviated, or the charms and wit of *Rosalind* be abated by time. There is indeed nothing perishable about him, except that very learning which he is said so much to want. He had not, it is true, enough for the demands of the age in which he lived, but he had perhaps too much for the reach of his genius, and the interest of his fame. *Milton* and he will carry the decayed remnants and fripperies of ancient mythology into more distant ages than they are by their own force intitled to extend; and the metamorphoses of *Ovid*, upheld by them, lay in a new claim to unmerited immortality.

Shakespeare is a name so interesting, that it is excusable to stop a moment, nay it would be indecent to pass him without the tribute of some admiration. He differs essentially from all other writers: him we may profess rather to feel than to understand; and it is safer to say, on many occasions, that we are possessed by him, than that we possess him. And no wonder;—he scatters the seeds of things, the principles of character and action, with so cunning a hand yet with so careless an air, and, master of our feelings, submits himself so little to our judgment, that every thing seems superior. We discern not his course, we see no connection of cause and effect, we are rapt in ignorant admiration, and claim no kindred with his abilities. All the incidents, all the parts, look like chance, whilst we feel and are sensible that the whole is design. His characters not only act and speak in strict conformity to nature, but in strict relation to us; just so much is shown as is requisite, just so much is impressed; he commands every passage to our heads and to our hearts, and moulds us as he pleases, and that with so much ease, that he never betrays his own exertions. We see these characters act from the mingled motives of passion, reason, interest, habit and complection, in all their proportions, when they are supposed to know it not themselves; and we are made to acknowledge that their actions and sentiments are, from those motives, the necessary result. He at once blends and distinguishes every thing;—every thing is complicated, every thing is plain. I restrain the furthest expressions of my admiration lest they should not seem applicable to man; but it is really astonishing that a mere human being, a part of humanity only, should so perfectly comprehend the whole; and that he should possess such exquisite art, that whilst every woman and every child shall feel the whole effect, his learned Editors and Commentators should yet so very frequently mistake or seem ignorant of the cause. A sceptre or a straw are in his hands of equal efficacy; he needs no selection; he converts everything into excellence; nothing is too great, nothing is too base. Is a character efficient like *Richard*, it is every thing we can wish: is it otherwise, like *Hamlet*, it is productive of equal admiration; action produces one mode of excellence and inaction another: the Chronicle, the Novel, or the Ballad; the king, or the beggar, the hero, the madman, the sot or the fool; it is all one;—nothing is worse, nothing is better: the same genius pervades and is equally admirable in all. Or, is a character to be shown in progressive change, and the events of years comprized within the hour;—with what a Magic hand does he prepare and scatter his spells! The Understanding must, in the first place be subdued; and lo! how the rooted prejudices of the child spring up to confound the man! The Weird sisters rise, and order is extinguished. The laws of nature give way, and leave nothing in our minds but wildness and horror. No pause is allowed us for reflection: horrid sentiment, furious guilt and compunction, air-drawn daggers, murders, ghosts, and inchantment, shake and *possess us wholly*. In the meantime the process is completed. *Macbeth* changes under our eye, *the milk of human kindness is converted to gall*; *he has supped full of horrors*, and his *May of life is fallen into the sear, the yellow leaf*; whilst we, the fools of amazement, are insensible to the shifting of place and the lapse of time, and till the curtain drops, never once wake to the truth of things, or recognize the laws of existence.—On such an occasion, a fellow, like *Rymer*, waking from his trance, shall lift up his Constable's staff, and charge this great Magician, this daring *practicer of arts inhibited*, in the name of *Aristotle*, to surrender; whilst *Aristotle* himself, disowning his wretched Officer, would fall prostrate at his feet and acknowledge his supremacy. O supreme of Dramatic excellence! (*might he say*,) not to me be imputed the insolence of fools. The bards of *Greece* were confined within the narrow circle of the Chorus, and hence they found themselves constrained to practise, for the most part, the precision, and copy the details of nature. I followed them, and knew not that a larger circle might be drawn, and the Drama extended to the whole reach of human genius. Convinced, I see that a more compendious *nature* may be obtained; a nature of *effects* only, to which neither the relations of place, or continuity of time, are always essential. Nature, condescending to the faculties and apprehensions of man, has drawn through human life a regular chain of visible causes and effects: but Poetry delights in surprise, conceals her steps, seizes at once upon the heart, and obtains the Sublime of things without betraying the rounds of her ascent: true Poesy is *magic*, not *nature*; an effect from causes hidden or unknown. To the Magician I prescribed no laws; his law and his power are one; his power is his law. Him, who neither imitates, nor is within the reach of imitation, no precedent can or ought to bind, no limits to contain. If his end is obtained, who shall question his course? Means, whether apparent or hidden, are justified in poesy by success; but then most perfect and most admirable when most concealed.

The reader must be sensible of something in the composition of Shakespeare's characters, which renders them essentially different from those drawn by other writers. The characters of every Drama must indeed be grouped; but in the groups of other poets the parts which are not seen, do not in fact exist. But there is a certain roundness and integrity in the forms of Shakespeare, which give them an independence as well as a relation, insomuch that we often meet with passages, which though perfectly felt, cannot be sufficiently explained in words, without unfolding the whole character of the speaker.

GEORGE III *Diary of Madame D'Arblay*. 1785.

'Was there ever such stuff as great part of Shakspeare? only one must not say so! But what think you?—What? Is there not sad stuff? What?—What?

I know it is not to be said! but it's true. Only it's Shakespeare, and nobody dare abuse him.'

ROMANTIC CRITICISM

GERVINUS *Shakespeare Commentaries*. 1850. (This passage is quoted here as it serves as an admirable introduction to German Romantic criticism.)

The man who first valued Shakespeare according to his full desert was indisputably Lessing. One single passage, where, in his 'Dramaturgie', he speaks of Romeo and Juliet, shows plainly that he apprehended his plays in their innermost nature, and this with the same unbiassed mind with which the poet wrote them. With all the force of a true taste, he pointed to Wieland's translation of the English dramatist, when scarcely anyone in Germany knew him. Not long before Shakespeare had been seriously compared amongst us with Gryphius; now Lessing appeared and discovered in the great tragic poet an accordance with the highest pretensions of Aristotle. The English editors and expositors of his works were yet under the Gallic yoke, when Lessing cast aside the French taste and the opinion of Voltaire, and with one stroke so transformed the age, that *we* now ridiculed the false sublimity of the French drama, as they had formerly laughed at English barbarism. Lessing's recommendation of the English poet was closely followed by Eschenburg's translation, and a completely altered taste among our young dramatists. A rude counterpoise to the exaggerations of French conventionality appeared for the moment necessary, in order to restore the even balance of judgment. In Goethe's youthful circle in Strasburg they spoke in Shakespeare's puns, jokes, and pleasantries; they wrote in his tone and style; they exhibited all the coarseness and nakedness of nature in contrast to French gloss and varnish, and felt themselves, from identity of character, as much at home with the Germanic nature of Shakespeare as with Hans Sachs. . . .

The distortion and extravagance of their early opinions passed in time from the minds of these men, who as poets and critics were equally prepared to take a wholly different view of the study of Shakespeare to that of the English commentators of old; the poet for the first time stands before us in the unassuming truth of nature. In 'Wilhelm Meister' Goethe produced that characteristic of Hamlet, which is like a key to all works of the poet; here all separate beauties are rejected, and the whole is explained by the whole, and we feel the soul of the outer frame-work and its animating breath, which created and organised the immortal work. . . .

While the Englishman lingered perhaps over isolated passages, we, on the contrary, destitute of all explanations, read rapidly on; we were careless about parts, and compared to the English reader we lost many separate beauties and ideas, but we enjoyed the whole more fully. For this enjoyment we were chiefly indebted to the translation of A. W. Schlegel, which even Englishmen read with admiration. . . . More than any other effort on behalf of the English poet, this translation has made him our own. Admiration reached a fresh point. And this rather with us than in England. . . .

However great were the merits of our Romanticists in having arranged Shakespeare's works for our enjoyment, even they have only slightly contributed to the inner understanding after which we seek, and to the unfolding of the human nature of the poet and the general value of his works. In A. W. Schlegel's 'Dramatic Lectures' the plays are singly discussed. All here testifies to poetic delicacy and sensibility; all is fair, alluring, inspiring—a panegyric of a totally different kind to the criticising characteristics of the English expositors. . . .

From 1811 to 1812 Coleridge had held lectures upon Shakespeare, so much in Schlegel's mind and manner, that a dispute arose as to the priority of merit of the two æsthetic philosophers. . . . He advanced the assertion— then a bold one in England—that not merely the splendour of different parts constituted the greatness of Shakespeare, by compensating for the barbarous shapelessness of the whole, but that he considered the æsthetic form of the whole equally admirable with the matter, and the judgment of the great poet not less deserving our wonder than his innate genius.

LESSING *Hamburgische Dramaturgie*. 1767.

Love itself dictated 'Zaire' to Voltaire! said a polite art critic. He would have been nearer the truth had he said gallantry; I know but one tragedy at which love itself has laboured and that is 'Romeo and Juliet' by Shakespeare. It is incontestable, that Voltaire makes his enamoured Zaire express her feelings with much nicety and decorum. But what is this expression compared with that living picture of all the smallest, most secret, artifices whereby love steals into our souls, all the imperceptible advantages it gains thereby, all the subterfuges with which it manages to supersede every other passion until it succeeds in holding the post of sole tyrant of our desires and aversions? Voltaire perfectly understands the—so to speak—official language of love; that is to say the language and the tone love employs when it desires to express itself with caution and dignity, when it would say nothing but what the prudish female sophist and the cold critic can justify. Still even the most efficient government clerk does not always know the most about the secrets of his government; or else if Voltaire had the same deep insight as Shakespeare into the essence of love, he would not exhibit it here, and therefore the poem has remained beneath the capacities of the poet.

Almost the same might be said of jealousy. His jealous Orosman plays a sorry figure beside the jealous Othello of Shakespeare. And yet Othello has unquestionably furnished the prototype of Orosman. Cibber says Voltaire avails himself of the brand that lighted the tragic pile of Shakespeare. I should have said: a brand from out of this flaming pile and moreover one that smoked more than it glowed or warmed. In Orosman we hear a jealous man speak and we see him commit a rash deed of jealousy, but of jealousy itself we learn neither more nor less than what we knew before. Othello on the contrary is a complete manual of this deplorable madness; there we can learn all that refers to it and how we may avoid it.

But is it always Shakespeare, always and eternally Shakespeare who understood everything better than the French, I hear my readers ask? That annoys us, because we cannot read him. I seize this opportunity to remind the public of what it seems purposely to have forgotten. We have a translation of Shakespeare. . . . The undertaking was a difficult one, and any other person than Herr Wieland would have made other slips in his haste, or have passed over more passages from ignorance or laziness, and what parts he has done well few will do better. Any way his rendering of Shakespeare is a book that cannot be enough commended among us. We have much to learn yet from the beauties he has given to us.

GOETHE *Wilhelm Meister.* 1795. (The rest of this famous passage on Hamlet is quoted on p. 213.)

Conceive a prince such as I have painted him, and that his father suddenly dies. Ambition and the love of rule are not the passions that inspire him. As a king's son he would have been contented: but now he is first constrained to consider the difference which separates a sovereign from a subject. The crown was not hereditary; yet a longer possession of it by his father would have strengthened the pretensions of an only son, and secured his hopes of the succession. In place of this, he now beholds himself excluded by his uncle, in spite of specious promises, most probably forever. He is now poor in goods and favour, and a stranger in the scene which from youth he had looked upon as his inheritance. His temper here assumes its first mournful tinge. He feels that now he is not more, that he is less, than a private nobleman; he offers himself as the servant of every one; he is not courteous and condescending, he is needy and degraded.

His past condition he remembers as a vanished dream. It is in vain that his uncle strives to cheer him, to present his situation in another point of view. The feeling of his nothingness will not leave him.

The second stroke that came upon him wounded deeper, bowed still more. It was the marriage of his mother. The faithful tender son had yet a mother, when his father passed away. He hoped, in the company of his surviving noble-minded parent, to reverence the heroic form of the departed; but his mother too he loses, and it is something worse than death that robs him of her. The trustful image, which a good child loves to form of its parents, is gone. With the dead there is no help; on the living no hold. She also is a woman, and her name is Frailty, like that of all her sex.

Now first does he feel himself completely bent and orphaned; and no happiness of life can repay what he has lost. Not reflective or sorrowful by nature, reflection and sorrow have become for him a heavy obligation. It is thus that we see him first enter on the scene. I do not think that I have mixed aught foreign with the piece, or overcharged a single feature of it.

A. W. SCHLEGEL *Über dramatische Kunst und Litteratur.* (Lectures delivered in Vienna in 1808, and published 1812.)

Never, perhaps, was there so comprehensive a talent for the delineation of character as Shakespeare's. It not only grasps the diversities of rank, sex, and age, down to the dawnings of infancy; not only do the king and the beggar, the hero and the pickpocket, the sage and the idiot speak and act with equal truth; not only does he transport himself to distant ages and foreign nations, and portray in the most accurate manner, with only a few apparent violations of costume, the spirit of the ancient Romans, of the French in their wars with the English, of the English themselves during a great part of their history, of the southern Europeans (in the serious part of many comedies) the cultivated society of that time, and the former rude and barbarous state of the North; his human characters have not only such depth and precision that they cannot be arranged under classes, and are inexhaustible, even in conception:—no— this Prometheus not merely forms men, he opens the gates of the magical world of spirits; calls up the midnight ghost; exhibits before us his witches amidst their unhallowed mysteries; peoples the air with sportive fairies and sylphs:—and these beings, existing only in imagination, possess such truth and consistency, that even when deformed monsters like Caliban, he extorts the conviction, that if there should be such beings, they would so conduct themselves. In a word, as he carries with him the most fruitful and daring fancy to the kingdom of nature,—on the other hand, he carries nature into the regions of fancy, lying beyond the confines of reality. We are lost in astonishment at seeing the extraordinary, the wonderful, and the unheard of, in such intimate nearness.

If Shakespeare deserves our admiration for his characters, he is equally deserving of it for his exhibition of passion, taking this word in its widest significance, as including every mental condition, every tone from indifference or familiar mirth to the wildest rage and despair. He gives us the history of minds; he lays open to us, in a single word, a whole series of preceding conditions. His passions do not at first stand displayed to us in all their height, as is the case with so many tragic poets, who, in the language of Lessing, are thorough masters of the legal style of love. He paints, in a most inimitable manner, the gradual progress from the first origin. 'He gives', as Lessing says, 'a living picture of all the most minute and secret artifices by which a feeling steals into our souls; of all the imperceptible advantages which it there gains; of all the stratagems by which every other passion is made subservient to it, till it becomes the sole tyrant of our desires and our aversions.' Of all poets, perhaps, he alone has portrayed the mental diseases,—melancholy, delirium, lunacy,—with such inexpressible, and, in every respect, definite truth, that the physician may enrich his observations from them in the same manner as from real cases.

LAMB *On the Tragedies of Shakspeare.* 1811.

It may seem a paradox, but I cannot help being of opinion that the plays of Shakspeare are less calculated for performance on a stage, than those of almost any other dramatist whatever. Their distinguishing excellence is a reason that they should be so. There is so much in them, which comes not under the province of acting, with which eye, and tone, and gesture, have nothing to do.

The glory of the scenic art is to personate passion, and the turns of passion: and the more coarse and palpable the passion is, the more hold upon the eyes and ears of the spectators the performer obviously possesses. For this reason, scolding scenes, scenes where two persons talk themselves into a fit of fury, and then in a surprising manner talk themselves out of it again, have always been the most popular upon our stage. And the reason is plain, because the spectators are here most palpably appealed to, they are the proper judges in this war of words, they are the legitimate ring that should be formed round such 'intellectual prize-fighters'. Talking is the direct object of the imitation here. But in all the best dramas, and in Shakspeare above all, how obvious it is, that the form of *speaking*, whether it be in soliloquy or dialogue, is only a medium, and often a highly artificial one, for putting the reader or spectator into possession of that knowledge of the inner structure and workings of mind in a character, which he could otherwise never have arrived at *in that form of composition* by any gift short of intuition. We do here as we do with novels written in the *epistolary form*. How many improprieties, perfect solecisms in letter-writing, do we put up with in Clarissa and other books, for the sake of the delight which that form upon the whole gives us.

But the practice of stage representation reduces everything to a controversy of elocution. Every character, from the boisterous blasphemings of Bajazet to the shrinking timidity of womanhood, must play the orator. The love-dialogues of Romeo and Juliet, those silver-sweet sounds of lovers' tongues by night; the more intimate and sacred sweetness of nuptial colloquy between an Othello or a Posthumus with their married wives, all those delicacies which are so delightful in the reading, as when we read of those youthful dalliances in Paradise—

> As beseem'd
> Fair couple link'd in happy nuptial league,
> Alone:

by the inherent fault of stage representation, how are these things sullied and turned from their very nature by being exposed to a large assembly; when such speeches as Imogen addresses to her lord, come drawling out of the mouth of a hired actress, whose courtship, though nominally addressed to the personated Posthumus, is manifestly aimed at the spectators, who are to judge of her endearments and her returns of love. . . .

The truth is, the Characters of Shakspeare are so much the objects of meditation rather than of interest or curiosity as to their actions, that while we are reading any of his great criminal characters,—Macbeth, Richard, even Iago,—we think not so much of the crimes which they commit, as of the ambition, the aspiring spirit, the intellectual activity, which prompts them to overleap those moral fences. Barnwell is a wretched murderer;

there is a certain fitness between his neck and the rope; he is the legitimate heir to the gallows; nobody who thinks at all can think of any alleviating circumstances in his case to make him a fit object of mercy. Or to take an instance from the higher tragedy, what else but a mere assassin is Glenalvon! Do we think of anything but of the crime which he commits, and the rack which he deserves? That is all which we really think about him. Whereas in corresponding characters in Shakspeare so little do the actions comparatively affect us, that while the impulses, the inner mind in all its perverted greatness, solely seems real and is exclusively attended to, the crime is comparatively nothing. But when we see these things represented, the acts which they do are comparatively every thing, their impulses nothing. The state of sublime emotion into which we are elevated by those images of night and horror which Macbeth is made to utter, that solemn prelude with which he entertains the time till the bell shall strike which is to call him to murder Duncan,—when we no longer read it in a book, when we have given up that vantage-ground of abstraction which reading possesses over seeing, and come to see a man in his bodily shape before our eyes actually preparing to commit a murder, if the acting be true and impressive, as I have witnessed it in Mr. K.'s performance of that part, the painful anxiety about the act, the natural longing to prevent it while it yet seems unperpetrated, the too close pressing semblance of reality, give a pain and an uneasiness which totally destroy all the delight which the words in the book convey, where the deed doing never presses upon us with the painful sense of presence: it rather seems to belong to history,—to something past and inevitable, if it has any thing to do with time at all. The sublime images, the poetry alone, is that which is present to our minds in the reading. . . .

It requires little reflection to perceive, that if those characters in Shakespeare which are within the precincts of nature, have yet something in them which appeals too exclusively to the imagination, to admit of their being made objects to the senses without suffering a change and a diminution,—that still stronger the objection must lie against representing another line of characters, which Shakspeare has introduced to give a wildness and a supernatural elevation to his senses, as if to remove them still farther from that assimilation to common life in which their excellence is vulgarly supposed to consist. When we read the incantations of those terrible beings the Witches in Macbeth, though some of the ingredients of their hellish composition savour of the grotesque, yet is the effect upon us other than the most serious and appalling that can be imagined? Do we not feel spell-bound as Macbeth was? Can any mirth accompany a sense of their presence? We might as well laugh under a consciousness of the principle of Evil himself being truly and really present with us. But attempt to bring these beings on to a stage, and you turn them instantly into so many old women, that men and children are to laugh at. Contrary to the old saying, that 'seeing is believing', the sight actually destroys the faith; and the mirth in which we indulge at their expense, when we see these creatures upon a stage, seems to be a sort of indemnification which we make to ourselves for the terror which they put us in when reading made them an object of belief,—when we surrendered up our reason to the poet, as children to their nurses and their elders; and we laugh at our fears, as children who thought they saw something in the dark, triumph when the bringing in of a candle discovers the vanity of their fears. For this exposure of supernatural agents upon a stage is truly bringing in a candle to expose their own delusiveness. . . .

The subject of Scenery is closely connected with that of the Dresses, which are so anxiously attended to on our stage. I remember the last time I saw Macbeth played, the discrepancy I felt at the changes of garment which he varied,—the shiftings and re-shiftings, like a Romish priest at mass. The luxury of stage-improvements, and the importunity of the public eye, require this. The coronation robe of the Scottish monarch was fairly a counterpart to that which our King wears when he goes to the Parliament-house,—just so full and cumbersome, and set out with ermine and pearls. And if things must be represented, I see not what to find fault with in this. But in reading, what robe are we conscious of? Some dim images of royalty—a crown and sceptre, may float before our eyes, but who shall describe the fashion of it? Do we see in our mind's eye what Webb or any other robe-maker could pattern? This is the inevitable consequence of imitating every thing, to make all things natural. Whereas the reading of a tragedy is a fine abstraction. It presents to the fancy just so much of external appearances as to make us feel that we are among flesh and blood, while by far the greater and better part of our imagination is employed upon the thoughts and internal machinery of the character. But in acting, scenery, dress, the most contemptible things, call upon us to judge of their naturalness.

Perhaps it would be no bad similitude, to liken the pleasure which we take in seeing one of these fine plays acted, compared with that quiet delight which we find in the reading of it, to the different feelings with which a reviewer, and a man that is not a reviewer, reads a fine poem. The accursed critical habit,—the being called upon to judge and pronounce, must make it quite a different thing to the former. In seeing these plays acted, we are affected just as judges. When Hamlet compares the two pictures of Gertrude's first and second husband, who wants to see the pictures? But in the acting, a miniature must be lugged out; which we know not to be the picture, but only to show how finely a miniature may be represented. The shewing of every thing, levels all things: it makes tricks, bows, and curtesies, of importance. Mrs. S. never got more fame by any thing than by the manner in which she dismisses the guests in the banquet-scene in Macbeth: it is as much remembered as any of her thrilling tones or impressive looks. But does such a trifle as this enter into the imaginations of the readers of that wild and wonderful scene? Does not the mind dismiss the feasters as rapidly as it can? Does it care about the gracefulness of the doing it? But by acting, and judging of acting, all these non-essentials are raised into an importance, injurious to the main interest of the play.

I have confined my observations to the tragic parts of Shakspeare. It would be no very difficult task to extend the enquiry to his comedies; and to shew why Falstaff, Shallow, Sir Hugh Evans, and the rest, are equally incompatible with stage representation.

KEATS *Letter to his brothers.* 22 Dec. 1817.

Several things dove-tailed in my mind, and at once it struck me what quality went to form a Man of Achievement, especially in Literature, and which Shakspeare possessed so enormously—I mean *Negative Capability*, that is, when a man is capable of being in uncertainties, mysteries, doubts, without any irritable reaching after fact and reason. Coleridge, for instance, would let go by a fine isolated verisimilitude caught from the Penetralium of mystery, from being incapable of remaining content with half-knowledge. This pursued through volumes would perhaps take us no further than this, that with a great poet the sense of Beauty overcomes every other consideration, or rather obliterates all consideration.

COLERIDGE *Essays and Lectures on Shakspeare.* 1818.

Shakspeare's Judgment Equal to his Genius

Thus then Shakspeare appears, from his Venus and Adonis and Rape of Lucrece alone, apart from all his great works, to have possessed all the conditions of the true poet. Let me now proceed to destroy, as far as may be in my power, the popular notion that he was a great dramatist by mere instinct, that he grew immortal in his own despite, and sank below men of second or third-rate power, when he attempted aught beside the drama— even as bees construct their cells and manufacture their honey to admirable perfection; but would in vain attempt to build a nest. Now this mode of reconciling a compelled sense of inferiority with a feeling of pride, began in a few pedants, who having read that Sophocles was the great model of tragedy, and Aristotle the infallible dictator of its rules, and finding that the Lear, Hamlet, Othello and other master-pieces were neither in imitation of Sophocles, nor in obedience to Aristotle,—and not having (with one or two exceptions) the courage to affirm, that the delight which their country received from generation to generation, in defiance of the alterations of circumstances and habits, was wholly groundless,—took upon them, as a happy medium and refuge, to talk of Shakspeare as a sort of beautiful *lusus naturæ*, a delightful monster,—wild, indeed, and without taste or judgment, but like the inspired idiots so much venerated in the East, uttering, amid the strangest follies, the sublimest truths. In nine places out of ten in which I find his awful name mentioned, it is with some epithet of 'wild', 'irregular', 'pure child of nature', &c. If all this be true, we must submit to it; though to a thinking mind it cannot but be painful to find any excellence, merely human, thrown out of all human analogy, and thereby leaving us neither rules for imitation, nor motives to imitate;—but if false, it is a dangerous falsehood;— for it affords a refuge to secret self-conceit,—enables a vain man at once to escape his reader's indignation by general swoln panegyrics, and merely by his *ipse dixit* to treat, as contemptible, what he has not intellect enough to comprehend, or soul to feel, without assigning any reason, or referring his opinion to any demonstrative principle;—thus leaving Shakspeare as a sort of grand Lama, adored indeed, and his very excrements prized as relics, but with no authority or real influence. I grieve that every late voluminous edition of his works would enable me to substantiate the present charge with a variety of facts one tenth of which would of themselves exhaust the time allotted to me. Every critic, who has or has not made a collection of black letter books— in itself a useful and respectable amusement,—puts on the seven-league boots of self-opinion, and strides at once from an illustrator into a supreme judge, and blind and deaf, fills his three-ounce phial at the waters of Niagara; and determines positively the greatness of the cataract to be neither more nor less than his three-ounce phial has been able to receive.

I think this is a very serious subject. It is my earnest desire—my passionate endeavour,—to enforce at various times and by various arguments and instances the close and reciprocal connexion of just taste with pure morality. Without that acquaintance with the heart of man, or that docility and child-like gladness to be made acquainted with it, which those only can have, who dare look at their own hearts—and that with a steadiness which religion only has the power of reconciling with sincere humility;—without this, and the modesty produced by it, I am deeply convinced that no man, however wide his erudition, however patient his antiquarian researches, can possibly understand, or be worthy of understanding, the writings of Shakspeare.

Assuredly that criticism of Shakspeare will alone be genial which is reverential. The Englishman, who without reverence, a proud and affectionate reverence, can utter the name of William Shakspeare, stands disqualified for the office of critic. He wants one at least of the very senses, the language of which he is to employ, and will discourse, at best, but as a blind man, while the whole harmonious creation of light and shade with all its subtle interchange of deepening and dissolving colours rises in silence to the silent *fiat* of the uprising Apollo. However inferior in ability I may be to some who have followed me, I own I am proud that I was the first in time who publicly demonstrated to the full extent of the position, that the supposed irregularity and extravagances of Shakspeare were the mere dreams of a pedantry that arraigned the eagle because it had not the dimensions of the swan. In all the successive courses of lectures delivered by me, since my first attempt at the Royal Institution, it has been, and it still remains, my object, to prove that in all points from the most important to the most minute, the judgment of Shakspeare is commensurate with his genius,—nay, that his genius reveals itself in his judgment, as in its most exalted form. And the more gladly do I recur to this subject from the clear conviction, that to judge aright, and with distinct consciousness of the grounds of our judgment, concerning the works of Shakspeare, implies the power and means of judging rightly of all other works of intellect, those of abstract science alone excepted. . . .

Let me, then, once more submit this question to minds emancipated alike from national, or party, or sectarian prejudice:—Are the plays of Shakspeare works of rude uncultivated genius, in which the splendour of the parts compensates, if aught can compensate, for the barbarous shapelessness and irregularity of the whole?—Or is the form equally admirable with the matter, and the judgment of the great poet, not less deserving our wonder than his genius?—Or, again, to repeat the question in other words:—Is Shakspeare a great dramatic poet on account only of those beauties and excellences which he possesses in common with the ancients, but with diminished claims to our love and honour to the full extent of his differences from them?—Or are these very differences additional proofs of poetic wisdom, at once results and symbols of living power as contrasted with lifeless mechanism—of free and rival originality as contra-distinguished from servile imitation, or, more accurately, a blind copying of effects, instead of a true imitation, of the essential principles?—Imagine not that I am about to oppose genius to rules. No! the comparative value of these rules is the very cause to be tried. The spirit of poetry, like all other living powers, must of necessity circumscribe itself by rules, were it only to unite power with beauty. It must embody in order to reveal itself; but a living body is of necessity an organized one; and what is organization but the connection of parts in and for a whole, so that each part is at once end and means? This is no discovery of criticism;—it is a necessity of the human mind; and all nations have felt and obeyed it, in the invention of metre, and measured sounds, as the vehicle and *involucrum* of poetry— itself a fellow-growth from the same life,—even as the bark is to the tree!

No work of true genius dares want its appropriate form, neither indeed is there any danger of this. As it must not, so genius cannot, be lawless; for it is even this that constitutes it genius—the power of acting creatively under laws of its own origination. How then comes it that not only single *Zoili*, but whole nations have combined in unhesitating condemnation of our great dramatist, as a sort of African nature, rich in beautiful monsters—as a wild heath where islands of fertility look the greener from the surrounding waste, where the loveliest plants now shine out among unsightly weeds, and now are choked by their parasitic growth, so intertwined that we cannot disentangle the weed without snapping the flower?—In this statement I have had no reference to the vulgar abuse of Voltaire, save as far as his charges are coincident with the decisions of Shakspeare's own commentators and (so they would tell you) almost idolatrous admirers. The true ground of the mistake lies in the confounding mechanical regularity with organic form. The form is mechanic, when on any given material we impress a pre-determined form, not necessarily arising out of the properties of the material;—as when to a mass of wet clay we give whatever shape we wish it to retain when hardened. The organic form, on the other hand, is innate; it shapes, as it develops, itself from within, and the fulness of its development is one and the same with the perfection of its outward form. Such as the life is, such is the form. Nature, the prime genial artist, inexhaustible in diverse powers, is equally inexhaustible in forms;—each exterior is the physiognomy of the being within,—its true image reflected and thrown out from the concave mirror;—and even such is the appropriate excellence of her chosen poet, of our own Shakspeare,— himself such a nature humanized, a genial understanding directing selfconsciously a power and an implicit wisdom deeper even than our consciousness.

I greatly dislike beauties and selections in general; but as proof positive of his unrivalled excellence, I should like to try Shakspeare by this criterion.

Make out your amplest catalogue of all the human faculties, as reason or the moral law, the will, the feeling of the coincidence of the two (a feeling *sui generis et demonstratio demonstrationum*) called the conscience, the understanding or prudence, wit, fancy, imagination, judgment,—and then of the objects on which these are to be employed, as the beauties, the terrors, and the seeming caprices of nature, the realities and the capabilities, that is, the actual and the ideal, of the human mind, conceived as an individual or as a social being, as in innocence or in guilt, in a play-paradise, or in a war-field of temptation;—and then compare with Shakspeare under each of these heads all or any of the writers in prose and verse that have ever lived! Who, that is competent to judge, doubts the result?—And ask your own hearts,—ask your own common sense—to conceive the possibility of this man being—I say not, the drunken savage of that wretched sciolist, whom Frenchmen, to their shame, have honoured before their elder and better worthies,—but the anomalous, the wild, the irregular, genius of our daily criticism! What! are we to have miracles in sport?—Or, I speak reverently, does God choose idiots by whom to convey divine truths to man?

The Characteristics of Shakspeare's Dramas

Having intimated that times and manners lend their form and pressure to genius, let me once more draw a slight parallel between the ancient and modern stage, the stages of Greece and of England. The Greeks were polytheists; their religion was local; almost the only object of all their knowledge, art and taste, was their gods; and, accordingly, their productions were, if the expression may be allowed, statuesque, whilst those of the moderns are picturesque. The Greeks reared a structure, which in its parts, and as a whole, filled the mind with the calm and elevated impression of perfect beauty, and symmetrical proportion. The moderns also produced a whole, a more striking whole; but it was by blending materials and fusing the parts together. And as the Pantheon is to York Minster or Westminster Abbey, so is Sophocles compared with Shakspeare; in the one a completeness, a satisfaction, an excellence, on which the mind rests with complacency; in the other a multitude of interlaced materials, great and little, magnificent and mean, accompanied, indeed, with a sense of a falling short of perfection, and yet, at the same time, so promising of our social and individual progression, that we would not, if we could, exchange it for that repose of the mind which dwells on the forms of symmetry in the acquiescent admiration of grace. This general characteristic of the ancient and modern drama might be illustrated by a parallel of the ancient and modern music;—the one consisting of melody arising from a succession of only pleasing sounds,—the modern embracing harmony also, the result of combination and the effect of a whole.

I have said, and I say it again, that great as was the genius of Shakespeare, his judgment was at least equal to it. Of this any one will be convinced, who attentively considers those points in which the dramas of Greece and England differ, from the dissimilitude of circumstances by which each was modified and influenced. . . .

The stage in Shakspeare's time was a naked room with a blanket for a curtain; but he made it a field for monarchs. That law of unity, which has its foundations, not in the factitious necessity of custom, but in nature itself, the unity of feeling, is every where and at all times observed by Shakspeare in his plays. Read Romeo and Juliet;—all is youth and spring;—youth and its follies, its virtues, its precipitancies;—spring with its odours, its flowers, and its transiency; it is one and the same feeling that commences, goes through, and ends the play. The old men, the Capulets and the Montagues, are not common old men; they have an eagerness, a heartiness, a vehemence, the effect of spring; with Romeo, his change of passion, his sudden marriage, and his rash death, are all the effects of youth;—whilst in Juliet love has all that is tender and melancholy in the nightingale, all that is voluptuous in the rose, with whatever is sweet in the freshness of spring; but it ends with a long deep sigh like the last breeze of the Italian evening. This unity of feeling and character pervades every drama of Shakspeare.

It seems to me that his plays are distinguished from those of all other dramatic poets by the following characteristics:

1. Expectation in preference to surprise. It is like the true reading of the passage:—'God said, Let there be light, and there was *light*';—not there *was* light. As the feeling with which we startle at a shooting star compared with that of watching the sunrise at the pre-established moment, such and so low is surprise compared with expectation.

2. Signal adherence to the great law of nature, that all opposites tend to attract and temper each other. Passion in Shakspeare generally displays libertinism, but involves morality; and if there are exceptions to this, they are, independently of their intrinsic value, all of them indicative of individual character, and, like the farewell admonitions of a parent, have an end beyond the parental relation. Thus the Countess's beautiful precepts to Bertram, by elevating her character, raise that of Helena her favorite, and soften down the point in her which Shakspeare does not mean us not to see, but to see and to forgive, and at length to justify. And so it is in Polonius, who is the personified memory of wisdom no longer actually possessed. This admirable character is always misrepresented on the stage. Shakspeare never intended to exhibit him as a buffoon; for although it was natural that Hamlet,—a young man of fire and genius, detesting formality, and disliking Polonius on political grounds, as imagining that he had assisted his uncle in his usurpation,—should express himself satirically,—yet this must not be taken as exactly the poet's conception of him. In Polonius a certain induration of character had arisen from long habits of business; but take his advice to Laertes, and Ophelia's reverence for his memory, and we shall see that he was meant to be represented as a statesman somewhat past his faculties,—his recollections of life all full of wisdom, and showing a knowledge of human nature, whilst what immediately takes place before him, and escapes from him, is indicative of weakness.

But as in Homer all the deities are in armour, even Venus; so in Shakspeare all the characters are strong. Hence real folly and dulness are made by him the vehicles of wisdom. There is no difficulty for one being a fool to imitate a fool; but to be, remain, and speak like a wise man and a great wit, and yet so as to give a vivid representation of a veritable fool,—*hic labor, hoc opus est*. A drunken constable is not uncommon, nor hard to draw; but see and examine what goes to make up a Dogberry.

3. Keeping at all times in the high road of life, Shakspeare has no innocent adulteries, no interesting incests, no virtuous vice;—he never renders that amiable which religion and reason alike teach us to detest, or clothes impurity in the garb of virtue, like Beaumont and Fletcher, the Kotzebues of the day. Shakspeare's fathers are roused by ingratitude, his husbands stung by unfaithfulness; in him, in short, the affections are wounded in those points in which all may, nay, must, feel. Let the morality of Shakspeare be contrasted with that of the writers of his own, or the succeeding, age, or of those of the present day, who boast their superiority in this respect. No one can dispute that the result of such a comparison is altogether in favour of Shakspeare;—even the letters of women of high rank in his age were often coarser than his writings. If he occasionally disgusts a keen sense of delicacy, he never injures the mind; he neither excites, nor flatters, passion, in order to degrade the subject of it; he does not use the faulty thing for a faulty purpose, nor carries on warfare against virtue, by causing wickedness to appear as no wickedness, through the medium of a morbid sympathy with the unfortunate. In Shakspeare vice never walks as in twilight; nothing is purposely out of its place;—he inverts not the order of nature and propriety,—does not make every magistrate a drunkard or glutton, nor every poor man meek, humane, and temperate; he has no benevolent butchers, nor any sentimental rat-catchers.

4. Independence of the dramatic interest on the plot. The interest in the plot is always in fact on account of the characters, not *vice versa*, as in almost all other writers; the plot is a mere canvass and no more. Hence arises the true justification of the same stratagem being used in regard to Benedict and Beatrice,—the vanity in each being alike. Take away from the Much Ado About Nothing all that which is not indispensable to the plot, either as having little to do with it, or, at best, like Dogberry and his comrades, forced into the service, when any other less ingeniously absurd watchmen and night-constables would have answered the mere necessities of the action;—take away Benedict, Beatrice, Dogberry, and the reaction of the former on the character of Hero,—and what will remain? In other writers the main agent of the plot is always the prominent character; in Shakspeare it is so, or is not so, as the character is in itself calculated, or not calculated, to form the plot. Don John is the main-spring of the plot of this play; but he is merely shown and then withdrawn.

5. Independence of the interest on the story as the ground-work of the plot. Hence Shakspeare never took the trouble of inventing stories. It was enough for him to select from those that had been already invented or recorded such as had one or other, or both, of two recommendations, namely, suitableness to his particular purpose, and their being parts of popular tradition,—names of which we had often heard, and of their fortunes, and as to which all we wanted was, to see the man himself. So it is just the man himself, the Lear, the Shylock, the Richard, that Shakspeare makes us for the

first time acquainted with. Omit the first scene in Lear, and yet every thing will remain; so the first and second scenes in the Merchant of Venice. Indeed it is universally true.

6. Interfusion of the lyrical—that which in its very essence is poetical—not only with the dramatic, as in the plays of Metastasio, where at the end of the scene comes the *aria* as the *exit* speech of the character,—but also in and through the dramatic. Songs in Shakspeare are introduced as songs only, just as songs are in real life, beautifully as some of them are characteristic of the person who has sung or called for them, as Desdemona's 'Willow', and Ophelia's wild snatches, and the sweet carollings in As You Like it. But the whole of the Midsummer Night's Dream is one continued specimen of the dramatized lyrical. And observe how exquisitely the dramatic of Hotspur:—

> Marry, and I'm glad on't with all my heart;
> I'd rather be a kitten and cry—mew, &c.

melts away into the lyric of Mortimore:—

> I understand thy looks: that pretty Welsh
> Which thou pourest down from these swelling heavens,
> I am too perfect in, &c.

7. The characters of the *dramatis personæ*, like those in real life, are to be inferred by the reader;—they are not told to him. And it is well worth remarking that Shakspeare's characters, like those in real life, are very commonly misunderstood, and almost always understood by different persons in different ways. The causes are the same in either case. If you take only what the friends of the character say, you may be deceived, and still more so, if that which his enemies say; nay, even the character himself sees himself through the medium of his character, and not exactly as he is. Take all together, not omitting a shrewd hint from the clown or the fool, and perhaps your impression will be right; and you may know whether you have in fact discovered the poet's own idea, by all the speeches receiving light from it, and attesting its reality by reflecting it.

Lastly, in Shakespeare the heterogeneous is united, as it is in nature. You must not suppose a pressure or passion always acting in or on a character!—passion in Shakspeare is that by which the individual is distinguished from others, not that which makes a different kind of him. Shakspeare followed the main march of the human affections. He entered into no analysis of the passions or faiths of men, but assured himself that such and such passions and faiths were grounded in our common nature, and not in the mere accidents of ignorance or disease. This is an important consideration, and constitutes our Shakspeare the morning star, the guide and the pioneer, of true philosophy.

HAZLITT *Lectures on the English Poets.* 1818.

The striking peculiarity of Shakespear's mind was its generic quality, its power of communication with all other minds—so that it contained a universe of thought and feeling within itself, and had no one peculiar bias, or exclusive excellence more than another. He was just like any other man, but that he was like all other men. He was the least of an egotist that it was possible to be. He was nothing in himself; but he was all that others were, or that they could become. He not only had in himself the germs of every faculty and feeling, but he could follow them by anticipation, intuitively, into all their conceivable ramifications, through every change of fortune or conflict of passion, or turn of thought. He had 'a mind reflecting ages past', and present:—all the people that ever lived are there. There was no respect of persons with him. His genius shone equally on the evil and on the good, on the wise and the foolish, the monarch and the beggar: 'All corners of the earth, kings, queens, and states, maids, matrons, nay, the secrets of the grave', are hardly hid from his searching glance. He was like the genius of humanity, changing places with all of us at pleasure, and playing with our purposes as with his own. He turned the globe round for his amusement, and surveyed the generations of men, and the individuals as they passed, with their different concerns, passions, follies, vices, virtues, actions, and motives—as well those that they knew, as those which they did not know, or acknowledge to themselves. The dreams of childhood, the ravings of despair, were the toys of his fancy. Airy beings waited at his cell, and came at his bidding. Harmless fairies 'nodded to him, and did him curtesies': and the night-hag bestrode the blast at the command of 'his so potent art'. The world of spirits lay open to him, like the world of real men and women: and there is the same truth in his delineations of the one as of the other; for if the preternatural characters he describes could be supposed to exist, they would speak, and feel, and act, as he makes them. He had only to think of any thing in order to become that thing, with all the circumstances belonging to it. When he conceived of a character, whether real or imaginary, he not only entered into all its thoughts and feelings, but seemed instantly, and as if by touching a secret spring, to be surrounded with all the same objects, 'subject to the same skyey influences', the same local, outward, and unforeseen accidents which would occur in reality. Thus the character of Caliban not only stands before us with a language and manners of its own, but the scenery and situation of the enchanted island he inhabits, the traditions of the place, its strange noises, its hidden recesses, 'his frequent haunts and ancient neighbourhood', are given with a miraculous truth of nature, and with all the familiarity of an old recollection. The whole 'coheres semblably together' in time, place, and circumstance. In reading this author, you do not merely learn what his characters say,—you see their persons. By something expressed or understood, you are at no loss to decypher their peculiar physiognomy, the meaning of a look, the grouping, the bye-play, as we might see it on the stage. A word, an epithet paints a whole scene, or throws us back whole years in the history of the person represented. So (as it has been ingeniously remarked) when Prospero describes himself as left alone in the boat with his daughter, the epithet which he applies to her, 'Me and thy *crying* self' flings the imagination instantly back from the grown woman to the helpless condition of infancy, and places the first and most trying scene of his misfortunes before us, with all that he must have suffered in the interval. . . . It is not 'a combination and a form' of words, a set speech or two, a preconcerted theory of a character, that will do this: but all the persons concerned must have been present in the poet's imagination, as at a kind of rehearsal; and whatever would have passed through their minds on the occasion, and have been observed by others, passed through his, and is made known to the reader. . . .

That which, perhaps, more than any thing else distinguishes the dramatic productions of Shakespear from all others, is this wonderful truth and individuality of conception. Each of his characters is as much itself, and as absolutely independent of the rest, as well as of the author, as if they were living persons, not fictions of the mind. The poet may be said, for the time, to identify himself with the character he wishes to represent, and to pass from one to another, like the same soul successively animating different bodies. By an art like that of the ventriloquist, he throws his imagination out of himself, and makes every word appear to proceed from the mouth of the person in whose name it is given. His plays alone are properly expressions of the passions, not descriptions of them. His characters are real beings of flesh and blood; they speak like men, not like authors. One might suppose that he had stood by at the time, and overheard what passed. As in our dreams we hold conversations with ourselves, make remarks, or communicate intelligence, and have no idea of the answer which we shall receive, and which we ourselves make, till we hear it: so the dialogues in Shakespear are carried on without any consciousness of what is to follow, without any appearance of preparation or premeditation. The gusts of passion come and go like sounds of music borne on the mind. Nothing is made out by formal inference and analogy, by climax and antithesis: all comes, or seems to come, immediately from nature. Each object and circumstance exists in his mind, as it would have existed in reality: each several train of thought and feeling goes on of itself, without confusion or effort. In the world of his imagination, every thing has a life, a place, and being of its own. . . .

Chaucer's characters are narrative, Shakespear's dramatic, Milton's epic. That is, Chaucer told only as much of his story as he pleased, as was required for a particular purpose. He answered for his characters himself. In Shakespear they are introduced upon the stage, are liable to be asked all sorts of questions, and are forced to answer for themselves. In Chaucer we perceive a fixed essence of character. In Shakespear there is a continual composition and decomposition of its elements, a fermentation of every particle in the whole mass, by its alternate affinity or antipathy to other principles which are brought in contact with it. Till the experiment is tried, we do not know the result, the turn which the character will take in its new circumstances. Milton took only a few simple principles of character, and raised them to the utmost conceivable grandeur, and refined them from every base alloy. His imagination, 'nigh sphered in Heaven', claimed kindred only with what he saw from that height, and could raise to the same elevation with itself. He sat retired and kept his state alone, 'playing with wisdom'; while Shakespear mingled with the crowd, and played the host, 'to make society the sweeter welcome'.

The passion in Shakespear is of the same nature as his delineation of character. It is not some one habitual feeling or sentiment preying upon itself, growing out of itself, and moulding every thing to itself; it is passion modified by passion, by all the other feelings to which the individual is liable, and to which others are liable with him; subject to all the fluctuations of caprice and accident; calling into play all the resources of the understanding and all the energies of the will; irritated by obstacles or yielding to them; rising from small beginnings to its utmost height; now drunk with hope, now stung to madness, now sunk in despair, now blown to air with a breath, now raging like a torrent. The human soul is made the sport of fortune, the prey of adversity: it is stretched on the wheel of destiny, in restless ecstasy. The passions are in a state of projection. Years are melted down to moments, and every instant teems with fate. We know the results, we see the process. Thus after Iago had been boasting to himself of the effect of his poisonous suggestions on the mind of Othello, 'which, with a little act upon the blood, will work like mines of sulphur', he adds—

> 'Look where he comes! not poppy nor mandragora,
> Nor all the drowsy syrups of the East,
> Shall ever medicine thee to that sweet sleep
> Which thou ow'dst yesterday.'—

And he enters at this moment, like the crested serpent, crowned with his wrongs and raging for revenge! The whole depends upon the turn of a thought. A word, a look, blows the spark of jealousy into a flame; and the explosion is immediate and terrible as a volcano. The dialogues in Lear, in Macbeth, that between Brutus and Cassius, and nearly all those in Shakespear, where the interest is wrought up to its highest pitch, afford examples of this dramatic fluctuation of passion. The interest in Chaucer is quite different; it is like the course of a river, strong, and full, and increasing. In Shakespear, on the contrary, it is like the sea, agitated this way and that, and loud-lashed by furious storms; while in the still pauses of the blast, we distinguish only the cries of despair, or the silence of death. . . .

Shakespear's imagination is of the same plastic kind as his conception of character or passion. 'It glances from heaven to earth, from earth to heaven.' Its movement is rapid and devious. It unites the most opposite extremes: or, as Puck says, in boasting of his own feats, 'puts a girdle round the earth in forty minutes'. He seems always hurrying from his subject, even while describing it, but the stroke, like the lightning's, is sure as it is sudden. He takes the widest possible range, but from that very range he has his choice of the greatest variety and aptitude of materials. He brings together images the most alike, but placed at the greatest distance from each other; that is, found in circumstances of the greatest dissimilitude. From the remoteness of his combinations, and the celerity with which they are effected, they coalesce the more indissolubly together. The more the thoughts are strangers to each other, and the longer they have been kept asunder, the more intimate does their union seem to become. Their felicity is equal to their force. Their likeness is made more dazzling by their novelty. They startle, and take the fancy prisoner in the same instant. I will mention one or two which are very striking, and not much known, out of Troilus and Cressida. Æneas says to Agamemnon,

> I ask that I may waken reverence,
> And on the cheek be ready with a blush
> Modest as morning, when she coldly eyes
> The youthful Phœbus.

Ulysses urging Achilles to shew himself in the field, says—

> No man is the lord of anything,
> Till he communicate his parts to others:
> Nor doth he of himself know them for aught,
> Till he behold them formed in the applause,
> Where they're extended! which like an arch reverberates
> The voice again, or like a gate of steel,
> Fronting the sun, receives and renders back
> Its figure and its heat.

Patroclus gives the indolent warrior the same advice.

> Rouse yourself; and the weak wanton Cupid
> Shall from your neck unloose his amorous fold,
> And like a dew-drop from the lion's mane
> Be shook to air.

Shakespear's language and versification are like the rest of him. He has a magic power over words: they come winged at his bidding; and seem to know their places. They are struck out at a heat, on the spur of the occasion, and have all the truth and vividness which arise from an actual impression of the objects. His epithets and single phrases are like sparkles, thrown off from an imagination, fired by the whirling rapidity of its own motion. His language is hieroglyphical. It translates thoughts into visible images. It abounds in sudden transitions and elliptical expressions. This is the source of his mixed metaphors, which are only abbreviated forms of speech. These, however, give no pain from long custom. They have, in fact, become idioms in the language. They are the building, and not the scaffolding to thought. We take the meaning and effect of a well-known passage entire, and no more stop to scan and spell out the particular words and phrases, than the syllables of which they are composed. In trying to recollect any other author, one sometimes stumbles, in case of failure, on a word as good. In Shakespear, any other word but the true one, is sure to be wrong. If any body, for instance, could not recollect the words of the following description,

> —Light thickens
> And the crow makes wing to the rooky wood,

he would be greatly at a loss to substitute others for them equally expressive of the feeling. These remarks, however, are strictly applicable only to the

impassioned parts of Shakespear's language, which flowed from the warmth
and originality of his imagination, and were his own. The language used for
prose conversation and ordinary business is sometimes technical, and involved in the affectation of the time. Compare, for example, Othello's apology
to the senate, relating 'his whole course of love', with some of the preceding
parts relating to his appointment, and the official dispatches from Cyprus.
In this respect, 'the business of the state does him offence'. His versification
is no less powerful, sweet, and varied. It has every occasional excellence, of
sullen intricacy, crabbed and perplexed, or of the smoothest and loftiest
expansion—from the ease and familiarity of measured conversation to the
lyrical sounds.

> —of ditties highly penned,
> Sung by a fair queen in a summer's bower,
> With ravishing division to her lute.

It is the only blank verse in the language, except Milton's, that for itself is
readable. It is not stately and uniformly swelling like his, but varied and
broken by the inequalities of the ground it has to pass over in its uncertain
course,

> And so by many winding nooks it strays,
> With willing sport to the wild ocean.

It remains to speak of the faults of Shakespear. They are not so many or
so great as they have been represented; what they are, are chiefly owing to
the following causes:—The universality of his genius was, perhaps, a disadvantage to his single works; the variety of his resources, sometimes diverting
him from applying them to the utmost effectual purposes. He might be said
to combine the powers of Æschylus and Aristophanes, of Dante and Rabelais,
in his own mind. If he had been only half what he was, he would perhaps
have appeared greater. The natural ease and indifference of his temper
made him sometimes less scrupulous than he might have been. He is relaxed
and careless in critical places; he is in earnest throughout only in Timon,
Macbeth, and Lear. Again, he had no models of acknowledged excellence
constantly in view to stimulate his efforts, and by all that appears, no love of
fame. He wrote for the 'great vulgar and the small', in his time, not for
posterity. If Queen Elizabeth and the maids of honour laughed heartily at
his worst jokes, and the catcalls in the gallery were silent at his best passages,
he went home satisfied, and slept the next night well. He did not trouble
himself about Voltaire's criticisms. He was willing to take advantage of the
ignorance of the age in many things; and if his plays pleased others, not to
quarrel with them himself. His very facility of production would make him
set less value on his own excellences, and not care to distinguish nicely between what he did well or ill. His blunders in chronology and geography do
not amount to above half a dozen, and they are offences against chronology
and geography, not against poetry. As to the unities, he was right in setting
them at defiance. He was fonder of puns than became so great a man. His
barbarisms were those of his age. His genius was his own. He had no objection to float down with the stream of common taste and opinion: he rose

above it by his own buoyancy, and an impulse which he could not keep under, in spite of himself or others, and 'his delights did shew most dolphin-like'.

He had an equal genius for comedy and tragedy; and his tragedies are better than his comedies, because tragedy is better than comedy. His female characters, which have been found fault with as insipid, are the finest in the world. Lastly, Shakespear was the least of a coxcomb of any one that ever lived, and much of a gentleman.

DE QUINCEY *On the Knocking at the Gate in Macbeth.* 1823.

From my boyish days I had always felt a great perplexity on one point in Macbeth. It was this: the knocking at the gate, which succeeds to the murder of Duncan, produced to my feelings an effect for which I never could account. The effect was, that it reflected back upon the murderer a peculiar awfulness and a depth of solemnity; yet, however obstinately I endeavoured with my understanding to comprehend this, for many years I never could see *why* it should produce such an effect.

Here I pause for one moment, to exhort the reader never to pay any attention to his understanding, when it stands in opposition to any other faculty of his mind. The mere understanding, however useful and indispensable, is the meanest faculty in the human mind, and the most to be distrusted; and yet the great majority of people trust to nothing else, which may do for ordinary life, but not for philosophical purposes. . . .

But to return from this digression, my understanding could furnish no reason why the knocking at the gate in Macbeth should produce any effect, direct or reflected. In fact, my understanding said positively that it could *not* produce any effect. But I knew better; I felt that it did; and I waited and clung to the problem until further knowledge should enable me to solve it. At length, in 1812, Mr. Williams made his *début* on the stage of Ratcliffe Highway, and executed those unparalleled murders which have procured for him such a brilliant and undying reputation. . . . Now it will be remembered, that in the first of these murders (that of the Marrs), the same incident (of a knocking at the door, soon after the work of extermination was complete) did actually occur, which the genius of Shakspere has invented; and all good judges, and the most eminent dilettanti, acknowledged the felicity of Shakspere's suggestion, as soon as it was actually realized. Here, then, was a fresh proof that I was right in relying on my own feeling, in opposition to my understanding; and I again set myself to study the problem; at length I solved it to my own satisfaction, and my solution is this. Murder, in ordinary cases, where the sympathy is wholly directed to the case of the murdered person, is an incident of coarse and vulgar horror; and for this reason, that it flings the interest exclusively upon the natural but ignoble instinct by which we cleave to life; an instinct which, as being indispensable to the primal law of self-preservation, is the same in kind (though different in degree) amongst all living creatures; this instinct, therefore, because it annihilates all distinctions, and degrades the greatest of men to the level of 'the poor beetle that we tread on', exhibits human nature in its most abject and humiliating attitude. Such an attitude would little serve the purposes of the poet. What then must he do? He must throw the interest on the murderer. Our sympathy must be with *him* (of course I mean a sympathy of comprehension, a sympathy by which we enter into his feelings, and are made to understand them,—not a sympathy of pity or approbation). In the murdered person, all strife of thought, all flux and reflux of passion and of purpose, are crushed by one overwhelming panic; the fear of instant death smites him 'with its petrific mace'. But in the murderer, such a murderer as a poet will condescend to, there must be raging some great storm of passion—jealousy, ambition, vengeance, hatred—which will create a hell within him; and into this hell we are to look.

In *Macbeth*, for the sake of gratifying his own enormous and teeming faculty of creation, Shakspere has introduced two murderers: and, as usual in his hands, they are remarkably discriminated: but, though in Macbeth the strife of mind is greater than in his wife, the tiger spirit not so awake, and his feelings caught chiefly by contagion from her,—yet, as both were finally involved in the guilt of the murder, the murderous mind of necessity is finally to be presumed in both. This was to be expressed; and on its own account, as well as to make it a more proportionable antagonist to the unoffending nature of their victim, 'the gracious Duncan', and adequately to expound 'the deep damnation of his taking off', this was to be expressed with peculiar energy. We were to be made to feel that the human nature, *i.e.*, the divine nature of love and mercy, spread through the hearts of all creatures, and seldom utterly withdrawn from man—was gone, vanished, extinct; and that the fiendish nature had taken its place. And, as this effect is marvellously accomplished in the *dialogues* and *soliloquies* themselves, so it is finally consummated by the expedient under consideration; and it is to this that I now solicit the reader's attention. If the reader has ever witnessed a wife, daughter, or sister in a fainting fit, he may chance to have observed that the most affecting moment in such a spectacle is *that* in which a sigh and a stirring announce the recommencement of suspended life. Or, if the reader has ever been present in a vast metropolis, on the day when some great national idol was carried in funeral pomp to his grave, and chancing to walk near the course through which it passed, has felt powerfully in the silence and desertion of the streets, and in the stagnation of ordinary business, the deep interest which at that moment was possessing the heart of man—if all at once he should hear the death-like stillness broken up by the sound of wheels rattling away from the scene, and making known that the transitory vision was dissolved, he will be aware that at no moment was his sense of the complete suspension and pause in ordinary human concerns so full and affecting, as at that moment when the suspension ceases, and the goings-on of human life are suddenly resumed. All action in any direction is best expounded, measured, and made apprehensible, by reaction. Now apply this to the case in Macbeth. Here, as I have said, the retiring of the human heart, and the entrance of the fiendish heart was to be expressed and made sensible. Another world has stept in; and the murderers are taken out of the region of human things, human purposes, human desires. They are transfigured: Lady Macbeth is 'unsexed';

Macbeth has forgot that he was born of woman; both are conformed to the image of devils; and the world of devils is suddenly revealed. But how shall this be conveyed and made palpable? In order that a new world may step in, this world must for a time disappear. The murderers, and the murder must be insulated—cut off by an immeasurable gulf from the ordinary tide and succession of human affairs—locked up and sequestered in some deep recess; we must be made sensible that the world of ordinary life is suddenly arrested—laid asleep—tranced—racked into a dreadful armistice; time must be annihilated; relation to things without abolished; and all must pass self-withdrawn into a deep syncope and suspension of earthly passion. Hence it is, that when the deed is done, when the work of darkness is perfect, then the world of darkness passes away like a pageantry in the clouds: the knocking at the gate is heard; and it makes known audibly that the reaction has commenced; the human has made its reflux upon the fiendish; the pulses of life are beginning to beat again; and the re-establishment of the goings-on of the world in which we live, first makes us profoundly sensible of the awful parenthesis that had suspended them.

O mighty poet! Thy works are not as those of other men, simply and merely great works of art; but are also like the phenomena of nature, like the sun and the sea, the stars and the flowers; like frost and snow, rain and dew, hail-storm and thunder, which are to be studied with entire submission of our own faculties, and in the perfect faith that in them there can be no too much or too little, nothing useless or inert—but that, the farther we press in our discoveries, the more we shall see proofs of design and self-supporting arrangement where the careless eye had seen nothing but accident!

LANDOR *Imaginary Conversations.* 1824.

Southey. In so wide and untrodden a creation as that of Shakspeare, can we wonder or complain that sometimes we are bewildered and entangled in the exuberance of fertility? Dry-brained men upon the Continent, the trifling wits of the theatre, accurate however and expert calculators, tell us that his beauties are balanced by his faults. The poetical opposition, puffing for popularity, cry cheerily against them, *his faults are balanced by his beauties*; when, in reality, all the faults that ever were committed in poetry would be but as air to earth, if we could weigh them against one single thought or image, such as almost every scene exhibits in every drama of this unrivalled genius. Do you hear me with patience?

Porson. With more; although at Cambridge we rather discourse on Bacon, for we know him better. He was immeasurably a less wise man than Shakspeare, and not a wiser writer: for he knew his fellow-man only as he saw him in the street and in the court, which indeed is but a dirtier street and a narrower: Shakspeare, who also knew him there, knew him everywhere else, both as he was, and as he might be.

Southey. There is as great a difference between Shakspeare and Bacon as between an American forest and a London timber-yard. In the timber-yard the materials are sawed and squared and set across: in the forest we have the natural form of the trees, all its growth, all its branches, all its leaves, all the mosses that grow about it, all the birds and insects that inhabit it; now deep shadows absorbing the whole wilderness; now bright bursting glades, with exuberant grass and flowers and fruitage; now untroubled skies; now terrific thunderstorms; everywhere multiformity, everywhere immensity.

VICTOR HUGO *Préface de Cromwell.* 1827.

Le moment est venu où l'équilibre entre les deux principes (le grotesque et le sublime) va s'établir. Un homme, un poète roi, *poeta soverano*, comme Dante le dit d'Homère, va tout fixer. Les deux génies rivaux unissent leur double flamme, et de cette flamme jaillit Shakspeare.

Nous voici parvenus à la sommité poétique des temps modernes. Shakspeare, c'est le Drame; et le drame, qui font sous un même souffle le grotesque et le sublime, le terrible et le bouffon, la tragédie at la comédie, le drame est le caractère propre de la troisième époque de poésie, de la littérature actuelle. . . .

Les personnages de l'ode sont des colosses: Adam, Caïn, Noé; ceux de l'épopée sont des géants: Achille, Atrée, Oreste; ceux du drame sont des hommes: Hamlet, Macbeth, Otello. L'ode vit de l'idéal, l'épopée du grandiose, le drame du réel. Enfin, cette triple poésie découle de trois grandes sources: la Bible, Homère, Shakspeare. . . .

Grâce à lui, point d'impressions monotones. Tantôt il jette du rire, tantôt de l'horreur dans la tragédie. Il fera rencontrer l'apothicaire à Roméo, les trois sorcières à Macbeth, les fossoyeurs à Hamlet. Parfois enfin il peut sans discordance, comme dans la scène du roi Lear et de son Fou, mêler sa voix criarde aux plus sublimes, aux plus lugubres, aux plus rêveuses musiques de l'âme.

Voilà ce qu'a su faire entre tous, d'une manière qui lui est propre et qu'il serait aussi inutile qu'impossible d'imiter, Shakspeare, ce dieu du théâtre, en qui semblent réunis, comme dans une trinité, les trois grands génies caractéristiques de notre scène: Corneille, Molière, Beaumarchais. . . .

Et puis, encore une fois, il y a de ces *fautes* qui ne prennent racine que dans les chefs-d'œuvre; il n'est donné qu'à certains génies d'avoir certains défauts. On reproche à Shakspeare l'abus de la métaphysique, l'abus de l'esprit, des scènes parasites, des obscénités, l'emploi des friperies mythologiques de mode dans son temps, de l'extravagance, de l'obscurité, du mauvais goût, de l'enflure, des aspérités de style. Le chêne, cet arbre géant que nous comparions tout à l'heure à Shakspeare et qui a plus d'une analogie avec lui, le chêne a le port bizarre, les rameaux noueux, le feuillage sombre, l'écorce âpre et rude; mais il est le chêne.

VICTORIAN CRITICISM

CARLYLE *On Heroes and Hero Worship.* 1840.

Well: this is our poor Warwickshire Peasant, who rose to be Manager of a Playhouse, so that he could live without begging; whom the Earl of South-

ampton cast some kind glances on; whom Sir Thomas Lucy, many thanks
to him, was for sending to the Treadmill! We did not account him a god,
like Odin, while he dwelt with us;—on which point there were much to be
said. But I will say rather, or repeat: In spite of the sad state Hero-worship
now lies in, consider what this Shakspeare has actually become among us.
Which Englishman we ever made, in this land of ours, which million of
Englishmen, would we not give up rather than the Stratford Peasant? There
is no regiment of highest Dignitaries that we would sell him for. He is the
grandest thing we have yet done. For our honour among foreign nations, as
an ornament to our English Household, what item is there that we would
not surrender rather than him? Consider now, if they asked us, Will you
give up your Indian Empire or your Shakspeare, you English; never have
had any Indian Empire, or never have had any Shakspeare? Really it were
a grave question. Official persons would answer doubtless in official language; but we, for our part too, should not we be forced to answer: Indian
Empire, or no Indian Empire; we cannot do without Shakspeare! Indian
Empire will go, at any rate, some day; but this Shakspeare does not go, he
lasts forever with us; we cannot give up our Shakspeare!

Nay, apart from spiritualities; and considering him merely as a real, market-
able, tangibly useful possession. England, before long, this Island of ours,
will hold but a small fraction of the English: in America, in New Holland,
east and west to the very Antipodes, there will be a Saxondom covering great
spaces of the Globe. And now, what is it that can keep all these together
into virtually one Nation, so that they do not fall out and fight, but live at
peace, in brotherlike intercourse, helping one another? This is justly regarded as the greatest practical problem, the thing all manner of sovereignties
and governments are here to accomplish: what is it that will accomplish
this? Acts of Parliament, administrative prime-ministers cannot. America is
parted from us, so far as Parliament could part it. Call it not fantastic, for
there is much reality in it: Here, I say, is an English King, whom no time
or chance, Parliament or combination of Parliaments, can dethrone! This
King Shakspeare, does not he shine, in crowned sovereignty, over us all, as
the noblest, gentlest, yet strongest of rallying signs; *in*destructible; really more
valuable in that point of view, than any other means or appliance whatsoever? We can fancy him as radiant aloft over all the Nations of Englishmen
a thousand years hence. From Paramatta, from New York, wheresoever,
under what sort of Parish-Constable soever, English men and women are,
they will say to one another: 'Yes, this Shakspeare is ours: we produced him,
we speak and think by him; we are of one blood and kind with him.' The
most common-sense politician, too, if he pleases, may think of that.

E. A. ABBOTT *A Shakespearian Grammar.* 1869.

It was an age of experiments, and the experiments were not always successful. . . . But for freedom, for brevity, and for vigour, Elizabethan is superior
to modern English. Many of the words employed by Shakespeare and his
contemporaries were the recent inventions of the age; hence they were used

with a freshness and exactness to which we are strangers. Again, the spoken English so far predominated over the grammatical English that it materially influenced the rhythm of the verse, the construction of the sentence, and even sometimes the spelling of words. Hence sprung an artless and unlaboured harmony which seems the natural heritage of Elizabethan poets, whereas such harmony as is attained by modern authors frequently betrays a painful excess of art. Lastly, the use of some few still remaining inflections (the subjunctive in particular), the lingering *sense* of many other inflections that had passed away leaving behind something of the old versatility and audacity in the arrangement of the sentence, the stern subordination of grammar to terseness and clearness, and the consequent directness and naturalness of expression, all conspire to give a liveliness and wakefulness to Shakespearian English which are wanting in the grammatical monotony of the present day. We may perhaps claim some superiority in completeness and perspicuity for modern English, but if we were to appeal on this ground to the shade of Shakespeare in the words of Antonio in the *Tempest*,—

'Do you not hear us speak?'

we might fairly be crushed with the reply of Sebastian—

'I do; and surely
It is a sleepy language.'

EDWARD DOWDEN *Shakspere: His Mind and Art.* 1875.

Over the beauty of youth and the love of youth, there is shed, in these plays of Shakspere's final period, a clear yet tender luminousness, not else-where to be perceived in his writings. In his earlier plays, Shakspere writes concerning young men and maidens, their loves, their mirths, their griefs, as one who is among them, who has a lively, personal interest in their concerns, who can make merry with them, treat them familiarly, and, if need be, can mock them into good sense. There is nothing in these early plays wonderful, strangely beautiful, pathetic about youth and its joys and sorrows. In the histories and tragedies, as was to be expected, more massive, broader, or more profound objects of interest engaged the poet's imagination. But in these latest plays, the beautiful pathetic light is always present. There are the sufferers, aged, experienced, tried—Queen Katharine, Prospero, Hermione. And over against these there are the children absorbed in their happy and exquisite egoism,—Perdita and Miranda, Florizel and Ferdinand, and the boys of old Belarius.

The same means to secure ideality for these figures, so young and beautiful, is in each case (instinctively perhaps rather than deliberately) resorted to. They are lost children—princes or a princess, removed from the court, and its conventional surroundings, into some scene of rare, natural beauty. There are the lost princes—Arviragus and Guiderius, among the mountains of Wales, drinking the free air, and offering their salutations to the risen sun. There is Perdita, the shepherdess-princess, 'queen of curds and cream', sharing with old and young her flowers, lovelier and more undying than

those that Proserpina let fall from Dis's waggon. There is Miranda, (whose
very name is significant of wonder), made up of beauty, and love, and womanly
pity, neither courtly nor rustic, with the breeding of an island of enchantment, where Prospero is her tutor and protector, and Caliban her servant,
and the prince of Naples her lover. In each of these plays we can see Shakspere, as it were, tenderly bending over the joys and sorrows of youth. We
recognise this rather through the total characterization, and through a feeling
and a presence, than through definite incident and statement. But some of
this feeling escapes in the disinterested joy and admiration of old Belarius
when he gazes at the princely youths, and in Camillo's loyalty to Florizel and
Perdita; while it obtains more distinct expression in such a word as that which
Prospero utters, when from a distance he watches with pleasure Miranda's
zeal to relieve Ferdinand from his task of log-bearing:—'Poor worm, thou art
infected.' . . .

A thought which seems to run through the whole of The Tempest, appearing here and there like a coloured thread in some web, is the thought
that the true freedom of man consists in service. Ariel, untouched by human
feeling, is panting for his liberty; in the last words of Prospero are promised
his enfranchisement and dismissal to the elements. Ariel reverences his great
master, and serves him with bright alacrity; but he is bound by none of our
human ties, strong and tender, and he will rejoice when Prospero is to him
as though he never were. To Caliban, a land-fish, with the duller elements
of earth and water in his composition, but no portion of the higher elements,
air and fire, though he receives dim intimations of a higher world,—a musical
humming, or a twangling, or a voice heard in sleep—to Caliban, service is
slavery. He hates to bear his logs; he fears the incomprehensible power of
Prospero, and obeys, and curses. The great master has usurped the rights of
the brute-power Caliban. And when Stephano and Trinculo appear, ridicu-
lously impoverished specimens of humanity, with their shallow understanding
and vulgar greeds, this poor earth-monster is possessed by a sudden *schwär-
merei*, a fanaticism for liberty!—

> 'Ban, 'ban, Ca'-Caliban,
> Has a new master; get a new man.
> Freedom, heydey! heydey, freedom! freedom! freedom, heydey, freedom!

His new master also sings his impassioned hymn of liberty, the *Marseillaise*
of the enchanted island:

> Flout 'em and scout 'em,
> And scout 'em and flout 'em;
> Thought is free.

The leaders of the revolution, escaped from the stench and foulness of the
horse-pond, King Stephano and his prime minister Trinculo, like too many
leaders of the people, bring to an end their great achievement on behalf of
liberty by quarrelling over booty,—the trumpery which the providence of
Prospero had placed in their way. Caliban, though scarce more truly wise

or instructed than before, at least discovers his particular error of the day and
hour:

> What a thrice-double ass
> Was I, to take this drunkard for a god,
> And worship this dull fool!

It must be admitted that Shakspere, if not, as Hartley Coleridge asserted,
'a Tory and a gentleman', had within him some of the elements of English
conservatism.

SWINBURNE *A Study of Shakespeare.* 1880.

We have now come to that point at the opening of the second stage in his
work where the supreme genius of all time begins first to meddle with the
mysteries and varieties of human character, to handle its finer and more
subtle qualities, to harmonise its more untuned and jarring discords; giving
here and thus the first proof of a power never shared in like measure by the
mightiest among the sons of men, a sovereign and serene capacity to fathom
the else unfathomable depths of spiritual nature, to solve its else insoluble
riddles, to reconcile its else irreconcilable discrepancies. In first stage Shakespeare had dropped his plummet no deeper into the sea of the spirit of man
than Marlowe had sounded before him; and in the channel of simple emotion
no poet could cast surer line with steadier hand than he. Further down in
the dark and fiery depths of human pain and mortal passion no soul could
search than his who first rendered into speech the aspirations and the agonies
of a ruined and revolted spirit. And until Shakespeare found in himself the
strength of eyesight to read and the cunning of handiwork to render those
wider diversities of emotion and those further complexities of character which
lay outside the range of Marlowe, he certainly cannot be said to have outrun
the winged feet, outstripped the fiery flight of his forerunner. In the heaven
of our tragic song the first-born star on the forehead of its herald god was not
outshone till the full midsummer meridian of that greater godhead before
whom he was sent to prepare a pathway for the sun. Through all the fore-
noon of our triumphant day, till the utter consummation and ultimate
ascension of dramatic poetry incarnate and transfigured in the master-singer
of the world, the quality of his tragedy was as that of Marlowe's, broad,
single, and intense; large of hand, voluble of tongue, direct of purpose. With
the dawn of its latter epoch a new power comes upon it, to find clothing and
expression in new forms of speech and after a new style. The language has
put off its foreign decorations of lyric and elegiac ornament; it has found
already its infinite gain in the loss of those sweet superfluous graces which
encumbered the march and enchained the utterance of its childhood. The
figures which it invests are now no more the types of a single passion, the
incarnations of a single thought. They now demand a scrutiny which tests
the power of a mind and tries the value of a judgment; they appeal to something more than the instant apprehension which sufficed to respond to the
immediate claim of those that went before them. Romeo and Juliet were
simply lovers, and their names bring back to us no further thought than of

their love and the lovely sorrow of its end; Antony and Cleopatra shall be
before all things lovers, but the thought of their love and its triumphant
tragedy shall recall other things beyond number—all the forces and all the
fortunes of mankind, all the chance and all the consequence that waited on
their imperial passion, all the infinite variety of qualities and powers wrought
together and welded into the frame and composition of that love which
shook from end to end all nations and kingdoms of the earth.

WALTER PATER *Appreciations*. 1889.

According to Johnson, *Richard the Second* is one of those plays which
Shakespeare has 'apparently revised'; and how doubly delightful Shakespeare
is where he seems to have revised! 'Would that he had blotted a thousand'—
a thousand hasty phrases, we may venture once more to say with his earlier
critic, now that the tiresome German superstition has passed away which
challenged us to a dogmatic faith in the plenary verbal inspiration of every
one of Shakespeare's clowns. Like some melodiously contending anthem of
Handel's, I said, of Richard's meek 'undoing' of himself in the mirror-scene;
and, in fact, the play of *Richard the Second* does, like a musical composition,
possess a certain concentration of all its parts, a simple continuity, an evenness
in execution, which are rare in the great dramatist. With *Romeo and Juliet*,
that perfect symphony (symphony of three independent poetic forms set in
a grander one[1] which it is the merit of German criticism to have detected)
it belongs to a small group of plays, where, by happy birth and consistent
evolution, dramatic form approaches to something like the unity of a lyrical
ballad, a lyric, a song, a single strain of music. Which sort of poetry we are to
account the highest, is perhaps a barren question. Yet if, in art generally,
unity of impression is a note of what is perfect, then lyric poetry, which in
spite of complex structure often preserves the unity of a single passionate
ejaculation, would rank higher than dramatic poetry, where, especially to the
reader, as distinguished from the spectator assisting at a theatrical performance, there must always be a sense of the effort necessary to keep the various
parts from flying asunder, a sense of imperfect continuity, such as the older
criticism vainly sought to obviate by the rule of the dramatic 'unities'. It
follows that a play attains artistic perfection just in proportion as it approaches
that unity of lyrical effect, as if a song or ballad were still lying at the root of
it, all the various expressions of the conflict of character and circumstance
falling at last into the compass of a single melody, or musical theme. As,
historically, the earliest classic drama arose out of the chorus, from which this
or that person, this or that episode, detached itself, so, into the unity of a
choric song the perfect drama ever tends to return, its intellectual scope
deepened, complicated, enlarged, but still with an unmistakable singleness,
or identity, in its impression on the mind. Just there, in that vivid single
impression left on the mind when all is over, not in any mechanical limitation
of time and place, is the secret of the 'unities'—the true imaginative unity—
of the drama.

[1] The Sonnet: the Aubade: the Epithalamium.

TWENTIETH-CENTURY CRITICISM

A. C. BRADLEY *Shakespearean Tragedy.* 1904.

A Shakespearean tragedy as so far considered may be called a story of exceptional calamity leading to the death of a man in high estate. But it is clearly much more than this, and we have now to regard it from another side. No amount of calamity which merely befell a man, descending from the clouds like lightning, or stealing from the darkness like pestilence, could alone provide the substance of its story. Job was the greatest of all the children of the east, and his afflictions were well-nigh more than he could bear; but even if we imagined them wearing him to death, that would not make his story tragic. Nor yet would it become so, in the Shakespearean sense, if the fire, and the great wind from the wilderness, and the torments of his flesh were conceived as sent by a supernatural power, whether just or malignant. The calamities of tragedy do not simply happen, nor are they sent; they proceed mainly from actions, and those the actions of men.

We see a number of human beings placed in certain circumstances; and we see, arising from the co-operation of their characters in these circumstances, certain actions. These actions beget others, and these others beget others again, until this series of inter-connected deeds leads by an apparently inevitable sequence to a catastrophe. The effect of such a series on imagination is to make us regard the sufferings which accompany it, and the catastrophe in which it ends, not only or chiefly as something which happens to the persons concerned, but equally as something which is caused by them. This at least may be said of the principal persons, and, among them, of the hero, who always contributes in some measure to the disaster in which he perishes.

This second aspect of tragedy evidently differs greatly from the first. Men, from this point of view, appear to us primarily as agents, 'themselves the authors of their proper woe'; and our fear and pity, though they will not cease or diminish, will be modified accordingly. We are now to consider this second aspect, remembering that it too is only one aspect, and additional to the first, not a substitute for it.

The 'story' or 'action' of a Shakespearean tragedy does not consist, of course, solely of human actions or deeds; but the deeds are the predominant factor. And these deeds are, for the most part, actions in the full sense of the word; not things done ''tween sleep and wake', but acts or omissions thoroughly expressive of the doer,—characteristic deeds. The centre of the tragedy, therefore, may be said with equal truth to lie in action issuing from character, or in character issuing in action.

Shakespeare's main interest lay here. To say that it lay in *mere* character, or was a psychological interest, would be a great mistake, for he was dramatic to the tips of his fingers. It is possible to find places where he has given a certain indulgence to his love of poetry, and even to his turn for general reflections; but it would be very difficult, and in his later tragedies perhaps impossible, to detect passages where he has allowed such freedom to the interest in character apart from action. But for the opposite extreme, for the abstraction of mere 'plot' (which is a very different thing from the tragic 'action'), for the kind of interest which predominates in a novel like *The Woman in White*, it is clear that he cared even less. I do not mean that this interest is absent from his dramas; but it is subordinate to others, and it is so interwoven with them that we are rarely conscious of it apart, and rarely feel in any great strength the half-intellectual, half-nervous excitement of following an ingenious complication. What we do feel strongly, as a tragedy advances to its close, is that the calamities and catastrophe follow inevitably from the deeds of men, and that the main source of these deeds is character. The dictum that, with Shakespeare, 'character is destiny' is no doubt an exaggeration, and one that may mislead (for many of his tragic personages, if they had not met with peculiar circumstances, would have escaped a tragic end, and might even have lived fairly untroubled lives); but it is the exaggeration of a vital truth.

Sir Walter Raleigh *Shakespeare*. 1907.

The vision, as it was seen by Shakespeare, is so solemn, and terrible, and convincing in its reality, that there are few, perhaps, among his readers, who have not averted or covered their eyes. 'I might relate', says Johnson, 'that I was many years ago so shocked by Cordelia's death, that I know not whether I ever endured to read again the last scenes of the play till I undertook to revise them as an editor.' For the better part of a century the feelings of play-goers were spared by alterations in the acting version. With readers of the play other protective devices have found favour. These events, they have been willing to believe, are a fable designed by Shakespeare to illustrate the possible awful consequences of error and thoughtlessness. Such things never happened; or, if they happened, at least we can be careful, and they never need happen again. So the reader takes refuge in morality, from motives not of pride, but of terror, because morality is within man's reach. The breaking of a bridge from faulty construction excites none of the panic fear that is produced by an earthquake.

But here we have to do with an earthquake, and good conduct is of no avail. Morality is not denied; it is overwhelmed and tossed aside by the in-rush of the sea. There is no moral lesson to be read, except accidentally, in any of Shakespeare's tragedies. They deal with greater things than man; with powers and passions, elemental forces, and dark abysses of suffering; with the central fire, which breaks through the thin crust of civilisation, and makes a splendour in the sky above the blackness of ruined homes. Because he is a poet, and has a true imagination, Shakespeare knows how precarious is man's tenure of the soil, how deceitful are his quiet orderly habits and his prosaic speech. At any moment, by the operation of chance, or fate, these things may be broken up, and the world given over once more to the forces that struggled in chaos.

It is not true to say that in these tragedies character is destiny. Othello is not a jealous man; he is a man carried off his feet, wave-drenched and blinded by the passion of love. Macbeth is not a murderous politician; he is a man possessed. Lear no doubt has faults; he is irritable and exacting, and the price that he pays for these weaknesses of old age is that they let loose hell. Hamlet is sensitive, thoughtful, generous, impulsive,—'a pure, noble, and most moral nature'—yet he does not escape the extreme penalty, and at the bar of a false criticism he too is made guilty of the catastrophe. But Shakespeare, who watched his heroes, awestruck, as he saw them being drawn into the gulf, passed no such judgment on them. In his view of it, what they suffer is out of all proportion to what they do and are. They are presented with a choice, and the essence of the tragedy is that choice is impossible. Coriolanus has to choose between the pride of his country and the closest of human affections. Antony stands poised between love and empire. Macbeth commits a foul crime; but Shakespeare's tragic stress is laid on the hopelessness of the dilemma that follows, and his great pity for mortality makes the crime a lesser thing. Hamlet fluctuates between the thought which leads nowhither and the action which is narrow and profoundly unsatisfying. Brutus, like Coriolanus, has to choose between his highest political hopes and the private ties of humanity. Lear's misdoing is forgotten in the doom that falls upon him; after his fit of jealous anger he awakes to find that he has no further choice, and is driven into the wilderness, a scapegoat for mankind. Othello—but the story of Othello exemplifies a further reach of Shakespeare's fearful irony— Othello, like Hamlet, suffers for his very virtues, and the noblest qualities of his mind are made the instruments of his crucifixion.

TOLSTOY *Shakespeare and the Drama*. 1906. (Trans. Aylmer Maude.)

I remember the astonishment I felt when I first read Shakespeare. I had expected to receive a great esthetic pleasure, but on reading, one after another, the works regarded as his best, *King Lear*, *Romeo and Juliet*, *Hamlet*, and *Macbeth*, not only did I not experience pleasure but I felt an insuperable repulsion and tedium, and a doubt whether I lacked sense, since I considered works insignificant and simply bad, which were regarded as the summit of perfection by the whole educated world; or whether the importance that educated world attributed to Shakespeare's works lacks sense. My perplexity was increased by the fact that I have always keenly felt the beauties of poetry in all its forms: why then did Shakespeare's works, recognised by the whole world as works of artistic genius, not only fail to please me, but even seem detestable? I long distrusted my judgment, and to check my conclusions, during fifty years, I repeatedly set to work to read Shakespeare in all possible forms—in Russian, in English, and in German in Schlegel's translation, as I was advised to. I read the tragedies, comedies, and historical plays, several times over, and I invariably experienced the same feelings— repulsion, weariness, and bewilderment. Now, before writing this article, as an old man of 75, wishing once more to check my conclusions, I have again read the whole of Shakespeare, including the historical plays, the *Henrys*, *Troilus and Cressida*, *The Tempest*, and *Cymbeline*, etc., and have experienced the same feeling still more strongly, no longer with perplexity but with a firm indubitable conviction that the undisputed fame Shakespeare enjoys as a great genius, which makes writers of our time imitate him and readers and spectators, distorting their esthetic and ethical sense, seek non-existent qualities in him, is a great evil—as every falsehood is. . . .

But not only are the characters in Shakespeare's plays placed in tragic positions which are quite impossible, do not result from the course of events, and are inappropriate to the period and the place, but they also behave in a way not in accord with their own definite characters and that is quite arbitrary. . . .

From the very beginning of reading any of Shakespeare's plays I was at once convinced that it was perfectly evident that he is lacking in the chief, if not the sole, means of portraying character, which is individuality of language—that each person should speak in a way suitable to his own character. That is lacking in Shakespeare. All his characters speak, not a language of their own but always one and the same Shakespearean, affected, unnatural language, which not only could they not speak, but which no real people could ever have spoken anywhere. . . .

Shakespeare's characters continually do and say what is not merely unnatural to them but quite unnecessary. I will not cite examples of this, for I think that a man who does not himself perceive this striking defect in all Shakespeare's dramas will not be convinced by any possible examples or proofs. It is sufficient to read *King Lear* alone, with the madness, the murders, the plucking out of eyes, Gloucester's jump, the poisonings, and the torrents of abuse—not to mention *Pericles*, *A Winter's Tale*—or *The Tempest*, to convince oneself of this. Only a man quite devoid of the sense of proportion and taste could produce the types of *Titus Andronicus* and *Troilus and Cressida*, and so mercilessly distort the old drama of *King Lear*. . . .

The content of Shakespeare's plays, as is seen by the explanations of his greatest admirers, is the lowest, most vulgar view of life, which regards the external elevation of the great ones of the earth as a genuine superiority; despises the crowd, that is to say, the working classes; and repudiates not only religious, but even any humanitarian, efforts directed towards the alteration of the existing order of society.

The second condition is also absent in Shakespeare except in his handling of scenes in which a movement of feeling is expressed. There is in his works a lack of naturalness in the situations, the characters lack individuality of speech, and a sense of proportion is also wanting, without which such works cannot be artistic.

The third and chief condition—sincerity—is totally absent in all Shakespeare's works. One sees in all of them an intentional artificiality; it is obvious that he is not in earnest but is playing with words. . . .

There is only one explanation of this astonishing fame: it is one of those epidemic suggestions to which people always have been and are liable. . . .

So that the first cause of Shakespeare's fame was that the Germans wanted to oppose something freer and more alive to the French drama of which they were tired, and which was really dull and cold. The second cause was that the young German writers required a model for their own dramas. The third and chief cause was the activity of the learned and zealous esthetic German critics who lacked esthetic feeling and formulated the theory of objective art, that is to say, deliberately repudiated the religious essence of the drama. . . .

A series of accidents brought it about that Goethe at the beginning of the last century, being the dictator of philosophic thought and esthetic laws, praised Shakespeare; the esthetic critics caught up that praise and began to write their long foggy erudite articles, and the great European public began to be enchanted by Shakespeare. The critics, responding to this public interest, laboriously vied with one another in writing fresh and fresh articles about Shakespeare, and readers and spectators were still further confirmed in their enthusiasm, and Shakespeare's fame kept growing and growing like a snowball, until in our time it has attained a degree of insane laudation that obviously rests on no other basis than suggestion. . . .

But above all, having assimilated that immoral view of life which permeates all Shakespeare's works he (a young man) loses the capacity to distinguish between good and evil. And the error of extolling an insignificant, inartistic, and not only non-moral but plainly immoral writer, accomplishes its pernicious work.

That is why I think that the sooner people emancipate themselves from this false worship of Shakespeare the better it will be—first because people when they are freed from this falsehood will come to understand that a drama which has no religious basis is not only not an important or good thing, as is now supposed, but is a most trivial and contemptible affair. And having understood this they will have to search for and work out a new form of modern drama—a drama which will serve for the elucidation and confirmation in man of the highest degree of religious consciousness. And secondly, because people when themselves set free from this hypnotic state, will understand that the insignificant and immoral works of Shakespeare and his imitators, aiming only at distracting and amusing the spectators, cannot possibly serve to teach the meaning of life, but that, as long as there is no real religious drama, guidance for life must be looked for from other sources.

LYTTON STRACHEY *Landmarks in French Literature.* 1912.

English dramatic literature is, of course, dominated by Shakespeare; and it is almost inevitable that an English reader should measure the value of other poetic drama by the standards which Shakespeare has already implanted in his mind. But, after all, Shakespeare himself was but the product and the crown of a particular dramatic convention; he did not compose his plays according to an ideal pattern; he was an Elizabethan, working so consistently according to the methods of his age and country that, as we know, he passed, 'unguessed at' among his contemporaries. But what were these methods and this convention? To judge of them properly we must look, not at Shakespeare's masterpieces, for they are transfused and consecrated with the light of transcendent genius, but at the average play of an ordinary Elizabethan playwright, or even at one of the lesser works of Shakespeare himself. And, if we look here, it will become apparent that the dramatic tradition of the Elizabethan age was an extremely faulty one. It allowed, it is true, of great richness, great variety, and the sublimest heights of poetry; but it also allowed of an almost incredible looseness of structure and vagueness of purpose, of dullness, of insipidity, and of bad taste. The genius of the Elizabethans was astonishing, but it was genius struggling with difficulties which were well-nigh insuperable; and, as a matter of fact, in spite of their amazing poetic and dramatic powers, their work has vanished from the stage, and is to-day familiar to but a few of the lovers of English literature. Shakespeare alone was not subdued to what he worked in. His overwhelming genius harmonised and ennobled the discordant elements of the Elizabethan tradition, and invested them not only with immortality, but with immortality understanded of the people. His greatest works will continue to be acted and applauded so long as there is a theatre in England. But even Shakespeare himself was not always successful. One has only to look at some of his secondary plays—at *Troilus and Cressida*, for instance, or *Timon of Athens*—to see at once how inveterate and malignant were the diseases to which the dramatic methods of the Elizabethans were a prey. Wisdom and poetry are intertwined with flatness and folly; splendid situations drift purposeless to impotent conclusions; brilliant psychology alternates with the grossest indecency and the feeblest puns. 'O matter and impertinency mixed!' one is inclined to exclaim at such a spectacle. And then one is blinded once more by the glamour of *Lear* and *Othello*; one forgets the defective system in the triumph of a few exceptions, and all plays seem intolerable unless they were written on the principle which produced *Pericles* and *Titus Andronicus* and the whole multitude of distorted and disordered works of genius of the Elizabethan age.

Racine's principles were, in fact, the direct opposite of these. 'Comprehension' might be taken as the watchword of the Elizabethans; Racine's was 'concentration'. His great aim was to produce, not an extraordinary nor a complex work of art, but a flawless one; he wished to be all matter and no impertinency. His conception of a drama was of something swift, simple, inevitable; an action taken at the crisis, with no redundancies however interesting, no complications however suggestive, no irrelevances however beautiful—but plain, intense, vigorous, and splendid with nothing but its own essential force. Nor can there be any doubt that Racine's view of what a drama should be has been justified by the subsequent history of the stage. The Elizabethan tradition has died out—or rather it has left the theatre, and become absorbed in the modern novel; and it is the drama of crisis—such as Racine conceived it—which is now the accepted model of what a stage-play should be. And, in this connection, we may notice an old controversy, which still occasionally raises its head in the waste places of criticism—the question of the three unities. In this controversy both sides have been content to repeat arguments which are in reality irrelevant and futile. It is irrelevant to consider whether the unities were or were not prescribed by Aristotle; and it is futile to ask whether the sense of probability is or is not more shocked by the scenic representation of an action of thirty-six hours than by one of twenty-four. The value of the unities does not depend either upon their traditional authority or—to use the French expression—upon their *vraisemblance*. Their true importance lies simply in their being a powerful means towards concentration. Thus it is clear that in an absolute sense they are neither good nor bad; their goodness or badness depends upon the kind of result which the dramatist is aiming at. If he wishes to produce a drama of the Elizabethan type—a drama of comprehension—which shall include as much as possible of the varied manifestations of human life, then obviously the observance of the unities must exercise a restricting and narrowing influence which would be quite out of place. On the other hand, in a drama of crisis they are not only useful but almost inevitable. If a crisis is to be a real crisis it must not drag on indefinitely; it must not last for more than a few hours, or—to put a rough limit—for more than a single day; in fact, the unity of time must be preserved. Again, if the action is to pass quickly, it must pass in one place, for there will be no time for the movement of the characters elsewhere; thus the unity of place becomes a necessity. Finally, if the mind is to be concentrated to the full upon a particular crisis, it must not be distracted by side issues; the event, and nothing but the event, must be displayed; in other words, the dramatist will not succeed in his object unless he employs the unity of action.

LEVIN L. SCHÜCKING *Character Problems in Shakespeare's Plays.* 1919, translated 1922.

After all this there can be no further doubts as to the popular character of Shakespeare's art. Indeed, it is proved by sufficient external evidence. . . . It is interesting to see what the eulogists of Beaumont and Fletcher in their laudatory poems in the introduction to their complete edition (1646) of these authors have to say about Shakespeare. They reproach him with the use of old-fashioned, indecent jokes, 'trunk-hose wit', as they call it.

All these things we must keep in mind in order to gain a firm foundation on which to base our judgment. It is remarkable in how many cases conclusions have been drawn without attention being paid to this standpoint. An example which brings this fault out in strong relief may be found in the treatment of *Troilus and Cressida*. Here the element that was for the most part unjustly looked upon by the critics of the nineteenth century as the 'parodistic tone' of the piece has been explained by Brandes as follows: 'From his very childhood his ears, as well as every one else's, had been filled with the splendour of the Trojan War. Every person who had taken part in it was the pattern of heroism, magnanimity, wisdom, venerableness, friendship and fidelity. As if such persons had ever existed! For the first time in his life he felt the keen desire to caricature as much as possible, put out his tongue, make a grimace, and show up the seamy side—the real side.' But did Shakespeare's company act before an audience of sixth-form schoolboys? What an absurdity to imagine that Shakespeare ever would or could have desired to summon the spectators of the Globe Theatre to a critical discussion on the (supposedly) traditional conception of the ethical value of the heroes of classical antiquity!

It is very evident that until this anachronistic point of view has been abandoned as absolutely untenable the correct historical contemplation of Shakespeare's art is out of the question. To read and interpret the Shakespearean drama in the light of the same standards as we do that of Ibsen would be as wrong as tacitly to identify the mental qualities of Shakespeare's audience with Ibsen's.

If now, in spite of the popular tone which we have traced in his creations, we find so much that offers a riddle to our intelligence, we must ask ourselves whether we have not, in many cases, lost a key to these riddles of which Shakespeare's contemporaries were in possession. The following exposition will make it clear that in a certain sense this is actually the case. Shakespearean exegesis has hitherto started almost exclusively with the most advanced side of his art, and has sought to judge all the rest from this. But Shakespeare's art-form is in fact a mixture of the most highly developed with quite primitive elements: on one side an inexpressible delicacy and subtlety in the portraiture of the soul, on the other aids and props to the understanding of the most antiquated description, as well as elements in the plot uncritically adopted and never properly fused into the play of character. Only the American scholar E. E. Stoll has lately, independently of the author, sought to promote this view—*i.e.*, that an historical understanding of Shakespeare is to be reached only by taking him much more literally than we have been wont to do, his art as more naïve, his methods as frequently far more primitive. . . .

It may perhaps be objected that the ultimate result of our method of historically correct criticism will not prove favourable to Shakespeare in the conventional sense. In this respect it is no mere chance that the name of Rümelin, the author of *Shakespeare-Studien eines Realisten*, will often be found in the following pages. This highly gifted and artistic critic has too often been regarded as a sort of Lucifer by the representatives of orthodox Shakespearean research, a rebel who in arrogant and infatuated delusion rose against the divinity of Shakespeare, thereby meriting to be hurled into the darkest depth of oblivion. But to be a worshipper of the letter is more often the result of a lack of judgment than of real piety. The man who, like the latest orthodox Shakespeareans, argues that to us Shakespeare can no longer be an object of criticism, but only a standard of art, will be little likely to forward a right understanding of him. Shakespearean research would have been more advanced to-day if it had in time taken up Rümelin's method of criticism and seriously dealt with the valuable suggestions contained in it by means of historical literary investigation.

T. S. ELIOT *Shakespeare and the Stoicism of Seneca.* 1927.

The last few years have witnessed a number of recrudescences of Shakespeare. There is the fatigued Shakespeare, a retired Anglo-Indian, presented by Mr. Lytton Strachey; there is the messianic Shakespeare, bringing a new philosophy and a new system of yoga, presented by Mr. Middleton Murry; and there is the ferocious Shakespeare, a furious Samson, presented by Mr. Wyndham Lewis in his interesting book, *The Lion and the Fox*. On the whole, we may all agree that these manifestations are beneficial. In any case, so important as that of Shakespeare, it is good that we should from time to time change our minds. The last conventional Shakespeare is banished from the scene, and a variety of unconventional Shakespeares take his place. About anyone so great as Shakespeare, it is probable that we can never be right; and if we can never be right, it is better that we should from time to time change our way of being wrong. Whether Truth ultimately prevails is doubtful and has never been proved; but it is certain that nothing is more effective in driving out error than a new error. Whether Mr. Strachey, or Mr. Murry, or Mr. Lewis, is any nearer to the truth of Shakespeare than Rymer, Morgann, or Webster, or Johnson, is uncertain; they are all certainly more sympathetic in this year 1927 than Coleridge, or Swinburne, or Dowden. If they do not give us the real Shakespeare—if there is one—they at least give us several up-to-date Shakespeares. If the only way to prove that Shakespeare did not feel and think exactly as people felt and thought in 1815, or in 1860, or in 1880, is to show that he felt and thought as we felt and thought in 1927, then we must accept gratefully that alternative. . . .

That Shakespeare deliberately took a 'view of life' from Seneca there seems to be no evidence whatever.

Nevertheless, there is, in some of the great tragedies of Shakespeare, a new attitude. It is not the attitude of Seneca, but it is derived from Seneca; it is slightly different from anything that can be found in French tragedy, in Corneille or in Racine; it is modern, and it culminates, if there is ever any culmination, in the attitude of Nietzsche. I cannot say that it is Shakespeare's 'philosophy'. Yet, many people have lived by it; though it may only have been Shakespeare's instinctive recognition of something of theatrical utility. It is the attitude of self-dramatization assumed by some of Shakespeare's heroes at moments of tragic intensity. It is not peculiar to Shakespeare; it is conspicuous in Chapman: Bussy, Clermont and Biron, all die in this way. Marston—one of the most interesting and least explored of all the Elizabethans—uses it; and Marston and Chapman were particularly Senecan. But Shakespeare, of course, does it very much better than any of the others, and makes it somehow more integral with the human nature of his characters. It is less verbal, more real. . . .

It is this general notion of 'thinking' that I would challenge. One has the difficulty of having to use the same words for different things. We say, in a vague way, that Shakespeare, or Dante, or Lucretius, is a poet who thinks, and that Swinburne is a poet who does not think, even that Tennyson is a poet who does not think. But what we really mean is not a difference in quality of thought, but a difference in quality of emotion. The poet who 'thinks' is merely the poet who can express the emotional equivalent of thought. But he is not necessarily interested in the thought itself. We talk as if thought was precise and emotion was vague. In reality there is precise emotion and there is vague emotion. To express precise emotion requires as great intellectual power as to express precise thought. But by 'thinking' I mean something very different from anything that I find in Shakespeare. Mr. Lewis, and other champions of Shakespeare as a great philosopher, have a great deal to say about Shakespeare's power of thought, but they fail to show that he thought to any purpose; that he had any coherent view of life, or that he recommended any procedure to follow. 'We possess a great deal of evidence', says Mr. Lewis, 'as to what Shakespeare thought of military glory and martial events.' Do we? Or rather, did Shakespeare think anything at all? He was occupied with turning human actions into poetry.

I would suggest that none of the plays of Shakespeare has a 'meaning', although it would be equally false to say that a play of Shakespeare is meaningless. All great poetry gives the illusion of a view of life. When we enter into the world of Homer, or Sophocles, or Virgil, or Dante, or Shakespeare, we incline to believe that we are apprehending something that can be expressed intellectually; for every precise emotion tends towards intellectual formulation.

G. Wilson Knight *The Wheel of Fire.* 1930.

Our reaction to great literature is a positive and dynamic experience. Crudely, sometimes ineffectually, interpretation will attempt to translate that experience in a spirit also positive and dynamic.

To do this we should regard each play as a visionary unit, close-knit in personification, atmospheric suggestion, and direct poetic-symbolism: three modes of transmission, equal in their importance. Too often the first of these alone receives attention: whereas, in truth, we should not be content even with all three, however clearly we have them in our minds, unless we can work back through them to the original vision they express. Each incident, each turn of thought, each suggestive symbol throughout *Macbeth* or *Lear* radiates inwards from the play's circumference to the burning central core without knowledge of which we shall miss their relevance and necessity: they relate primarily, not directly to each other, nor to the normal appearances of human life, but to this central reality alone. The persons of Shakespeare have been analysed carefully in point of psychological realism. But in giving detailed and prolix attention to any one element of the poet's expression, the commentator, starting indeed from a point on the circumference, instead of working into the heart of the play, pursues a tangential course, riding, as it were, on his own life-experiences farther and farther from his proper goal. Such is the criticism that finds 'fault' with the Duke's decisions at the close of *Measure for Measure*: if we are to understand the persons of Shakespeare we should consider always what they do rather than what they might have done. Each person, event, scene, is integral to the poetic statement: the removing, or blurring, of a single stone in the mosaic will clearly lessen our chance of visualizing the whole design. . . .

I will now shortly formulate what I take to be the main principles of right Shakespearian interpretation:

(i) Before noticing the presence of faults we should first regard each play as a visionary unit bound to obey none but its own self-imposed laws. To do this we should attempt to preserve absolute truth to our own imaginative reaction, whithersoever it may lead us in the way of paradox and unreason. We should at all costs avoid selecting what is easy to understand and forgetting the superlogical.

(ii) We should thus be prepared to recognize what I have called both the 'temporal' and 'spatial' elements: that is, to relate any given incident or speech either to the time-sequence of story or the peculiar atmosphere, intellectual or imaginative, which binds the play. Being aware of this new element we should not look for perfect verisimilitude to life, but rather see each play as an expanded metaphor, by means of which the original vision has been projected into forms roughly correspondent with actuality, conforming thereto with greater or less exactitude according to the demands of its own nature. It will then usually appear that many difficult actions and events become coherent and, within the scope of their own universe, natural.

(iii) We should analyse the use and meaning of direct poetic symbolism—that is, events whose significance can hardly be related to the normal processes of actual life. Also the minor symbolic imagery of Shakespeare, which is extremely consistent, should receive careful attention. Where certain images continually recur in the same associative connexion, we can, if we have reason to believe that this associative force is strong enough, be ready to see the presence of the associative value when the images occur alone. Nor should we neglect the symbolic value of aural effects such as the discharge of cannon in *Hamlet* and *Othello* or the sound of trumpets in *Measure for Measure* and *Lear*.

(iv) The plays from *Julius Cæsar* (about 1599) to *The Tempest* (about 1611) when properly understood fall into a significant sequence. This I have called 'the Shakespeare Progress'. Therefore in detailed analysis of any one play it may sometimes be helpful to have regard to its place in the sequence, provided always that thought of this sequence be used to illuminate, and in no sense be allowed to distort, the view of the play under analysis. Particular notice should be given to what I have called the 'Hate-theme' which is turbulent throughout most of these plays: an especial mood of cynicism towards love, disgust at the physical body, and dismay at the thought of death; a revulsion from human life caused by a clear sight of its limitations—more especially limitations imposed by time.

E. E. STOLL *Art and Artifice in Shakespeare*. 1933.

Drama, therefore, if we are to judge of it from the foregoing, is no 'document'. (Not a social document, of course—that question has not here arisen—but not even a 'human' one.) Most of the misinterpretation of it, whether that of Shakespeare or of Æschylus, has been more or less due to our taking it to be such. Whether as story or as character, it is, as Mr. Bridges says of Shakespeare's alone, 'not nature in the sense of being susceptible of the same analysis as that by which the assumptions of science would investigate nature'; and the tendency so to conceive of it is really the same spirit of literalism that prompted the sixteenth- and seventeenth-century critics to establish the canon of the unities—the consideration that they afford, not (as they do) a more compact and effective structure, but a greater *vraisemblance*. The human figures certainly are not, as a recent writer has declared them to be, 'copied with little alteration from the population of the world'; and thank Heaven that they are not. Still less are they examples or illustrations of our psychology. But they are not always even perfect copies of the inner vision, that 'higher reality' which, as Goethe observes, great art represents. They are a compromise, an accommodation, a simplification, to suit the structure and particular conception of the whole. 'The spirit of man cannot be satisfied but with truth, or at least verisimility', says Dryden, echoing Aristotle; but only verisimility is what art, drama, and more especially, among great drama, that of Shakespeare, bestow. It is not reality, or even perfect consistency, but an illusion, and, above all, an illusion whereby the spirit of man shall be moved. The greatest of dramatists is careful, not so much for the single character, as for the drama; indeed, he observes not so much the probabilities of the action, or the psychology of the character, as the psychology of the audience, for whom both action and character are framed. Writing hastily, but impetuously, to be played, not read, he seizes upon almost every means of imitation and opportunity for excitement which this large liberty affords. For everything he would give us, not only (in effect) life as we know it is, but (and far more) drama as we would have it be; yet remembers, no man so constantly, that the attention of his audience—the liberty of his art—has limits. Like all dramatists, he must have a situation; like all the greater dramatists, an intense one. He would, as would Dryden, 'work up the pity to a greater height'. Therefore, like them, he has, necessarily, had to start with premises or postulates, and provoke intrusions, human or super-human, whereby the hero, still keeping our sympathy, can be put in a plight. And just because of the largeness of the undertaking—the whole story and an old one, many characters and situations, and times and places, not a few, and all the form and pressure, sound and colour, of existence—he has necessarily had—for consistency of illusion, swiftness of movement, and intensity of effect—to contrive more audaciously and variously, and (in turn) to make such amends or adjustments as he could, sometimes even by artifices which are scarcely art. He evades and hedges, he manœuvres and manipulates, he suppresses or obscures. But his most noble and effectual amends is positive—his poetry. The premise sets him free for it—*præcipitandus est liber spiritus*—and he walks not soberly afoot, like your philosopher, but flies. And Shakespeare is the greatest of dramatists because the illusion he offers is the widest and highest, the emotion he arouses the most irresistible and overwhelming.

By poetry, an imaginative conquest, he works the wonder—by rhythm and recurrence, acceleration and retardation, swelling and subsidence, and this in the structure, the rhetoric, or the metre; also (for obviously drama is not music) by the seizing and ordering of such thoughts and sentiments, such words and images, as belong together, though never together in this world before; and (above all) in the characters, by both the one process and the other—and who knows by what other besides?—as a vitalising, differentiating power. His imitation is creation; what with us is dull and solid fact, assumes, still recognizable, the potency and liberty of fiction. So it is, in some measure, with the Greeks as well, and with Racine and Ibsen, who one and all are poets, yet not in such signal and pre-eminent measure, not to such dramatic—both airy and substantial—effect. They have less amends to make, but less resources wherewith to make them. Shakespeare's characters, more unmistakably than anyone else's, are, from the outset, given voices, accents, of their own—and not individual only, but beautiful—a fact which inveigles us, throughout the play, and even (witness the critics) afterwards, into accepting, not them only, but also the incredible things that they not infrequently do. They speak—like human beings, though none we know or hear of—*therefore* they are; and then, if for nothing else, their story is— 'for the moment'—credible.

CAROLINE SPURGEON *Shakespeare's Imagery*. 1935.

It has not, so far as I know, ever yet been noticed that recurrent images play a part in raising, developing, sustaining, and repeating emotion in the tragedies, which is somewhat analogous to the action of a recurrent theme or 'motif' in a musical fugue or sonata, or in one of Wagner's operas.

Perhaps, however, a more exact analogy to the function of Shakespeare's images in this respect is the unique work of another great artist, of the peculiar quality of which they constantly remind one, that is, Blake's illustrations to his prophetic books. These are not, for the most part, illustrations in the ordinary sense of the term, the translation by the artist of some incident in the narrative into a visual picture; they are rather a running accompaniment to the words in another medium, sometimes symbolically emphasizing or interpreting certain aspects of the thought, sometimes supplying frankly only decoration or atmosphere, sometimes grotesque and even repellent, vivid, strange, arresting, sometimes drawn with an almost unearthly beauty of form and colour. Thus, as the leaping tongues of flame which illuminate the pages of *The Marriage of Heaven and Hell* show the visual form which Blake's thought evoked in his mind, and symbolize for us the purity, the beauty, and the two-edged quality of life and danger in his words, so the recurrent images in *Macbeth* or *Hamlet* reveal the dominant picture or sensation—and for Shakespeare the two are identical—in terms of which he sees and feels the main problem or theme of the play, thus giving us an unerring clue to the way he looked at it, as well as a direct glimpse into the working of his mind and imagination.

These dominating images are a characteristic of Shakespeare's work throughout, but whereas in the earlier plays they are often rather obvious and of set design, taken over in some cases with the story itself from a hint in the original narrative; in the later plays, and especially in the great tragedies, they are born of the emotions of the theme, and are, as in *Macbeth*, subtle, complex, varied, but intensely vivid and revealing; or as in *Lear*, so constant and all pervading as to be reiterated, not only in the word-pictures, but also in the single words themselves.

Any reader, of course, must be aware of certain recurrent symbolic imagery in Shakespeare, such as that of a tree and its branches, and of planting, lopping, or rooting up, which runs through the English historical plays; they are conscious of the imaginative effect of the animal imagery in *Lear*, or of the flash of explosives in *Romeo and Juliet*, but it was not until the last few years, when in the course of an intensive study of Shakespeare's imagery I had listed and classified and card-indexed and counted every image in every play thrice over, that the actual facts as to these dominating pictures stared me in the face.

I found that there is a certain range of images, and roughly a certain proportion of these, to be expected in every play, and that certain familiar categories, of nature, animals, and what one may call 'everyday' or 'domestic', easily come first. But in addition to this normal grouping, I have found, especially in the tragedies, certain groups of images which, as it were, stick out in each particular play and immediately attract attention because they are peculiar either in subject or quantity, or both.

These seem to form the floating image or images in Shakespeare's mind called forth by that particular play, and I propose now, as briefly as possible, just to look at the tragedies from the point of view of these groups of images only.

In *Romeo and Juliet* the beauty and ardour of young love is seen by Shakespeare as the irradiating glory of sunlight and starlight in a dark world. The dominating image is *light*, every form and manifestation of it; the sun, moon, stars, fire, lightning, the flash of gunpowder, and the reflected light of beauty and of love; while by contrast we have night, darkness, clouds, rain, mist, and smoke. . . .

In *Hamlet*, naturally, we find ourselves in an entirely different atmosphere, and if we look closely we see this is partly due to the number of images of sickness, disease, or blemish of the body in the play, and we discover that the idea of an ulcer or tumour, as descriptive of the unwholesome condition of Denmark morally, is, on the whole, the dominating one.

E. M. W. TILLYARD *Shakespeare's History Plays*. 1944.

Most readers of Shakespeare know that his own version of order or degree is in Ulysses's speech on the topic in *Troilus and Cressida*; not all would grant that it states the necessary setting of the Histories; and few realize how large a body of thought it epitomises or hints at. (May I here ask the reader to have before him a text of this speech?)

Its doctrine is primarily political but evidently goes far beyond mere practical politics. First, we learn that the order which prevails in the heavens is duplicated on earth, the king corresponding to the sun; then that disorder in the heavens breeds disorder on earth, both in the physical sublunary organization and in the commonwealth of men. When Shakespeare calls degree the ladder to all high designs he probably has another correspondence in mind: that between the ascending grades of man in his social state and the ladder of creation or chain of being which stretched from the meanest piece of inanimate matter in unbroken ascent to the highest of the archangels. The musical metaphor in 'Take but degree away, untune that string, and hark what discord follows' is far more than a metaphor; it implies the traditional Platonic doctrine that (in Dryden's words)

> From harmony, from heavenly harmony
> This universal frame began,

and that at the world's last hour

> Music shall untune the sky.

Finally, when an Elizabethan audience heard the words 'chaos, where degree is suffocate', the educated element at least would understand chaos in a more precise sense than we should naturally do. They would understand it as a parallel in the state to the primitive warring of the elements from which the universe was created and into which it would fall if the constant pressure of God's ordering and sustaining will were relaxed. . . .

The Elizabethan conception of world-order was in its outlines medieval although it had discarded much medieval detail. The universe was a unity, in which everything had its place, and it was the perfect work of God. Any imperfection was the work not of God but of man; for with the fall of man the universe underwent a sympathetic corruption. But for all the corruption the marks of God's perfection were still there, and one of the two great roads to salvation was through the study of created things. But though the idea of unity was basic, the actual order of the world presented itself to the Elizabethans under three different, though often related, appearances: a chain, a series of corresponding planes, and a dance to music. . . .

The Elizabethan political order, the Golden Age brought in by the Tudors, is nothing apart from the cosmic order of which it is a part. If this is Davies's[1] faith, is it not contrariwise the more likely that when Shakespeare deals with the concrete facts of English history he never forgets the principle of order behind all the terrible manifestations of disorder, a principle sometimes fulfilled, however imperfectly, even in the kingdoms of this world?

S. L. BETHELL *Shakespeare and the Popular Dramatic Tradition.* 1944.

Every approach to Shakespeare has in it something of value, but I am convinced of the fundamental importance of the words themselves—of the poetry—and of the great, though secondary, importance of a knowledge of Elizabethan stage conditions. My own particular approach, considered in these pages, can be undertaken only in the closest association with pure literary criticism and a consideration of Shakespeare's stagecraft.

I have stressed the element of convention in Shakespeare, since it is generally overlooked. But it is necessary also to insist that Shakespeare and his contemporaries worked to no thought-out conventional system; indeed, their conventions are successful just because they are traditional and unconscious.

[1] Sir John Davies, author of the poem *Orchestra.*

Moreover, being unconscious, they were by no means rigidly adhered to: the Elizabethan playwright varies his position on the scale between conventionalism and naturalism, even in the course of a single play. This rapidity of adjustment is a principal component in Shakespeare's remarkable subtlety. Lapses into naturalism are especially frequent in Shakespeare: they are probably a major cause of his continuous popularity on the stage. . . .

What then is the essence of this popular dramatic tradition—of the perennial psychology of the popular audience? . . . Miss Bradbrook has adumbrated a capacity of the Elizabethan audience, which I regard as fundamentally important: the ability to keep simultaneously in mind two opposite aspects of a situation. . . .

Characters, without being themselves made up of incompatible qualities, may evoke distinct and separate responses from the audience. Thus Falstaff is (a) amusing, and (b) morally reprehensible: an Elizabethan audience would applaud his wit, but approve his final dismissal. . . . Not only character, but every aspect of the Elizabethan drama, is shot through with this quality of dual awareness. The mixture of conventionalism and naturalism demands a dual mode of attention. Awareness of the play as play implies the dual awareness of play-world and real world: upon this depends the piquancy of a play-within-the-play, or of the situation in which a boy plays the part of a girl playing the part of a boy (Julia, Jessica, Rosalind, Viola, Imogen). And the Elizabethan apparently enjoyed a song, when it broke the continuity of the play, perhaps criticising the performer's voice ('A mellifluous voice' (*T.N.* II. iii. 54)) before taking up the play again where he dropped it for the counter-attraction of music. . . .

And the audience responds in this complex way without conscious effort. This is the core of my present thesis: that a popular audience, uncontaminated by abstract and tendentious dramatic theory, will attend to several diverse aspects of a situation, simultaneously yet without confusion. . . .

That the playwright should avail himself of this fact is a prerequisite of all dramatic subtlety. Conditions in the Elizabethan theatre were ideal. Shakespeare's Globe was a truly national theatre, with the cultural stratification one of degree only—not of kind, as it is to-day; and the playwright, who was presumably producer also, and frequently an actor in the company, would find himself in an intimate relationship with an unified and habitual audience. . . .

To sum up, I believe I am justified in asserting that there *is* a popular dramatic tradition, and that its dominant characteristic is the audience's ability to respond spontaneously and unconsciously on more than one plane of attention at the same time. I shall call this the principle of multi-consciousness.

H. B. CHARLTON *Shakespearian Tragedy*, 1948. (The Clark Lectures delivered at Cambridge.)

In the field of interpretation, the most striking trend of the last generation has been the assault on Andrew Bradley. On the one hand, we are told, he is too little of a historian and too much of a philosopher; he lifts Shakespeare out of his Tudor theatre, making no allowance for Elizabethan stage conventions, and assuming in his innocence that words and scenes mean what they seem to mean. On the other hand, he is assailed because he takes Shakespeare's dramas as plays and not as poems; he accepts the persons of them at their face value as semblable men and women, and not as plastic symbols in an arabesque of esoteric imagery, nor as rhythmic ripples intoned in a chromatic ritual. The position of these neo-Shakespearians perturbs me because I cannot understand it. Much of it is Cantabrigian in origin, or in orientation, though perhaps less so in quality. I cite a few characteristic passages without naming their source, well knowing that a Cambridge audience would recognise them. When, for instance, I read that *Hamlet* 'so far from being Shakespeare's masterpiece . . . is certainly an artistic failure', I feel that English is a language which I do not know. When I am told that to attain the 'soul-experience' of a Shakespeare play is 'a process which forces us to cut below the crust of plot and character, and to expose those riches of poetic imagination too often buried in our purely unconscious enjoyment of Shakespeare's art', I applaud the recognition of the mystery of poetic genius, but I ask whether the crust has not itself some meaning, whether in fact it is not the means to meaning chosen by the poet, whether it be not indeed part of the form which has attained identity with its substance. Moreover, I feel entitled to demand whether the values of these treasure-troves from the unconscious should not be expressed in a recognised coinage of critical currency. Again, I am told how to approach Shakespeare if I am to participate with the elect in their mystic rites. 'We start with so many lines of verse on a printed page which we read as we should read any other poem. We have to elucidate the meaning (using Dr. Richards' fourfold definition) and to unravel ambiguities; we have to estimate the kind and quality of the imagery and determine the precise degree of evocation of particular figures; we have to allow full weight to each word, exploring its "tentacular roots", and to determine how it controls and is controlled by the rhythmic movement of the passage in which it occurs.' All seems as systematic, as precise, and as rigorous as a measurement in the Cavendish Laboratory. But how does one estimate 'the kind and quality of imagery'? By what test does one establish that it has been 'truly' estimated? What instrument measures the 'precise degree' of evocation, and on what principles does one determine how a word 'controls and is controlled by the rhythmic movement of the passage in which it occurs'? Are not critics of this school using the façade of the Cavendish to hide a conventicle of impressionist anarchists? The abracadabra apparently most potent in all these neo-Shakespearian conjurations is some such phrase as 'organic poetic structure' or the even more gnomic 'objective correlative'. These can presumably be recognised infallibly, and are sufficient warrant for distorting the plain sense of the words of the text and for discarding the apparent meaning of the incidents of the scene. *In excelsis*, the doctrine asserts that Shakespeare can mean nothing to us to-day unless we happen to hold the peculiar tenets of a relatively small theological sect, and have withal a peculiarly idiosyncratic intuition for chromatic and tonic values. 'The difficulty is for a modern dichotomised mind to comprehend the organic functioning of minds free from our own pathological division.' The terms of the diagnosis suggest what may well be the mainspring of the new creed: the resurgence of the cult of the Middle Ages. . . .

Such seems to be the metaphysic of the neo-Shakespearians. It is a comprehensive dogma, and the most characteristically dogmatic articles of it are the assertion that it is we who miss Shakespeare, and that it is they alone who have caught him since he passed from the bodily presence of his contemporaries. Who was it then that was seen by Dryden and Johnson and Coleridge and Goethe and Hazlitt and Arnold and Meredith and Bradley and uncountable hosts of normal sensible men throughout the last three centuries?

For my own part, I am a devout Bradleyite.

F. E. HALLIDAY *Shakespeare and his Critics*. 1st edition, 1949.

Yet in spite of their apparent reality Shakespeare's characters are not real; like Cézanne's paintings they are a representation of life, not a reproduction of it. As a painter has to work within the spatial limits of his canvas, so Shakespeare has to force a play within the temporal limits of a two hours' traffic, 'turning the accomplishment of many years into an hour-glass'. He himself explains his difficulty in the Choruses of *Henry V*, and he implores the audience to use their imaginations, 'to brook abridgment', and to mind 'true things by what their mockeries be'. Here, it is true, he is referring primarily to limitation of space, to the cramping effect of this unworthy scaffold, this cockpit, this wooden O of the Globe theatre. But he has to overcome a similar difficulty of time, to compress within two or three hours the story of Macbeth's degeneration, and of Othello's change from a man possessed by love to one possessed by hate. To secure this end he has to resort to violent abridgment, compression and distortion. His problem resembles that of the painter, and his solution is similar. The painter cannot compete with nature, for his pigments from white to black are only a fraction of her immense range which starts with the blinding light of the sun, so that he has to pitch his painting in a lower key with subtler gradations of intensity. Shakespeare also, limited by time, cannot compete with nature, but he equals her range and represents her by more violent transitions and rapid foreshortenings, by abstracting everything that is not dramatically relevant. It is as absurd therefore to complain, as did Rymer and Tolstoy, that Shakespeare's tragedies are not true to life as to complain that Van Gogh's paintings of the sun are no more like the sun than Shakespeare's mistress's eyes. They are works of art, not nature, and give the effect of reality only because they are distortions, like the huge and wonderful figures in the clerestory windows of Chartres cathedral.

Consider the case of *Othello*. The speed of the first act is comparatively leisurely; in Act II the pace quickens and Iago begins his attack obliquely by sapping Cassio's position; but it is not until Act III Scene iii that he launches his direct assault on Othello. It begins at line 90 when Desdemona and Emilia go out:

Oth. Excellent wretch! Perdition catch my soul,
But I do love thee! and when I love thee not,
Chaos is come again.
    Iago. My noble lord . . .

And at the end of the scene, perhaps the most terrible scene in literature, Othello cries in agony:

Damn her, lewd minx! O, damn her!
Come, go with me apart: I will withdraw,
To furnish me with some swift means of death
For the fair devil.

And all within four hundred lines! It is not, of course, true to life; a man like Othello, so many fathom deep in love, could not so simply and so speedily be convinced of his wife's infidelity. But it is true as a work of art; within the limitations under which Shakespeare had to work, when time must be closed up like a fan, it is terribly and inevitably true. It is a representation of life in a purer yet intenser element than ours, an element from which all baser matter has been exhausted and into which is packed that only which makes Othello's agony, and time itself is huddled. Yet, lest the audience should be distressed by this abstraction of irrelevance and concentration of relevance, Shakespeare is careful to introduce when necessary a character who, by voicing our possible protests, relieves our feelings and prepares us to accept the dramatic and poetic truth. Thus Emilia, by expressing our feelings, alleviates our resentment and horror at Othello's blind credulity:

I durst, my lord, to wager she is honest,
Lay down my soul at stake:

and again when, though too late, she cries:

Thou art rash as fire, to say
That she was false: O, she was heavenly true! . . .
            O gull! O dolt!
As ignorant as dirt! thou hast done a deed—

all our indignation is spent and pity alone is left. Then, when Iachimo, in a scene remarkably like that between Iago and Othello, convinces Posthumus that Imogen is faithless, Philario in the character of Chorus speaks for the audience:

Sir, be patient:
This is not strong enough to be believed
Of one persuaded well of—

So does that satisfactory lady Paulina in *The Winter's Tale*:

Good queen, my lord,
Good queen: I say good queen;
And would by combat make her good, so were I
A man, the worst about you.

And Kent speaks to Lear even more bluntly than does Paulina to Leontes.

J. I. M. Stewart *Character and Motive in Shakespeare.* 1949.

If we seek through the many phases of Shakespeare criticism for some cardinal assertion in the truth of which most great names in every century concur we shall arrive, I think, at this: Shakespeare understood the passions and described, or conveyed, their several and conjoined operations with certainty, subtlety and power. It is the opinion of Dryden, the father of our criticism and a dramatist having good cause to discriminate men and dummies; of Johnson, a moralist ceaselessly curious in conduct and the best of Shakespeare's comprehensive critics; of Coleridge of the dispersed and incomparable perceptions; of Andrew Bradley, whose book is at once so lucid and so profound; and of Sigmund Freud, who distinguished in the plays a regular consonance with the radical workings of the mind of real men and women. Here, one may fairly claim, is the classical line in Shakespeare criticism, and those who would depart from it must show their credentials. Some of these credentials I shall do my best to examine in the present book.

It would be foolish to deny the bracing influence which historical and comparative method has had upon the æsthetic criticism of Shakespeare, or the need for many modifications of our received opinions which recent scholarship has exposed. I am far from thinking that *Shakespearean Tragedy*, for example, can continue to stand without qualification in face of such researches as Professor Elmer Edgar Stoll's. But I believe that the 'realists' (as they have come to be called) are mistaken on the whole in the emphasis of their criticism, and that if they do indeed sometimes show that there is less in the plays than Bradley supposes, yet inquiries in quite other fields powerfully suggest that there is more—more, I mean, of that insight into the 'obscurer regions of man's being' which Bradley asserts and which the realists are inclined to deny. . . .

If in particular we suspect that Shakespearian character is not at this late date to be written off as drastically as some would urge, it must yet be admitted that we are to-day conscious of problems which critics in the classical line have to some extent ignored or obscured. I do not like to find Bradley spoken of as a 'character-monger' or Coleridge treated with a pained indulgence as a neurotic scribbler in the margins of an art he misunderstcod. Nevertheless I believe both these would have been better critics, and would have spared lesser men many fumbling efforts, if they had paused to consider more strictly the nature not of tragedy indeed but of poetic drama, together with the conception and treatment of character appropriate to the kind. . . .

Keats and Mr. Eliot clearly regard the poetry and the drama as inseparable: and their report is positive. We must conclude that the poetry, if operative, enters into and transforms the fable; or rather, and more strictly, that it acts directly and continuously upon the spectator or reader in some way which conditions the whole experience. Tolstoy in a sense was right. The poetry is mildly hypnogenic. We are put into a state which would be inappropriate for the reception of realistic prose drama, but in which such a drama as Shakespeare's can best operate according to its own proper laws. . . .

Now, if this be true, everything the poetic dramatist contrives, proper to his art, will intuitively take account of the special sort of awareness induced by the poetry, and of the deeper or occult aspects of human action and character from the acknowledgment of which most of the spectator's ultimate pleasure and satisfaction is to arise. The poetic dramatist is thus constructing as for contemplation through some optical instrument which may reveal to a vision failing to adjust itself only distortion and improbability. It is in this way that I would account for the hit-or-miss quality of Shakespeare's art as instanced in the opinions of Keats and Tolstoy on *King Lear*. Poetry, as Bradley said, must be read poetically; and drama, we may add, must be viewed through its right optical r lium. If we regard the drama as it were disenchantedly—intellectually and without the co-presence of the emotions designed—it is only by a laborious analysis that we shall account for impressions which we imperfectly remember as having come to us when not disenchanted. Thus in an unpoetical reading motives may often appear confused or inadequate, and Angelo or Leontes may seem not a man but a monster.

The characters, then (but I mean chiefly those major characters with whom the imagination of the dramatist is deeply engaged), have often the superior reality of individuals exposing the deepest springs of their action. But the superior reality is manifested through the medium of situations which are sometimes essentially symbolical; and these may be extravagant or merely fantastic when not interpreted by the quickened imagination, for it is only during the prevalence of a special mode of consciousness, the poetic, that the underlying significance of these situations is perceived. Moreover powerful forces—the mandates of our culture—stand ready here to step in with a sort of censorship when they can. This is why, in Mr. Wilson Knight's phrase, 'the memory will always try to reject the imagination' . . .

And it is when the poetic drama is no longer with any readiness read poetically that the way is opened for such vagaries of historical criticism as I am to discuss. Communication has become muted or imperfect and the critic senses this. He takes the play from the shelf and cannot discern or decide what is really there. So what, he asks, is *likely* to be there? Criticism holds no more fatal question.

L. C. KNIGHTS *King Lear and the Great Tragedies.* From *The Age of Shakespeare*, edited by Boris Ford, 1955.

It is an obvious fact that the appreciation of Shakespeare, the kind of thing men have got from Shakespeare, has varied enormously at different periods. Of course no single mode of appreciation was ever completely dominant; and between critics sharing a roughly similar manner of approach there have been great differences of critical intelligence, of degree of exposure to the plays, so that the good critic of any one phase remains valuable long after that phase has passed. But from time to time major shifts of attention occur, and not the least significant and fruitful of these is the one that has been taking place in our own time and that scholars and critics of very different kinds have helped to bring about. Conceptions of the nature and function of poetic drama have

been radically revised; the essential structure of the plays has been sought in
the poetry rather than in the more easily extractable elements of 'plot' and
'character'; and our whole conception of Shakespeare's relation to his work,
of the kind of thing he was trying to do as an artist whilst simultaneously
satisfying the demands of the Elizabethan theatre—this conception is under-
going a revolutionary change. The 'new' Shakespeare, I should say, is much
less impersonal than the old. Whereas in the older view Shakespeare was the
god-like creator of a peopled world, projecting—it is true—his own spirit
into the inhabitants, but remaining essentially the analyst of 'their' passions,
he is now felt as much more immediately engaged in the action he puts before
us. If the verse has now moved well into the centre of the picture, this is
because linguistic vitality is now felt as the chief clue to the urgent personal
themes that not only shape the poetic-dramatic structure of each play but
form the figure in the carpet of the canon as a whole.

The essential structure of Shakespeare's plays is poetic. That is easily said;
what is meant is something that can only be grasped in relation to individual
plays or not grasped at all. We may take as an example Macbeth's 'aside'
when he has been greeted as Thane of Cawdor:

> This supernatural soliciting
> Cannot be ill; cannot be good: if ill,
> Why hath it given me earnest of success,
> Commencing in a truth? I am thane of Cawdor:
> If good, why do I yield to that suggestion
> Whose horrid image doth unfix my hair
> And make my seated heart knock at my ribs,
> Against the use of nature? Present fears
> Are less than horrible imaginings:
> My thought, whose murder yet is but fantastical
> Shakes so my single state of man, that function
> Is smother'd in surmise, and nothing is
> But what is not.   (I. iii)

This is temptation, presented with concrete force. Even if we attend only to
the revelation of Macbeth's spiritual state, our recognition of the body—the
very feel—of the experience, is a response to the poetry, to such things as the
sickening see-saw rhythm ('Cannot be ill; cannot be good . . .'), changing to
the rhythm of the pounding heart, the overriding of grammar ('My thought
whose murder yet is but fantastical'), as thought is revealed in the very process of formation, and so on. But the poetry makes further claims, and if we
attend to them we find that the words do not only point inward to the
presumed state of Macbeth's mind but, as it were, outward to the play as a
whole. The equivocal nature of temptation, the commerce with phantoms
consequent upon false choice, the resulting sense of unreality ('nothing is but
what is not'), which has yet such power to 'smother' vital function, the un-
naturalness of evil ('against the use of nature'), and the relation between
disintegration in the individual ('my single state of man') and disorder in the
larger social organism—all these are major themes of the play which are

mirrored in the speech under consideration. They emerge as themes because they are what the poetry—reinforced by action and symbolism—again and again insists on. And the interrelations we are forced to make take us outside the speeches of the protagonists to the poetry of the play as a whole. That 'smother'd', for example, takes us forward not only to Lady Macbeth's 'blanket of the dark' but to such things as Ross's choric comment after the murder of Duncan:

> . . . by the clock 'tis day,
> And yet dark night strangles the travelling lamp:
> Is't night's predominance, or the day's shame,
> That darkness does the face of earth entomb,
> When living light should kiss it?   (II. iv)

It is in an explicit recognition of the dense verbal texture of the greater plays that one of the main services of recent Shakespeare criticism lies. Yet there are misunderstandings to be guarded against. It would, for example, be a mistake to regard the meaning of a play as residing exclusively or even predominantly in the imagery. Recurrent imagery certainly plays a large part in shaping the meanings with which we are concerned; but a too insistent concentration on imagery, let alone a mechanical classification of images, can only defeat its own purpose. What we attend to is not only the imagery but all the organic components of the living verse; and the verse in turn works in conjunction with the dramatic action and our sense of what the different persons of the drama stand for as each play develops. The greater Shakespeare plays thus demand an unusual activity of attention, forcing the reader to respond with the whole of his active imagination. It is only when the mind of the reader is thoroughly 'roused and awakened' that meanings from below the level of 'plot' and 'character' crystallize out and form themselves into a living structure. If that structure of meaning seems especially closely connected with recurring and interrelated imagery, that is not because possible associations and recurrences are puzzled out by the intellect, but because the mind at a certain pitch of activity and responsiveness combines the power of focusing lucidly on what is before it with an awareness of before and after, sensing the whole in the part, and with a triumphant energy relating part to part in a living whole. But it is only in relation to that larger all-embracing meaning—determined by the 'plain sense' of what is said, and by its overtones, by the dramatic situation and the progress of the action, by symbols and by the interplay of different attitudes embodied in the different persons of the drama—it is only in relation to this total meaning that the imagery, or any other component that may be momentarily isolated, takes on its full significance. We only hear Shakespeare's deeper meanings when we listen with the whole of ourselves.

CHAPTER III

THE PLAYS AND THEIR CRITICS

IN the following pages the plays are printed in chronological order, or at least in an order that must approximate to the one in which they were written. It is that given by E. K. Chambers in his *William Shakespeare*, 1930, which, with a few modifications, is generally accepted as authoritative. The sequence, however, is not absolutely certain; it is difficult, for example, to place exactly *The Merry Wives, The Taming of the Shrew, All's Well* and *Timon of Athens*. There is no other play that can be dated as accurately as *Henry V* with its references to Essex's Irish expedition of 1599, but for most of the plays it is possible to fix dates between which they must have been written. For example, if a play is mentioned by Meres it must have been written before September 7th, 1598, when his *Palladis Tamia* was registered (see p. 45); if it is not mentioned, it is probable that it was written after that date. For the plays published as Quartos precise final dates are fixed by entries in the Stationers' Register, less precise ones by the year of publication on the title-page. Other external evidence of final dates is afforded by the records of performances and by contemporary mention. Internal evidence fixing a date after which a play must have been written is sometimes given by topical allusions: for instance, the reference in *King Lear* to the eclipses of the sun and moon in the autumn of 1605. Where such evidence is meagre or lacking the date has to be decided on stylistic grounds, and this is where the research of nineteenth-century scholars into Shakespeare's verse has been valuable— and also where there is occasion for dispute. It should be noted that there is a tendency among modern scholars, notably T. W. Baldwin, to push back the dates of the early plays.

The following table indicates the chief sources used by Shakespeare:

1.	2 Henry VI.	Holinshed.
2.	3 Henry VI.	Holinshed.
3.	1 Henry VI.	Holinshed.
4.	Richard III.	Holinshed.
5.	Comedy of Errors.	Plautus: *Menæchmi.*
6.	Titus Andronicus.	Seneca and Ovid.
7.	Taming of the Shrew.	*Taming of a Shrew.*
8.	Two Gentlemen of Verona.	Montemayor: *Diana Enamorada.*
9.	Love's Labour's Lost.	Shakespeare.
10.	Romeo and Juliet.	Arthur Brooke: *Romeus and Juliet.*
11.	Richard II.	Holinshed.
12.	Midsummer Night's Dream.	Shakespeare.

13. King John.	*The Troublesome Raigne of Iohn.*
14. Merchant of Venice.	Ser Giovanni: *Il Pecorone.*
15. 1 Henry IV.	Holinshed and *The Famous Victories*
16. 2 Henry IV.	*of Henry V.*
17. Much Ado about Nothing.	Bandello: *Timbreo and Fenicia.*
18. Henry V.	Holinshed, and *The Famous Victories of Henry V.*
19. Julius Cæsar.	Plutarch: *Lives.*
20. As You Like It.	Thomas Lodge: *Rosalynde.*
21. Twelfth Night.	Riche: *Apolonius and Silla.*
22. Hamlet.	Belleforest: *Histoires Tragiques.*
23. Merry Wives of Windsor.	Shakespeare.
24. Troilus and Cressida.	Chaucer: *Troilus and Criseyde.*
25. All's Well.	Boccaccio: *Giglietta di Nerbona.*
26. Measure for Measure.	Whetstone: *Promos and Cassandra.*
27. Othello.	Cinthio: *Hecatommithi.*
28. King Lear.	*King Leir.*
29. Macbeth.	Holinshed.
30. Antony and Cleopatra.	Plutarch: *Lives.*
31. Coriolanus.	Plutarch: *Lives.*
32. Timon of Athens.	Plutarch: *Lives.*
(33. Pericles.	Gower: *Apollonius of Tyre.*)
34. Cymbeline.	Boccaccio: *Decameron*, and Holinshed.
35. Winter's Tale.	Robert Greene: *Pandosto.*
36. The Tempest.	Jourdan: *A Discovery of the Bermudas.*
37. Henry VIII.	Holinshed.
(38. Two Noble Kinsmen.	Chaucer: *The Knight's Tale.*)

Shakespeare, like the other Elizabethan dramatists, rarely invented his plots. There was an urgent demand for new plays, and if they were to be turned out quickly an obvious method of saving time was to work up a ready-made story. This Shakespeare did, and it will be seen that he drew on four main sources for his material: old plays, Holinshed's *Chronicles*, Plutarch's *Lives*, and romances derived from the Italian Novel.

The old anonymous plays of *The Taming of a Shrew*, *The Troublesome Reign of John*, *The Famous Victories of Henry V*, and *King Leir and his Three Daughters* were all pressed into service, but for their plots only; there is little or no resemblance between their texts and those that Shakespeare made from them. They are completely rewritten, new characters are added, the action is made dramatic, and the plot itself of *King Leir* is radically altered. In *The Famous Victories* the secondary plot of *Henry IV* is crudely sketched, as is the character of Sir John Oldcastle, the original, if such a shadowy figure may so be called, of Falstaff. Here is a short scene from the old play:

Hen. But Ned, so soone as I am King, the first thing I wil do, shal be to put my Lord chiefe Iustice out of office. And thou shalt be my Lord chiefe Iustice of England.

Ned. Shall I be Lord chiefe Iustice?

By gogs wounds, ile be the brauest Lord chiefe Iustice of England.

Hen. Then Ned, Ile turne all these prisons into fence Schooles, and I will endue thee with them, with landes to maintaine them withall: then I wil haue a bout with my Lord chiefe Iustice, thou shalt hang none but picke purses and horse stealers, and such base minded villaines, but that fellow that wil stand by the high way side couragiously with his sword and buckler and take a purse, that fellow giue him commendations, beside that, send him to me and I wil giue him an anuall pension out of my Exchequer, to maintaine him all the dayes of his life.

Iohn. Nobly spoken Harry, we shall neuer haue a mery world til the old king be dead.

It used to be thought that 2, 3 *Henry VI* as printed in the Folio were adaptations by Shakespeare of other men's work, *The First Part of the Contention*, and *The True Tragedy*, but it now seems certain that these Quartos were pirated editions of Shakespeare's own text. All the evidence goes to show that when Shakespeare used a play as a source he did not merely patch and adapt it, he rewrote it.

Holinshed's *Chronicles of England, Scotlande, and Irelande* were published in 1578 and contained inexhaustible material to satisfy the feverish nationalism of London citizens, and Shakespeare made use of it in all his Histories, and in two Tragedies and a Romance as well. But Holinshed supplied only the framework: the language, the characterisation, and many of the characters themselves are Shakespeare's; he found no material for the sub-plot of *Henry IV* in Holinshed and little for the Hotspur theme. Only when bored or uninspired did Shakespeare transcribe Holinshed at length, as in the tedious dissertation on the 'law Salike', and the list of prisoners in *Henry V*.

Plutarch, however, is another matter. Sir Thomas North's translation of Amyot's French version of Plutarch had appeared in 1579 as *The Lives of the Noble Grecians and Romanes*, so that Shakespeare must have been acquainted with the book from his youth. When therefore he turned from comedy and history to the tragedy of character it was natural that he should turn to Plutarch's dramatic biographies and North's inspiring prose. Sometimes he would borrow an anecdote or an incident, as in *Timon of Athens*, v. i. 195–221:

'My Lords of Athens, I have a little yard in my house where there groweth a fig tree, on the which many citizens have hanged themselves: and, because I mean to make some building on the place, I thought good to let you all understand it, that, before the fig tree be cut down, if any of you be desperate, you may there in time go hang yourselves.' He died in the city of Halæ, and was buried upon the seaside.

Sometimes a few words appear to inspire a whole passage, like Charmian's in North's movingly simple account of Cleopatra's death, v. ii. 324–6 (but note the magic of Shakespeare's final touch, 'Ah, soldier!')

Her death was very sudden. For those whom Cæsar sent unto her ran thither in all haste possible, and found the soldiers standing at the gate, mistrusting nothing, nor understanding of her death. But when they had opened the doors they found Cleopatra stark dead, laid upon a bed of gold, attired and arrayed in her royal robes, and one of her two women, which was called Iras, dead at her feet: and her other woman called Charmion half-dead, and trembling, trimming the diadem which Cleopatra ware upon her head. One of the soldiers, seeing her, angrily said unto her: 'Is that well done, Charmion?' 'Very well', said she again, 'and meet for a princess descended from the race of so many noble kings.' She said no more, but fell down dead by the bed.

Sometimes Shakespeare would follow North closely and at length, as in the description of the meeting of Coriolanus and Aufidius, IV. v.:

It was even twilight when he entered the city of Antium, and many people met him in the streets, but no man knew him. So he went directly to Tullus Aufidius' house, and when he came thither, he got him up straight to the chimney hearth, and sat him down, and spake not a word to any man, his face all muffled over. They of the house, spying him, wondered what he should be, and yet they durst not bid him rise. For ill-favouredly muffled and disguised as he was, yet there appeared a certain majesty in his countenance, and in his silence: whereupon they went to Tullus, who was at supper, to tell him of the strange disguising of this man. Tullus rose presently from the board, and, coming towards him, asked him what he was, and wherefore he came. Then Martius unmuffled himself, and after he had paused a while, making no answer, he said unto him: 'If thou knowest me not yet, Tullus, and, seeing me, dost not perhaps believe me to be the man I am indeed, I must of necessity bewray myself to be that I am. I am Caius Martius, who hath done to thyself particularly, and to all the Volscians generally, great hurt and mischief, which I cannot deny for my surname of Coriolanus that I bear. For I never had other benefit nor recompense of all the true and painful service I have done, and the extreme dangers I have been in, but this only surname: a good memory and witness of the malice and displeasure thou shouldst bear me. Indeed the name only remaineth with me: for the rest the envy and cruelty of the people of Rome have taken from me, by the sufferance of the dastardly nobility and magistrates, who have forsaken me, and let me be banished by the people. This extremity hath now driven me to come as a poor suitor to take thy chimney hearth, not of any hope I have to save my life thereby. For, if I had feared death, I would not have come hither to have put my life in hazard: but pricked forward with spite and desire I have to be revenged of them that thus have banished me, whom now I begin to be avenged on, putting my person between my enemies.'

It is not often that Shakespeare follows as literally and lengthily as this, though North's noble account of 'the wonderful sumptuousness of Cleopatra, queen of Egypt, going unto Antonius', and Shakespeare's parallel passage are well known. Shakespeare's debt to North is a great one, and it would be ungracious to deny it, but it would be equally unfair to maintain that Shakespeare merely transcribed—even North: nearly always he adds some touch that transfigures the whole. That this is so, in one notable instance at least, is shown by Middleton Murry in his analysis of Enobarbus's speech quoted on p. 266.

Shakespeare's debt to the Italian novel is different. The light and flimsy stories could be adapted and woven together at pleasure: Claudio and Hero taken from Bandello, hints for Benedick and Beatrice perhaps extracted from Castiglione, while the humour of Dogberry 'he happened to take at Grendon in Bucks'; or to a mixture of Secchi, Bandello, and Cinthio, add Malvolio, Feste, Sir Toby, and Sir Andrew, and the piercing poetry of Viola, and call it what you will; or Holinshed's *Chronicles* might richly and strangely be grafted on to the *Decameron* of Boccaccio. Here there is no question of transcription; the plots only are plundered, what is precious abstracted, then mingled, new situations and vital characters added, and the whole swept into a unity and integrated by the poetry and spirit of Shakespeare.

It is only what we should expect from genius in a hurry; Shakespeare thankfully accepted the materials, and if the foundations were partly laid and the scaffolding satisfactorily erected so much the better; but whatever the beginnings—an old play, Holinshed, an Italian or English novel, or one of Plutarch's *Lives*—the building, the work of art, was his own.

The critical extracts are examples of eighteenth-century, Romantic, Victorian and twentieth-century criticism, the representatives of the first two periods nearly always being Johnson, Coleridge, and Hazlitt, who give continuity and unity to the whole. In addition, when possible, there are extracts from contemporary and later seventeenth-century critics, notably Dryden, as well as from the rare and sensitive Lamb and de Quincey.

Unless otherwise stated, the extracts from Johnson are from his *General Observations on the Plays of Shakspeare*; those from Coleridge from *Notes and Lectures upon Shakspeare and some of the Old Dramatists*; and those from Hazlitt from *Characters of Shakespear's Plays*.

THE SHAKESPEAREAN CANON

The Plays of the First Folio, 1623

HENRY THE SIXTH, PART II

WRITTEN   1590–1. Not mentioned by Meres, 1598.

PERFORMED   No record of an early performance.

REGISTERED   1594 March 12 by Thomas Millington . . . 'the firste parte of the Contention'.

PUBLISHED   1594 Q1. 'The First part of the Contention betwixt the two famous Houses of Yorke and Lancaster.' A 'bad' Quarto.
1600 Q2.
1619 Q3. 'The Whole Contention betweene the two Famous Houses, Lancaster and Yorke . . . Diuided into two Parts: And newly corrected and enlarged. Written by William Shakespeare, Gent.'
1623 F1. as 'The Second part of King Hen. the Sixt'. A third as long again as the Quartos.

SOURCES   Mainly from the *Chronicles* of Holinshed and Hall.

HENRY THE SIXTH, PART III

WRITTEN   1590–1. Not mentioned by Meres, 1598.

PERFORMED   Before Sept. 1592 when Greene in his *Groatsworth of Wit* parodied the line 'O tiger's heart wrapped in a woman's hide'.
(see p. 45).

REGISTERED   No original entry, but assigned by Millington to Pavier in 1602.

PUBLISHED   1595 Q1. 'The true Tragedie of Richard Duke of Yorke . . . as it was sundrie times acted by the Right Honourable the Earle of Pembroke his seruants.' A 'bad' Quarto.
1600 Q2.
1619 Q3. Jaggard's reprint with 'The First Part of the Contention' as 'The Whole Contention'.
1623 F1. as 'The Third part of King Henry the sixt'. A third as long again as the Quartos.

SOURCES   Mainly the *Chronicles* of Holinshed and Hall.

King. Thàt is to fee how deepe my graue is made,
For with his foule fled all my worldly folace :
For feeing him, I fee my life in death.

War. As furely as my foule intends to liue
With that dread King that tooke our ftate vpon him,
To free vs from his Fathers wrathfull curfe,
I do beleeue that violent hands were laid
Vpon the life of this thrice-famed Duke.

Suf. A dreadfull Oath, fworne with a folemn tongue:
What inftance giues Lord Warwicke for his vow.

War. See how the blood is fetled in his face.
Oft haue I feene a timely-parted Ghoft,
Of afhy femblance, meager, pale, and bloodleffe.
Being all defcended to the labouring heart,
Who in the Conflict that it holds with death,
Attracts the fame for aydance 'gainft the enemy,
Which with the heart there cooles, and ne're returneth,
To blufh and beautifie the Cheeke againe.
But fee, his face is blacke, and full of blood :
His eye-balles further out. than when he liued,
Staring full gaftly, like a ftrangled man :
His hayre vprear'd, his noftrils ftretcht with ftrugling :
His hands abroad difplay'd, as one that grafpt
And tugg'd for Life, and was by ftrength fubdude.
Looke on the fheets his haire (you fee) is fticking,
His well proportion'd Beard, made ruffe and rugged,
Like to the Summers Corne by Tempeft lodged :
It cannot be but he was murdred heere,
The leaft of all thefe fignes were probable.

Suf. Why Warwicke, who fhould do the D. to death?
My felfe and *Beauford* had him in protection,
And we I hope fir, are no murtherers.

War. But both of you were vowed D. Humfries foes,
And you (forfooth) had the good Duke to keepe :
Tis like you would not feaft him like a friend,
And 'tis well feene, he found an enemy.

Queen. Than you belike fufpect thefe Noblemen,
As guilty of Duke *Humfries* timeleffe death.

                                              War.

2 *HENRY VI*, III, ii. FROM THE FOLIO.

It used to be thought that *The First Part of the Contention* and the *True Tragedy* were old plays revised and expanded into the *Henry VI, Parts* 2 and 3 of the Folio. But in 1929 Peter Alexander showed that they are 'bad' Quartos the texts of which were reproduced from memory by actors or a prompter, and that the Folio text is the original play printed probably from the prompt-copy. There may have been collaboration, but there is no reason why Shakespeare should not have been the sole author.

HENRY THE SIXTH, PART I

WRITTEN   1591–2. Not mentioned by Meres, 1598.

PERFORMED   1592. In his *Diary* Henslowe records a performance on
            March 3 of a new play, 'Harey the vj', performed by Lord
Strange's Men, probably at the Rose. See also Nashe's reference below. This may be Shakespeare's play, or one that he revised.

REGISTERED   1623 Nov. 8. One of the 16 plays registered by Blount and
            Jaggard before their publication of the Folio. It is entered as
'The thirde parte of Henry ye Sixt', but the entry must refer to 1 *Henry VI*.

PUBLISHED   1623 F 1, as 'The First part of King Henry the Sixt'.

SOURCES   Mainly the *Chronicles* of Holinshed and Hall.

There appears to be more than one style in the play. Perhaps Shakespeare's part is confined to II. iv and IV. ii, though he may be the sole author.

THOMAS NASHE   How would it have ioyed braue *Talbot* (the terror of the
            French) to thinke that after he had lyne two hundred
yeares in his Tombe, hee should triumphe againe on the Stage, and haue his bones newe embalmed with the teares of ten thousand spectators at least, (at seuerall times) who, in the Tragedian that represents his person, imagine they behold him fresh bleeding?

Pierce Penilesse, 1592.

JOHNSON   From mere inferiority nothing can be inferred; in the productions
            of wit there will be inequality. Sometimes judgment will err, and
sometimes the matter itself will defeat the artist. Of every author's works one will be the best, and one will be the worst. The colours are not equally pleasing, nor the attitudes equally graceful, in all the pictures of Titian or Reynolds.

Dissimilitude of style, and heterogeneousness of sentiment, may sufficiently show that a work does not really belong to the reputed author. But in these plays no such marks of spuriousness are found. The diction, the versification, and the figures, are Shakespeare's. These plays, considered, without regard to characters and incidents, merely as narratives in verse, are more happily conceived, and more accurately finished, than those of King John,

Richard II, or the tragic scenes of Henry IV and V. If we take these plays from Shakespeare, to whom shall they be given? What author of that age had the same easiness and fluency of numbers? . . .

Of these three plays I think the second the best. The truth is, that they have not sufficient variety of action, for the incidents are too often of the same kind; yet many of the characters are well discriminated. . . .

The old copies of the two latter parts of Henry VI and of Henry V are so apparently imperfect and mutilated, that there is no reason for supposing them the first draughts of Shakespeare. I am inclined to believe them copies taken by some auditor who wrote down, during the representation, what the time would permit, then, perhaps, filled up some of his omissions at a second or third hearing, and when he had by this method formed something like a play, sent it to the printer. [This is a remarkable anticipation of modern textual criticism.]

COLERIDGE 1 Henry VI. Act i. sc. i. Bedford's speech:

> Hung be the heavens with black, yield day to night!
> Comets, importing change of times and states,
> Brandish your crystal tresses in the sky;
> And with them scourge the bad revolting stars
> That have consented unto Henry's death!
> King Henry the fifth, too famous to live long!
> England ne'er lost a king of so much worth.

Read aloud any two or three passages in blank verse even from Shakespeare's earliest dramas, as Love's Labour's Lost, or Romeo and Juliet; and then read in the same way this speech, with especial attention to the metre; and if you do not feel the impossibility of the latter having been written by Shakspeare, all I dare suggest is, that you may have ears,—for so has another animal,—but an ear you cannot have, *me judice*.

HAZLITT During the time of the civil wars of York and Lancaster, England was a perfect bear-garden, and Shakespear has given us a very lively picture of the scene. The three parts of Henry VI convey a picture of very little else, and are inferior to the other historical plays. They have brilliant passages; but the general groundwork is comparatively poor and meagre, the style 'flat and unraised'.

LOGAN PEARSALL SMITH And if we read the historical plays in the order of their composition, we are aware again of the same stupendous stride of genius. The four earliest of these, the three *Henry VI* plays and *Richard III*, are what the Patriot King called 'stuff'; they are woven of the stuff of the common Elizabethan drama, and whether Shakespeare really wrote them has been often doubted. And yet from my reading of these four plays I remember a few scenes which I feel he must have written

—a few gleams through the morning mists from the 'glory hereafter to be revealed', from the sun still below the horizon, of his ascending genius. Touched by these gleams of dawn, I see looming faintly, to borrow his own words,

> The baby figure of the giant mass
> Of things to come at large.

In the musings of the poor mild King in the third *Henry VI* play, on the happiness of the shepherd's lot (II, v), we find a soliloquy and a poetic day-dream that no one but Shakespeare could have written, and in the death of Cardinal Beaufort (2 *Henry VI*, III, iii) the note of Shakespearean tragedy is first sounded in that scene of despair and dreadful death. Cade in this play is almost a living figure, and even more alive is his derisive follower, Smith, 'the weaver', who, when Cade tells Sir Humphrey Stafford that his father was of royal blood, though stolen at birth and trained as a bricklayer, Smith ironically confirms this boast by declaring 'Sir, he made a chimney in my father's house, and the bricks are alive at this day to testify it; therefore deny it not' (IV, ii).

On Reading Shakespeare, 1923.

E. M. W. TILLYARD So much for Shakespeare's use in his tetralogy [1, 2, 3 *Henry VI* and *Richard III*] of the conceptions of world order and the processes of history: the ideas that appear so little in the Chronicle Plays and seem to have been the property of a select and educated class, that ally Shakespeare with Chapman and Daniel and Sir John Hayward. His use of them illustrates the academic side of himself that was so prominent in his early years. It is to his History Plays what the Plautine form is to the *Comedy of Errors* and the Senecan and Ovidian elements and conventions to *Titus Andronicus*.

But Shakespeare was not only academic in his first historical tetralogy: he was a popular dramatist too. Not that the populace would have objected to his superior opinions on history; they would have been willing to be impressed if they also got the things they expected: which they most certainly did. And first, for this popular material, there is what I have called sometimes Higden and sometimes Holinshed: the mediation of sheer fact. For though Shakespeare did see history in an intelligible pattern he compressed into a popular and lively form an astonishing quantity of sheer historical fact. . . .

Shakespeare also satisfied the popular taste in setting forth the great popular political theme, the horror of civil war, and in giving his plays the required chauvinist tone. Joan of Arc is a bad enough woman, Margaret of Anjou an intriguing enough queen; an Englishman is worth a sufficient number of Frenchmen; Frenchmen are sufficiently boastful and fickle, to satisfy every popular requirement.

Finally, Shakespeare occasionally satisfies the taste for the startling but irrelevant anecdote; the pieces of sensation that pleased the people but could be spared from the play. There is for example the scene in 1 *Henry VI* (II. 3) where the Countess of Auvergne plots Talbot's death by inviting him to her house and he prevents her by summoning his men by a blast from his horn; and a scene in 2 *Henry VI* (I. 4) where Bolingbroke the conjurer calls up spirits at the command of the Duchess of Gloucester.

In sum Shakespeare in his first effort could beat the writers of Chronicle Plays on their own ground. . . .

To redress this wrong emphasis [on the Cade scenes] we must think of yet another strain in this tetralogy: that of formalism and stylisation. It is something archaic, inherited from the Morality Play. But it is the very feature through which the essential life of the poetry is expressed. When we encounter an unnatural and stylised balance of incident or an artificial pattern of speech we must not think that here is merely an archaic survival: we must accept them as things having contemporary vitality and must make them the norm of the play. We must in fact be good Aristotelians, for the moment, and believe that the soul of the play is in plot rather than in character. The realism of the Jack Cade scenes is not their main point but a subsidiary enrichment. Their main point is to make half a pattern, the other half being implied by the blameless orderliness of Iden. We are apt to praise the Cade scenes for being realistic and jeer at Iden for being a dummy, when we should merge praise and blame into the appreciation of a piece of stylisation which includes the whole. . . . The most moving of all the scenes in the tetralogy, the ghosts visiting the sleeps of Richard III and Richmond in *Richard III*, is perhaps the most rigidly patterned and most grossly unrealistic of any. What could be remoter from actuality than the juxtaposition of the two tents and the liturgical chantings of each ghost as it passes? But to object to this scene on these grounds is as stupid as to blame the *Eumenides* of Aeschylus for being deficient in the realistic psychology of the *Electra* of Euripides. When this principle has been grasped and accepted the tetralogy comes out a much more assured and solid affair than it is generally thought to be.

But if the Morality Play prompted the formality of Shakespeare's first tetralogy it also supplied a single pervasive theme; one which overrides but in no way interferes with the theme he derived from Hall. In none of the plays is there a hero: and one of the reasons is that there is an unnamed protagonist dominating all four. It is England, or in Morality terms Respublica. Just as London, which appears only in the prologue, is the hero of Wilson's *Three Lords and Three Ladies of London* (itself more a Morality Play than a developed Elizabethan drama), so England, though she is now quite excluded as a character, is the true hero of Shakespeare's first tetralogy. . . .

Finally Shakespeare reinforces the structural unity which the themes of the Morality and of Hall create, by sowing in one play the seeds that are to germinate in the next and by constant references back from a later play to an earlier. . . .

For all the inequality of execution, the vast crowding in of historical incident (some of it inorganic), Shakespeare planned his first historical tetralogy greatly, reminding one of Hardy in the *Dynasts*. When we consider how deficient his fellow-dramatists were in the architectonic power, we can only conclude that this was one of the things with which he was conspicuously endowed by nature. Far from being the untidy genius, Shakespeare was in one respect a born classicist.

Shakespeare's History Plays, 1944.

RICHARD THE THIRD

WRITTEN   1592–3. Mentioned by Meres, 1598.

PERFORMED 1593 Dec. 30. The play of 'Buckingham' recorded by Henslowe in his *Diary* may refer to *Richard III*. It was not noted as 'new', and was performed by Sussex's Men.

1633. 'On Saterday, the 17th of Novemb. being the Queens birthday, Richarde the Thirde was acted by the K. players at St James, wher the king and queene were present, it being the first play the queene sawe since her Maiestys delivery of the Duke of York.' (*Office Book* of Sir Henry Herbert.)

REGISTERED 1597 Oct 20 by Andrew Wise.

PUBLISHED   1597 Q1. 'As it hath beene lately Acted by the Right honourable the Lord Chamberlaine his seruants.'

1598 Q2. 'By William Shakespeare.'
1602 Q3. 'Newly augmented,' though there are no additions.
1605 Q4, 1612 Q5. 'As it hath been lately Acted by the Kings Maiesties Seruants.'
1622 Q6.
1623 F1.
Each Q is printed from its predecessor. F1 is printed from Q6 with reference to another source, possibly the original MS.

SOURCE   Mainly the *Chronicles* of Holinshed and Hall.

The authenticity of the play is doubted by the disintegrators. J. M. Robertson attributes it to Marlowe, Kyd, and Heywood, Shakespeare contributing only six or seven speeches. E. K. Chambers 'finds nothing here which might not be Shakespeare'.

In 1700 Colley Cibber adapted the play, adding more love-interest and violence, and his melodramatic version held the stage until quite recent times.

Sir Laurence Olivier's film version contains snatches of Cibber.

ANON.   *Burbage*. I like your face, and the proportion of your body for *Richard* the 3. I pray, M. *Phil*. let me see you act a little of it.
Philomusus. 'Now is the winter of our discontent,
            Made glorious summer by the sonne of Yorke.'
                        Returne from Parnassus II. 1601?

JOHN MANNINGHAM   Vpon a tyme when Burbidge played Rich. 3. there was a citizen greue soe farr in liking with him, that before

she went from the play shee appointed him to come that night vnto hir by
the name of Ri: the 3. Shakespeare overhearing their conclusion went before,
was intertained, and at his game ere Burbidge came. Then message being
brought that Rich. the 3d was at the dore, Shakespeare caused returne to be
made that William the Conqueror was before Richard the 3.

Diary, 1602.

JOHNSON This is one of the most celebrated of our author's performances;
        yet I know not whether it has not happened to him as to others,
to be praised most, when praise is not most deserved. That this play has
scenes noble in themselves, and very well contrived to strike in the exhibition,
cannot be denied. But some parts are trifling, others shocking, and some
improbable.

THOMAS WHATELY Thus, from the beginning of their history to their last
              moments, are the characters of Macbeth and Richard
preserved entire and distinct: and though probably Shakespeare, when he was
drawing the one, had no attention to the other; yet, as he conceived them to
be widely different, expressed his conceptions exactly, and copied both from
nature, they necessarily became contrasts to each other; and, by seeing them
together, that contrast is more apparent, especially where the comparison is
not between opposite qualities, but arises from the different degrees, or from
a particular display, or total omission, of the same quality. This must often
happen, as the character of Macbeth is much more complicated than that of
Richard; and therefore, when they are set in opposition, the judgment of the
poet shows itself as much in what he has left out of the latter as in what he
has inserted. The picture of Macbeth is also, for the same reason, much the
more highly finished of the two; for it required a greater variety, and a greater
delicacy of painting, to express and to blend with consistency all the several
properties which are ascribed to him. That of Richard is marked by more
careless strokes, but they are, notwithstanding, perfectly just. Much bad
composition may indeed be found in the part; it is a fault from which the best
of Shakespeare's plays are not exempt, and with which this Play particularly
abounds; and the taste of the age in which he wrote, though it may afford
some excuse, yet cannot entirely vindicate the exceptionable passages. After
every reasonable allowance, they must still remain blemishes ever to be
lamented; but happily, for the most part, they only obscure, they do not dis-
figure his draughts from nature. Through whole speeches and scenes, character is often wanting; but in the worst instances of this kind, Shakespeare is but
insipid; he is not inconsistent; and in his peculiar excellence of drawing
characters, though he often neglects to exert his talents, he is very rarely
guilty of perverting them.

Remarks on some of the Characters of Shakespeare, 1785.

COLERIDGE This play should be contrasted with Richard II. Pride of intel-
          lect is the characteristic of Richard, carried to the extent of even
boasting to his own mind of his villany, whilst others are present to feed his

pride of superiority. Shakspeare here, as in all his great parts, developes in a tone of sublime morality the dreadful consequences of placing the moral, in subordination to the mere intellectual, being. In Richard there is a predominance of irony, accompanied with apparently blunt manners to those immediately about him, but formalized into a more set hypocrisy towards the people as represented by their magistrates.

HAZLITT The Richard of Shakespear is towering and lofty; equally impetuous and commanding; haughty, violent, and subtle; bold and treacherous; confident in his strength as well as in his cunning; raised high by his birth, and higher by his talents and his crimes; a royal usurper, a princely hypocrite, a tyrant and a murderer of the house of Plantagenet.

> But I was born so high:
> Our aery buildeth in the cedar's top,
> And dallies with the wind, and scorns the sun.

The idea conveyed in these lines (which are indeed omitted in the miserable medley acted for Richard III) is never lost sight of by Shakespear, and should not be out of the actor's mind for a moment. The restless and sanguinary Richard is not a man striving to be great, but to be greater than he is; conscious of his strength of will, his power of intellect, his daring courage, his elevated station; and making use of these advantages to commit unheard-of crimes, and to shield himself from remorse and infamy. . . .

The manner in which Shakespear's plays have been generally altered or rather mangled by modern mechanists, is a disgrace to the English stage. The patch-work Richard III which is acted under the sanction of his name, and which was manufactured by Cibber, is a striking example of this remark.

The play itself is undoubtedly a very powerful effusion of Shakespear's genius. The ground-work of the character of Richard, that mixture of intellectual vigour with moral depravity, in which Shakespear delighted to show his strength—gave full scope as well as temptation to the exercise of his imagination.

LAMB I am almost disposed to deny to Garrick the merit of being an admirer of Shakespeare. A true lover of his excellences he certainly was not; for would any true lover of them have admitted into his matchless scenes such ribald trash as Tate and Cibber, and the rest of them, that

> 'With their darkness durst affront his light',

have foisted into the acting plays of Shakespeare? I believe it impossible that he could have had a proper reverence for Shakespeare, and have condescended to go through that interpolated scene in Richard III, in which Richard tries to break his wife's heart by telling her he loves another woman, and says, 'if she survives this she is immortal'. Yet I doubt not he delivered this vulgar stuff with as much anxiety of emphasis as any of the genuine parts: and for acting, it is as well calculated as any.

On the Tragedies of Shakespeare, 1811.

SIR EDMUND CHAMBERS Nor do I see any adequate reason for assuming two hands. There are 'dull' scenes, but the style is uniform throughout. It is a highly mannered rhetorical style, extravagant in utterance, with many appeals and exclamations. There is much violent and vituperative speech; the word 'blood' runs like a *leit-motif* through the play. Epithets, and sometimes nouns, are piled up, in pairs, with or without a conjunction; in triplets or even greater numbers. Types of line-structure tend to recur. One is based on such a triplet; another is the 'balanced' line, of noun and epithet against noun and epithet. A 'clinching' line at the end of a speech is also common. There are 'cumulative' passages of parallel lines with parisonic beginnings or ending. Words and phrases are repeated for emphasis. There is much 'ringing of the changes' on individual words, between line and line and speech and speech. Sometimes this is progressive, as new words are introduced. Sometimes it takes the form of a bitter pun. There is rhetorical structure, in antithesis, antiphon, stichomythia. Some of it is ultimately of Senecan origin. All these features occur individually in pre-Shakespearean plays and recur in later Shakespearean plays, with diminishing frequency. But I do not think that they are quite so massed and multiplied elsewhere. I find nothing here which might not be Shakespeare, at an early stage of development, and while he is still much under the influence of his predecessors. Perhaps I should make a qualification. I am not certain that the extremely ineffective speeches of the ghosts may not be a spectacular theatrical addition.

William Shakespeare: A Study of Facts and Problems, 1930.

THE COMEDY OF ERRORS

WRITTEN   1592–3. Mentioned by Meres, 1598.

PERFORMED   1594 Dec. 28, at Gray's Inn.
            1604 At Court. 'By his Maiesties plaiers. On Inosents night The plaie of Errors. Shaxberd.' (*Revels Account.*)

REGISTERED 1623. One of the 16 plays that had not already been published as Quartos registered by Blount and Jaggard before the publication of the Folio.

PUBLISHED   1623 F1. A fair text, probably based on Shakespeare's MS.

SOURCE   The *Menæchmi*, a comedy by Plautus.

'The play (1,777 lines) is Shakespeare's shortest, and was probably meant to precede a mask, jig, or other afterpiece.'

GRAY'S INN RECORDS The next grand Night was intended to be upon *Innocents-Day* at Night. . . . The Ambassador [of the Inner Temple] came . . . about Nine of the Clock at Night . . . there arose such a disordered Tumult and Crowd upon the Stage, that there was no Opportunity to effect that which was intended. . . . The Lord Ambassador and his Train thought that they were not so kindly entertained as was before expected, and thereupon would not stay any longer at that time, but, in a sort, discontented and displeased. After their Departure the Throngs and Tumults did somewhat cease, although so much of them continued, as was able to disorder and confound any good Inventions whatsoever. In regard whereof, as also for that the Sports intended were especially for the gracing of the *Templerians*, it was thought good not to offer any thing of Account, saving Dancing and Revelling with Gentlewomen; and after such Sports, a Comedy of Errors (like to *Plautus* his *Menechmus*) was played by the Players. So that Night was begun, and continued to the end, in nothing but Confusion and Errors; whereupon, it was ever afterwards called, *The Night of Errors.* . . . We preferred Judgments . . . against a Sorcerer or Conjuror that was supposed to be the Cause of that confused Inconvenience. . . . And Lastly, that he had foisted a Company of base and common Fellows, to make up our Disorders with a Play of Errors and Confusions; and that that Night had gained to us Discredit, and itself a Nickname of Errors.

Gesta Grayorum, Dec. 28th, 1594.

HAZLITT This comedy is taken very much from the Menæchmi of Platus, and is not an improvement on it. Shakespear appears to have bestowed no great pains on it, and there are but a few passages which bear the decided stamp of his genius. He seems to have relied on his author, and on the interest arising out of the intricacy of the plot. The curiosity excited is certainly very considerable, though not of the most pleasing kind. We are teazed as with a riddle, which notwithstanding we try to solve. . . . This play leads us not to feel much regret that Shakespear was not what is called a classical scholar. We do not think his *forte* would ever have lain in imitating or improving on what others invented, so much as in inventing for himself, and perfecting what he invented,—not perhaps by the omission of faults, but by the addition of the highest excellencies. His own genius was strong enough to bear him up, and he soared longest and best on unborrowed plumes. . . .

Pinch the conjuror is also an excrescence not to be found in Plautus. He is indeed a very formidable anachronism.

> They brought one Pinch, a hungry lean-fac'd villain,
> A mere anatomy, a mountebank,
> A thread-bare juggler and a fortune-teller;
> A needy, holy-ey'd, sharp-looking wretch,
> A living dead man.

This is exactly like some of the Puritanical portraits to be met with in Hogarth.

COLERIDGE The myriad-minded man, our, and all men's, Shakespeare, has in this piece presented us with a legitimate farce in exactest consonance with the philosophical principles and character of farce, as distinguished from comedy and from entertainments. A proper farce is mainly distinguished from comedy by the license allowed, and even required, in the fable, in order to produce strange and laughable situations. The story need not be probable, it is enough that it is possible. A comedy would scarcely allow even the two Antipholuses; because, although there have been instances of almost indistinguishable likeness in two persons, yet these are mere individual accidents, *casus ludentis naturæ*, and the *verum* will not excuse the *inverisimile*. But farce dares add the two Dromios, and is justified in so doing by the laws of its end and constitution. In a word, farces commence in a postulate, which must be granted.

JOHN MASEFIELD The *Menæchmi* of Plautus is a piece of very skilful theatrical craft. It is almost heartless. In bringing it out of the Satanic kingdom of comedy into the charities of a larger system Shakespeare shows for the first time a real largeness of dramatic instinct. In his handling of the tricky ingenious plot he achieves (what, perhaps, he wrote the play to get) a dexterous, certain play of mind. He strikes the ringing note time after time. It cannot be said that the verse, or the sense of character, or the invention is better than in the other early plays. It is not. The play is on a lower plane than any of his other works. It is the only Shakespearean play without a deep philosophical idea. . . . It is also the first play that shows a fine, sustained power of dramatic construction.

William Shakespeare, 1911.

TITUS ANDRONICUS

WRITTEN   1593–4. Mentioned by Meres, 1598.

PERFORMED 1592 April 11, 'ne. Tittus & Vespacia'. By Strange's Men.
           1594 Jan 24, 'ne Titus & Ondronicous'. By Sussex's Men.
1594 June 14, 'Andronicous'. By Admiral's and Chamberlain's Men.
(Henslowe's *Diary*.)

REGISTERED 1594 Feb 6 by John Danter.

PUBLISHED 1594 Q1. 'As it was Plaide by the Right Honourable the Earle of Darbie, Earle of Pembrooke, and Earle of Sussex their Seruants.'
1600 Q2. 'As it hath sundry times been playde by . . . and the Lorde Chamberlaine theyr Seruants.'
1611 Q3. 'As it hath sundry times beene plaide by the Kings Maiesties Seruants.'
1623 F1. Set up from Q3 with the addition of III. ii.

SOURCES   Seneca, *Thyestes* and *Troades*. Ovid, *Metamorphoses*. The themes of the murderous Moor, and of the marriage of Moor and white woman were common. (Cf. *Othello*.)

If the play were really new in 1594 it is crude work for Shakespeare at so late a date. If, however, the *Tittus and Vespacia* of 1592 refers to *Titus*

Andronicus it is more reasonable to attribute it to Shakespeare. J. D. Wilson thinks it a play by Peele, revised by Shakespeare.

In 1678 Edward Ravenscroft wrote an adaptation of *Titus Andronicus*, even more full of horrors than the original. His *Address* to his play contains the only piece of external evidence (which need not be taken too seriously) against the authenticity of any play in the First Folio.

Titus Andronicus was revived by Sir Laurence Olivier at Stratford in 1955.

BEN JONSON He that will swear *Jeronimo* or *Andronicus* are the best plays
　　　　　　　yet shall pass unexcepted at here, as a man whose judgment shows it is constant and hath stood still these five and twenty or thirty years.
Induction to Bartholomew Fair, 1614.

RAVENSCROFT I think it a greater theft to rob the dead of their praise than
　　　　　　　　the living of their money. That I may not appear guilty of such a crime, 'tis necessary I should acquaint you, that there is a play in Mr. Shakespeare's volume under the name of *Titus Andronicus*, from whence I drew part of this. I have been told by some anciently conversant with the stage, that it was not originally his, but brought by a private author to be acted, and he only gave some master-touches to one or two of the principal parts or characters; this I am apt to believe, because 'tis the most incorrect and indigested piece in all his works; it seems rather a heap of rubbish than a structure.
Address to *Titus Andronicus, or the Rape of Lavinia*, 1678.

JOHNSON All the editors and critics agree with Mr. Theobald in supposing
　　　　　　this play spurious. I see no reason for differing from them; for the colour of the style is wholly different from that of the other plays, and there is an attempt at regular versification and artificial closes, not always inelegant, yet seldom pleasing. The barbarity of the spectacles, and the general massacre, which are here exhibited, can scarcely be conceived tolerable to any audience; yet we are told by Jonson, that they were not only borne, but praised. That Shakespeare wrote any part, though Theobald declares it incontestable, I see no reason for believing.

SCHLEGEL This tragedy, it is true, is framed according to a false idea of the
　　　　　　　tragic, which by an accumulation of cruelties and enormities degenerates into the horrible, and yet leaves no deep impression behind. . . . In detail there is no want of beautiful lines, bold images, nay, even features which betray the peculiar conception of Shakespeare. Among these we may reckon the joy of the treacherous Moor at the blackness and ugliness of his child begot in adultery; and in the compassion of Titus Andronicus, grown childish through grief, for a fly which had been struck dead, and his rage afterwards when he imagines he discovers in it his black enemy, we recognise the future poet of *Lear*.
Lectures on Dramatic Poetry.

HAZLITT *Titus Andronicus* is certainly as unlike Shakespear's usual style as it is possible. It is an accumulation of vulgar physical horrors, in which the power exercised by the poet bears no proportion to the repugnance excited by the subject. The character of Aaron the Moor is the only thing which shews any originality of conception; and the scene in which he expresses his joy 'at the blackness and ugliness of his child begot in adultery', the only one worthy of Shakespear. Even this is worthy of him only in the display of power, for it gives no pleasure. Shakespear managed these things differently. Nor do we think it a sufficient answer to say that this was an embryo or crude production of the author. In its kind it is full grown, and its features decided and overcharged. It is not like a first imperfect essay, but shows a confirmed habit, a systematic preference of violent effect to everything else. There are occasional detached images of great beauty and delicacy, but these were not beyond the powers of other writers then living.

SIR WALTER RALEIGH There is an attractive simplicity about the criticism which attributes all that is good to Shakespeare, and all that is bad 'to an inferior hand'. On this principle *Titus Andronicus* has been stoutly alleged to contain no single line of Shakespeare's composing. But if once we are foolishly persuaded to go behind the authority of Heminge and Condell (reinforced, in the case of *Titus*, by the testimony of Francis Meres), we have lost our only safe anchorage, and are afloat upon a wild and violent sea, subject to every wind of doctrine. No critical ear, however highly respected, can safely set itself up against the evidence of Shakespeare's friends. It is wiser to believe that the plays in the Folio were attributed to Shakespeare either because they were wholly his, or because they were recast and rewritten by him, or, lastly, because they contain enough of his work to warrant the attribution.

Shakespeare, 1907.

M. C. BRADBROOK *Titus Andronicus* and *The Rape of Lucrece*, Shakespeare's two 'tragical discourses' were in their time extremely well thought on. We have Ben Jonson's word that the public enjoyed *Titus*, and Gabriel Harvey's that the judicious read *Lucrece*.[1] They are now among the least studied of his work, and *Titus* has often been rejected from the canon, though its many echoes of *The Rape of Lucrece* should alone be enough to retain it.

In these two works, where Shakespeare was trying his hand in the high style, he models from accepted designs. Early Elizabethan tragedy was closely connected with the non-dramatic Complaint: *Lucrece* is comparable with Daniel's *Rosamund's Complaint*, and *Titus* is largely a dramatic lament. The Complaint was a late medieval form: in *The Mirror for Magistrates* the medieval tradition was transmitted to the Elizabethans. The Vergilian journey to the underworld, the allegorical figures and wailing ghosts, the imagery of hell and judgment and the demonstration of the turn of Fortune's wheel as Chaucer described it:

[1] See p. 47.

> Tragedy is to seyn a certeyn storie . . .
> Of hym that stood in greet prosperitee
> And is yfallen out of high degree
> Into myserie and endeth wrecchedly—

are all transferred to the stage in the early revenge play, the other parent-stock from which *Titus Andronicus* derives. Kyd's *Spanish Tragedy* provides the dramatic model: Ovid's *Metamorphoses*, part of the story, which is based on the Rape of Philomel. Shakespeare was drawing on as many good authorities as he could: but the Senecan influence is now generally disallowed.

There is an emblematic or heraldic quality about all the characters of *Titus Andronicus*. Formal grouping appears with the first great scene of lament where, after the procession of Titus's condemned sons, Lucius, his banished heir, stands with sword drawn, whilst Titus kneels and pleads with the stones under his feet.

> A stone is silent and offendeth not,
> And tribunes with their tongues doom men to death,

he says, working out the emblematic contrast of the stony-hearted men at great length. Next, the ravished Lavinia is brought to her father; he invites the whole family to sit on the earth together and wipe one another's eyes in a kind of ballet of lamentation. . . .

The moral heraldry of *Titus Andronicus* is not confined to grouping and imagery. The figure of Aaron is the only one which beside Titus has any life in it. He is portentous and diabolic: his blackness an outward symbol of his diabolic nature, recognized by all. . . . Aaron is half-symbol, half stage-formula. The medieval devil, witty and exuberant, has contributed to his character, and so has the conscienceless Machiavel, with his delight in plots, his manipulation of the poor victims to engineer their own undoing, and his rapid action by violence when policy will not serve. He is an atheist, of course, and regards an oath as 'popish'.

His wit throws the laments of the tragic characters into high relief—whether he is crying 'weke, weke' as he stabs the nurse ('so cries a pigge prepared to the spit'), 'almost splitting his sides with extreme laughter' as Titus mutilates himself, or dandling the coal-black baby which Tamora bears him, and defying her sons:

> Yee white limde walles, yee alehouse painted signes . . .

But when the Revenge action is on foot, Titus becomes witty and ironic in turn, sends his ominous presents to the young princes, shoots his arrows at the gods, and outplays Aaron at his own game of countermining. . . .

Titus Andronicus is then more like a pageant than a play. But unlike such pageants as those at the end of the third book of the *Faerie Queene*, it is not provided with an interpretation, and no doubt it was enjoyed by the ground-lings as an atrocity play. They would take what it had in common with *Lust's Dominion* and ignore what was different. This learned and decorous work may have achieved popular success only through misunderstanding of the young author's intentions.

It is quite possible that Shakespeare himself did not know exactly what he meant by this play. But in the laments of Titus, which are the core of the piece, can be felt some faint foreshadowing of the pain and madness that were ultimately to issue in *King Lear*. The play seems a first crude attempt to portray some experience that Shakespeare was only to recognize, understand and embody in a 'lively image' at a much later stage. Because that later image exists, we may guess at the unfulfilled intention of the earlier writing, where the meaning is given in terms of doctrine, not of experience: stated, not realized: shadowed, not portrayed.

Shakespeare and Elizabethan Poetry, 1951.

THE TAMING OF THE SHREW

WRITTEN   1593–4. Not mentioned by Meres, 1598, unless it is the unknown 'Loue labours wonne'.

PERFORMED   *A Shrew* was acted 'sundry times' before its publication in 1594. On June 13th, 1594, Henslowe received 9s. for a performance of '*the Tamynge of A Shrowe*'.
The first definite reference to *The Shrew* is: 'On Tusday night at Saint James, the 26 of Novemb. 1633, was acted before the Kinge and Queene, The Taminge of the Shrewe. Likt.' (*Office Book* of Sir Henry Herbert.)

REGISTERED   1594 May 2nd, by Peter Short, 'the Tayminge of a Shrowe'.
1607. Transferred to Nicholas Ling, and then to John Smethwick.

These entries refer to the older anonymous play, *The Taming of* A *Shrew*, which was published in 1594 'As it was sundry times acted by the Right honorable the Earle of Pembrook his seruants', and again in 1596 and 1607. Some think *A Shrew* is a 'bad' Quarto of *The Shrew*.
In their composite entry for the Folio in 1623, of Shakespeare's plays that had not previously been published, Blount and Jaggard omit *The Taming of The Shrew* and *King John*, presumably because they passed as reprints of the older plays *The Taming of A Shrew*, and *The Troublesome Reign of King John*.

PUBLISHED   1623 F1. Probably set up from MS used as the prompt-copy.
1631 Q. 'A Wittie and Pleasant Comedie Called The Taming of the Shrew. As it was acted by his Maiesties Seruants at the Blacke Friers and the Globe. Written by Will. Shakespeare.' Set up from F1.

SOURCES   *The Taming of A Shrew*, and Ariosto's *I Suppositi*, translated by George Gascoigne as *The Supposes*.

It seems possible that Shakespeare collaborated in this play: that he wrote the Petruchio-Katharine scenes and the Sly episode with its Warwickshire references, while his unknown collaborator wrote the Bianca sub-plot.
Soon after the Restoration John Lacy wrote a coarse prose version called *Sauny the Scot*. It was also adapted by Garrick.

SIR ASTON COKAIN

> *Shakspeare* your *Wincot*-Ale hath much renownd,
> That fox'd a Beggar so (by chance was found
> Sleeping) that there needed not many a word
> To make him to believe he was a Lord:
> But you affirm (and in it seem most eager)
> 'Twill make a Lord as drunk as any Beggar.
> Bid *Norton* brew such Ale as *Shakspeare* fancies
> Did put *Kit Sly* into such Lordly trances:
> And let us meet there (for a fit of Gladness)
> And drink our selves merry in sober sadness.
>
>   *To Mr. Clement Fisher of Wincott*, 1658.

PEPYS To the King's house, and there saw 'The Tameing of a Shrew', which hath some very good pieces in it, but generally is but a mean, play; and the best part, 'Sawny', done by Lacy; and hath not half its life, by reason of the words, I suppose, not being understood, at least by me. (9 *April* 1667.)

To the King's playhouse, and there saw a silly play and an old one, 'The Taming of a Shrew'. (2 *Nov.* 1667.)

JOHNSON Of this play the two plots are so well united, that they can hardly be called two, without injury to the art with which they are interwoven. The attention is entertained with all the variety of a double plot, yet is not distracted by unconnected incidents.

The part between Catharine and Petruchio is eminently sprightly and diverting. At the marriage of Bianca, the arrival of the real father, perhaps produces more perplexity than pleasure. The whole play is very popular and diverting.

HAZLITT *The Taming of the Shrew* is almost the only one of Shakespeare's comedies that has a regular plot, and downright moral. It is full of bustle, animation, and rapidity of action. It shows admirably how self-will is only to be got the better of by stronger will, and how one degree of ridiculous perversity is only to be driven out by another still greater. Petruchio is a madman in his senses; a very honest fellow, who hardly speaks a word of truth, and succeeds in all his tricks and impostures. He acts his assumed character to the life, with the most fantastical extravagance, with complete presence of mind, with untired animal spirits, and without a particle of ill humour from beginning to end. . . .

We have heard the *Honey-Moon* called 'an elegant Katherine and Petruchio'. We suspect we do not understand this word *elegant* in the sense that many people do. But in our sense of the word, we should call Lucentio's description of his mistress elegant.

> Tranio, I saw her coral lips to move,
> And with her breath she did perfume the air:
> Sacred and sweet was all I saw in her.

When Biondello tells the same Lucentio for his encouragement, 'I knew a wench married in an afternoon as she went to the garden for parsley to stuff a rabbit, and so may you, sir'—there is nothing elegant in this, and yet we hardly know which of the two passages is the best. . . .

The character of Sly and the remarks with which he accompanies the play are as good as the play itself . . . 'The Slies are no rogues', as he says of himself. We have a great predilection for this representative of the family; and what makes us like him the better is, that we take him to be of kin (not many degrees removed) to Sancho Panza.

GERVINUS The scenes between Petruchio and Katherine might be converted into a mere joke, and that of the commonest order. It is sad to think that a man like Garrick has done this. He contracted the piece, under the title of Katherine and Petruchio, into a play of three acts; he expunged the more refined part, the plot for the wooing of Bianca, and he debased the coarse remainder into a clumsy caricature. The acting of the pair was coarsely extravagant, according to the custom which has subsequently maintained its ground; Woodward at the same period acted Petruchio with such fury, that he ran the fork into the finger of his fellow actress (Mrs. Clive), and when he carried her off the stage, threw her down. Thus is the piece still performed in London as a concluding farce, with all disgusting overloadings of vulgar buffoonery, even after the genuine play was acted again at the Haymarket in 1844, and was received with applause.[1] . . .

The wooer, Petruchio, is fashioned out of coarse clay; he comes not to Padua as Lucentio does, for the sake of study, but to marry for gold. The rich shrew is offered to him in jest, and he enters upon his courtship in a spirit of good-humoured bravado. . . .

Katherine, whom he undertakes to woo, is like a wasp, like a foal that kicks from its halter—pert, quick and determined, but full of good heart; Petruchio already takes pleasure in her nature, because her honest heart overflows in the right place, as in the last act with the widow.

Shakespeare Commentaries, 1850.

G. I. DUTHIE It is essential to a right understanding of Shakespeare to realize that the fundamental antithesis between order and disorder is ubiquitous in his work. We find it in comedies, histories, and tragedies. Consider it in *The Taming of the Shrew*, a play which is liable to be seriously misunderstood by the modern reader if he does not bear in mind the order-disorder antithesis. Some readers find the play to a considerable extent repellent. What is it about? One might perhaps say, it is about a vivid, spirited woman who is cowed into abject submission by the violence of an egregious bully. The spectacle of the 'taming' is not amusing, but disgusting. So the matter may perhaps appear to some modern readers. It did not appear so to Shakespeare.

[1] This refers to Benjamin Webster's remarkable production: remarkable because of its truth and simplicity at a time when scenery was beginning to overwhelm the plays.

We have seen that according to the doctrine of the hierarchical universe every existing thing (apart from the very highest and the very lowest) occupies a position in the scale above one thing and below another. Everything rules one thing and is ruled by another. As regards the domestic milieu, the husband rules the wife, and the wife's duty is to obey the husband implicitly. This may be foreign to our modern idea of marriage: but we must, in order to interpret the play properly, try to see things as Shakespeare saw them. In refusing to accord her husband implicit obedience, Katharine is offending against the divinely established order of things—her conduct is unnatural. And when at last she does stand forth as the obedient wife *par excellence*, we are witnessing the triumph of enlightenment—the triumph of right over error—the establishment of the most desirable state of affairs. When towards the close of the play Katharine gives her remarkable display of wifely obedience, Lucentio says, 'Here is a wonder, if you talk of a wonder.' Hortensio replies, 'And so it is: I wonder what it bodes.' And Petruchio declares:

> Marry, peace it bodes, and love and quiet life,
> And awful rule and right supremacy;
> And, to be short, what not, that's sweet and happy?

'Awful rule', 'right supremacy'—because according to the doctrine of order the wife must subject herself to the husband. But, this having been granted, what we have is peace, love, happiness, harmony. That is what is established at the end of *The Taming of the Shrew*. It is as if in the little kingdom of Petruchio's family there had been a civil war: a subject (Katharine) rebelled against the king (Petruchio): the king quelled the revolt by force: the subject admitted error: and now all is well.

Katharine's last speech in the play is an enunciation of the doctrine of order as applied to the domestic milieu, and includes a reference to the doctrine of correspondences. The speech explicitly states the 'moral' of the play, and it is not stated in a cowed tone but surely with fervent conviction. Katharine has learned the truth. To Hortensio's wife, who is disobedient to her husband, she says:

> Thy husband is thy lord, thy life thy keeper,
> Thy head, thy sovereign; . . .
> Such duty as the subject owes the prince
> Even such a woman oweth to her husband;
> And when she is froward, peevish, sullen, sour,
> And not obedient to his honest will,
> What is she but a foul contending rebel
> And graceless traitor to her loving lord?

According to the doctrine of correspondences, the relationship of husband to wife is the same as the relationship of king to subject, or of the head to the rest of the body. An insubordinate wife corresponds to a rebellious subject. We may take the hint and go further. The sin of Satan was that he rebelled against God: a rebellious wife is acting correspondingly to that. . . .

We have seen that when order was destroyed on one plane of reality it was considered possible that there would be an associated destruction of order on other planes of reality. The ultimate result might be universal disintegration. This ultimate result is nowhere even hinted at in *The Taming of the Shrew*. Shakespeare is writing a comedy. He is not concerned with horror. He does not want to arouse in his audience emotions such as are aroused by tragedy. But I have little doubt that the sophisticated member of his contemporary audience would say that this spectre of universal disintegration was there, hovering in the background, even in *The Taming of the Shrew*. For Shakespeare's contemporaries it was there, as an ultimate most grievous possibility, since order had been assailed on one plane of reality. But in the comedy this possibility is not mentioned at all, for that would have destroyed the mood of the play altogether. Order is established at the end before any fundamental damage is done.

Shakespeare, 1951.

THE TWO GENTLEMEN OF VERONA

WRITTEN   1594–5. Mentioned by Meres, 1598.

PERFORMED   No record of an early performance.

REGISTERED 1623 Nov. 8 by Blount and Isaak Jaggard. One of the 16 plays registered before the publication of the Folio.

PUBLISHED   1623: F1. The text is rather short, but fairly correct.

SOURCE   *La Diana Enamorada*: a prose romance in Spanish by Jorge de Montemayor.

JOHNSON In this play there is a strange mixture of knowledge and ignorance, of care and negligence. The versification is often excellent, the allusions are learned and just; but the author conveys his heroes by sea from one inland town to another in the same country; he places the emperor at Milan, and sends his young men to attend him, but never mentions him more; he makes Proteus, after an interview with Silvia, say he has only seen her picture; and, if we may credit the old copies, he has, by mistaking places, left his scenery inextricable. The reason of all this confusion seems to be, that he took his story from a novel, which he sometimes followed, and sometimes forsook, sometimes remembered, and sometimes forgot.

HAZLITT This is little more than the first outlines of a comedy loosely sketched in. It is the story of a novel dramatised with very little labour or pretension; yet there are passages of high poetical spirit, and of inimitable quaintness of humour, which are undoubtedly Shakespear's, and there is throughout the conduct of the fable a careless grace and felicity which marks it for his. . . . The style of the familiar parts of this comedy is indeed made up of conceits—low they may be for what we know, but then they are not poor, but rich ones. The scene of Launce with his dog (not that in the second, but that in the fourth act) is a perfect treat in the way of farcical drollery and invention; nor do we think Speed's manner of proving his master to be in love deficient in wit or sense, though the style may be criticised as not simple enough for the modern taste. . . .

The tender scenes in this play, though not so highly wrought as in some others, have often much sweetness of sentiment and expression. . . .

> *Lucetta.*   I do not seek to quench your love's hot fire,
> But qualify the fire's extreme rage,
> Lest it should burn above the bounds of reason.
> *Julia.*   The more thou damm'st it up, the more it burns.
> The current that with gentle murmur glides,
> Thou know'st, being stopped, impatiently doth rage;
> But when his fair course is not hindered,
> He makes sweet music with the enamelled stones,
> Giving a gentle kiss to every sedge
> He overtaketh in his pilgrimage;
> And so by many winding nooks he strays,
> With willing sport, to the wild ocean.
> Then let me go, and hinder not my course:
> I'll be as patient as a gentle stream,
> And make a pastime of each weary step,
> Till the last step have brought me to my love
> And there I'll rest, as after much turmoil
> A blessed soul doth in Elysium.

If Shakespear indeed had written only this and other passages in The Two Gentlemen of Verona, he would *almost* have deserved Milton's praise of him—

> And sweetest Shakespear, Fancy's child,
> Warbles his native wood-notes wild.

But as it is, he deserves rather more praise than this.

LOGAN PEARSALL SMITH And yet it is curious to note that the supremest gift of language, that gift of the magic and evocatory phrase, which has made Shakespeare the master-magician of the world was by no means with him as with many young poets a natural endowment; and we find few traces of it in the long poems he so carefully composed when nearly thirty. His earliest plays are written in the common poetic diction of his time—that style of the day which as Swinburne says all great poets begin by writing and lesser poets write all their lives. In the earlier historical plays, where Shakespeare's authorship is disputed, it is hardly possible to discriminate by any criterion of style which parts are of his composition. In the powerful rhetoric and plangent declamation of certain passages in these plays we seem to be first aware of Shakespeare's gift of language; but it is only in *The Two Gentlemen of Verona*, with the Song 'Who is Silvia', with the line:

> *The uncertain glory of an April day,*

and the passage about the brook that makes sweet music as it strays, that his power over words becomes a magic power, and his golden mastery of speech begins to almost blind us with its beauty.

On Reading Shakespeare, 1933.

LOVE'S LABOUR'S LOST

WRITTEN   1594–5. Mentioned by Meres, 1598.

PUBLISHED   1598 Q1. 'A Pleasant Conceited Comedie Called, Loues labors lost. As it was presented before her Highnes this last Christmas. Newly corrected and augmented By W. Shakespere.'
Not a 'bad' Quarto, but a badly printed text. The fact that there was no entry in the Stationers' Register before Q1 suggests that there may have been an earlier, surreptitious Quarto from which Q1 was 'newly corrected and augmented', though it is possible that Shakespeare rewrote the play for its publication in 1598. It is the first play to be published with his name.
1623 F1. Set up from Q1. There are many corrections, but many new errors are introduced.
1631 Q2. 'A Wittie and Pleasant Comedie, As it was Acted by his Maiesties Seruants at the Blacke-Friers and the Globe. Written by William Shakespeare.'

PERFORMED   If the title-page of Q1 is not the repetition of an earlier one 'it was presented before her Highnes this last Christmas', i.e. 1597–8, though of course it was probably acted as soon as written.
1605. 'By his Maiesties plaiers. Betwin Newers Day and Twelfe day A play of Loues Labours Lost.' (*Revels Account.*)

REGISTERED   1607 Jan. 22, by Nicholas Ling.

SOURCES   The plot appears to be Shakespeare's own, though there are many topical allusions: the Duc de Biron and the Duc de Longueville were supporters of Henry of Navarre.

J. D. Wilson thinks that the play as we have it is a revision of an early version that was acted at the Earl of Southampton's house in the plague year 1593–4. It certainly seems to be written for a courtly rather than a popular audience.

SIR WALTER COPE   I have sent and bene all thys morning huntyng for players Juglers & Such kinde of Creaturs, but fynde them harde to finde, wherfore Leavinge notes for them to seeke me, Burbage ys

A PLEASANT

Conceited Comedie
CALLED,
Loues labors lost.

As it vvas presented before her Highnes
this last Christmas.

Newly corrected and augmented
By W. Shakespere.

Imprinted at London by *W.W.*
for *Cutbert Burby.*
1598.

TITLE-PAGE OF THE FIRST QUARTO

come, & sayes ther ys no new playe that the quene hath not seene, but they have revyved an olde one, Cawled *Loves Labore lost*, which for wytt & mirthe he sayes will please her exceedingly. And Thys ys apointed to be playd to Morowe night at my Lord of Sowthamptons, unless yow send a wrytt to Remove the Corpus Cum Causa to your howse in Strande. Burbage ys my messenger Ready attendyng your pleasure.

Letter to Robert Cecil, 1604.

JOHNSON In this play, which all the editors have concurred to censure, and some have rejected as unworthy of our poet, it must be confessed that there are many passages mean, childish and vulgar; and some which ought not to have been exhibited, as we are told they were, to a maiden queen. But there are scattered through the whole many sparks of genius; nor is there any play that has more evident marks of the hand of Shakespeare.

COLERIDGE The characters in this play are either impersonated out of Shakspeare's own multiformity by imaginative self-position or out of such as a country town and schoolboy's observation might supply,—the curate, the schoolmaster, the Armado, (who even in my time was not extinct in the cheaper inns of North Wales) and so on. The satire is chiefly on follies of words. Biron and Rosaline are evidently the pre-existent state of Benedict and Beatrice, and so, perhaps, is Boyet of Lafeu, and Costard of the Tapster in Measure for Measure; and the frequency of the rhymes, the sweetness as well as the smoothness of the metre, and the number of acute and fancifully illustrated aphorisms, are all as they ought to be in a poet's youth. True genius begins by generalizing and condensing; it ends in realizing and expanding. It first collects the seeds.

Yet if this juvenile drama had been the only one extant of our Shakspeare, and we possessed the tradition only of his riper works, or accounts of them in writers who had not even mentioned this play,—how many of Shakspeare's characteristic features might we not still have discovered in Love's Labour's Lost, though as in a portrait taken of him in his boyhood?

I can never sufficiently admire the wonderful activity of thought throughout the whole of the first scene of the play, rendered natural, as it is, by the choice of the characters, and the whimsical determination on which the drama is founded. . . .

The same kind of intellectual action is exhibited in a more serious and elevated strain in many other parts of this play. Biron's speech at the end of the fourth act is an excellent specimen of it. It is logic clothed in rhetoric;— but observe how Shakspeare, in his two-fold being of poet and philosopher, avails himself of it to convey profound truths in the most lively images,—the whole remaining faithful to the character supposed to utter the lines, and the expressions themselves constituting a further developement of that character:

> Other slow arts entirely keep the brain:
> And therefore finding barren practisers,
> Scarce shew a harvest of their heavy toil:
> But love, first learned in a lady's eyes,

> Lives not alone immured in the brain;
> But, with the motion of all elements,
> Courses as swift as thought in every power;
> And gives to every power a double power,
> Above their functions and their offices. . . .

This is quite a study;—sometimes you see this youthful god of poetry connecting disparate thoughts purely by means of resemblances in the words
expressing them,—a thing in character in lighter comedy, especially of that
kind in which Shakspeare delights, namely, the purposed display of wit,
though sometimes, too, disfiguring his graver scenes;—but more often you
may see him doubling the natural connection or order of logical consequence
in the thoughts by the introduction of an artificial and sought-for resemblance
in the words, as, for instance, in the third line of the play,—

> And then grace us in the disgrace of death;—

this being a figure often having its force and propriety, as justified by the law
of passion, which, inducing in the mind an unusual activity, seeks for means
to waste its superfluity,—when in the highest degree—in lyric repetitions
and sublime tautology.

HAZLITT If we were to part with any of the author's comedies, it should be
this. Yet we would be loth to part with Don Adriano de Armado,
that mighty potentate of nonsense, or his page, that handful of wit; with
Nathaniel the curate, or Holofernes the schoolmaster, and their dispute after
dinner on 'the golden cadences of poesy'; with Costard the clown, or Dull the
constable. Biron is too accomplished a character to be lost to the world, and
yet he could not appear without his fellow courtiers and the king: and if we
were to leave out the ladies, the gentlemen would have no mistresses. So that
we believe we may let the whole play stand as it is, and we shall hardly
venture to 'set a mark of reprobation on it'. Still we have some objections to
the style, which we think savours more of the pedantic spirit of Shakespear's
time than of his own genius, more of controversial divinity, and the logic of
Peter Lombard, than of the inspiration of the Muse. It transports us quite
as much to the manners of the court, and the quirks of courts of law, as to
the scenes of nature or the fairy-land of his own imagination. Shakespear has
set himself to imitate the tone of polite conversation then prevailing among
the fair, the witty, and the learned, and he has imitated it but too faithfully.
It is as if the hand of Titian had been employed to give grace to the curls of
a full-bottomed periwig, or Raphael had attempted to give expression to the
tapestry figures in the House of Lords.

WALTER PATER It is this foppery of delicate language, this fashionable plaything of his time, with which Shakespeare is occupied in
Love's Labour's Lost. He shows us the manner in all its stages; passing from
the grotesque and vulgar pedantry of Holofernes, through the extravagant
but polished caricature of Armado, to become the peculiar characteristic of

a real though still quaint poetry in Biron himself, who is still chargeable even at his best with just a little affectation. As Shakespeare laughs broadly at it in Holofernes or Armado, so he is the analyst of its curious charm in Biron; and this analysis involves a delicate raillery by Shakespeare himself at his own chosen manner. . . .

As happens with every true dramatist, Shakespeare is for the most part hidden behind the persons of his creation. Yet there are certain of his characters in which we feel that there is something of self-portraiture. And it is not so much in his grander, more subtle and ingenious creations that we feel this—in *Hamlet* and *King Lear*—as in those slighter and more spontaneously developed figures, who, while far from playing principal parts, are yet distinguished by a peculiar happiness and delicate ease in the drawing of them; figures which possess, above all, that winning attractiveness which there is no man but would willingly exercise, and which resemble those works of art which, though not meant to be very great or imposing, are yet wrought of the choicest material. Mercutio in *Romeo and Juliet*, belongs to this group of Shakespeare's characters—versatile, mercurial people, such as make good actors, and in whom the

'Nimble spirits of the arteries',

the finer but still merely animal elements of great wit, predominate. A careful delineation of minor, yet expressive traits seems to mark them out as the characters of his predilection; and it is hard not to identify him with these more than with others. Biron, in Love's Labour's Lost, is perhaps the most striking member of this group. In this character, which is never quite in touch, never quite on a perfect level of understanding, with the other persons of the play, we see, perhaps, a reflex of Shakespeare himself, when he has just become able to stand aside from and estimate the first period of his poetry.

Appreciations, 1889.

H. GRANVILLE-BARKER Here is a fashionable play; now, by three hundred years, out of fashion. Nor did it ever, one supposes, make a very wide appeal. It abounds in jokes for the elect. Were you not numbered among them you laughed, for safety, in the likeliest places. A year or two later the elect themselves might be hard put to it to remember what the joke was. . . .

Drama, as Shakespeare will come to write it, is, first and last, the projection of character in action; and devices for doing this, simple and complex, must make up three-quarters of its artistry. We can watch his early discovery that dialogue is waste matter unless it works to this end; that wit, epigram, sentiment are like paper and sticks in a fireplace, the flaring and crackling counting for nothing if the fire itself won't light, if these creatures in whose mouths the wit is sounded won't 'come alive'. To the last he kept his youthful delight in a pun; and he would write an occasional passage of word-music with a minimum of meaning to it (but of maximum emotional value, it will be found, to the character that has to speak it). His development of verse to dramatic use is a study in itself. He never ceased to develop it, but for a while the dramatist had a hard time with the lyric poet. The early plays abound, besides, in elaborate embroidery of language done for its own sake. This was a fashionable literary exercise and Shakespeare was an adept at it. To many young poets of the time their language was a new-found wonder; its very handling gave them pleasure. The amazing things it could be made to do! He had to discover that they were not much to his purpose; but it is not easy to stop doing what you do so well. Yet even in this play we may note the difference between the Berowne of

> Light seeking light doth light of light beguile;
> So ere you find where light in darkness lies
> Your light grows dark by losing of your eyes!

and of the soliloquy beginning

> And I forsooth in love . . .

Turn also from one of the many sets of wit to Katharine's haunting answer when Rosaline twits her with rebellion against Cupid:

Rosaline.   You'll ne'er be friends with him; he kill'd your sister.
Katharine.   He made her melancholy, sad, and heavy:
   And so she died: had she been light, like you,
   Of such a merry, nimble, stirring spirit,
   She might have been a grandam ere she died
   And so may you, for a light heart lives long.

Compare it with the set of wit that follows:

Rosaline.   What's your dark meaning, mouse, of this light word?
Katharine.   A light condition in a beauty dark.
Rosaline.   We need more light to find your meaning out.
Katharine.   You'll mar the light, by taking it in snuff;
   Therefore I'll darkly end the argument.

But Rosaline won't let her, and they manage to get five more rather spicier exchanges. It is all very charming, and a 'set of wit' describes it well. Get a knowledge of the game and it may be as attractive to watch for a little as are a few sets of tennis. But pages on pages of such smart repartee will not tell us as much of the speakers as those few simple lines of Katharine's tell us —of herself and her love for her sister, and of Rosaline too.

Prefaces to Shakespeare: First Series, 1927.

ROMEO AND JULIET

WRITTEN   1594–5. Mentioned by Meres, 1598.

PERFORMED   'Often plaid publiquely' before Q1 1597.

PUBLISHED   1597 Q1. 'An Excellent conceited Tragedie of Romeo and
        Iuliet. As it hath been often (with great applause) plaid
publiquely, by the right Honourable the L. of Hunsdon his Seruants.' A
'bad' Quarto, apparently reproduced from memory by two or three actors
who had played in a shortened version.
1599 Q2. 'Newly corrected, augmented, and amended: As it hath bene
sundry times publiquely acted, by the right Honourable the Lord Chamberlaine his Seruants.' Q2 contains many errors, but may have been set up from
the original MS with some reference to a corrected Q1. Q2 has 'Enter Will
Kemp' for Q1's 'Enter Peter' (IV. v. 102).
1609 Q3. 'As it hath beene sundrie times publiquely Acted, by the Kings
Maiesties Seruants at the Globe.' Set up from Q2.
Q4. 'Written by W. Shake-speare.' No date. Set up from Q3.
1623 F1. Set up from Q3.

REGISTERED   1607 Jan 22, by Nicholas Ling.

SOURCES   Arthur Brooke's poem, *The Tragicall Historye of Romeus and
        Juliet* (1562), and William Painter's prose version in his
Palace of Pleasure (1567). Both these come from a novella by Bandello.

In 1680 Otway adapted *Romeo and Juliet* in his *Caius Marius*. The scene
is Rome, and Juliet (Lavinia) wakes before Romeo (Marius) dies. Garrick
returned to the original, though he retained the scene between the dying
lovers, this version being played until Kemble's time.

LEONARD DIGGES
        Nor shall I e're beleeue, or thinke thee dead
        (Though mist) untill our bankrout Stage be sped
        (Impossible) with some new strain 't out-do
        Passions of *Iuliet*, and her *Romeo*.
                                        First Folio, 1623.

PEPYS   To the Opera, and there saw 'Romeo and Juliet', the first time it was
        ever acted, but it is a play of itself the worst that ever I heard, and
the worst acted that ever I saw these people do, and I am resolved to go no
more to see the first time of acting, for they were all of them out more or less.
[Betterton played Romeo, and his wife Juliet.]
                                        1 *March* 1662.

DRYDEN *Shakespear* show'd the best of his skill in his *Mercutio*, and he said
himself, that he was forc'd to kill him in the third Act, to prevent
being kill'd by him. But, for my part, I cannot find he was so dangerous a
person: I see nothing in him but what was so exceeding harmless, that he
might have liv'd to the end of the Play, and dy'd in his bed, without offence
to any man.

On the Dramatique Poetry of the Last Age, 1684.

JOHNSON This play is one of the most pleasing of our author's performances.
The scenes are busy and various, the incidents numerous and important, the catastrophe irresistibly affecting, and the process of the action
carried on with such probability, at least with such congruity to popular
opinions, as tragedy requires.

Here is one of the few attempts of Shakespeare to exhibit the conversation
of gentlemen, to represent the airy sprightliness of juvenile elegance. Mr.
Dryden mentions a tradition, which might easily reach his time, of a declaration made by Shakespeare, that 'he was obliged to kill Mercutio in the third
act, lest he should have been killed by him'. Yet he thinks him 'no such
formidable person, but that he might have lived through the play, and died
in his bed', without danger to the poet. Dryden well knew, had he been in
quest of truth, that, in a pointed sentence, more regard is commonly had to
the words than the thought, and that it is very seldom to be rigorously understood. Mercutio's wit, gaiety and courage, will always procure him friends
that wish him a longer life; but his death is not precipitated, he has lived out
the time allotted him in the construction of the play; nor do I doubt the ability
of Shakespeare to have continued his existence, though some of his sallies are,
perhaps, out of reach of Dryden; whose genius was not very fertile of merriment, nor ductile to humour, but acute, argumentative, comprehensive and
sublime.

The nurse is one of the characters in which the author delighted; he has,
with great subtilty of distinction, drawn her at once loquacious and secret,
obsequious and insolent, trusty and dishonest.

His comic scenes are happily wrought, but his pathetic strains are always
polluted with some unexpected depravations. His persons, however distressed, have a conceit left them in their misery, a miserable conceit.

HAZLITT *Romeo and Juliet* is the only tragedy which Shakespear has written
entirely on a love-story. It is supposed to have been his first play,
and it deserves to stand in that proud rank. There is the buoyant spirit of
youth in every line, in the rapturous intoxication of hope, and in the bitterness of despair. It has been said of *Romeo and Juliet* by a great critic,[1] that
'whatever is most intoxicating in the odour of a southern spring, languishing
in the song of the nightingale, or voluptuous in the first opening of the rose,
is to be found in this poem'. The description is true; and yet it does not
answer to our idea of the play. For if it has the sweetness of the rose, it has
its freshness too; if it has the languor of the nightingale's song, it has also its

[1] Coleridge.

giddy transport; if it has the softness of a southern spring, it is as glowing and as bright. There is nothing of a sickly and sentimental cast. Romeo and Juliet are in love, but they are not love-sick. Everything speaks the very soul of pleasure, the high and healthy pulse of the passions: the heart beats, the blood circulates and mantles throughout. . . .

Romeo is Hamlet in love. There is the same rich exuberance of passion and sentiment in the one, that there is of thought and sentiment in the other. Both are absent and self-involved, both live out of themselves in a world of imagination. Hamlet is abstracted from everything; Romeo is abstracted from everything but his love, and lost in it. His 'frail thoughts dally with faint surmise', and are fashioned out of the suggestions of hope, 'the flatteries of sleep'. He is himself only in his Juliet; she is his only reality, his heart's true home and idol. The rest of the world is to him a passing dream.

COLERIDGE I have previously had occasion to speak at large on the subject of the three unities of time, place, and action, as applied to the drama in the abstract, and to the particular stage for which Shakspeare wrote, as far as he can be said to have written for any stage but that of the universal mind. I hope I have in some measure succeeded in demonstrating that the former two, instead of being rules, were mere inconveniences attached to the local peculiarities of the Athenian drama; that the last alone deserved the name of a principle, and that in the preservation of this unity Shakspeare stood pre-eminent. Yet, instead of unity of action, I should greatly prefer the more appropriate, though scholastic and uncouth words homogeneity, proportionateness, and totality of interest,—expressions, which involve the distinction, or rather the essential difference, betwixt the shaping skill of mechanical talent, and the creative, productive, life-power of inspired genius. In the former each part is separately conceived, and then by a succeeding act put together;—not as watches are made for wholesale—(for there each part supposes a preconception of the whole in some mind)—but more like pictures on a motley screen. Whence arises the harmony that strikes us in the wildest natural landscapes,—in the relative shapes of rocks, the harmony of colours in the heaths, ferns, and lichens, the leaves of the beech, and the oak, the stems and rich brown branches of the birch and other mountain trees, varying from verging autumn to returning spring,—compared with the visual effect from the greater number of artificial plantations?—From this, that the natural landscape is effected, as it were, by a single energy modified *ab intra* in each component part. And as this is the particular excellence of the Shakspearian drama generally, so it is especially characteristic of the Romeo and Juliet. . . .

Mercutio is a man possessing all the elements of a poet: the whole world was, as it were, subject to his law of association. Whenever he wishes to impress anything, all things become his servants for the purpose: all things tell the same tale, and sound in unison. This faculty, moreover, is combined with the manners and feelings of a perfect gentleman, himself utterly unconscious of his powers. By his loss it was contrived that the whole catastrophe of the tragedy should be brought about: it endears him to Romeo, and gives to the death of Mercutio an importance which it could not otherwise have acquired.

I say this in answer to an observation, I think by Dryden (to which indeed Dr. Johnson has fully replied), that Shakspeare having carried the part of Mercutio as far as he could, till his genius was exhausted, had killed him in the third Act, to get him out of the way. What shallow nonsense! As I have remarked, upon the death of Mercutio the whole catastrophe depends; it is produced by it. The scene in which it occurs serves to show how indifference to any subject but one, and aversion to activity on the part of Romeo, may be overcome and roused to the most resolute and determined conduct. Had not Mercutio been rendered so amiable and so interesting, we could not have felt so strongly the necessity for Romeo's interference, connecting it immediately, and passionately, with the future fortunes of the lover and his mistress. . . .

Shakspeare has described this passion in various states and stages, beginning, as was most natural, with love in the young. Does he open his play by making Romeo and Juliet in love at first sight—at the first glimpse, as any ordinary thinker would do? Certainly not: he knew what he was about, and how he was to accomplish what he was about: he was to develope the whole passion, and he commences with the first elements—that sense of imperfection, that yearning to combine itself with something lovely. Romeo became enamoured of the idea he had formed in his own mind, and then, as it were, christened the first real being of the contrary sex as endowed with the perfections he desired. He appears to be in love with Rosaline; but, in truth, he is in love only with his own idea. He felt that necessity of being beloved which no noble mind can be without. Then our poet, our poet who so well knew human nature, introduces Romeo to Juliet, and makes it not only a violent, but a permanent love—a point for which Shakspeare has been ridiculed by the ignorant and unthinking. Romeo is first represented in a state most susceptible of love, and then, seeing Juliet, he took and retained the infection.

SIR WALTER RALEIGH Since the rise of Romantic criticism, the appreciation of Shakespeare has become a kind of auction, where the highest bidder, however extravagant, carries off the prize. To love and to be wise is not given to man; the poets themselves have run to wild extremes in their anxiety to find all Shakespeare in every part of him; so that it has become to be almost a mark of insensibility to consider his work rationally and historically as a whole. Infinite subtlety of purpose has been attributed to him in cases where he accepted a story as he found it, or half contemptuously threw in a few characters and speeches to suit the requirements of his Elizabethan audience. Coleridge, for example, finds it 'a strong instance of the fineness of Shakespeare's insight into the nature of the passions, that Romeo is introduced already love-bewildered', doting on Rosaline. Yet the whole story of Romeo's passion for Rosaline is set forth in Arthur Brooke's poem, from which Shakespeare certainly drew the matter of his play. Again, the same great critic asserts that 'the low soliloquy of the Porter' in *Macbeth* was 'written for the mob by some other hand, perhaps with Shakespeare's consent', and that 'finding it take, he with the remaining ink of a pen otherwise employed, just interpolated the words—"I'll devil-porter it no further: I had thought to have let in some of all professions, that go the primrose way to the everlasting bonfire". Of the rest not one syllable has the ever-present being of Shakespeare.' That is to say, Coleridge does not like the Porter's speech, so he denies it to Shakespeare. But one sentence in it is too good to lose, so Shakespeare must be at hand to write it. This is the very ecstasy of criticism, and sends us back to the cool and manly utterances of Dryden, Johnson, and Pope with a heightened sense of the value of moderation and candour.

Shakespeare, 1907.

H. B. CHARLTON The plot of *Romeo and Juliet* is pure fiction. . . . Moreover the hero and the heroine had none of the pomp of historic circumstance about them; they were socially of the minor aristocracy who were to stock Shakespeare's comedies, and their only political significance was an adventitious rôle in the civic disturbance of a small city-state. Romeo and Juliet were in effect just a boy and a girl in a novel; and as such they had no claim to the world's attention except through their passion and their fate.

To choose such folk as these for tragic heroes was æsthetically wellnigh an anarchist's gesture; and the dramatist provided a sort of programme-prologue to prompt the audience to see the play from the right point of view. In this play-bill the dramatist draws special attention to two features of his story. First, Verona was being torn by a terrible, bloodthirsty feud which no human endeavour had been able to settle; this was the direct cause of the death of the lovers, and but for those deaths it never would have been healed. Second, the course of the young lovers' lives is from the outset governed by a malignant destiny; fatal, star-crossed, death-marked, they are doomed to piteous destruction.

The intent of this emphasis is clear. The tale will end with the death of two ravishingly attractive young folk; and the dramatist must exonerate himself from all complicity in their murder lest he be found guilty of pandering to a liking for a human shambles. He disowns responsibility and throws it on Destiny, Fate. The device is well warranted in the tragic tradition and especially in its Senecan models. But whether in fact it succeeds is a matter for further consideration. The invocation of Fate is strengthened by the second feature scored heavily in the prologue, the feud. The feud is so to speak the means by which Fate acts. The feud is to provide the sense of immediate, and Fate that of ultimate, inevitability. For it may happen that, however the dramatist deploys his imaginative suggestions, he may fail to summon up a Fate sufficiently compelling to force itself upon the audience as unquestioned shaper of the tragic end. In such circumstance Romeo's and Juliet's death would be by mere chance, a gratuitous intervention by a dramatist exercising his homicidal proclivities for the joy of his audience. Hence the feud has a further function. It will be the dramatist's last plea for exculpation or for mercy; and it will allow his audience to absolve him or to forgive him without loss of its own 'philanthropy'; for through death came the healing of the feud, and with it, the removal of the threat to so many other lives. . . .

But with what conviction could a sixteenth-century spectator take over these ancient figures? Even the human beings of an old mythology may lose their compelling power; 'what's Hecuba to him, or he to Hecuba?' But the gods are in a much worse case; pagan, they had faded before the God of the Christians: *Vicisti, Galilæe*! Fate was no longer a deity strong enough to carry the responsibility of a tragic universe; at most, it could intervene casually as pure luck, and bad luck as a motive turns tragedy to mere chance. It lacks entirely the ultimate tragic ἀνάγκη. It fails to provide the indispensable inevitability.

Is then Shakespeare's *Romeo and Juliet* an unsuccessful experiment? To say so may seem not only profane but foolish. In its own day, as the dog's-eared Bodley Folio shows, and ever since, it has been one of Shakespeare's most preferred plays. It is indeed rich in spells of its own. But as a pattern of the idea of tragedy, it is a failure. Even Shakespeare appears to have felt that, as an experiment, it had disappointed him. At all events, he abandoned tragedy for the next few years and gave himself to history and to comedy; and even afterwards, he fought shy of the simple theme of love, and of the love of anybody less than a great political figure as the main matter for his tragedies.

Nevertheless it is obvious that neither sadism nor masochism is remotely conscious in our appreciation of *Romeo and Juliet*, nor is our 'philanthropy' offended by it. But the achievement is due to the magic of Shakespeare's poetic genius and to the intermittent force of his dramatic power rather than to his grasp of the foundations of tragedy. . . .

This earth, it would seem, has no place for passion like Romeo's and Juliet's. And so, stirred to sympathy by Shakespeare's poetic power, we tolerate, perhaps even approve, their death. At least for the moment.

But tragedy lives not only for its own moment, nor by long 'suspensions of disbelief'. There is the inevitable afterthought and all its 'obstinate questionings'. Our sentiments were but momentarily gratified. And finally our deeper consciousness protests. Shakespeare has but conquered us by a trick: the experiment carries him no nearer to the heart of tragedy.

Shakespearian Tragedy, 1948.

RICHARD THE SECOND

WRITTEN   1595–6. Mentioned by Meres, 1598.

PERFORMED   1595. Sir Edward Hoby invited Sir Robert Cecil to see a performance of 'K. Richard' on Dec. 9th.

1601. 7 Feb. At the Globe.

1631. Revived at the Globe.

REGISTERED   1597. Aug 29, by Andrew Wise.

PUBLISHED   1597 Q1. 'As it hath beene publikely acted by the right
                 Honourable the Lorde Chamberlaine his Seruants.'
A 'good' Quarto, probably printed from Shakespeare's MS.
1598 Q2. 'By William Shake-speare.' Printed from Q1.
1598 Q3. Printed from Q2.
1608 Q4. 'With new additions of the Parliament Sceane, and the deposing
of King Richard, As it hath been lately acted by the Kinges Majesties seruants,
at the Globe.' Printed from Q3. The 'deposition scene' appears to have been
part of the original play which was cut when Q1 was printed. The version
in Q4 seems to be a shorthand report.
1615 Q5. Printed from Q4.
1623 F1. Printed from Q3 or Q5.

SOURCE   Holinshed's *Chronicles*.

The Elizabethans saw parallels between the reigns of Richard II and
Elizabeth. The Earl of Essex was charged with High Treason 'for the dis-
posing and settling to himself Aswell the Crowne of England, as of the king-
dome of Ireland'. On the day before his rebellion, 8 Feb 1601, his supporters persuaded Shakespeare's company to revive *Richard II* at the Globe.
Nahum Tate and Theobald made adaptations of *Richard II*.

SIR EDWARD COKE I protest upon my soul and conscience I doe beleeve she
                 should not have long lived after she had been in your
power. Note but the precedents of former ages, how long lived Richard the
Second after he was surprised in the same manner?
                 Speech at the Trial of the Earl of Essex, 1601.

FRANCIS BACON The afternoone before the rebellion, Merricke, with a great
               company of others, that afterwards were all in the action,
had procured to bee played before them, the play of deposing King Richard
the second. Neither was it casuall, but a play bespoken by Merrick. And
not so onely, but when it was told him by one of the players, that the playe
was olde, and they should haue losse in playing it, because fewe would come
to it: there was fourty shillings extraordinarie giuen to play it, and so thereupon playd it was. So earnest hee was to satisfie his eyes with the sight of
that tragedie which hee thought soone after his lord should bring from the
stage to the state, but that God turned it vpon their owne heads.
A Declaration of the Treasons by Robert late Earle of Essex, 1601.

DRYDEN I cannot leave this subject, before I do justice to that divine poet,
        by giving you one of his passionate descriptions: 'tis of Richard the
Second when he was deposed, and led in triumph through the streets of
London by Henry of Bullingbrook: the painting of it is so lively, and the
words so moving, that I have scarce read anything comparable to it in any
other language. Suppose you have seen already the fortunate usurper passing
through the crowd, and followed by the shouts and acclamations of the people;

and now behold King Richard entering upon the scene: consider the wretchedness of his condition, and his carriage in it; and refrain from pity, if you can—

> As in a theatre, the eyes of men,
> After a well-graced actor leaves the stage,
> Are idly bent on him that enters next,
> Thinking his prattle to be tedious:
> Even so, or with much more contempt, men's eyes
> Did scowl on Richard: no man cried, God save him:
> No joyful tongue gave him his welcome home,
> But dust was thrown upon his sacred head,
> Which with such gentle sorrow he shook off,
> His face still combating with tears and smiles
> (The badges of his grief and patience),
> That had not God (for some strong purpose) steel'd
> The hearts of men, they must perforce have melted,
> And barbarism itself have pitied him.

Preface to Troilus and Cressida, 1679.

JOHNSON Jonson, who, in his Catiline and Sejanus, has inserted many
speeches from the Roman historians, was, perhaps, induced to that
practice by the example of Shakespeare, who had condescended sometimes
to copy more ignoble writers. But Shakespeare had more of his own than
Jonson, and, if he sometimes was willing to spare his labour, showed by what
he performed at other times, that his extracts were made by choice or idleness
rather than necessity.

This play is one of those which Shakespeare revised; but as success in works
of invention is not always proportionate to labour, it is not finished at last
with the happy force of some other of his tragedies, nor can be said much to
affect the passions or enlarge the understanding.

COLERIDGE I have stated that the transitional link between the epic poem
and the drama is the historic drama; that in the epic poem a
pre-announced fate gradually adjusts and employs the will and the events as
its instruments, whilst the drama, on the other hand, places fate and will in
opposition to each other, and is then most perfect, when the victory of fate
is obtained in consequence of imperfections in the opposing will, so as to
leave a final impression that the fate itself is but a higher and a more intelligent
will.

From the length of the speeches, and the circumstance that, with one
exception, the events are all historical, and presented in their results, not
produced by acts seen by, or taking place before, the audience, this tragedy
is ill suited to our present large theatres. But in itself, and for the closet, I
feel no hesitation in placing it as the first and most admirable of all Shakespeare's purely historical plays. For the two parts of Henry IV form a
species of themselves, which may be named the mixed drama. The distinction does not depend on the mere quantity of historical events in the play

compared with the fictions; for there is as much history in Macbeth as in Richard, but in the relation of the history to the plot. In the purely historical plays, the history forms the plot; in the mixed, it directs it; in the rest, as Macbeth, Hamlet, Cymbeline, Lear, it subserves it. But, however unsuited to the stage this drama may be, God forbid that even there it should fall dead on the hearts of jacobinized Englishmen! Then, indeed, we might say— *præteriit gloria mundi!* For the spirit of patriotic reminiscence is the all-permeating soul of this noble work. It is, perhaps, the most purely historical of Shakespeare's dramas. There are not in it, as in the others, characters introduced merely for the purpose of giving a greater individuality and real-ness, as in the comic parts of Henry IV, by presenting, as it were, our very selves. Shakspeare avails himself of every opportunity to effect the great object of the historic drama, that, namely, of familiarizing the people to the great names of their country, and thereby of exciting a steady patriotism, a love of just liberty, and a respect for all those fundamental institutions of social life, which bind men together. . . .

Richard is not meant to be a debauchee; but we see in him that sophistry which is common to man, by which we can deceive our own hearts, and at one and the same time apologize for, and yet commit, the error. Shakspeare has represented this character in a very peculiar manner. He has not made him amiable with counterbalancing faults; but has openly and broadly drawn those faults without reserve, relying on Richard's disproportionate sufferings and gradually emergent good qualities for our sympathy; and this was possible, because his faults are not positive vices, but spring entirely from defect of character. . . .

No doubt, something of Shakspeare's punning must be attributed to his age, in which direct and formal combats of wit were a favourite pastime of the courtly and accomplished. It was an age more favourable, upon the whole, to vigour of intellect than the present, in which a dread of being thought pedantic dispirits and flattens the energies of original minds. But indepen-dently of this, I have no hesitation in saying that a pun, if it be congruous with the feeling of the scene, is not only allowable in the dramatic dialogue, but oftentimes one of the most effectual intensives of passion.

HAZLITT *Richard II* is a play little known compared with *Richard III*, which last is a play that every unfledged candidate for theatrical fame chuses to strut and fret his hour upon the stage in; yet we confess that we prefer the nature and feeling of the one to the noise and bustle of the other; at least, as we are so often forced to see it acted. In *Richard II* the weakness of the king leaves us leisure to take a greater interest in the mis-fortunes of the man. After the first act, in which the arbitrariness of his behaviour only proves his want of resolution, we see him staggering under the unlooked-for blows of fortune, bewailing his loss of kingly power, not pre-venting it, sinking under the aspiring genius of Bolingbroke, his authority trampled on, his hopes failing him, and his pride crushed and broken down under insults and injuries, which his own misconduct had provoked, but which he has not courage or manliness to resent. The change of tone and behaviour in the two competitors for the throne according to their change of fortune, from the capricious sentence of banishment passed by Richard upon Bolingbroke, the suppliant offers and modest pretensions of the latter on his return, to the high and haughty tone with which he accepts Richard's resignation of the crown after the loss of all his power, the use which he makes of the deposed king to grace his triumphal progress through the streets of London, and the final intimation of his wish for his death, which immediately finds a servile executioner, is marked throughout with complete effect and without the slightest appearance of effort. The steps by which Bolingbroke mounts the throne are those by which Richard sinks into the grave. We feel neither respect nor love for the deposed monarch; for he is as wanting in energy as in principle: but we pity him, for he pities himself. His heart is by no means hardened against himself, but bleeds afresh at every new stroke of mischance, and his sensibility, absorbed in his own person, and unused to misfortune, is not only tenderly alive to its own sufferings, but without the fortitude to bear them. He is, however, human in his distresses; for to feel pain, and sorrow, weakness, disappointment, remorse and anguish, is the lot of humanity, and we sympathise with him accordingly. The sufferings of the man make us forget that he ever was a king.

LAMB The reluctant pangs of abdicating royalty in Edward furnished hints which Shakspeare scarce improved in his Richard the Second; and the death scene of Marlowe's king moves pity and terror beyond any scene ancient or modern with which I am acquainted.

Specimens of English Dramatic Poets.

GEORGE SAINTSBURY The whole *ordonnance* and handling of the play, whether we look at plot, character, diction, or versification, speak a period at which the poet has already learned a great deal, but has not learned everything. He has already acquired the full disposition of the chronicle-play after a fashion which nobody but himself had yet shown; but he has not discovered the full secret of diversifying and adorning it. The historic page is translated into a dramatic one with the indefinable mastery— in adjusting to the theatre the 'many actions of many men' at many places and times—which perhaps no other dramatist has ever fully shown. But, to mention nothing else, there is a want of tragi-comic relief: the history, interesting as it is, is still too much of a *mere* history. So, in the second respect, the poet has left his predecessors, and even to some extent himself, far behind in the art of breathing a soul into the figures of the historic tapestry; but he has not yet made it, as he was to make it later, a wholly complete and individual soul. Of the central figure we shall speak anon; but it is almost more important that the accessories, though never mere 'supers', still lack that full Shakespearean individuality 'in the round' of which the poet is so prodigal later. . . . They have, many of them, the rudiments of the great Shakespearean quality of 'setting the principal character going'; but as that character itself is not fully worked out, so their powers are not fully called into action. . . .

The same interesting character of transition is over the diction, in the

wider sense, and the verse. The latter is far advanced beyond the chaos of
the earliest plays, where rhyme and blank verse, 'fourteeners' and sheer
doggerel, lyrical measures and prose, jostle each other as Shakespeare successively and impartially experiments with the imperfect implements of his
predecessors. The blank verse itself has made great strides; it is one of the
most noticeable points of that contrast with Marlowe, to which we shall
come presently, that Shakespeare has improved upon the stately staccato of
the 'dead shepherd' almost as much as Marlowe himself had improved in his
normal passages on the not even stately stump of 'Gorboduc'. But it is still
not perfectly flexible and cursive; it has not completely mastered the secrets
of the pause, and the varied trisyllabic and disyllabic foot, and the consequent
verse paragraph. There is more rhyme than there need be; there is even the
quatrain, which hardly even Dryden, in his first flush of passion for rhyme on
the stage, would have ventured to endorse. And on the other hand, there is
no (or next to no) prose—that remarkable provider of relief, appetite, and
many other good things in the intervals of tragic verse. The longer speeches
still possess something, nay much, of that *tirade* character—that rhetorical
rather than poëtical *ordonnance*—which disappears so marvellously in the
tragedies of the greatest time even where rhetoric was almost excusable.

The diction of the play, from the present point of view, is a subject almost
more interesting, but much more delicate and uncertain. Speaking from many
years' reading, I should say that 'Richard II' is the most *carefully* written of
all Shakespeare's plays. A certain constraint is over almost all of it. . . . There
is nothing of the almost riotous variety and license of the earliest dramas.
There is marked abstinence, as a rule—of course with exceptions—from that
play on words which, as some would have it, was the very breath of Shakespeare's nostrils. The Marlowesque magniloquence appears; but it is almost
always studiously toned, adjusted, clarified. In short, in this, as in other
matters, the poet is between his two periods of freedom, and in one, as it
were, almost of pupilage. He is afraid, perhaps he does not even wish, to 'let
himself go'. He breaks away and soars sometimes, but not very often, in the
direction of sublimity; he scarcely ever breaks away in the other direction of
homeliness. He is, on the lines which he is following, almost 'correct'. And
the worst that can be said of the play is that this approach to correctness
brings with it the inevitable concomitant of a certain loss of colour.

It is probable that this correctness—not less relatively certain because it is
not according to the Three Unities—has done the piece harm with some
critics in the inevitable comparison with Marlowe's 'Edward II'. Shakespeare
has despised, as he always did despise, the illegitimate attractions; and there
is nothing answering to Edward's fatal passion for Gaveston to excuse—if it
can be called excuse—the misdoings of Edward's great-grandson. And
Shakespeare was already discarding, though he had not yet quite discarded,
the *incomprehensibleness* of Marlowe. That mighty but incomplete and far
from universal genius always, as his continuer in the next generation said,
'threw himself headlong into clouds' and abode in them, with the profit as
with the disadvantage of his dwelling-place. Lamb may be right in taking
the pathos of Edward's ghastly and degrading end as greater than that of the

final moment, which becomes Richard better than any passage of his happier life. But the decision is at least open to argument. Lamb, exquisite critic as he was, was always a little liable to the exquisite critics' sin of preferring what the vulgar do not know to what they do, and in his time Marlowe was all but utterly unknown. In almost every other respect 'Richard II' seems to me to have the advantage.

Introduction to Richard II, c. 1900.

A MIDSUMMER NIGHT'S DREAM

WRITTEN   1595–6. Mentioned by Meres, 1598.

PERFORMED   'Sundry times publickely acted' before Q1, 1600.
            1604. 'On New yeares night we had a play of Robin goode-
fellow.' (From a *Letter* of Dudley Carleton to John Chamberlain.)

REGISTERED 1600, Oct. 8th, by Thomas Fisher.

PUBLISHED   1600 Q1. 'As it hath beene sundry times publickely acted, by
            the Right honourable, the Lord Chamberlaine his seruants.
Written by William Shakespeare.' A fairly good text, possibly printed from Shakespeare's MS.
1619 Q2. Dated 1600. One of the ten plays published by Jaggard in 1619, many of them with false dates. Set up from Q1.
1623 F1. Set up from Q2, but with a few additional stage directions.

SOURCES   The fantasy is essentially Shakespeare's, but the following books
            may have furnished hints:
Theseus and Hippolyta: Plutarch's *Life of Theseus,* and Chaucer's *Knight's Tale.*
Pyramus and Thisbe and the name 'Titania': Ovid's *Metamorphoses.*
Robin Goodfellow: Scot's *Discovery of Witchcraft.*
Oberon: Greene's *James IV.*
    It is probable that *A Midsummer Night's Dream* was written for a wedding entertainment and converted into a play for the public stage by some altera-tions to the last act.
    In 1692 Betterton produced *The Fairy Queen* at Dorset Garden Theatre, an adaptation of the Fairy and Clown elements of *A Midsummer Night's Dream* with music by Purcell, dancing, and elaborate spectacle. Garrick adapted it, and so did Frederic Reynolds in 1816.

JOHN SPENCER Forasmuch as this Courte hath beene informed, by Mr
            Comisary general, of a great misdemenor committed in the
house of the right honorable Lo. Bishopp of Lincolne, by entertaining into his house divers Knights and Ladyes, with many other householders servants, uppon the 27th Septembris (1631), being the Saboth day, to see a playe or

tragidie there acted; which began aboute tenn of the clocke at night, and ended about two or three of the clocke in the morning:

Wee do therefore order, and decree, that the Rt honorable John, Lord Bishopp of Lincolne, shall, for his offence, erect a free Schoole in Eaton, or else at Greate Staughton, and endowe the same with 20¹ per ann. for the maintenance of the schoolmaster for ever. . . .

Likewis wee doe order that Mr Wilson, because hee was a speciall plotter and contriver of this business, and did in such a brutishe manner acte the same with an Asses head (The playe, *M. Nights Dr*¹); and therefore hee shall, upon Tuisday next, from 6 of the clocke in the morning till six of the clocke at night, sitt in the Porters Lodge at my Lords Bishopps House, with his feete in the stocks, and attyred with his asse head, and a bottle of hay sett before him, and this subscription on his breast:

> Good people I have played the beast,
>   And brought ill things to passe:
> I was a man, but thus have made
>   My selfe a silly Asse.

A Copie of the Order or Decree (ex officio Comisarii generalis).

PEPYS To the King's Theatre, where we saw 'Midsummer's Night's Dream', which I had never seen before, nor shall ever again, for it is the most insipid, ridiculous play that ever I saw in my life.
Diary, 29th Sept. 1662.

JOHNSON Wild and fantastical as this play is, all the parts, in their various modes, are well written, and give the kind of pleasure which the author designed. Fairies in his time were much in fashion; common tradition had made them familiar, and Spenser's poem had made them great.

COLERIDGE Helena's speech:

> I will go tell him of fair Hermia's flight, &c.

I am convinced that Shakespeare availed himself of the title of this play in his own mind, and worked upon it as a dream throughout, but especially, and, perhaps, unpleasingly, in this broad determination of ungrateful treachery in Helena, so undisguisedly avowed to herself, and this, too, after the witty cool philosophizing that precedes. The act itself is natural, and the resolve so to act is, I fear, likewise too true a picture of the lax hold which principles have on a woman's heart, when opposed to, or even separated from, passion and inclination. . . . Still, however, just in itself, the representation of this is not poetical; we shrink from it, and cannot harmonize it with the ideal.

HAZLITT It is astonishing that Shakespear should be considered, not only by foreigners, but by many of our own critics, as a gloomy and heavy

---

¹ These words are written in the margin, in another hand.

writer, who painted nothing but 'gorgons and hydras, and chimeras dire'. His subtlety exceeds that of all other dramatic writers, insomuch that a celebrated person of the present day said that he regarded him rather as a metaphysician than a poet. His delicacy and sportive gaiety are infinite. In the *Midsummer Night's Dream* alone, we should imagine, there is more sweetness and beauty of description than in the whole range of French poetry put together. What we mean is this, that we will produce out of that single play ten passages, to which we do not think any ten passages in the works of the French poets can be opposed, displaying equal fancy and imagery. . . .

It has been suggested to us, that the *Midsummer Night's Dream* would do admirably to get up as a Christmas after-piece; and our prompter proposed that Mr. Kean should play the part of Bottom, as worthy of his great talents. . . .

Alas the experiment has been tried, and has failed; not through the fault of Mr. Kean, who did not play the part of Bottom, nor of Mr. Liston, who did, and who played it well, but from the nature of things. The *Midsummer Night's Dream*, when acted, is converted from a delightful fiction into a dull pantomime. The spectacle was grand; but the spirit was evaporated, the genius was fled.—Poetry and the stage do not agree well together. The attempt to reconcile them in this instance fails not only of effect, but of decorum. The *ideal* can have no place upon the stage, which is a picture without perspective; everything there is in the foreground. That which was merely an airy shape, a dream a passing thought, immediately becomes an unmanageable reality. Where all is left to the imagination (as in the case of reading) every circumstance, near or remote, has an equal chance of being kept in mind, and tells according to the mixed impression of all that has been suggested. But the imagination cannot sufficiently qualify the actual impressions of the senses. Any offence given to the eye is not to be got rid of by explanation. Thus Bottom's head in the play is a fantastic illusion, produced by magic spells: on the stage it is an ass's head, and nothing more; certainly a very strange costume for a gentleman to appear in. Fancy cannot be embodied any more than a simile can be painted; and it is as idle to attempt it as to personate *Wall* or *Moonshine*. Fairies are not incredible, but fairies six feet high are so. Monsters are not shocking, if they are seen at a proper distance. When ghosts appear at mid-day, when apparitions stalk along Cheapside, then may the *Midsummer Night's Dream* be represented without injury at Covent Garden or at Drury Lane. The boards of a theatre and the regions of fancy are not the same thing.

BENEDETTO CROCE The quintessence of all these comedies (as we may say of *Hamlet* in respect of the great tragedies) is the *Midsummer Night's Dream*. Here the quick ardours, the inconstancies, the caprices, the illusions, the delusions, every sort of love folly, become embodied and weave a world of their own, as living and as real as that of those who are visited by these affections, tormented or rendered ecstatic, raised on high or hurled downward by them, in such a way that everything is equally real or equally fantastic, as you may please to call it. The sense of dream, of a dream-reality persists and prevents our feeling the chilly sense of allegory or of apology. The little drama seems born of a smile, so delicate, refined and ethereal it is. Graceful and delicate to a degree is also the setting of the dream the celebration of the wedding of Theseus and Hippolyta and the theatrical performance of the artisans, for these are not merely ridiculous in their clumsiness, they are also childlike and ingenuous, arousing a sort of gay pity: we do not laugh at them: we smile. Oberon and Titania are at variance owing to reciprocal wrongs, and trouble has arisen in the world. Puck obeys the command of Oberon and sets to work, teasing, punishing and correcting. But in performing this duty of punishing and correcting, he too makes mistakes, and the love intrigue becomes more complicated and active. Here we find a resemblance to the rapid passage into opposite states and the strange complications that arose in Italian knightly romances, as the result of drinking the water from one of two opposite fountains whereof one filled the heart with amorous desires, the other turned first ardours to ice.

Ariosto, Shakespeare, and Corneille (trans. Douglas Ainslie), 1920.

KING JOHN

WRITTEN   1596–7. Mentioned by Meres, 1598.

PERFORMED   First recorded performance 1737.

REGISTERED   No entry. On Nov. 8th 1623 Blount and Jaggard entered for their copy of all Shakespeare's plays that had not previously been published as Quartos, except *King John* and *The Taming of the Shrew*, possibly because they passed as reprints of the older plays *The Troublesome Reign* and *The Taming of A Shrew*.

PUBLISHED   1623 F1. A fairly good text.

SOURCES   *The Troublesome Raigne of Iohn King of England, with the discouerie of King Richard Cordelions Base sonne (vulgarly named, The Bastard Fawconbridge): also the death of King Iohn at Swinstead Abbey*, 1591.
The Second part of the troublesome Raigne of King Iohn, conteining the death of Arthur Plantaginet, the landing of Lewes, and the poysning of King Iohn at Swinstead Abbey, 1591.
In 1611 the two parts were printed together as being 'Written by W. Sh.'; in 1622 they were reprinted and openly ascribed to 'W. Shakespeare'.
The author of *The Troublesome Reign* is unknown, but may have been Shakespeare himself. He follows the action of the old play fairly closely, but entirely rewrites it.
    King John was revived by Rich in 1737, and Colley Cibber adapted it as *Papal Tyranny* at the time of the '45 Rebellion.

Johnson The tragedy of King John, though not written with the utmost
power of Shakespeare, is varied with a very pleasing interchange of
incidents and characters. The lady's grief is very affecting, and the character
of the Bastard contains that mixture of greatness and levity which this author
delighted to exhibit.

Hazlitt *King John* is the last of the historical plays we shall have to speak
of; and we are not sorry that it is. If we are to indulge our imaginations, we had rather do it upon an imaginary theme; if we are to find subjects
for the exercise of our pity and terror, we prefer seeking them in fictitious
danger and fictitious distress. It gives a *soreness* to our feelings of indignation
or sympathy, when we know that in tracing the progress of sufferings and
crimes, we are treading upon real ground, and recollect that the poet's dream
'*denoted a foregone conclusion*'—irrevocable ills, not conjured up by fancy, but
placed beyond the reach of poetical justice. That the treachery of King John,
the death of Arthur, the grief of Constance, had a real truth in history,
sharpens the sense of pain, while it hangs a leaden weight on the heart and the
imagination. Something whispers us that we have no right to make a mock
of calamities like these, or to turn the truth of things into the puppet and
plaything of our fancies. 'To consider thus' may be 'to consider too curiously';
but still we think that the actual truth of the particular events, in proportion
as we are conscious of it, is a drawback on the pleasure as well as the dignity
of tragedy. . . .

This, like the other plays taken from English history, is written in a remarkably smooth and flowing style, very different from some of the tragedies.
Macbeth for instance. The passages consist of a series of single lines, not
running into one another. This peculiarity in the versification, which is most
common in the three parts of *Henry VI*, has been assigned as a reason why
those plays were not written by Shakespear. But the same structure of verse
occurs in his other undoubted plays, as in *Richard II* and in *King John*.

Richard Garnett This mailed tragedy stands to Shakespeare's other plays
of English history in the relation of a prologue, not
merely as first in order of period, but as depicting a rudimentary condition
of English society. It is Shakespeare's one purely mediæval play, for by
Henry IV's time a modern element has come in, and Richard II is rather a
study of character than a delineation of contemporary manners. 'King John',
on the other hand, gives 'the very form and pressure of the time'. It is therefore distinguished by the overwhelming force of the passions represented, and
also by their simplicity. Every leading character has a single object, which
he pursues with no more deviation than the stress of circumstances demands.
John would save his crown and Faulconbridge his country; Constance would
vindicate her son's rights and Pandulph would subjugate England to the
Pope. There is no complication of motives, no hesitation or qualification;
passion is primitive, simple, and Titanic. The language is consequently high
pitched throughout, but without exaggeration. Everything is on the grand

scale, as it ought to be when the interlocutors are kings, queens, princesses, nobles, and cardinals, and there is hardly a person of humble birth or low calling in the piece.

Introduction to King John, c. 1900.

LILY B. CAMPBELL What I hope to show is that just as there is in the Shake-pearean tragedies a dominant ethical pattern of passion opposed to reason, so there is in the history plays a dominant political pattern characteristic of the political philosophy of his age. . . .

The play [*King John*] is concerned, not with mirroring the whole conflict of Elizabeth and the Catholic church, but with reflecting that part of the conflict which centred about Mary [Queen of Scots]. Therefore Shakespeare weaves together the troubles of King John with Arthur and his troubles with the church and his troubles with the rebel nobles in support of a foreign power in the pattern familiar to his contemporaries, slighting other aspects of the long contest.

Events crowd the stage in the last scenes to hurry the play to its end. The armado intended to supply the French is wrecked, even as was the Spanish Armada, the nobles are returned to their allegiance by the warning of Melun, rule passes to Prince Henry as John dies, poisoned. Peace is once more in sight as Faulconbridge utters the famous words . . .

> This England never did, nor never shall,
> Lie at the proud foot of a conqueror,
> But when it first did help to wound itself.
> Now these her princes are come home again,
> Come the three corners of the world in arms,
> And we shall shock them. Nought shall make us rue,
> If England to itself do rest but true.

It is fitting that Faulconbridge should thus sum up the significance of the play, for it is he who acts as chorus to the play. Many students, bothered by the unheroic hero, have, like Professor Dover Wilson, tried to set up Faulcon-bridge as hero. With admirable consistency some of the same critics would make Falstaff the hero of the Henry IV plays. It is true that Faulconbridge is, like Falstaff, generally considered the most interesting character of the play, and that, unlike Falstaff, he is certainly the most heroic. But *King John* with Faulconbridge as hero is a play without form and void, signifying nothing. He is outside the structure of the play as he is outside it historically. He avenges his father's death. He acts as a foil to the king in his more unkingly moments. He loots the monasteries—off stage. But he is remembered chiefly because, as chorus, he says some of the most admirable things in the play. It should be noted, however, that his comments are in the nature of political comments. Our familiar quotations from the play are from his words of political wisdom on the nature of political opportunism and treachery, on the political significance of Arthur's death, on the true secret of England's weak-ness and strength. In the plot he is only important as was the vice in the old moralities, in pricking others on to action.

The truth of the matter is that the history play was not often privileged to reflect a hero in its mirror, for that was not the mission of the history play. That Shakespeare was able to depict King John in his conflict with the church as speaking his eloquent defiance of the pope and the foreign priest without making him the great Christian warrior reflects the greatness of Shakespeare and of his understanding of the genre in which he was writing.

Shakespeare's 'Histories': Mirrors of Elizabethan Policy, 1947.

THE MERCHANT OF VENICE

WRITTEN   1596–7. Mentioned by Meres, 1598.

PERFORMED   It had 'beene diuers times acted by the Lord Chamberlaine his Seruants' before Q1, 1600.

1605. According to the Revels Account it was twice performed at Court (Whitehall) by 'His Maiesties plaiers': 'on Shrousunday', and 'On Shroutus-day A play Cauled the Martchant of Venis Againe Commanded By the Kings Maiestie', by 'Shaxberd'.

REGISTERED   1598. July 22 'James Robertes. Entred for his copie . . . a booke of the Marchaunt of Venyce. . . . Prouided, that yt bee not prynted by the said James Robertes or anye other whatsoeuer without lycence first had from the Right honorable the lord Chamberlen.'

1600 '28 Octobris. Thomas Haies . . . by Consent of master Robertes. A booke called the booke of the merchant of Venyce.'

PUBLISHED   1600 Q1. 'The most excellent Historie of the Merchant of Venice. With the extreame cruelty of Shylocke the Iewe towards the sayd Merchant, in cutting a iust pound of his flesh: and the obtayning of Portia by the choyse of three chests. As it hath beene diuers times acted by the Lord Chamberlaine his Seruants. Written by William Shakespeare.' Q1 is a 'good' Quarto, probably printed from Shakespeare's MS. 1619 Q2. One of the ten plays issued by William Jaggard, some of them with false dates. This Q is dated 1600. Set up from Q1.

1623 F1. Set up from Q1.

SOURCES   The Bond theme came from *Il Pecorone* (The Simpleton), by Ser Giovanni Fiorentino; the Casket theme from the 66th story of Richard Robinson's version of the *Gesta Romanorum*. Shakespeare may have worked from an earlier play, *The Jew*, which has been lost, and apparently combined the two themes. There are some parallels to Marlowe's *Jew of Malta*. The Jew, Roderigo Lopez, was executed in 1594 for the attempted poisoning of Queen Elizabeth and Don Antonio of Portugal.

In 1701 George Granville adapted the *Merchant of Venice* in his *Jew of Venice* which included a masque, Shylock being acted by the comedian Dogget. Macklin and Garrick restored much of Shakespeare and treated Shylock more seriously.

NICHOLAS ROWE To these I might add, that incomparable Character of
Shylock the *Jew*, in the *Merchant of* Venice; but tho' we
have seen that Play Receiv'd and Acted as a Comedy, and the part of the
Jew perform'd by an Excellent Comedian, yet I cannot but think it was
design'd Tragically by the Author. There appears in it such a deadly Spirit
of Revenge, such a savage Fierceness and Fellness, and such a bloody designa-
tion of Cruelty and Mischief, as cannot agree either with the Stile or Characters of Comedy. The Play it self, take it all together, seems to me to be
one of the most finish'd of any of Shakespear's. The Tale indeed, in that
Part relating to the Caskets, and the extravagant and unusual kind of Bond
given by *Antonio*, is a little too much remov'd from the Rules of Probability:
But taking the Fact for granted, we must allow it to be very beautifully
written. There is something in the Friendship of *Antonio* to *Bassanio* very
Great, Generous and Tender. The whole fourth Act, supposing, as I said,
the Fact to be probable, is extremely Fine. But there are two Passages that
deserve a particular Notice. The first is, what *Portia* says in praise of Mercy,
and the other on the Power of Musick.

Preface to Shakespeare, 1709.

JOHNSON Of The Merchant of Venice the style is even and easy, with few
peculiarities of diction, or anomalies of construction. The comick
part raises laughter, and the serious fixes expectation. The probability of
either one or the other story cannot be maintained. The union of the two
actions in one event is, in this drama, eminently happy.

HAZLITT This is a play that in spite of the change of manners and prejudices
still holds undisputed possession of the stage. Shakespear's malignant has outlived Mr. Cumberland's benevolent Jew. In proportion as
Shylock has ceased to be a popular bugbear, 'baited with the rabble's curse',
he becomes a half-favourite with the philosophical part of the audience, who
are disposed to think that Jewish revenge is at least as good as Christian
injuries. Shylock is *a good hater*; 'a man no less sinned against than sinning'.
If he carries his revenge too far, yet he has strong grounds for 'the lodged
hate he bears Anthonio', which he explains with equal force of eloquence
and reason. . . .
Portia is not a very great favourite with us; neither are we in love with her
maid, Nerissa. Portia has a certain degree of affectation and pedantry about
her, which is very unusual in Shakespeare's women, but which perhaps was
a proper qualification for the office of a 'civil doctor', which she undertakes
and executes so successfully. The speech about Mercy is very well; but there
are a thousand finer ones in Shakespear. We do not admire the scene of the
caskets: and object entirely to the Black Prince, Morocchius. We should
like Jessica better if she had not deceived and robbed her father, and Lorenzo,
if he had not married a Jewess, though he thinks he has a right to wrong a
Jew. . . .
When we first went to see Mr. Kean in Shylock, we expected to see, what
we had been used to see, a decrepit old man, bent with age and ugly with

mental deformity, grinning with deadly malice, with the venom of his heart congealed in the expression of his countenance, sullen, morose, gloomy, inflexible, brooding over one idea, that of his hatred, and fixed on one unalterable purpose, that of his revenge. We were disappointed, because we had taken our idea from other actors, not from the play. There is no proof there that Shylock is old, but a single line, 'Anthonio and *old* Shylock, both stand forth,'—which does not imply that he is infirm with age—and the circumstance that he has a daughter marriageable, which does not imply that he is old at all. It would be too much to say that his body should be made crooked and deformed to answer to his mind which is bowed down and warped with prejudices and passion. That he has but one idea, is not true; he has more ideas than any other person in the piece; and if he is intense and inveterate in the pursuit of his purpose, he shews the utmost elasticity, vigour, and presence of mind, in the means of attaining it. But so rooted was our habitual impression of the part from seeing it caricatured in the representation, that it was only from a careful perusal of the play itself that we saw our error. The stage is not in general the best place to study our author's characters in. It is too often filled with traditional commonplace conceptions of the part, handed down from sire to son, and suited to the taste of *the great vulgar and the small.*—"Tis an unweeded garden: things rank and gross do merely gender in it!' If a man of genius comes once in an age to clear away the rubbish, to make it fruitful and wholesome, they cry, "Tis a bad school: it may be like nature, it may be like Shakespear, but it is not like us.' Admirable critics!

HEINE When I saw a performance of this play at Drury Lane, a beautiful pale-faced English woman stood behind me in the box and wept profusely at the end of the fourth act, and called out repeatedly: 'The poor man is wronged.' Her face was of the noblest Greek cast, and her eyes were big and dark. I have never been able to forget those big dark eyes weeping for Shylock.

But thinking of those tears I must count *The Merchant of Venice* among the tragedies, although the framework of the play is ornamented with the gayest masks, satires and love episodes, and the author's real intention was to write a comedy. Perhaps Shakespeare had in mind to create, for the entertainment of the masses, a trained werewolf, a loathsome fabulous monster thirsting for blood, and thereby losing his daughter and his ducats, and becoming a laughing stock. But the genius of the poet, the universal spirit which inspires him is always above his individual will, and so it happened that he expressed in Shylock, in spite of all his glaring grotesqueness, the vindication of an ill-fortuned sect, whom Providence for mysterious reasons has made the butt of the hatred of high and low, and who have not always shown loving kindness in return.

But what am I saying? The genius of Shakespeare rises above the petty jealousies of two religious factions, and his drama shows us really neither Jew nor Christian, but oppressor and oppressed, and the savage rejoicing of the latter when he can pay back with interest the suffered injuries to his callous tormentor. There is not the slightest trace of religious differences in this play: in Shylock Shakespeare merely represents a man whom Nature compels to hate his enemy, and in Antonio and his friends he portrays by no means the disciples of that divine teaching which tells us to love our enemies. . . . In fact, Shakespeare would have written a satire on Christianity if he intended it to be represented by those characters who are hostile to Shylock, and yet are hardly worthy of unlacing his shoes. The bankrupt Antonio is a weakling without energy, without strong hates and also without strong likes, a dull worm's-heart, whose flesh is really not fit for anything but to bait fish withal. Besides he never returns the borrowed three thousand ducats to the duped Jew. Nor does Bassanio refund his money, and he is a true fortune-hunter, as one English critic calls him; he borrows money to buy fine clothes and entice a wife with a fat dowry. . . .

As for Lorenzo, he is the accomplice of one of the most infamous burglaries, and according to Prussian criminal law he would be pilloried and sentenced to fifteen years hard labour; although he is not only the receiver of stolen ducats and jewels, but also receptive to beauty, to moonlit landscapes and music. As for the other Venetians who appear as Antonio's companions, they do not seem to abhor money either, and when their own friend is in distress they have nothing but words, coined air, for him. . . . However much we must hate Shylock, we cannot blame even him if he despises those people a little.

Shakespeares Mädchen und Frauen, 1839.

LOGAN PEARSALL SMITH *The Merchant of Venice* is not for many lovers of Shakespeare one of their favourite plays. Its theatricality and stage-effectiveness puts a cheat upon them which they afterwards resent. But the other day, when I happened to look into it—'The moon shines bright'—these first words of the last Act put a kind of magic on me:

> In such a night as this,
> When the sweet wind did gently kiss the trees
> And they did make no noise,—
> > In such a night
> Stood Dido with a willow in her hand
> Upon the wild sea banks, and waft her love
> To come again to Carthage,—

when Lorenzo and Jessica were out-nighting each other in such a night as this, what could I do but revel in the moonlight and enchanted echoes of this scene?

> Sit, Jessica: look, how the floor of heaven
> Is thick inlaid with patines of bright gold:
> There's not the smallest orb which thou behold'st
> But in his motion like an angel sings,
> Still quiring to the young-eyed cherubins;
> Such harmony is in immortal souls;
> But, whilst this muddy vesture of decay
> Doth grossly close it in, we cannot hear it.

Poetry was given to man, Goethe said, to make him satisfied with himself and with his lot. Certainly for me poetry, either in verse or prose, exquisitely performs this function. I may be old and cross and ill, a wasted life may lie behind me, and the grave yawn close in front. I may have lost my faith, my illusion, my teeth, my reputation and umbrella. What does it matter? It doesn't matter in the least! Reading Lorenzo's words,

> Come, ho! and wake Diana with a hymn!

off I go into the enchanted forest, into the Age of Gold. Life ceases to be brief, sad, enigmatic; I am perfectly satisfied with it. What more is there indeed to ask for? I taste a joy beyond the reach of fate; *le bonheur, l'impossible bonheur*, is mine. I am (to express myself in sober terms) simply kidnapped into heaven. I sit with the Gods and quaff their nectar; quaff indeed a nectar more generous than their own, since I, alone of the immortals, taste the aroma of this aromatic floating, orchard plot of earth, which, could they but sip its fragrance, how gladly would the Gods descend from their golden chairs, take upon themselves the burden of earthly sin, and provoke another Flood! Even that 'fading mansion', my aching, coughing body, becomes a vehicle and instrument of music, and like a battered old violin, shivers and vibrates with tunable delight. 'Therefore the poet', as Lorenzo went on to tell Jessica,

> 'Did feign that Orpheus drew trees, stones, and flood;
> Since naught so stockish, hard, and full of rage,
> But music for the time doth change his nature.'

If ever again I am so stockish or full of rage as to deny the genius of Shakespeare, the music of this scene will, in the magical five minutes it takes to read it through, charm me back from my backsliding.

On Reading Shakespeare, 1933.

HENRY THE FOURTH, PART I

WRITTEN   1597–8. Meres mentions 'Henry the 4', 1598.

PERFORMED   1600 March 6th. The Lord Chamberlain entertained an Ambassador with the play *Sir John Old Castell*.

1613. Both *Sir John Falstaffe* and *The Hotspur* were acted at 'The Magnificent Marriage of Frederick Count Palatine and the Lady Elizabeth'.

1625. The *First Part of Sir John Falstaff* at Whitehall.

1638. 'At the Cocpit the 29th of May the princes berthnyght—ould Castel.

REGISTERED   1598 Feb. 25th. by Andrew Wise; transferred to Matthew Law in 1603.

PUBLISHED   1598 Q1. 'The History of Henrie the Fourth; With the battell at Shrewsburie, betweene the King and Lord Henry Percy, surnamed Henrie Hotspur of the North. With the humorous conceits of Sir

Iohn Falstaffe.' Q 1 is the authoritative text, later Quartos being set up from
their immediate predecessors.

1599 Q 2. 'Newly corrected by W. Shake-speare.'

1604 Q 3; 1608 Q 4; 1613 Q 5; 1622 Q 6; 1632 Q 7; 1639 Q 8.

1623 F 1. Set up from Q 5.

HENRY THE FOURTH, PART II

WRITTEN   1597–8. Meres mentions 'Henry the 4', 1598.

PERFORMED   'Sundrie times publikely acted' before Q, 1600.
            1619. At Court?

REGISTERED 1600 Aug. 23rd. by Andrew Wise and William Aspley.

PUBLISHED   1600 Q. 'The Second Part of Henrie the fourth, continuing
            to his death, and coronation of Henrie the fift. With the
humours of sir Iohn Falstaffe, and swaggering Pistoll. As it hath been sundrie
times publikely acted by the right honourable, the Lord Chamberlaine his
seruants. Written by William Shakespeare.' Probably set up from a MS used
as a prompt-copy.

1623 F 1. Contains 168 lines omitted from Q, but leaves out 40 lines of Q.
Probably set up from a theatrical MS, possibly that used for Q which had
been modified.

SOURCES   Holinshed's *Chronicle* for the historical theme. *The Famous
            Victories of Henry the Fifth*, an anonymous play, gave hints for
the comic scenes.

In the play as Shakespeare originally wrote it Sir John Falstaff must have
been called Sir John Oldcastle. This is apparent from the play on the word
in Part I (I. ii), where Falstaff is called 'my old lad of the castle', and from the
unmetrical line 'Away, good Ned, Falstaff sweats to death'. Shakespeare
probably took the name from the anonymous play *The Famous Victories of
Henry the Fifth*, and then in deference to the Lords Cobham, who were
descendants of Oldcastle and prominent at Court, changed it to Falstaff
before publication. He chose the new name for two reasons: Falstaff like
Oldcastle was 'Sir John' and this would necessitate fewer alterations; and Sir
John Fastolfe in 1 *Henry VI* had a kind of alacrity in running away. Unfortunately for Shakespeare the real Sir John Fastolfe was no more a coward
than Sir John Oldcastle, and the substitution led to new protests.

LEONARD DIGGES

> Yet these sometimes, even at a friend's desire
> Acted, have scarce defraied the Seacoale fire,
> And doore-keepers: when let but *Falstaffe* come,
> *Hall, Poines*, the rest you scarce shall have a roome
> All is so pester'd.
>   *Commendatory Verses to Shakespeare's Poems*, 1604.

RICHARD JAMES A young Gentle Lady of your acquaintance, having read
ye works of Shakespeare, made me this question. How Sr
John Falstaffe, or Fastolf, as he is written in ye Statute Book of Maudlin
Colledge in Oxford, where everye day that society were bound to make
memorie of his soul, could be dead in ye time of Harrie ye Fift and again
live in ye time of Harrie ye Sixt to be banished for cowardice: Whereto I
made answear that it was one of those humours and mistakes for which Plato
banisht all poets out of his commonwealth. That Sr John Falstaffe was in
those times a noble valiaunt souldier, as apeeres by a book in ye Heralds
Office dedicated unto him by a Herald who had binne with him, if I well
remember, for the space of 25 yeeres in ye French wars; that he seems also
to have binne a man of learning, because, in a Library of Oxford, I find a
book of dedicating Churches sent from him for a present unto Bishop Wain-
flete, and inscribed with his own hand. That in Shakespeares first shew of
Harrie the fift, the person with which he undertook to playe a buffone was
not Falstaffe, but Sir Jhon Oldcastle, and that offence beinge worthily taken
by Personages descended from his title (as peradventure by many others allso
whoe ought to have him in honourable memorie) the poet was putt to make
an ignorant shifte of abusing Sir Jhon Falstophe, a man not inferior of Vertue,
though not so famous in pietie as the other, who gave witnesse unto the
truth of our reformation with a constant and resolute Martyrdom, unto
which he was pursued by the Priests, Bishops, Moncks, and Friers of those
days.

Epistle to Sir Harry Bourchier, c. 1625.

THOMAS FULLER John Fastolfe Knight—the *Stage* hath been overbold with
his memory, making him a *Thrasonical Puff*, & emblem of
Mock-valour.

True it is, *Sir John Oldcastle* did first bear the brunt of the one, being
made the *make-sport* in all plays for a *coward*. It is easily known out of what
purse this black *peny* came. The *Papists* railed on him for a *Heretick*, and
therefore he must also be a *coward*, though indeed he was a *man* of *arms*,
every inch of him, and as valiant as any of his age.

Now as I am glad that *Sir John Oldcastle* is *put out*, so I am sorry that
Sir John Fastolfe is *put in*, to relieve his memory in this base service, to be
the *anvil* for every *dull wit* to strike upon. Nor is our Comedian excusable,
by some alteration of his name, writing him *Sir John Falstafe* (and making
him the *property* of *pleasure* for King *Henry* the fifth, to abuse) seeing the
vicinity of sounds intrench on the memory of *that worthy Knight*, and few
do heed the *inconsiderable difference* in spelling of their name.

Worthies of England, 1662.

PEPYS In Paul's Church-yard I bought the play of Henry the Forth, and
so went to the new Theatre [Killigrew's] and saw it acted; but my
expectation being too great, it did not please me, as otherwise I believe it
would; and my having a book, I believe did spoil it a little. (31 *Dec.* 1660.)

From thence to the Theatre, and saw Harry the 4th, a good play. (4 *June* 1661.)

To the King's playhouse, and there saw 'Henry the Fourth': and, contrary to expectation, was pleased in nothing more than in Cartwright's speaking of Falstaffe's speech about 'What is Honour?' ... It was observable how a gentleman of good habit sitting just before us, eating of some fruit in the midst of the play, did drop as dead, being choked; but with much ado Orange Moll did thrust her finger down his throat, and brought him to life again. (2 *Nov.* 1667.)

So I to the other two playhouses into the pit, to gaze up and down, and there did by this means, for nothing, see an act in 'The Schoole of Compliments' at the Duke of York's house, and 'Henry the Fourth' at the King's house; but, not liking either of the plays, I took my coach again, and home. (7 *Jan.* 1668.)

To the King's house, and saw a piece of 'Henry the Fourth'. (18 *Sept.* 1668.)

DRYDEN As for Falstaff, he is not properly one humour, but a miscellany of humours or images, drawn from so many several men: that wherein he is singular is his wit, or those things he says *præter expectatum*, unexpected by the audience; his quick evasions, when you imagine him surprised, which, as they are extremely diverting of themselves, so receive a great addition from his person; for the very sight of such an unwieldy old debauched fellow is a comedy alone.

An Essay of Dramatic Poesy, 1668.

JOHNSON None of Shakespeare's plays are more read than the first and second parts of Henry IV. Perhaps no author has ever in two plays afforded so much delight. The great events are interesting, for the fate of kingdoms depends upon them; the slighter occurrences are diverting, and, except one or two, sufficiently probable; the incidents are multiplied with wonderful fertility of invention, and the characters diversified with the utmost nicety of discernment, and the profoundest skill in the nature of man.

The prince, who is the hero both of the comick and tragick part, is a young man of great abilities and violent passions, whose sentiments are right, though his actions are wrong; whose virtues are obscured by negligence, and whose understanding is dissipated by levity. In his idle hours he is rather loose than wicked; and when the occasion forces out his latent qualities, he is great without effort, and brave without tumult. The trifler is roused into a hero, and the hero again reposes in the trifler. The character is great, original and just.

Percy is a rugged soldier, cholerick and quarrelsome, and has only the soldier's virtues, generosity and courage.

But Falstaff, unimitated, unimitable Falstaff, how shall I describe thee! thou compound of sense and vice; of sense which may be admired, but not esteemed; of vice which may be despised, but hardly detested. Falstaff is a character loaded with faults, and with those faults which naturally produce contempt. He is a thief and a glutton, a coward and a boaster, always ready to cheat the weak, and prey upon the poor; to terrify the timorous, and insult the defenceless. At once obsequious and malignant, he satirizes in their absence those whom he lives by flattering. He is familiar with the prince only as an agent of vice, but of this familiarity he is so proud, as not only to be supercilious and haughty with common men, but to think his interest of importance to the duke of Lancaster. Yet the man thus corrupt, thus despicable, makes himself necessary to the prince that despises him, by the most pleasing of all qualities, perpetual gaiety, by an unfailing power of exciting laughter, which is the more freely indulged, as his wit is not of the splendid or ambitious kind, but consists in easy scapes and sallies of levity, which make sport, but raise no envy. It must be observed, that he is stained with no enormous or sanguinary crimes, so that his licentiousness is not so offensive but that it may be borne for his mirth.

The moral to be drawn from this representation is, that no man is more dangerous than he that, with a will to corrupt, hath the power to please; and that neither wit nor honesty ought to think themselves safe with such a companion, when they see Henry seduced by Falstaff.

MAURICE MORGANN Tho' I have considered *Falstaff's* character as relative only to one single quality, yet so much has been said, that it cannot escape the reader's notice that he is a character made up by *Shakespeare* wholly of incongruities;—a man at once young and old, enterprizing and fat, a dupe and a wit, harmless and wicked, weak in principle and resolute by constitution, cowardly in appearance and brave in reality; a knave without malice, a liar without deceit; and a knight, a gentleman, and a soldier, without either dignity, decency, or honour: This is a character, which, though it may be decompounded, could not, I believe, have been formed, nor the ingredients of it duly mingled upon any receipt whatever: It required the hand of *Shakespeare* himself to give to every particular part a relish of the whole, and of the whole to every particular part;—alike the same incongruous, identical *Falstaff*, whether to the grave Chief Justice he vainly talks of his youth, and offers to *caper for a thousand*; or cries to Mrs. Doll, '*I am old, I am old*', though she is seated on his lap, and he is courting her for busses. How *Shakespeare* could furnish out sentiment of so extraordinary a composition, and supply it with such appropriated and characteristic language, humour and wit, I cannot tell; but I may, however, venture to infer, and that confidently, that he who so well understood the uses of incongruity, and that laughter was to be raised by the opposition of qualities in the same man, and not by their agreement or conformity, would never have attempted to raise mirth by showing us Cowardice in a Coward unattended by Pretence, and softened by every excuse of age, corpulence, and infirmity: And of this we cannot have a more striking proof than his furnishing this very character, on one instance of real terror, however excusable, with boast, braggadocio, and pretence, exceeding that of all other stage Cowards the whole length of his superior wit, humour, and invention.

On the Dramatic Character of Sir John Falstaff, 1777.

HAZLITT If Shakespear's fondness for the ludicrous sometimes led to faults in his tragedies (which was not often the case) he has made us amends by the character of Falstaff. This is perhaps the most substantial comic character that ever was invented. Sir John carries a most portly presence in the mind's eye; and in him, not to speak it profanely, 'we behold the fulness of the spirit of wit and humour bodily.' We are as well acquainted with his person as his mind, and his jokes come upon us with double force and relish from the quantity of flesh through which they make their way, as he shakes his fat sides with laughter, or 'lards the lean earth as he walks along'. Other comic characters seem, if we approach and handle them, to resolve themselves into air, 'into thin air'; but this is embodied and palpable to the grossest apprehension: it lies 'three fingers deep upon the ribs', it plays about the lungs and the diaphragm with all the force of animal enjoyment. His body is like a good estate to his mind, from which he receives rents and revenues of profit and pleasure in kind, according to its extent, and the richness of the soil. Wit is often a meagre substitute for pleasurable sensation; an effusion of spleen and petty spite at the comforts of others, from feeling none in itself. Falstaff's wit is an emanation of a fine constitution; an exuberance of good-humour and good-nature; an overflowing of his love of laughter and good-fellowship; a giving vent to his heart's ease, and over-contentment with himself and others. He would not be in character, if he were not so fat as he is; for there is greatest keeping in the boundless luxury of his imagination and the pampered self-indulgence of his physical appetites. He manures and nourishes his mind with jests, as he does his body with sack and sugar. He carves out his jokes, as he would a capon or a haunch of venison, where there is *cut and come again*; and pours out upon them the oil of gladness. His tongue drops fatness, and in the chambers of his brain 'it snows of meat and drink'. He keeps up perpetual holiday and open house, and we live with him in a round of invitations to a rump and dozen.—Yet we are not to suppose that he was a mere sensualist. All this is as much in imagination as in reality. His sensuality does not engross and stupefy his other faculties, but 'ascends me into the brain, clears away all the dull, crude vapours that environ it, and makes it full of nimble, fiery, and delectable shapes'. His imagination keeps up the ball after his senses have done with it. He seems to have even a greater enjoyment of the freedom from restraint, of good cheer, of his ease, of his vanity, in the ideal exaggerated description which he gives of them, than in fact. He never fails to enrich his discourse with allusions to eating and drinking, but we never see him at table. He carries his own larder about with him, and he is himself 'a tun of man'. His pulling out the bottle in the field of battle is a joke to shew his contempt for glory accompanied with danger, his systematic adherence to his Epicurean philosophy in the most trying circumstances. Again, such is his deliberate exaggeration of his own vices, that it does not seem quite certain whether the account of his hostess's bill, found in his pocket, with such an out-of-the-way charge for capons and sack with only one half-penny-worth of bread, was not put there by himself as a trick to humour the jest upon his favourite propensities, and as a conscious caricature of himself. He is represented as a liar, a braggart, a coward, a glutton, etc., and yet we are not offended but delighted with him; for he is all these as much to amuse others as to gratify himself. He openly assumes all these characters to shew the humorous part of them. The unrestrained indulgence of his own ease, appetites, and convenience, has neither malice nor hypocrisy in it. In a word, he is an actor in himself almost as much as upon the stage, and we no more object to the character of Falstaff in a moral point of view than we should think of bringing an excellent comedian, who should represent him to the life, before one of the police offices. We only consider the number of pleasant lights in which he puts certain foibles (the more pleasant as they are opposed to the received rules and necessary restraints of society) and do not trouble ourselves about the consequences resulting from them, for no mischievous consequences do result. Sir John is old as well as fat, which gives a melancholy retrospective tinge to the character; and by the disparity between his inclinations and his capacity for enjoyment, makes it still more ludicrous and fantastical.

The secret of Falstaff's wit is for the most part a masterly presence of mind, an absolute self-possession, which nothing can disturb. His repartees are involuntary suggestions of his self-love; instinctive evasions of everything that threatens to interrupt the career of his triumphant jollity and self-complacency. His very size floats him out of all his difficulties in a sea of rich conceits; and he turns round on the pivot of his convenience, with every occasion and at a moment's warning. His natural repugnance to every unpleasant thought or circumstance, of itself makes light of objections, and provokes the most extravagant and licentious answers in his own justification. His indifference to truth puts no check upon his invention, and the more improbable and unexpected his contrivances are, the more happily does he seem to be delivered of them, the anticipation of their effect acting as a stimulus to the gaiety of his fancy. The success of one adventurous sally gives him spirits to undertake another: he deals always in round numbers, and his exaggerations and excuses are 'open, palpable, monstrous as the father that begets them'. . . .

The heroic and serious part of these two plays founded on the story of Henry IV is not inferior to the comic and farcical. The characters of Hotspur and Prince Henry are two of the most beautiful and dramatic, both in themselves and from contrast, that ever were drawn. They are the essence of chivalry. We like Hotspur the best upon the whole, perhaps because he was unfortunate. . . .

The truth is, that we never could forgive the Prince's treatment of Falstaff; though perhaps Shakespear knew what was best, according to the history, the nature of the times, and of the man. We speak only as dramatic critics. Whatever terror the French in those days might have of Henry V, yet, to the readers of poetry at present, Falstaff is the better man of the two. We think of him and quote him oftener.

GEORG BRANDES Shakespeare felt himself attracted to the hero, the young Prince, by some of the most deep-rooted sympathies of his nature. We have seen how vividly and persistently the contrast between appearance and reality preoccupied him; we saw it last in *The Merchant of*

Venice. In proportion as he was irritated and repelled by people who try to pass for more than they are, by creatures of affectation and show, even by women who resort to artificial colours and false hair in quest of a beauty not their own, so his heart beat warmly for any one who had appearances against him, and concealed great qualities behind an unassuming and misinterpreted exterior. His whole life, indeed, was just such a paradox—his soul was replete with the greatest treasures, with rich humanity and inexhaustible genius, while externally he was little better than a light-minded mountebank, touting, with quips and quiddities, for the ha'pence of the mob. Now and then, as his Sonnets show, the pressure of this outward prejudice so weighed upon him that he came near to being ashamed of his position in life, and of the tinsel world in which his days were passed; and then he felt with double force the inward need to assure himself how great may be the gulf between the apparent and the real worth of human character.

Moreover, this view of his material gave him an occasion, before tuning the heroic string of his lyre, to put in a word for the right of high-spirited youth to have its fling, and indirectly to protest against the hasty judgments of narrow-minded moralists and Puritans. He would here show that great ambitions and heroic energy could pass unscathed through the dangers even of exceedingly questionable diversions. This Prince of Wales was 'merry England' and 'martial England' in one and the same person.

William Shakespeare (trans. William Archer), 1898.

J. I. M. STEWART Now, anthropologists are always telling us of countries gone waste and barren under the rule of an old, impotent and guilty king, who must be ritually slain and supplanted by his son or another before the saving rains can come bringing purification and regeneration to the land. Is not Henry IV in precisely the situation of this king? Dover Wilson avers that it is so, without any thought of magical implication:

. . . his reign and all his actions are overhung with the consciousness . . . of persona guilt . . . a fact that Shakespeare never misses an opportunity of underlining. . . . We see him first at the beginning of act 3 crushed beneath the disease that afflicts his body and the no less grievous diseases that make foul the body of his kingdom.

Perhaps, then, we glimpse here a further reason why the rejection of Falstaff is inevitable—not merely traditionally and moralistically inevitable but symbolically inevitable as well. And this may be why, when in the theatre, we do not really rebel against the rejection; why we find a fitness too in its being sudden and catastrophic. As long as we are in the grip of drama it is profoundly fit that Hal, turning king and clergyman at once, should run bad humours on the knight, should kill his heart. For the killing carries something of the ritual suggestion, the obscure *pathos*, of death in tragedy.

I suggest that Hal, by a displacement common enough in the evolution of ritual, kills Falstaff instead of killing the king, his father. In a sense Falstaff *is* his father; certainly is a 'father-substitute' in the psychologist's word; and this makes the theory of a vicarious sacrifice more colourable. All through the play there is a strong implicit parallelism between Henry Bolingbroke and his policies and Falstaff and *his* policies; and at one point in the play the two fathers actually, as it were, fuse (like Leonardo's two mothers in his paintings of the Virgin and St Anne), and in the Boar's Head tavern King Falstaff sits on his throne while his son Prince Henry kneels before him. And Falstaff, in standing for the old king, symbolises all the accumulated sin of the reign, all the consequent sterility of the land. But the young king draws his knife at the altar—and the heart of that grey iniquity, that father ruffian, is as fracted and corroborate as Pistol avers. Falstaff's rejection and death are very sad, but Sir James Frazer would have classed them with the Periodic Expulsion of Evils in a Material Vehicle, and discerned beneath the skin of Shakespeare's audience true brothers of the 'people of Leti, Moa and Lakor.

If this addition of another buried significance to the composite myth of Hal and Falstaff should seem extravagant, or an injudicious striving after Morgann's 'lightness of air', let it be remembered that drama, like religious ritual, plays upon atavic impulses of the mind. All true drama penetrates through representative fiction to the condition of myth. And Falstaff is in the end the dethroned and sacrificed king, the scapegoat as well as the sweet beef. For Falstaff, so Bacchic, so splendidly with the Maenads Doll and Mistress Quickly a creature of the wine-cart and the cymbal, so fit a sacrifice (as Hal early discerns) to lard the lean, the barren earth, is of that primitive and magical world upon which all art, even if with a profound unconsciousness, draws.

Character and Motive in Shakespeare, 1949.

MUCH ADO ABOUT NOTHING

WRITTEN   1598–9.

PERFORMED   'Sundrie times publikely acted' before Q, 1600.
    Much Ado was twice performed at Whitehall at the wedding festivities of the Count Palatine and Elizabeth, daughter of James I, 1613.

REGISTERED   1600. '4 Augusti
    The Commedie of muche A doo about $\left.\right\}$ to be staied.'
nothing a booke
This may have been an attempt by the Chamberlain's Men to prevent piratical publication.
1600. '23 Augusti. Andrew Wise William Aspley. Entred for their copies vnder the handes of the wardens Two bookes, the one called Muche a Doo about nothinge . . . Wrytten by master Shakespeare. xij^d.'
This is the first appearance of Shakespeare's name in the Stationers' Register.

PUBLISHED   1600 Q. 'As it hath been sundrie times publikely acted by the right honourable, the Lord Chamberlaine his seruants. Written by William Shakespeare.'
A 'good' Quarto. In IV. ii, Dogberry is called Kempe, and Verges is called

Cowley. Will Kempe and Richard Cowley were both actors in Shakespeare's company.

1623 F1. set up from a copy of Q that had been used as a prompt-copy: instead of the 'Enter Musicke' of Q, F prints 'Enter Iacke Wilson', the singer, II. i.

SOURCES   The Claudio-Hero plot occurs in a novella by Bandello, *Timbreo and Fenicia*, translated by Belleforest in his *Histoires Tragiques*; in Ariosto's *Orlando Furioso*, translated by Sir John Harington, and in the *Faerie Queene* II. iv. The Beatrice-Benedick plot is Shakespeare's own, as is Dogberry-Verges. According to Aubrey (*c.* 1681) 'The Humour of the Constable in a Midsomernight's Dreame [Much Ado], he happened to take at Grendon in Bucks which is the roade from London to Stratford'.

In 1662 Davenant combined *Measure for Measure* and the Beatrice-Benedick theme of *Much Ado* in his *Law Against Lovers*. Benedick was one of Garrick's favourite parts. He first played it at Drury Lane in 1748, and for the last time in 1776.

LEONARD DIGGES
>   let but Beatrice
> And Benedicke be seene, loe in a trice
> The Cockpit Galleries, Boxes, all are full.
>   *Commendatory Verses to Shakespeare's Poems,* 1640.

PEPYS   I went to the Opera, and saw 'The Law against Lovers', a good play and well performed, especially the little girl's, whom I never saw act before, dancing and singing; and were it not for her, the losse of Roxalana would spoil the house.[1]

[1] 'The little girl' and 'Roxalana' (Elisabeth Davenport) are representative of the actresses now for the first time appearing on the public stage.

Diary, Feb. 18*th*, 1662.

CHARLES GILDON   This Fable is as full of Absurdities, as the Writing is full of Beauties: The first I leave to the Reader to find out by the Rules I have laid down; the second I shall endeavour to shew, and point out some few of the many that are contain'd in the Play. *Shakespear* indeed had the misfortune, which other of our poets have since had, of laying his scene in a warm Climate, where the Manners of the People are very different from ours; and yet has made them talk and act generally like Men of a colder Country. . . .

This Play we must call a Comedy, tho some of the Incidents, and Discources too, are more in a Tragick Strain: and that of the Accusation of *Hero* is too shocking for either Tragedy or Comedy; nor cou'd it have come off in Nature, if we regard the Country, without the Death of more than *Hero*. . . . Besides which, there is such a pleasing Variety of Characters in the Play, and those perfectly maintain'd, as well as distinguish'd, that you lose the Absurdities of the Conduct in the Excellence of the Manners, Sentiments, Diction, and Topicks. *Benedict* and *Beatrice* are two sprightly, witty, talkative Characters; and tho of the same nature, yet perfectly distinguished; and you have no need to read the Names to know who speaks. . . .

To quote all the Comick Excellencies of this Play would be to transcribe three parts of it. For all that passes betwixt *Benedict* and *Beatrice* is admirable. . . . Nay, the variety and natural Distinction of the vulgar Humours of this Play, are remarkable.

The Scenes of this Play are something obscure; for you can scarce tell where the Place is in the two first Acts, tho the Scenes in them seem pretty entire, and unbroken. But those are things that we ought not to look much for in *Shakespear*. Yet whilst he is out in the Dramatick Imitation of the Fable, he always draws Mén and Women so perfectly, that when we read, we can scarce persuade ourselves but that the Discourse is real and no Fiction.

An Essay on the Art, Rise, and Progress of the Stage, 1714.

COLERIDGE The interest of the plot is always in fact on account of the characters, not *vice versa*, as in almost all other writers; the plot is a mere canvass and no more. Hence arises the true justification of the same strategem being used in regard to Benedict and Beatrice,—the vanity in each being alike. Take away from the Much Ado About Nothing all that which is not indispensable to the plot, either as having little to do with it, or, at best, like Dogberry and his comrades, forced into the service, when any other less ingeniously absurd watchmen and night-constables would have answered the mere necessities of the action;—take away Benedict, Beatrice, Dogberry, and the reaction of the former on the character of Hero,—and what will remain? In other writers the main agent of the plot is always the prominent character; in Shakespeare it is so, or is not so, as the character is in itself calculated, or not calculated, to form the plot. Don John is the main-spring of the plot of this play; but he is merely shown and then withdrawn.

HAZLITT This admirable comedy used to be frequently acted till of late years. Mr. Garrick's Benedick was one of his most celebrated characters; and Mrs. Jordan, we have understood, played Beatrice very delightfully. The serious part is still the most prominent here, as in other instances that we have noticed. Hero is the principal figure in the piece, and leaves an indelible impression on the mind by her beauty, her tenderness, and the hard trial of her love. . . .

The principal comic characters in Much Ado About Nothing, Benedick and Beatrice, are both essences in their kind. His character as a woman-hater is admirably supported, and his conversion to matrimony is no less happily effected by the pretended story of Beatrice's love for him. . . .

Perhaps that middle point of comedy was never more nicely hit in which the ludicrous blends with the tender, and our follies, turning round against themselves in support of our affections, retain nothing but their humanity.

Dogberry and Verges in this play are inimitable specimens of quaint blundering and misprisions of meaning; and are a standing record of that formal gravity of pretension and total want of common understanding, which Shakespear no doubt copied from real life, and which in the course of two hundred years appear to have ascended from the lowest to the highest offices in the state.

J. Dover Wilson The manuscript, then, which Sims and his compositors handled in 1600 was, we hold, an old play which had been worked over and recast somewhere towards the end of 1598 or the beginning of 1599. . . . 'The 'old play', therefore, as far as the internal evidence takes us, was an early play by Shakespeare himself.

Once the fact of revision is established, it is possible to frame a theory, which we may claim to be at least plausible, as to the general lines on which Shakespeare carried it out. We may premise at the outset, without fear of contradiction, that the characters which would interest him most in 1598-9 would be Beatrice and Benedick, and, secondly, that economical as ever of his energies and his material he would be likely to retain as much of the old version as he conveniently could. In his desire to bring Beatrice and Benedick more into the foreground of the picture, he would be obliged, we must suppose, to re-write and greatly to expand their 'parts', especially when they were present together on the stage. This meant a corresponding curtailment in other sections of the play, which must be kept more or less within its original proportions; but while there would be abridgment and compression Shakespeare would avoid more re-writing in these sections than was absolutely necessary. Further, since three-quarters of the received text is in prose and the verse-scenes are almost entirely concerned with the Hero and Claudio plot, we infer that the 1598-9 revision was a prose one and that the verse belongs to the old play. This inference is supported by the distinction between the prose and verse as regards punctuation, which we have noted above. It finds support also in the style of the verse, which so far from resembling what we should expect Shakespeare to be writing at the very end of the century is all strongly reminiscent of *The Two Gentlemen* and *Romeo and Juliet*, as we shall point out in detail in our notes. Moreover there are many indications that the verse-scenes have been abridged; for they contain not only many broken lines of verse but also those imperfectly deleted passages which we have previously dealt with. But a consideration of the plot will perhaps furnish us with the most interesting and conclusive evidence of the way in which the revision was carried out. . . .

The Copy for Much Ado About Nothing, 1923.

HENRY THE FIFTH

WRITTEN   1598–9. J. Dover Wilson argues that Falstaff was in the play as
                originally written, but that Kempe's departure left Shakespeare
without a suitable actor, so that before production he had to fill in with fresh
episodes, and substituted Pistol for Falstaff in the leek-eating scene.

PERFORMED   'Sundry times played' before Q1 1600. It may have been the
                first play to have been performed in the newly built Globe
theatre, 'This wooden O' of the Prologue.

1605 Jan. 7th: a performance at Whitehall 'By his Maiesties plaiers'.

REGISTERED   1600. '4 Augusti. Henry the ffift, a booke, to be staied.' This
                may have been an attempt by the Chamberlain's Men to prevent
piratical publication.

1600. 14 August. Thomas Pavier entered for his copy.

PUBLISHED   1600 Q1. 'The Chronicle History of Henry the fift, With his
                battel fought at Agin Court in France. Togither with Auntient
Pistoll. As it hath bene sundry times playd by the Right honorable the Lord
Chamberlaine his seruants. Printed by Thomas Creede, for Tho. Millington,
and Iohn Busby.' A 'bad' Quarto: a reported version, possibly that of an actor
who played either Gower, Exeter, or the Governor of Harfleur. The fact
that the Prologue, Epilogue, Choruses, three scenes, and long passages are
omitted suggests that the report was based on a shortened version.

1602 Q2. Set up from Q1.

1619 Q3. Set up from Q1. Dated 1608. One of the ten plays published in
1619 by Jaggard, many of them with false dates.

1623 F1. A fair text.

SOURCES   Holinshed's *Chronicle*.
                The Famous Victories of Henry the fifth. (The wooing scene
occurs in this play.)

William Fluellen and George Bardolfe were fellow recusants with Shakespeare's father, John, in 1592.

Henry V was adapted by Aaron Hill in 1723. The 'noble play of Henry
the Fifth' seen by Pepys was written by Lord Orrery.

SIR THOMAS HANMER   Most of those passages are here thrown to the bottom
                of the page, and rejected as spurious, which were
stigmatized as such in Mr. Pope's edition; and it were to be wished that more
had then undergone the same sentence. The promoter of the present edition
hath ventured to discard but few more upon his own judgment, the most
considerable of which is that wretched piece of ribaldry in *King Henry the
Fifth*, put into the mouths of the French princess and an old gentlewoman,
improper enough as it is all in French, and not intelligible to an English
audience, and yet that perhaps is the best thing that can be said of it. There

can be no doubt but a great deal more of that low stuff, which disgraces the work of this great author, was foisted in by the players after his death, to please the vulgar audiences by which they subsisted: and though some of the poor witticisms and conceits must be supposed to have fallen from his pen, yet as he hath put them generally into the mouths of low and ignorant people, so it is to be remembered that he wrote for the stage, rude and unpolished as it then was; and the vicious taste of the age must stand condemned for them, since he hath left upon record a signal proof how much he despised them.

Preface to his edition of Shakespeare, 1744.

JOHNSON This play has many scenes of high dignity, and many of easy merriment. The character of the king is well supported, except in his courtship, where he has neither the vivacity of Hal, nor the grandeur of Henry. The humour of Pistol is very happily continued; his character has, perhaps, been the model of all the bullies that have yet appeared on the English stage.

The lines given to the chorus have many admirers; but the truth is, that in them a little may be praised, and much must be forgiven: nor can it be easily discovered why the intelligence given by the chorus is more necessary in this play than in many others where it is omitted. The great defect of this play is the emptiness and narrowness of the last act, which a very little diligence might have easily avoided.

HAZLITT Henry V is a very favourite monarch with the English nation, and he appears to have been also a favourite with Shakespear, who labours hard to apologise for the actions of the king, by shewing us the character of the man, as 'the king of good fellows'. He scarcely deserves this honour. He was fond of war and low company: we know little else of him. He was careless, dissolute and ambitious;—idle, or doing mischief. In private, he seemed to have no idea of the common decencies of life, which he subjected to a kind of regal licence; in public affairs, he seemed to have no idea of any rule of right or wrong, but brute force, glossed over with a little religious hypocrisy and archiepiscopal advice. His principles did not change with his situation and professions. His adventure on Gadshill was a prelude to the affair of Agincourt, only a bloodless one; Falstaff was a puny prompter of violence and outrage, compared with the pious and politic Archbishop of Canterbury, who gave the king *carte blanche*, in a genealogical tree of his family, to rob and murder in circles of latitude and longitude abroad—to save the possessions of the Church at home. This appears in the speeches in Shakespear, where the hidden motives that actuate princes and their advisers in war and policy are better laid open than in speeches from the throne or woolsack. Henry, because he did not know how to govern his own kingdom, determined to make war upon his neighbours. Because his own title to the crown was doubtful, he laid claim to that of France. Because he did not know how to exercise the enormous power, which had just dropped into his hands, to any one good purpose, he immediately undertook (a cheap and obvious resource of sovereignty) to do all the mischief he could. . . . Henry declares his resolution 'when France is his, to bend it to his awe, or break it all to pieces'—a resolution worthy of a conqueror, to destroy all that he cannot enslave; and what adds to the joke, he lays all the blame of the consequences of his ambition on those who will not submit tamely to his tyranny . . . Henry V, it is true, was a hero, a king of England, and the conqueror of the king of France. Yet we feel little love or admiration for him. He was a hero, that is, he was ready to sacrifice his own life for the pleasure of destroying thousands of other lives: he was a king of England, but not a constitutional one, and we only like kings according to the law; lastly he was a conqueror of the French king, and for this we dislike him less than if he had conquered the French people. How then do we like him? We like him in the play. There he is a very amiable monster, a very splendid pageant. As we like to gaze at a panther or a young lion in their cages in the Tower, and catch a pleasing horror from their glistening eyes, their velvet paws, and dreadless roar, so we take a very romantic, heroic, patriotic, and poetical delight in the boasts and feats of our younger Harry, as they appear on the stage and are confined to lines of ten syllables; where no blood follows the stroke that wounds our ears, where no harvest bends beneath horses' hoofs, no city flames, no little child is butchered, no dead men's bodies are found piled on heaps and festering the next morning—in the orchestra! . . .

It is worth observing that in all these plays, which give an admirable picture to the spirit of the *good old times*, the moral inference does not at all depend upon the nature of the actions, but on the dignity or meanness of the persons committing them. 'The eagle England' has a right 'to be in prey', but 'the weazel Scot' has none 'to come sneaking to her nest', which she has left to pounce upon others. Might was right, without equivocation or disguise, in that heroic and chivalrous age. . . .

The comic parts of *Henry V* are very inferior to those of *Henry IV*. Falstaff is dead, and without him, Pistol, Nym, and Bardolph are satellites without a sun.

SIR SIDNEY LEE Shakespeare's 'Henry V' is as far as possible removed from what is generally understood by drama. It is without intrigue or entanglement; it propounds no problems of psychology; its definite motive is neither comic nor tragic; women play in it the slenderest part; it lacks plot in any customary sense. In truth, the piece is epic narrative, or rather heroic biography, adapted to the purposes of the stage. The historical episodes—political debate, sieges, encampments, battles, diplomatic negotiations—with which the scenes deal, are knit together by no more complex bond than the chronological succession of events, the presence in each of the same *dramatis personæ* and the predominance in each of the same character—the English King, in whose mouth the dramatist sets nearly a third of all the lines of the play. A few of the minor personages excite genuine interest, and there are some attractive scenes of comic relief, but these have no organic connection with the central thread of the play. Shakespeare's efforts were mainly concentrated on the portraiture of 'this star of England', King Henry, whom he deliberately chose out of the page of history as the fittest representative of the best distinctive type of English character. . . .

Broadly speaking, Shakespeare has in no other play cast a man so entirely in the heroic mould as King Henry. Such failings as are indicated are kept in the background. On his virtues alone a full blaze of light is shed. Flawless heroines Shakespeare had depicted in plenty, but Henry is his only male character who, when drawn at full length, betrays no crucial or invincible defect of will, or mind, or temper. The Bastard in 'King John' approaches him most closely in heroic stature, but the Bastard is not drawn at full length. Certainly no other of Shakespeare's monarchs is comparable with Henry V. In the rest of his English historical plays he tells sad stories of the deaths of the kings, who are ruined mainly by moral flaws in their character. 'Richard II', 'Richard III', 'King John', even 'Henry IV', illustrate the unworthiness of those who thirst for kingly glory, the brittleness rather than the brilliance of the royal estate. Only Henry V proves himself deserving of truly royal prosperity, of which the last scene of the play seems to guarantee him lasting enjoyment. Alone in Shakespeare's gallery of English monarchs does Henry's portrait evoke at once a joyous sense of satisfaction in the high potentialities of human character and a sense of pride among Englishmen that a man of his mettle is of English race.

Introduction to Henry V, c. 1900.

JOHN MASEFIELD The play ought to be seen and judged as a part of the magnificent tragic series. Detached from its place, as it has been, it loses all its value. It is not greatly poetical in itself. It is popular. It is about a popular hero who is as common as those who love him. But in its place it is tremendous. Henry V is the one commonplace man in the eight plays. He alone enjoys success and worldly happiness. He enters Shakespeare's vision to reap what his broken-hearted father sowed. He passes out of Shakespeare's vision to beget the son who dies broken-hearted after bringing all to waste again.

'Hear him but reason in divinity',

cries the admiring archbishop. Yet this searcher of the spirit woos his bride like a butcher, and jokes among his men like a groom. He has the knack of life that fits human beings for whatever is animal in human affairs.

William Shakespeare, 1911.

G. I. DUTHIE The essentials of the design of the trilogy [*Richard II, Henry IV* and *Henry V*] may perhaps, at the risk of . . . over-simplification, be stated as follows. We begin with a thoroughly bad king—a disordered personality in which 'will doth mutiny with wit's regard'. He produces disorder in the state by unkingly conduct. England is being ruined by him. To continue to tolerate him is to invite further ruin. But to depose him would be a crime against the law of God. England is in a dilemma. The true moral course is for her to endure Richard, to leave him to God's vengeance for betrayal of trust, even if she has to accept the role of martyrdom.

But he *is* deposed—that crime is committed: and then he is murdered. Henry IV becomes king. Though coming to the throne by a disorderly deed, he wants to produce order in the kingdom. In his personality will does not mutiny with wit's regard; but he is a guilty man, and he is dogged by Nemesis. He has to contend with rebellion from his former supporters: prophecies of woe uttered by Richard and others are fulfilled: and the dissoluteness of his son and heir may be thought of as part of the retribution for the crime of usurpation. It looks as if when Henry V becomes king he will be like Richard, and as if he will be deposed in his turn by Hotspur or another such. But the Prince, a prodigal son figure, repents and emerges as the good king *par excellence*. He embraces the ideal of law and order which he had previously flouted. But more than this. The *Richard II* and *Henry IV* plays present us with various kinds of character and various ways of life, and we find ourselves comparing them in the light of the question, what is the nature of the ideal king?

Richard, though legitimately king, is disfigured by personality disorder. Henry IV has no such personality disorder as Richard. He uses 'policy', and we feel that calculation, keeping his eye on the main chance, is too prominent a part of his character for us to sympathize with him fully. He is not sufficiently warm-hearted. Hotspur detests him as a 'vile politician'. But Hotspur is open to criticism on other grounds. If Hotspur were ever to become king he would not be successful. He is animated by a noble ideal of chivalric honour, but he is immoderate, rash, imprudent, lacking in discretion. Hotspur is criticized by, among others, Falstaff (who is opposed to Henry IV's values also). Falstaff, the misleader of youth, represents a way of life that culminates in diseases. The prince rightly gives it up. But from it, it may be suggested, he retains a sense of fellow-being with the humble and low which contributes beneficially to his character as king. We have a chain of character-comparisons: as regards values, we have Henry IV opposed to Richard II; opposed to Henry IV we have, in different ways, Hotspur and Falstaff; Falstaff is opposed to Hotspur; and Falstaff himself is rejected. The ideal king, Henry V, exemplifies both 'policy' and chivalry, but he is not a second Henry IV nor a second Hotspur. Something of both there is in him: but, unlike either of them, he is a properly balanced personality, a sympathetically conceived order-figure. If at one point he talks as Henry IV might, he is yet, unlike Henry IV, essentially a frank and warm-hearted personality, a fully human personality. If at another point he talks as Hotspur might, he is yet, unlike Hotspur, a man of judgment and discretion.

Shakespeare, 1951.

JULIUS CÆSAR

WRITTEN   1599–1600.

PERFORMED   1599, Sept. 21st. Thomas Platter, a German doctor, saw a play
           of *Julius Cæsar*, though not necessarily Shakespeare's, at a
Bankside theatre.
1613. One of the plays—'Cæsars Tragedy'—acted at the 'Magnificent
Marriage' of the Count Palatine to the Lady Elizabeth.
1636, Jan 31st, at 'St. James'.
1638, Nov. 13th, at 'the Cocpit'.

REGISTERED   1623. 8th November. One of the 16 plays registered by Blount
            and Jaggard before publishing F1.

PUBLISHED   1623 F1. A very good text. In IV. iii, Brutus's account of
           Portia's death may be revision, the later report by Messala the
undeleted original version.

SOURCE   Plutarch's *Lives* of Brutus, Cæsar, and Antony, translated by
           Sir Thomas North (1579) from the French of Jacques Amyot
(1559).

THOMAS PLATTER After dinner on September 21st [1599], at about two
           o'clock, I went across the river with my companions, and
in the 'strewn roof-house' [streüwinen Dachhaus] saw the Tragedy of the
first Emperor Julius Cæsar, with at least fifteen characters, acted very well.
At the end of the play two of the actors in men's clothes and two in women's
clothes performed a dance, as is their custom, wonderfully well together.

                                                              1599.

JOHN WEEVER
           The many-headed multitude were drawne
           By *Brutus* speach, that *Cæsar* was ambitious,
           When eloquent *Mark Antonie* had showne
           His vertues, who but *Brutus* then was vicious?
                                  The Mirror of Martyrs, 1601.

BEN JONSON His wit was in his owne power; would the rule of it had beene
           so too. Many times hee fell into those things, could not escape
laughter: As when hee said in the person of *Cæsar* one speaking to him;
Cæsar thou dost me wrong. Hee replyed: *Cæsar did never wrong but with
just cause* and such like: which were ridiculous.
                                  Discoveries 1623–37.

LEONARD DIGGES

> So have I seene when Cesar would appeare
> And on the Stage at halfe-sword parley were,
> *Brutus* and *Cassius*: oh how the Audience,
> Were ravish'd, with what wonder they went thence,
> When some new day they would not brooke a line,
> Of tedious (though well laboured) *Catiline*.

Commendatory Verses to Shakespeare's Poems, 1640.

DRYDEN:

> Our author, by experience, finds it true,
> 'Tis much more hard to please himself than you . . .
> And to confess a truth, though out of time,
> Grows weary of his long-loved mistress, Rhyme.
> Passion's too fierce to be in fetters bound,
> And nature flies him like enchanted ground:
> What verse can do, he has perform'd in this,
> Which he presumes the most correct of his;
> But spite of all his pride, a secret shame
> Invades his breast at Shakspeare's sacred name:
> Awed when he hears his godlike Romans rage,
> He, in a just despair, would quit the stage;
> And to an age less polish'd, more unskill'd,
> Does, with disdain, the foremost honours yield.

Prologue to 'Aurengzebe', 1676.

RYMER In the former Play [*Othello*], our Poet might be the bolder, the persons being all his own Creatures, and meer fiction. But here he sins not against Nature and Philosophy only, but against the most known History, and the memory of the Noblest Romans, that ought to be sacred to all Posterity. He might be familiar with *Othello* and *Jago*, as his own natural acquaintance: but *Cæsar* and *Brutus* were above his conversation. To put them in Fools Coats, and make them Jack-puddens in the *Shakespear* dress, is a *Sacriledge*, beyond anything in *Spelman*. The truth is, this authors head was full of villainous, unnatural images, and history has only furnish'd him with great names, thereby to recommend them to the World, by writing over them, *This is* Brutus; *this is* Cicero; *this is* Cæsar. . . .

For indeed, that Language which *Shakespear* puts in the Mouth of *Brutus* wou'd not suit, or be convenient, unless from some son of the Shambles, or some natural offspring of the Butchery. But never any Poet so boldly and so barefac'd flounced along from contradiction to contradiction. . . .

This may shew with what indignity our Poet treats the noblest *Romans*. But there is no other cloth in this Wardrobe. Every one must be content to wear a Fools Coat, who comes to be dressed by him.

A Short View of Tragedy, 1693.

JOHNSON Of this tragedy many particular passages deserve regard, and the
            contention and reconcilement of Brutus and Cassius is universally
celebrated; but I have never been strongly agitated in perusing it, and think
it somewhat cold and unaffecting, compared with some other of Shakespeare's
plays; his adherence to the real story, and to Roman manners, seems to have
impeded the natural vigour of his genius.

COLERIDGE I know no part of Shakspeare that more impresses on me the
            belief of his genius being superhuman, than this scene between
Brutus and Cassius. In the Gnostic heresy it might have been credited with
less absurdity than most of their dogmas, that the Supreme had employed him
to create, previously to his function of representing, characters.

HAZLITT *Julius Cæsar* is not equal as a whole, to either of his other plays
            taken from the Roman history. It is inferior in interest to *Corio-
lanus*, and both in interest and power to *Antony and Cleopatra*. It however
abounds in admirable and affecting passages, and is remarkable for the profound knowledge of character, in which Shakespear could scarcely fail. If
there is any exception to this remark, it is in the hero of the piece himself.
We do not much admire the representation here given of Julius Cæsar, nor
do we think it answers to the portrait given of him in the Commentaries.
He makes several vapouring and rather pedantic speeches, and does nothing.
Indeed, he has nothing to do. So far, the fault of the character is the fault of
the plot. . . .

Shakespear has in this play and elsewhere shown the same penetration into
political character and the springs of public events as into those of every-day
life. For instance, the whole design of the conspirators to liberate their country
fails from the generous temper and over-weening confidence of Brutus in
the goodness of their cause and the assistance of others. Thus it has always
been. Those who mean well themselves think well of others, and fall a prey
to their security. That humanity and honesty which dispose men to resist
injustice and tyranny render them unfit to cope with the cunning and power
of those who are opposed to them . . . Cassius was better cut out for a con-
spirator. His heart prompted his head. His watchful jealousy made him fear
the worst that might happen and his irritability of temper added to his
inveteracy of purpose and sharpened his patriotism. The mixed nature of
his motives made him fitter to contend with bad men.

SIR EDMUND CHAMBERS These conflicting theories [about the authorship of
                        Julius Cæsar] may perhaps be left to cancel each other
out. I believe them to be all equally misconceived, and to rest partly upon
characteristic Shakespearean inconsistencies in the handling of detail, and
partly upon the special features of the play. One is that, while Shakespeare's
later tragedies move in a single curve to a catastrophe in the death of the title-
character, the action of *Julius Cæsar* has two peaks, one in the Capitol and
the other at Philippi, and the psychological interest is at least as much in

Brutus as in Cæsar. The effect of a double theme is therefore given. The other is that Shakespeare is deliberately experimenting in a classical manner, with an extreme simplicity both of vocabulary and of phrasing. This has already been noted by Bradley, *Shakespearean Tragedy*, 85. It is often admirably telling, but sometimes it leads to a stiffness, perhaps even a baldness, of diction, which may awake reminiscences of pre-Shakespearean plays. I do not see any special resemblance to Marlowe; the constant use of mid-line speech endings and mid-line pauses is not pre-Shakespearean at all. As for Beaumont, it is merely a matter of verbal parallels, and the derivation of Beaumont's diction from Shakespeare's has long been recognized. The element of simple dignity in the style of *Julius Cæsar*, although we have no particular reason to suppose that he knew it otherwise than upon the stage, seems to have made a special appeal to him.

William Shakespeare, 1930.

J. C. Maxwell   *Julius Cæsar* is a play which well deserves study for its own sake, though its place in Shakespeare's development as a tragic dramatist has often, reasonably enough, been the centre of interest. Shakespeare has evidently carried over to a different subject some of the methods used in the English history plays. He is, however, freed from certain limitations. Especially in the first history plays, though even there he re-models his historical material, he has to work within an annalistic framework; and up to the end of the series the king's reign remains the unit of construction. In *Julius Cæsar* there is no restriction of this kind. He can take the momentous event as the centre of his play, and the peculiarities of construction in *Julius Cæsar* arise largely from the fact that it is the Shakespeare play which takes its unity most notably from a single event: the death of Cæsar, the central secular event in world history. This is the simplest way of describing how the play hangs together: it has been elaborated by critics who have remarked that the 'spirit of Cæsar' is more powerful than the living Cæsar had been, and Shakespeare himself makes this point: 'O Julius Cæsar, thou art mighty yet!' (V. iii. 94). It seems wiser to stop short of invoking such an abstraction as 'Cæsarism'; Shakespeare shows conspicuous discretion in not raising in our minds the question of what Cæsar's rule would really have been like. What matters for the play is people's hopes and fears about it, and the brutality and incompetence of the triumvirs' rule which takes its place.

So much for the relation of the play to the English history plays. The other element in it which has been discussed in relation to Shakespeare's development is the figure of Brutus. The notion of Brutus as an embryo Hamlet has been specially popular. The comparison is legitimate so long as it does not seek to establish an exclusive line of development; more than *Hamlet* is foreshadowed by *Julius Cæsar* as a whole, and Wilson Knight has done a service by pointing out how much of Macbeth, too, can be seen in Brutus. But one Shakespearian theme which becomes predominant in *Hamlet* certainly makes its first notable appearance in the presentation of Brutus in *Julius Cæsar*: the notion of a disparity between the man and what he does.

This notion still seems somewhat intrusive: the play is not built round it as *Hamlet* is. The result is (to exaggerate a little) that where Hamlet is a mystery Brutus is a puzzle. Two factors contribute to make this so. The first is that, as I have said, Shakespeare is attempting something new. The second is that, as has often been pointed out, he is committed to presenting a doctrinaire intellectual, and one whose doctrine (classical republicanism) is one with which he has no spontaneous imaginative sympathy. Yet he is surprisingly successful in making something positive out of his limitations. The best example is Brutus's soliloquy in II. i. Coleridge's difficulties with this were the difficulties of a true critic; Shakespeare seems here to be whittling away the whole meaning of theoretic republicanism, and it is not an adequate answer to point to the monarchical assumptions of Shakespeare's day. Brutus in this soliloquy is and is not a republican, and the obscurities in the speech, though in part the result of Shakespeare's lack of sympathy with the ideas involved, also convey 'the instinct of a man over the threshold of whose awareness a terrible doubt perpetually threatens to lap'.[1]

Enough has been said about the links between *Julius Cæsar* and some of Shakespeare's earlier and later work. Among its qualities considered as an independent play, I shall single out only one—its moral and political realism. When Shakespeare wrote, there was already a large body of interpretations of the fall of Cæsar, both in drama and elsewhere, and there was by no means a single orthodox view. But there was a tradition of partisan interpretation, whether on the republican or the monarchical side. Shakespeare shows his preference for a more humanized treatment by taking Plutarch as his starting-point rather than any of the sixteenth-century dramatic versions. He does show the influence of the latter as well, but the bombastic elements in Cæsar himself which have given offence, and have raised doubts as to Shakespeare's intentions, are markedly toned down from earlier Senecan dramas in Latin, and from that curious anonymous play—academic but with strong affinities to Marlowe—*Cæsar's Revenge* (*c.* 1592–6). But in the latter the whole play is bombastic in tone. Shakespeare has modified the traditional stage Cæsar, but he has modified the staple of the play's language far more, so that Cæsar himself stands out. The exact purpose of this treatment is open to dispute, but what seems clear is that Cæsar speaks as he does because of some realistic and psychological intention on Shakespeare's part, perhaps, as Stewart suggests, to convey 'the impression of one physically fretted to decay, and opposing to the first falterings of the mind an increasingly rigid and absolute assertion of the Cæsar idea'.

Here, then, there is psychological realism. Equally pronounced is the moral realism with which the conspiracy is viewed. Whatever may be the ideological veneer, murder remains murder. There are greater and more complex things in Shakespeare, but there is nothing which better displays clarity and sanity of moral vision than Act III of *Julius Cæsar*, with Brutus's high-minded sacrificial attitude towards murder displayed without comment and condemning itself simply by expressing itself

---

[1] J. I. M. Stewart, *Character and Motive in Shakespeare* (1949), p. 52.

> Stoop, Romans, stoop,
> And let us bathe our hands in Caesar's blood
> Up to the elbows, and besmear our swords;
> Then walk we forth even to the market-place,
> And waving our red weapons o'er our heads,
> Let's all cry, 'Peace, freedom, and liberty'.

Pope was shocked by this from Brutus, and transferred it to Casca. But Shakespeare knew better. And after self-revelation, the working-out of the consequences in action: Antony's servant comes with a message; Antony himself echoes and parodies the assassins' horrible self-exaltation—'whilst your purpled hands to reek and smoke. . . . The choice and master spirits of this age.' But they are so infatuated that they cannot see themselves aright in the mirror held up to them, and we realize that their fate is sealed.

> *Shakespeare: the Middle Plays.* From *The Age of Shakespeare,* edited by Boris Ford, 1955.

AS YOU LIKE IT

WRITTEN   1599–1600.

PERFORMED   1603. There is evidence that *As You Like It* was the play acted on Dec 2 1603, when the Court was at Wilton House.

REGISTERED 1600. '4 Augusti. As you like yt, a booke, to be staid.' Possibly an attempt by the Chamberlain's Men to prevent piratical publication.
1623. 8 November. One of the 16 plays registered by Blount and Jaggard before publishing F 1.

PUBLISHED   1623 F 1. A fair text, set up from the prompt-book.

SOURCES   Thomas Lodge's novel, *Rosalynde, or Euphues' Golden Legacy,* based on the 14th century *Tale of Gamelyn.*

JOHNSON Of this play the fable is wild and pleasing. I know not how the ladies will approve the facility with which both Rosalind and Celia give away their hearts. To Celia much may be forgiven for the heroism of her friendship. The character of Jaques is natural and well preserved. The comic dialogue is very sprightly, with less mixture of low buffoonery than in some other plays; and the graver part is elegant and harmonious. By hastening to the end of his work, Shakespeare suppressed the dialogue between the usurper and the hermit, and lost an opportunity of exhibiting a moral lesson, in which he might have found matter worthy of his highest powers.

EDWARD CAPELL A traditional story was current some years ago about Stratford,—that a very old man of that place,—of weak

intellects, but yet related to Shakespeare,—being ask'd by some of his neighbours, what he remember'd about him; answer'd,—that he saw him once
brought on the stage, upon another man's back; which answer was apply'd
by the hearers, to his having seen him perform in this scene the part of Adam:
That he should have done so, is made not unlikely by another constant
tradition,—that he was no extraordinary actor, and therefore took no parts
upon him but such as this: for which he might also be peculiarly fitted by an
accidental lameness, which,—as he himself tells us twice in his 'Sonnets',
v. 37, and 89,—befell him in some part of life; without saying how, or when,
of what sort, or in what degree; but his expressions seem to indicate—latterly.

Commentary, 1774.

HAZLITT Shakespear has here converted the forest of Arden into another
Arcadia, where they 'fleet the time carelessly, as they did in the
golden world'. It is the most ideal of any of this author's plays. It is a pastoral
drama, in which the interest arises more out of the sentiments and characters
than out of the actions or situations. It is not what is done, but what is said,
that claims our attention. Nursed in solitude, 'under the shade of melancholy
boughs', the imagination grows soft and delicate, and the wit runs riot in
idleness, like a spoiled child, that is never sent to school. Caprice and fancy
reign and revel here, and stern necessity is banished to the court. The mild
sentiments of humanity are strengthened with thought and leisure; the echo
of the cares and noise of the world strikes upon the ear of those 'who have
felt them knowingly', softened by time and distance. 'They hear the tumult
and are still.' The very air of the place seems to breathe a spirit of philosophical poetry: to stir the thoughts, to touch the heart with pity, as the drowsy
forest rustles to the sighing gale. Never was there such beautiful moralising,
equally free from pedantry or petulance.

Jaques is the only purely contemplative character in Shakespear. He thinks,
and does nothing. His whole occupation is to amuse his mind, and he is
totally regardless of his body and his fortunes. He is the prince of philosophical idlers; his only passion is thought; he sets no value upon anything
but as it serves as food for reflection. . . . He resents Orlando's passion for
Rosalind as some disparagement of his own passion for abstract truth.

EDWARD DOWDEN Jaques died, we know not how, or when, or where; but
he came to life again a century later, and appeared in the
world as an English clergyman; we need stand in no doubt as to his character,
for we all know him under his later name of Lawrence Sterne. Mr Yorick
made a mistake about his family tree; he came not out of the play of Hamlet,
but out of As You Like It. In Arden he wept and moralised over the wounded
deer; and at Namport his tears and sentiment gushed forth for the dead
donkey. . . .

Upon the whole, As You Like It is the sweetest and happiest of all Shakspere's comedies. No one suffers; no one lives an eager intense life; there is
no tragic interest in it as there is in the Merchant of Venice, as there is in
Much Ado about Nothing. It is mirthful, but the mirth is sprightly, graceful,

exquisite; there is none of the rollicking fun of Sir Toby here; the songs are not 'coziers' catches' shouted in the night time, 'without any mitigation or remorse of voice', but the solos and duets of pages in the wild-wood, or the noisier chorus of foresters. The wit of Touchstone is not mere clownage, nor has it any indirect serious significances; it is a dainty kind of absurdity worthy to hold comparison with the melancholy of Jacques. And Orlando in the beauty and strength of early manhood, and Rosalind,

> A gallant curtle-axe upon her thigh,
> A boar-spear in her hand,

and the bright, tender, loyal womanhood within—are figures which quicken and restore our spirits, as music does, which is neither noisy nor superficial, and yet which knows little of the deep passion and sorrow of the world.

Shakspere, when he wrote this idyllic play, was himself in his forest of Arden. He had ended one great ambition—the historical plays—and not yet commenced his tragedies. It was a resting-place. He sends his imagination into the woods to find repose. Instead of the court and camps of England, and the embattled plains of France, here was this woodland scene, where the palm-tree, the lioness, and the serpent are to be found; possessed of a flora and fauna that flourish in spite of physical geographers. There is an open-air feeling throughout the play. The dialogue, as has been observed, catches freedom and freshness from the atmosphere. 'Never is the scene within-doors except when something discordant is introduced to heighten as it were the harmony.' After the trumpet-tones of Henry V comes the sweet pastoral strain, so bright, so tender. Must it not be all in keeping? Shakspere was not trying to control his melancholy. When he needed to do that, Shakspere confronted his melancholy very passionately, and looked it full in the face. Here he needed refreshment, a sunlight tempered by forest-boughs, a breeze upon his forehead, a stream murmuring in his ears.

Shakspere, His Mind and Art, 1875.

S. L. Bethell The true explanation of Touchstone's behaviour lies in the psychology, not of Touchstone himself, but of the audience. Professional jesters are witty, but they are also fools: they are to be laughed *at* as well as *with*; and if they 'wear not motley in their brains', it is up to them not to let their public behaviour be unduly influenced by their natural good sense. The audience would expect to laugh at Touchstone, the court jester—not to sympathise with him. Shakespeare makes him witty because we do not tire of wit as we do of the 'natural'. William and Audrey provide the dullness—but again, a highly stylised dullness, funnier than nature—and they have very little of the dialogue. Touchstone, in a fat part, must have wit; but there is no reason why he should not be a fool also, in the matter of Audrey, and so constitute a double source of amusement. The psychological difficulty is brushed aside, and we are given a character wise in speech and foolish in action—which seems to have been the character usually assumed by a court jester. The audience is thus required to attend simultaneously to two diverse aspects of a situation, and to keep the two strands of attention separate; to enjoy the folly and the wit without any naturalistic sense of their incompatibility.

The conventions of depersonalisation and of 'double nature' (both the Claudius and Touchstone varieties) obviously depend upon a dual consciousness of play-world and real world; but even in a conventional theatre, they are not entirely satisfactory. Ideally, plot, character and dialogue should be closely interrelated, and the themes of a play be expressed through their fusion at every point. When a single character is made to do double service, the associations gathered around his first personality have to be thrust aside for his second personality to function; uncertainty and a degree of disharmony are bound to result. Significantly, it is in the earlier plays that these conventions occur most frequently, and in plays which are not organised into a complete poetic and dramatic unity. I have mentioned the uncertain structure of *Hamlet*; and in *As You Like It* there is some discontinuity between the levels of plot, character and dialogue. Its deeper themes are conveyed mainly in the dialogue, and almost incidentally: the concern with court *versus* country, and the question of literary pastoral. There is a triple burlesque: of the courtiers who sigh for the country (the Duke at the end leaves his 'sermons in stones' with an indecent haste); of the pastoral convention in literature (in the dialogue of Silvius and Phebe); and of the country itself (in the clod-hopping rudeness of William and Audrey). It is the serious tone distinguishing at times his treatment of Corin and Adam that leads us to see where Shakespeare's true sympathies lie—with the old rural order, which in his own lifetime was being rapidly displaced by commercial enterprise. . . .

Rosalind in Arden may perhaps represent the true blend of court and country, but there is no inevitable relationship between the romantic plot and what I take to be the underlying theme. Shakespeare's chief purpose was entertainment, his deeper purpose only incidental, and so it would be wrong to take everything in the play as equally significant. In such circumstances, there is no harm in Touchstone's double nature; we are not to treat matters of character very seriously. Sometimes Touchstone's dialogue is relevant to the deeper theme, and we must not reject this incidental wisdom because of his foolish behaviour on other occasions.

Shakespeare and the Popular Dramatic Tradition, 1944.

TWELFTH NIGHT

WRITTEN   1599–1600.

PERFORMED   1601 Jan 6th? Leslie Hotson argues that the play was first presented at Whitehall when Queen Elizabeth entertained Don Virginio Orsino, Duke of Bracciano, on Twelfth Night, 1601. (See *The First Night of Twelfth Night.* 1954.)

1602 Feb 2nd, in the Middle Temple.

1618 'before his Maiesty on Easter Monday.' (*Chamber Account.*)

1623 'At Candlemas Malvolio was acted at court, by the kings servants.'
(*Office Book of Sir Henry Herbert.*)

REGISTERED 1623 Nov 8th. One of the 16 plays registered by Blount and
              Jaggard before publishing F1.

PUBLISHED   1623 F1. A good text, set up from the prompt-copy.

SOURCES   The Olivia-Orsino, Viola-Sebastian plot from the story of
              Apolonius and Silla in Barnabe Riche's *Farewell to Militarie
profession* (1581). This is an adaptation of Belleforest's French version of a
novella by Bandello, based on the Sienese comedy of *Gl'Ingannati*. The sub-
plot and its characters are Shakespeare's creation.

   In 1703 William Burnaby vulgarised *Twelfth Night* in his *Love Betray'd*.

JOHN MANNINGHAM At our feast wee had a play called 'Twelue Night, or
                  What You Will', much like the Commedy of Errores,
or Menechmi in Plautus, but most like and neere to that in Italian called
Inganni. A good practise in it to make the Steward beleeue his Lady widdowe
was in love with him, by counterfeyting a letter as from his Lady in generall
termes, telling him what shee liked best in him, and prescribing his gesture
in smiling, his apparaile, &c., and then when he came to practise making him
beleeue they tooke him to be mad.

Diary, Feb. 2, 1602.

LEONARD DIGGES

                        Loe in a trice
        The Cockpit Galleries, Boxes, all are full.
        To heare Maluoglio that crosse garter'd Gull.
              Commendatory Verses to Shakespeare's Poems, 1640.

PEPYS Observed at the Opera a new play, 'Twelfth Night', was acted there,
        and the King there: so I, against my own mind and resolution, could
not forbear to go in, which did make the play seem a burthern to me; and I
took no pleasure at all in it. (*Sept.* 11, 1661.)

   To the Duke's house, and there saw Twelfth-Night acted well, though it
be but a silly play, and not relating at all to the name or day. (*Jan.* 6, 1663.)

   To the Duke of York's house, and saw 'Twelfth Night', as it is now revived, but, I think, one of the weakest plays that ever I saw on the stage.
(*Jan.* 20, 1669.)

JOHNSON This play is, in the graver part, elegant and easy, and, in some of
          the lighter scenes, exquisitely humorous. Aguecheek is drawn with
great propriety, but his character is, in a great measure, that of natural
fatuity, and is, therefore, not the proper prey of a satirist. The soliloquy of
Malvolio is truly comic; he is betrayed to ridicule merely by his pride. The
marriage of Olivia, and the succeeding perplexity, though well enough contrived to divert in the stage, wants credibility, and fails to produce the proper
instruction required in the drama, as it exhibits no just picture of life.

Lamb Malvolio is not essentially ludicrous. He becomes comic but by
accident. He is cold, austere, repelling; but dignified, consistent, and,
for what appears, rather of an over-stretched morality. . . . But his morality
and his manners are misplaced in Illyria. He is opposed to the proper *levities*
of the piece, and falls in the unequal contest. Still his pride, or his gravity,
(call it what you will,) is inherent, and native to the man, not mock or affected,
which latterly only are the fit objects to excite laughter. His quality is at the
best unlovely, but neither buffoon nor contemptible. His bearing is lofty, a
little above his station, but probably not much above his deserts. We see no
reason why he should not have been brave, honourable, accomplished. . . .
His dialect on all occasions is that of a gentleman and a man of education.
We must not confound him with the eternal old, low steward of comedy. . . .
Even in his absurd state of chains and darkness a sort of greatness seems never
to desert him. He argues highly and well with the supposed Sir Topas and
philosophises gallantly upon his straw. There must have been some shadow
of worth about the man; he must have been something more than a mere
vapour—a thing of straw or Jack in office—before Fabian and Maria could
have ventured sending him upon a courting errand to Olivia There was
some consonancy (as he would say) in the undertaking, or the jest would have
been too bold even for that house of misrule.

Bensley, accordingly, threw over the part an air of Spanish loftiness. He
looked, spake, and moved like an old Castilian. He was starch, spruce,
opinionated, but his superstructure of pride seemed bottomed upon a sense
of worth. There was something in it beyond the coxcomb. It was big and
swelling, but you could not be sure that it was hollow. You might wish to
see it taken down, but you felt that it was upon an elevation. He was magnificent from the outset; but when the decent sobrieties of the character began
to give way, and the poison of self-love, in his conceit of the Countess's
affection, gradually to work, you would have thought that the hero of La
Mancha in person stood before you. . . . I confess that I never saw the catastrophe of this character, while Bensley played it, without a kind of tragic
interest.

On Some of the Old Actors.

Hazlitt This is justly considered as one of the most delightful of Shakespear's comedies. It is full of sweetness and pleasantry. It is
perhaps too good-natured for comedy. It has little satire, and no spleen. It
aims at the ludicrous rather than the ridiculous. It makes us laugh at the
follies of mankind, not despise them, and still less bear any ill-will towards
them. Shakespear's comic genius resembles the bee rather in its power of
extracting sweets from weeds or poisons, than in leaving a sting behind it.
He gives the most amusing exaggeration of the prevailing foibles of his
characters, but in a way that they themselves, instead of being offended at,
would almost join in to humour; he rather contrives opportunities for them
to shew themselves off in the happiest lights, than renders them contemptible
in the perverse construction of the wit or malice of others.—There is a certain
stage of society in which people become conscious of their peculiarities and

absurdities, affect to disguise what they are, and set up pretensions to what they are not. This gives rise to a corresponding style of comedy, the object of which is to detect the disguises of self-love, and to make reprisals on these preposterous assumptions of vanity, by marking the contrast between the real and the affected character as severely as possible, and denying to those, who would impose on us for what they are not, even the merit which they have. This is the comedy of artificial life, of wit and satire, such as we see it in Congreve, Wycherley, Vanbrugh, etc. To this succeeds a state of society from which the same sort of affectation and pretence are banished by a greater knowledge of the world or by their successful exposure on the stage; and which by neutralising the materials of comic character, both natural and artificial, leaves no comedy at all—but *the sentimental*. Such is our modern comedy. There is a period in the progress of manners anterior to both these, in which the foibles and follies of individuals are of nature's planting, not the growth of art or study; in which they are therefore unconscious of them themselves, or care not who knows them, if they can but have their whim out; and in which, as there is no attempt at imposition, the spectators rather receive pleasure from humouring the inclinations of the persons they laugh at, than wish to give them pain by exposing their absurdity. This may be called the comedy of nature, and it is the comedy which we generally find in Shakespear.—Whether the analysis here given be just or not, the spirit of his comedies is evidently quite distinct from that of the authors above mentioned, as it is in its essence the same with that of Cervantes, and also very frequently of Molière, though he was more systematic in his extravagance than Shakespear. Shakespear's comedy is of a pastoral and poetical cast. Folly is indigenous to the soil, and shoots out with native, happy, unchecked, luxuriance. Absurdity has every encouragement afforded it; and nonsense has room to flourish in. Nothing is stunted by the churlish, icy hand of indifference or severity. The poet runs riot in a conceit, and idolises a quibble. His whole object is to turn the meanest or rudest objects to a pleasurable account. The relish which he has of a pun, or of the quaint humour of a low character, does not interfere with the delight with which he describes a beautiful image, or the most refined love. . . .

In a word, the best turn is given to everything, instead of the worst. There is a constant infusion of the romantic and enthusiastic, in proportion as the characters are natural and sincere; whereas in the more artificial style of comedy, everything gives way to ridicule and indifference, there being nothing left but affectation on one side, and incredulity on the other.—Much as we like Shakespear's comedies, we cannot agree with Dr. Johnson that they are better than his tragedies; nor do we like them half so well. If his inclination to comedy sometimes led him to trifle with the seriousness of tragedy, the poetical and impassioned passages are the best parts of his comedies. The great and secret charm of *Twelfth Night* is the character of Viola. Much as we like catches and cakes and ale, there is something that we like better. We have a friendship for Sir Toby; we patronise Sir Andrew; we have an understanding with the Clown, a sneaking kindness for Maria and her rogueries; we feel a regard for Malvolio, and sympathise with his gravity, his smiles, his cross garters, his yellow stockings, and imprisonment in the stocks. But there is something that excites in us a stronger feeling than all this—it is Viola's confession of her love.

SIR EDMUND CHAMBERS Thus we are left with the exquisite pendants of *As You Like It* and *Twelfth Night*, two plays whose common serenity of golden temper is indeed only a reflex of their single intention. The parallels between them are easy to draw. The ordered gardens of the Boccaccio-like villa in Illyria and the pastoral glades of the forest of Arden serve equally well for images of that civilized and sheltered society wherein alone, according to Meredith, comedy obtains its real scope; and each lends an appropriate setting to those wilful departures from the way of right reason which it is the proper and special mission of comedy to correct. The plays are as physicians set to heal kindred ailments of an idle brain; the affectations of the fields here and there of the town. *As You Like It* is the comedy of the romantics, of the imagination which runs away with the facts of life and frames impossible ideals on the extravagant assumption that human nature in a forest is something wholly different from human nature in a court. *Twelfth Night* in its turn is the comedy of the sentimentalists, of the tendency of minds pent in the artificial atmosphere of cities to a spiritual self-deception, whereby they indulge in the expression of emotions not because they really have them, but because they have come to be regarded by themselves or others as modish or delightful emotions to have.

Shakespeare: A Survey, 1925.

HAMLET

WRITTEN   1600–1.

PERFORMED   1602, July; it had then been 'latelie Acted'.
          1603. It had been acted at Cambridge and Oxford.
1607, acted on board Captain Keeling's East Indiaman.
1608, 'I [Keeling] envited Captain Hawkins to a ffishe dinner and had Hamlet acted abord me: which I permitt to keepe my people from idlenes and unlawful games, or sleepe.'
1619–20, at Court.
1637, at Hampton Court, 24 January, 'before the kinge and Queene'.

REGISTERED   1602 'xxvj^{to} Julij. James Robertes. Entred for his Copie . . .
          A booke called the Revenge of Hamlett Prince Denmarke as yt was latelie Acted by the Lord Chamberleyne his servantes'.

PUBLISHED   1603 Q1. 'The Tragicall Historie of Hamlet Prince of Denmarke By William Shake-speare. As it hath beene diuerse times acted by his Highnesse seruants in the Cittie of London: as also in the two Vniuersities of Cambridge and Oxford, and else-where.' A 'bad' Quarto,

The Tragicall Hiſtorie of
HAMLET
Prince of Denmarke.

Enter two Centinels. { now call'd *Bernardo*
{ & *Francisco* —

1. STand: who is that?
2. STis I.
1. O you come moſt carefully vpon your watch,
2. And if you meete *Marcellus* and *Horatio,*
The partners of my watch, bid them make haſte.
1. I will: See who goes there.
    Enter Horatio and Marcellus.
Hor. Friends to this ground.
Mar. And leegemen to the Dane,
O farewell honeſt ſouldier, who hath releeued you?
1. *Barnardo* hath my place, giue you good night.
Mar. Holla, *Barnardo.*
2. Say, is *Horatio* there?
Hor. A peece of him.
2. Welcome *Horatio,* welcome good *Marcellus.*
Mar. What hath this thing appear'd againe to night.
2. I haue ſeene nothing.
Mar. *Horatio* ſayes tis but our fantaſie,
And wil not let beliefe take hold of him,
Touching this dreaded ſight twice ſeene by vs,
    B   There-

THE TRAGEDIE OF
HAMLET, Prince of Denmarke.

Actus Primus. Scæna Prima.

Enter Barnardo and Francisco two Centinels.

Barnardo.

Ho's there?

Fran. Nay answer me: Stand & vnfold
your selfe.

Bar. Long liue the King.

Fran. Barnardo?

Bar. He.

Fran. You come most carefully vpon your houre.

Bar. Tis now strook twelue, get thee to bed Francisco.

Fran. For this releefe much thankes: 'Tis bitter cold,
And I am sicke at heart.

Barn. Haue you had quiet Guard?

Fran. Not a Mouse stirring.

Barn. Well, goodnight. If you do meet Horatio and
Marcellus, the Riuals of my Watch, bid them make hast.

Enter Horatio and Marcellus.

Fran. I thinke I heare them. Stand: who's there?

Hor. Friends to this ground.

Mar. And Leige-men to the Dane.

Fran. Giue you good night.

Mar. O farewel honest Soldier, who hath relieu'd you?

Fra. Barnardo ha's my place: giue you goodnight.

Exit Fran.

Mar. Holla Barnardo.

Bar. Say, what is Horatio there?

Hor. A peece of him.

Bar. Welcome Horatio, welcome good Marcellus.

Mar. What, ha's this thing appear'd againe to night.

Bar. I haue seene nothing.

Mar. Horatio saies, 'tis but our Fantasie,
And will not let beleefe take hold of him
Touching this dreaded sight, twice seene of vs,
Therefore I haue intreated him along
With vs, to watch the minutes of this Night,
That if againe this Apparition come,
He may approue our eyes, and speake to it.

Hor. Tush, tush, 'twill not appeare.

Bar. Sit downe a while,
And let vs once againe assaile your eares,
That are so fortified against our Story,
What we two Nights haue seene.

Hor. Well, sit we downe,
And let vs heare Barnardo speake of this.

Barn. Last night of all,
When yond same Starre that's Westward from the Pole
Had made his course t'illume that part of Heauen

Where now it burnes, Marcellus and my selfe,
The Bell then beating one.

Mar. Peace, breake thee of:
Looke where it comes againe.

Enter the Ghost

Barn. In the same figure, like the King that's dead.

Mar. Thou art a Scholler; speake to it Horatio.

Barn. Lookes it not like the King? Marke it Horatio.

Hora. Most like: It harrowes me with feat & wonder

Barn. It would be spoke too.

Mar. Question it Horatio.

Hor. What art thou that vsurp'st this time of night,
Together with that Faire and Warlike forme
In which the Maiesty of buried Denmarke
Did sometimes march: By Heauen I charge thee speake.

Mar. It is offended.

Barn. See, it stalkes away.

Hor. Stay: speake; speake: I Charge thee, speake.

Exit the Ghost.

Mar. 'Tis gone, and will not answer.

Barn. How now Horatio? You tremble & look pale:
Is not this something more then Fantasie?
What thinke you on't?

Hor. Before my God, I might not this beleeue
Without the sensible and true auouch
Of mine owne eyes.

Mar. Is it not like the King?

Hor. As thou art to thy selfe,
Such was the very Armour he had on,
When th'Ambitious Norwey combatted:
So frown'd he once, when in an angry parle
He smot the sledded Pollax on the Ice.
'Tis strange.

Mar. Thus twice before, and iust at this dead houre,
With Martiall stalke, hath he gone by our Watch.

Hor. In what particular thought to work, I know not:
But in the grosse and scope of my Opinion,
This boades some strange eruption to our State.

Mar. Good now sit downe, & tell me he that knowes
Why this same strict and most obseruant Watch,
So nightly toyles the subiect of the Land,
And why such dayly Cast of Brazon Cannon
And Forraigne Mart for Implements of warre:
Why such impresse of Ship-wrights, whose sore Taske
Do's not diuide the Sunday from the weeke,
What might be toward, that this sweaty hast
Doth make the Night ioynt-Labourer with the day:
Who is't that can informe me?

Hor. That can I,

A 2

less than half the length of Q2. A reported text, possibly by the actor who played Marcellus in performances based on the transcript underlying F1.

1604 Q2. 'Newly imprinted and enlarged to almost as much againe as it was, according to the true and perfect Coppie.' The longest version, possibly set up from the original MS. 85 lines which appear in F1 were omitted probably in deference to Anne of Denmark, the Queen.

1611 Q3, set up from Q2; Q4 (undated) from Q3; Q5 (1637) from Q4. 1623 F1. Probably set up from a transcript of the Q2 MS, which had been used as a prompt-copy. It is 200 lines shorter than Q2, probably owing to cuts.

SOURCES   Belleforest's French version in his *Histoires Tragiques* (1576) of the *Historiæ Danicæ* of Saxo Grammaticus. There was an old play of Hamlet, now lost, acted in 1594, which may have been written by Kyd and used by Shakespeare.

In 1772 Garrick refined *Hamlet* in a version that was never printed, omitting the grave-diggers and making his own part still larger.

PHILIP HENSLOWE In the name of god Amen begininge at Newington my Lord Admeralle men & my Lorde Chamberlen men As ffolowethe 1594.

June	3.		Heaster & Asheweros	viijˢ.
	4.		the Jewe of Malta	xˢ.
	5.		Andronicous	xijˢ.
	6.		Cutlacke	xjˢ.
	8.	ne	Bellendon	xvijˢ.
	9.		Hamlet	viijˢ.
	10.		Heaster	vˢ.
	11.		the Tamynge of A Shrowe	ixˢ.
	12.		Andronicous	vijˢ.
	13.		the Jewe	iiijˢ.

(This reference by Henslowe in his *Diary* to a performance of *Hamlet* refers to the lost play, or *Ur-Hamlet*, which may have been written by Kyd. The disintegrators maintain that Q1 is a version of this play revised by Shakespeare, and that even in Q2 fragments of the old *Hamlet* are incorporated and account for certain dramatic difficulties.)

GABRIEL HARVEY The younger sort takes much delight in Shakespeares Venus, & Adonis: but his Lucrece, & his tragedie of Hamlet, Prince of Denmarke, haue it in them, to please the wiser sort.
                                                                Marginalia, 1598–1601.

ANTHONY SCOLOKER It should be like the *Neuer-too-well read Arcadia*, where the *Prose* and *Verce* (*Matter* and *Words*) are like his *Mistresses* eyes, one still excelling another and without Coriuall: or to come home to the vulgars *Element*, like *Friendly Shakespeare's Tragedies*, where the *Commedian* rides, when the *Tragedian* stands on Tip-toe: Faith it should please all, like Prince *Hamlet*. But in sadnesse, then it were to be feared he would runne mad.

Epistle to Daiphantus, 1604.

PEPYS To the Opera, and there saw 'Hamlet, Prince of Denmarke', done with scenes very well, but above all, Betterton did the Prince's part beyond imagination. (24 *August* 1661.)

To the Theatre, and there saw 'Hamlett' very well done. (27 *Nov.* 1661.)

By water to the Royal Theatre; but that was so full they told us we could have no room. And so to the Duke's house; and there saw 'Hamlett' done, giving us fresh reason never to think enough of Betterton. Who should we see come upon the stage but Gosnell, my wife's maid, but neither spoke, danced, nor sung; which I was sorry for. (28 *May* 1663.)

With my wife within doors, and getting a speech out of Hamlett, 'to bee or not to bee', without book. (*Nov.* 13, *Lord's Day*, 1664.)

To the Duke of York's playhouse, and saw 'Hamlet', which we have not seen this year before, or more; and mightily pleased with it, but, above all, with Betterton, the best part, I believe, that ever man acted. (30 *August* 1668.)

CHARLES GILDON I have been told that he writ the scene of the Ghost in *Hamlet*, at his House which bordered on the Charnel-House and Church-Yard.

Lives and Characters, 1698.

JOHN DOWNES The Tragedy of *Hamlet*; *Hamlet* being Perform'd by Mr. *Betterton*, Sir *William* [Davenant] (having seen Mr. *Taylor* of the *Black-Fryars* Company Act it, who being Instructed by the Author Mr. *Shakespear*) taught Mr. *Betterton* in every Particle.

Roscius Anglicanus, 1708.

NICHOLAS ROWE His admirable Wit, and the natural Turn of it to the Stage, soon distinguish'd him, if not as an extraordinary Actor, yet as an excellent Writer. His Name is Printed, as the Custom was in those Times, amongst those of the other Players, before some old Plays, but without any particular Account of what sort of Parts he us'd to play; and tho' I have inquir'd, I could never meet with any further Account of him this way, than that the top of his performance was the Ghost in his own *Hamlet*. . . .

I cannot leave *Hamlet*, without taking notice of the Advantage with which we have seen this Master-piece of *Shakespear* distinguish it self upon the Stage, by Mr *Betterton's* fine Performance of that Part . . . I must own a particular Obligation to him, for the most considerable part of the Passages relating to his Life, which I have here transmitted to the Publick; his Veneration for the Memory of *Shakespear* having engaged him to make a Journey into *Warwickshire*, on purpose to gather up what Remains he could of a Name for which he had so great a value.

Works of Shakespeare, 1709.

JOHNSON If the dramas of Shakespeare were to be characterized, each by the particular excellence which distinguishes it from the rest, we must allow to the tragedy of Hamlet the praise of variety. The incidents are so numerous, that the argument of the play would make a long tale. The scenes are interchangeably diversified with merriment and solemnity; with merriment, that includes judicious and instructive observations; and solemnity, not strained by poetical violence above the natural sentiments of man. New characters appear from time to time in continual succession, exhibiting various forms of life and particular modes of conversation. The pretended madness of Hamlet causes much mirth, the mournful distraction of Ophelia fills the heart with tenderness, and every personage produces the effect intended, from the apparition that, in the first act, chills the blood with horror, to the fop, in the last, that exposes affectation to just contempt.

The conduct is, perhaps, not wholly secure against objections. The action is, indeed, for the most part, in continual progression, but there are some scenes which neither forward nor retard it. Of the feigned madness of Hamlet there appears no adequate cause, for he does nothing which he might not have done with the reputation of sanity. He plays the madman most, when he treats Ophelia with so much rudeness, which seems to be useless and wanton cruelty.

Hamlet is, through the whole piece, rather an instrument than an agent. After he has, by the stratagem of the play, convicted the king, he makes no attempt to punish him; and his death is at last effected by an incident which Hamlet has no part in producing.

The catastrophe is not very happily produced; the exchange of weapons is rather an expedient of necessity, than a stroke of art. A scheme might easily have been formed to kill Hamlet with the dagger, and Laertes with the bowl.

The poet is accused of having shown little regard to poetical justice, and may be charged with equal neglect of poetical probability. The apparition left the regions of the dead to little purpose; the revenge which he demands is not obtained, but by the death of him that was required to take it; and the gratification, which would arise from the destruction of an usurper and a murderer, is abated by the untimely death of Ophelia, the young, the beautiful, the harmless, and the pious.

VOLTAIRE Je suis bien loin assurément de justifier en tout la tragédie d'Hamlet: c'est une pièce grossière et barbare, qui ne serait pas supportée par la plus vile populace de la France et de l'Italie. Hamlet y devient fou au seconde acte, et sa maîtresse folle au troisième; le prince tue le père de sa maîtresse, feignant de tuer un rat, et l'héröine se jette dans la rivière. On fait sa fosse sur le théâtre; des fossoyeurs disent des *quolibets* dignes d'eux, en tenant dans leurs mains des têtes de morts; le print Hamlet répond à leurs grossièretés abominables par des folies non moins dégoûtantes. Pendant ce temps-là, un des acteurs fait la conquête de la Pologne. Hamlet, sa mère, et son beau-père boivent ensemble sur le théâtre; on chante à table, on sy' querelle, on se bat, on se tue: on croirait que cet ouvrage est le fruit de l'imagination d'un sauvage ivre.

Préface de Sémiramis, 1748.

MALONE Oldys, in one of his manuscripts, says that Shakespeare received but
five pounds for his *Hamlet*; whether from the players who first
acted it, or the printer or bookseller who first published it, is not distinguished.
Supplementary Observations, 1780.

GOETHE Figure to yourselves this youth, this son of princes; conceive him
vividly, bring his state before your eyes, and then observe him
when he learns that his father's spirit walks; stand by him in the terrors of
the night, when the venerable ghost itself appears before him. A horrid
shudder passes over him; he speaks to the mysterious form; he sees it beckon
him; he follows it, and hears. The fearful accusation of his uncle rings in his
ears; the summons to revenge, and the piercing oft-repeated prayer, Remember me!

And when the ghost has vanished, who is it that stands before us? A young
hero panting for vengeance? A prince by birth, rejoicing to be called to
punish the usurper of his crown? No! trouble and astonishment take hold of
the solitary young man: he grows bitter against smiling villains, swears that
he will not forget the spirit, and concludes with the significant ejaculation:

> The time is out of joint: O cursed spite,
> That ever I was born to set it right!

In these words, I imagine, will be found the key to Hamlet's whole procedure. To me it is clear that Shakespeare meant, in the present case, to
represent the effects of a great action laid upon a soul unfit for the performance
of it. In this view the whole piece seems to me to be composed. There is an
oak-tree planted in a costly jar, which should have borne only pleasant
flowers in its bosom; the roots expand, the jar is shivered.

A lovely, pure, noble and most moral nature, without the strength of nerve
which forms a hero sinks beneath a burden which it cannot bear and must
not cast away. All duties are holy for him; the present is too hard. Impossibilities have been required of him; not in themselves impossibilities, but such
for him. He winds, and turns, and torments himself; he advances and recoils;
is ever put in mind, ever puts himself in mind; at last does all but lose his
purpose from his thoughts; yet still without recovering his peace of mind.
(See also p. 76.)

Wilhelm Meister, 1795.

COLERIDGE The seeming inconsistencies in the conduct and character of
Hamlet have long exercised the conjectural ingenuity of critics;
and, as we are always loth to suppose that the cause of defective apprehension
is in ourselves, the mystery has been too commonly explained by the very
easy process of setting it down as in fact inexplicable, and by resolving the
phenomenon into a misgrowth or *lusus* of the capricious and irregular genius
of Shakspeare. The shallow and stupid arrogance of these vulgar and indolent
decisions I would fain do my best to expose. I believe the character of Hamlet
may be traced to Shakspeare's deep and accurate science in mental philosophy.
Indeed, that this character must have some connection with the common

fundamental laws of our nature may be assumed from the fact, that Hamlet has been the darling of every country in which the literature of England has been fostered. In order to understand him, it is essential that we should reflect on the constitution of our own minds. Man is distinguished from the brute animals in proportion as thought prevails over sense: but in the healthy processes of the mind, a balance is constantly maintained between the impressions from outward objects and the inward operations of the intellect;— for if there be an overbalance in the contemplative faculty, man thereby becomes the creature of mere meditation, and loses his natural power of action. Now one of Shakspeare's modes of creating characters is, to conceive any one intellectual or moral faculty in morbid excess, and then to place himself, Shakspeare, thus mutilated or diseased, under given circumstances. In Hamlet he seems to have wished to exemplify the moral necessity of a due balance between our attention to the objects of our senses, and our meditation on the workings of our minds,—an *equilibrium* between the real and the imaginary worlds. In Hamlet this balance is disturbed: his thoughts, and the images of his fancy, are far more vivid than his actual perceptions, and his very perceptions, instantly passing through the *medium* of his contemplations, acquire, as they pass, a form and a colour not naturally their own. Hence we see a great, an almost enormous, intellectual activity, and a proportionate aversion to real action, consequent upon it, with all its symptoms and accompanying qualities. This character Shakspeare places in circumstances, under which it is obliged to act on the spur of the moment:—Hamlet is brave and careless of death, but he vacillates from sensibility, and procrastinates from thought, and loses the power of action in the energy of resolve. Thus it is that this tragedy presents a direct contrast to that of Macbeth; the one proceeds with the utmost slowness, the other with a crowded and breathless rapidity.

LAMB The character of Hamlet is perhaps that by which, since the days of Betterton, a succession of popular performers have had the greatest ambition to distinguish themselves. The length of the part may be one of their reasons. But for the character itself, we find it in a play, and therefore we judge it a fit subject of dramatic representation. The play itself abounds in maxims and reflections beyond any other, and therefore we consider it as a proper vehicle for conveying moral instruction. But Hamlet himself— what does he suffer meanwhile by being dragged forth as a public schoolmaster, to give lectures to the crowd! Why, nine parts in ten of what Hamlet does, are transactions between himself and his moral sense; they are the effusions of his solitary musings, which he retires to holes and corners and the most sequestered parts of the palace to pour forth; or rather, they are the silent meditations with which his bosom is bursting, reduced to words for the sake of the reader, who must else remain ignorant of what is passing there. These profound sorrows, these light-and-noise-abhorring ruminations, which the tongue scarce dares utter to deaf walls and chambers, how can they be represented by a gesticulating actor, who comes and mouths them out before an audience, making four hundred people his confidants at once! I say not that it is the fault of the actor so to do; he must pronounce them *ore rotundo*; he must accompany them with his eye; he must insinuate them into his auditory by some trick of eye, tone, or gesture,—or he fails. *He must be thinking all the while of his appearance, because he knows that all the while the spectators are judging of it.* And this is the way to represent the shy, negligent, retiring Hamlet!

On the Tragedies of Shakspeare, 1811.

HAZLITT Hamlet is a name; his speeches and sayings but the idle coinage of the poet's brain. What then, are they not real? They are as real as our own thoughts. Their reality is in the reader's mind. It is *we* who are Hamlet. . . .

The character of Hamlet stands quite by itself. It is not a character marked by strength of will or even of passion, but by refinement of thought and sentiment. Hamlet is as little of the hero as a man can well be: but he is a young and princely novice, full of high enthusiasm and quick sensibility —the sport of circumstances, questioning with fortune and refining on his own feelings, and forced from the natural bias of his disposition by the strangeness of his situation. He seems incapable of deliberate action, and is only hurried into extremities on the spur of the occasion, when he has no time to reflect. . . . At other times, when he is most bound to act, he remains puzzled, undecided, and sceptical, dallies with his purposes, till the occasion is lost, and finds out some pretence to relapse into indolence and thoughtfulness again. . . .

He is the prince of philosophical speculators; and because he cannot have his revenge perfect, according to the most refined idea his wish can form, he declines it altogether. So he scruples to trust the suggestions of the ghost, contrives the scene of the play to have surer proof of his uncle's guilt, and then rests satisfied with this confirmation of his suspicions, and the success of his experiment, instead of acting upon it. Yet he is sensible of his own weakness, taxes himself with it, and tries to reason himself out of it. Still he does nothing; and this very speculation on his own infirmity only affords him another occasion for indulging it. It is not from any want of attachment to his father or abhorrence of his murder that Hamlet is thus dilatory, but it is more to his taste to indulge his imagination in reflecting upon the enormity of the crime and refining on his schemes of vengeance, than to put them into immediate practice. His ruling passion is to think, not to act: and any vague pretext that flatters this propensity instantly diverts him from his previous purposes. . . .

We do not like to see our author's plays acted, and least of all, *Hamlet.* There is no play that suffers so much in being transferred to the stage. Hamlet himself seems hardly capable of being acted. Mr. Kemble unavoidably fails in this character from a want of ease and variety. The character of Hamlet is made up of undulating lines; it has the yielding flexibility of 'a wave o' th' sea'. Mr. Kemble plays it like a man in armour, with a determined inveteracy of purpose, on one undeviating straight line, which is as remote from the natural grace and refined susceptibility of the character as the sharp angles and abrupt starts which Mr. Kean introduces into the part. Mr. Kean's Hamlet is as much too splenetic and rash as Mr. Kemble's is too deliberate and formal. His manner is too strong and pointed. He throws a severity, approaching to virulence, into the common observations and answers. There is nothing of this in Hamlet. He is, as it were, wrapped up in his reflections, and only *thinks aloud*. There should therefore be no attempt to impress what he says upon others by a studied exaggeration of emphasis or manner; no *talking at* his hearers. There should be as much of the gentleman and scholar as possible infused into the part, and as little of the actor. A pensive air of sadness should sit reluctantly upon his brows, but no appearance of fixed and sullen gloom. He is full of weakness and melancholy, but there is no harshness in his nature. He is the most amiable of misanthropes.

A. C. BRADLEY We come next to what may be called the sentimental view of Hamlet, a view common both among his worshippers and among his defamers. Its germ may perhaps be found in an unfortunate phrase of Goethe's (who of course is not responsible for the whole view): 'a lovely, pure and most moral nature, *without the strength of nerve which forms a hero*, sinks beneath a burden which it cannot bear and must not cast away.' When this idea is isolated, developed and popularised, we get the picture of a graceful youth, sweet and sensitive, full of delicate sympathies and yearning aspirations, shrinking from the touch of everything gross and earthly; but frail and weak, a kind of Werther, with a face like Shelley's and a voice like Mr. Tree's. And then we ask in tender pity, how could such a man perform the terrible duty laid on him?

How, indeed! And what a foolish Ghost even to suggest such a duty! But this conception, though not without its basis in certain beautiful traits of Hamlet's nature, is utterly untrue. It is too kind to Hamlet on one side, and it is quite unjust to him on another. The 'conscience' theory at any rate leaves Hamlet a great nature which you can admire and even revere. But for the 'sentimental' Hamlet you can feel only pity not unmingled with contempt. Whatever else he is, he is no *hero*.

But consider the text. This shrinking, flower-like youth—how could he possibly have done what we *see* Hamlet do? What likeness to him is there in the Hamlet who, summoned by the Ghost, bursts from his terrified friends with the cry:

> Unhand me, gentlemen!
> By heaven, I'll make a ghost of him that lets me;

the Hamlet who scarcely once speaks to the King without an insult, or to Polonius without a gibe; the Hamlet who storms at Ophelia and speaks daggers to his mother; the Hamlet who, hearing a cry behind the arras, whips out his sword in an instant and runs the eavesdropper through; the Hamlet who sends his 'school-fellows' to their death and never troubles his head about them more; the Hamlet who is the first man to board a pirate ship, and who fights with Laertes in the grave; the Hamlet of the catastrophe, an omnipotent fate, before whom all the court stands helpless, who, as the truth breaks upon him, rushes on the King, drives his foil right through his body, then seizes the poisoned cup and forces it violently between the wretched man's lips, and in the throes of death has force and fire enough to wrest the cup from Horatio's hand ('By heaven, I'll have it!') lest he should drink and die? This man, the Hamlet of the play, is a heroic, terrible figure. He would have been formidable to Othello or Macbeth. If the sentimental Hamlet had crossed him, he would have hurled him from his path with one sweep of his arm.

This view, then, or any view that approaches it, is grossly unjust to Hamlet, and turns tragedy into mere pathos. But on the other side, it is too kind to him. It ignores the hardness and cynicism which were indeed no part of his nature, but yet, in this crisis of his life, are indubitably present and painfully marked. . . .

There remains, finally, that class of view which may be named after Schlegel and Coleridge. According to this, *Hamlet* is the tragedy of reflection. The cause of the hero's delay is irresolution; and the cause of this irresolution is excess of the reflective or speculative habit of mind. . . .

On the whole, the Schlegel-Coleridge theory is the most widely received view of Hamlet's character. . . . Nevertheless this theory fails to satisfy. And it fails not merely in this or that detail, but as a whole. . . . And thus, I must maintain, it degrades Hamlet and travesties the play. For Hamlet, according to all the indications in the text, was not naturally or normally such a man, but rather, I venture to affirm, a man who at any *other* time and in any *other* circumstances than those presented would have been perfectly equal to his task; and it is, in fact, the very cruelty of his fate that the crisis of his life comes on him at the one moment when he cannot meet it, and when his highest gifts, instead of helping him, conspire to paralyse him. . . .

Under the conditions of a peculiar kind, Hamlet's reflectiveness certainly might prove dangerous to him, and his genius might even (to exaggerate a little) become his doom. Suppose that violent shock to his moral being of which I spoke;[1] and suppose that under this shock, any possible action being denied to him, he began to sink into melancholy; then, no doubt, his imaginative and generalising habit of mind might extend the effects of this shock through his whole being and mental world. And if, the state of melancholy being thus deepened and fixed, a sudden demand for difficult and decisive action in a matter connected with the melancholy arose, this state might well have for one of its symptoms an endless and futile mental dissection of the required deed. And, finally, the futility of this process, and the shame of this delay, would further weaken him and enslave him to his melancholy still more. Thus the speculative habit would be *one* indirect cause of the morbid state which hindered action; and it would also reappear in a degenerate form as one of the *symptoms* of this morbid state.

Shakespearean Tragedy, 1904.

[1] It was the moral shock of the sudden ghastly disclosure of his mother's true nature, falling on him when his heart was aching with love, and his body doubtless weakened by sorrow.

J. Dover Wilson   We are driven, therefore, to conclude with Loening, Bradley, Clutton-Brock and other critics that Shakespeare meant us to imagine Hamlet suffering from some kind of mental disorder throughout the play. Directly, however, such critics begin trying to define the exact nature of the disorder, they go astray. Its immediate origin cannot be questioned; it is caused, as we have seen, by the burden which fate lays upon his shoulders. We are not, however, at liberty to go outside the frame of the play and seek remoter origins in his past history. It is now well known, for instance, that a breakdown like Hamlet's is often due to seeds of disturbance planted in infancy and brought to evil fruition under the influence of mental strain of some kind in later life. Had Shakespeare been composing *Hamlet* to-day, he might conceivably have given us a hint of such an infantile complex. But he knew nothing of these matters and to write as if he did is to beat the air. We may go further. It is entirely misleading to attempt to describe Hamlet's state of mind in terms of modern psychology at all, not merely because Shakespeare did not think in these terms, but because—once again—Hamlet is a character in a play, not in history. He is part only, if the most important part, of an artistic masterpiece, of what is perhaps the most successful piece of dramatic illusion the world has ever known. And at no point of the composition is the illusion more masterly contrived than in the matter of his distraction. . . .

I call the 'sore distraction' melancholy because that is the name which Hamlet gives it, and the name by which Shakespeare and his audience no doubt thought of it. The character of Hamlet, like so many other dramatic characters of the period, was a study in melancholy; and melancholy was a condition of mind to which men in the late sixteenth century and throughout the seventeenth gave much thought. . . . But though Shakespeare relates his Hamlet to contemporary notions about melancholy, just as he sets his Ghost in a framework of references and allusions to the demonology of the day, neither is composed according to any prescribed pattern or recipe; and they are as greatly mistaken who seek the origin of Hamlet's character in Elizabethan psychology as those who attempt to fathom it in terms of Freudian psychopathology. . . .

I believe, as many others have believed, that this conception first came to Shakespeare from the career and personality of his patron's hero, the brilliant, melancholy and ill-fated Earl of Essex, who met his death upon the scaffold some six to twelve months before *Hamlet*, as we now have it, appeared upon the stage. Apart from the question of its probability, which I have argued elsewhere, the theory has the merit of explaining why Shakespeare set out to surround his Prince with an atmosphere of mystery. The character of Essex was also a mystery, the most baffling and widely discussed of the age, and if audiences at the beginning of the seventeenth century saw the features of the Earl in those of Shakespeare's Hamlet, so far from worrying about the mystery as modern critics do, they would expect it and accept it as a matter of course. But, while the theory explains the historical origin of Hamlet's mystery, it does nothing to reveal its true nature. If Shakespeare made Hamlet mysterious partly in order to increase his likeness to Essex, he secured the effect not by psychological analysis but through dramatic illusion. Even if the historians could recapture for us the very soul of Essex and hand it over for examination to psychologists endowed with finer instruments than have yet been or are ever likely to be fashioned, the diagnosis would not help us a whit with Hamlet. For Hamlet is not Essex; he is not even Essex as reflected in the mind of Shakespeare; he is that reflection, sufficiently life-like to be recognisable by Shakespeare's contemporaries, but moulded, adapted and remade for the purposes of dramatic art.

In fine, we were never intended to reach the heart of the mystery. That it has a heart is an illusion; the mystery itself is an illusion; Hamlet is an illusion. The secret that lies behind it all is not Hamlet's, but Shakespeare's: the technical devices he employed to create this supreme illusion of a great and mysterious character, who is at once mad and the sanest of geniuses, at once a procrastinator and a vigorous man of action, at once a miserable failure and the most adorable of heroes. The character of Hamlet, like the appearance of his successive impersonators on the stage, is a matter of 'make-up'.

What Happens in Hamlet, 1935.

F. E. HALLIDAY It is dramatically important that Claudius should be a formidable opponent; we must feel that Hamlet is confronted physically with a difficult task or his delay will make us merely impatient; the smaller the stature of the king the smaller that of Hamlet. That Claudius is an adulterer and a villain is of the essence of the play, the main premise on which the rest depends; Hamlet calls him 'a mildewed ear', 'a vice of kings', a 'bloody, bawdy villain', but Hamlet is, to put it moderately, prejudiced, and in a less frenzied mood calls him a 'mighty opposite'. The truth is that Shakespeare is at pains to show us the better qualities of the king; though he is a deep drinker he can carry his Rhenish and we never see him drunk; though he seduced Gertrude his love seems to be more than sensual appetite; and though he murdered his brother he tries to repent. It is not suggested that Claudius is not vicious, but he has virtues too; he is clever, quick-witted, resolute and brave, and we must do him justice if we are to do justice to Hamlet. Shakespeare does so, and as he makes tragic heroes of Macbeth and King John by the poetry that he gives them to speak, so does he make Claudius a more worthy opponent of Hamlet:

> In the corrupted currents of this world
> Offence's gilded hand may shove by justice,
> And oft 'tis seen the wicked prize itself
> Buys out the law: but 'tis not so above;
> There is no shuffling . . .

The speech illustrates another quality of the poetry: the pervasive assonance, a threatening and muttered undertone of short *u*'s that runs throughout as prologue to the omen coming on. Thus, the principal assonantal sequence of Claudius—*corrupted currents, justice, shuffling, shove, above*—remarkably resembles that of Hamlet's soliloquy, two of the words, indeed, being common to both: *suffer, troubles, shuffled, undiscovered country, puzzles, currents, rub, grunt*. As another example there is the king's,

> the people muddied,
> Thick and unwholsome in their thoughts and whispers,
> For good Polonius' death; and we have done but greenly
> In hugger-mugger to inter him: poor Ophelia
> Divided from herself and her fair judgment . . .

And in prose there is Hamlet's, 'It is such a kind of gaingiving as would perhaps trouble a woman'.

This subdued and ominous utterance is only one element in the pervading atmosphere, not so much of revenge and blood, as of mystery; another is the poetry as a whole. All poetry is mysterious both in its origin and in itself, and the greater the poetry the more disturbing its strange reverberations of meaning. But Shakespeare himself was haunted by the mysteries of life and death, and nowhere does he express this feeling more powerfully and beautifully than in *Hamlet*, particularly, of course, in the character of Hamlet himself, and this is perhaps the main secret of the almost universal appeal of the tragic hero and his poetry.

Hamlet describes this feeling when he compares himself to a recorder, his 'mystery', of course, being very much more than his secret knowledge of his father's murder: 'You would play upon me; you would seem to know my stops; you would pluck out the heart of my mystery; you would sound me from my lowest note to the top of my compass: and there is much music in this little organ: yet cannot you make it speak.' Then, in the more powerful medium of verse:

> The dread of something after death,
> The undiscovered country from whose bourn
> No traveller returns.

Yet Hamlet dies on a note of certitude, his assurance emphasised by the unexpected latinisms so exquisitely set between lines of homely monosyllables:

> If thou didst ever hold me in thy heart,
> Absent thee from felicity awhile,
> And in this harsh world draw thy breath in pain,
> To tell my story.

It is out of this poetry, this synthesis of lyric, epic and elegy, subdued and made dramatic, that the best-loved of Shakespeare's characters is fashioned; for by now it is axiomatic that poetry is character, and this poetry *is* Hamlet.

The Poetry of Shakespeare's Plays, 1954.

THE MERRY WIVES OF WINDSOR

WRITTEN   1600–1. But see the extract from Leslie Hotson's *Shakespeare versus Shallow*, printed below.

PERFORMED   'Divers times acted' before Q1, 1602.
        1604 Nov. 4th, at Whitehall, 'By his Maiesties plaiers'.
1638 Nov. 15th, 'At the Cocpit'.

REGISTERED   1602 Jan. 18th, by John Busby, and assigned to Arthur Johnson.

PUBLISHED   1602 Q1. 'A Most pleasant and excellent conceited Comedie, of Syr Iohn Falstaffe, and the merrie Wiues of Windsor Enter-mixed with sundrie variable and pleasing humors, of Syr Hugh the Welch Knight, Iustice Shallow, and his wise Cousin M. Slender. With the swagger-ing vaine of Auncient Pistoll, and Corporall Nym. By William Shakespeare. As it hath bene diuers times Acted by the right Honorable my Lord Chamber-laines seruants. Both before her Maiestie, and else-where.' A 'bad' Quarto, based on a report, probably that of the actor who played the Host.
1619 Q2. One of the ten plays printed by Jaggard in 1619, many of them with false dates. Set up from Q1.
1623 F1. A good text.

SOURCES   The plot is essentially Shakespeare's. The theme of the lover hidden by the unfaithful wife is common enough in the literature of the period.
    There are obvious references to the visit of the Count of Mömpelgart to England, including Windsor, in 1592, and to that of his ambassador (also to Windsor) in 1595, who urged his master's claim to the Garter promised by Elizabeth. Mömpelgart was elected to the Order in 1597; in 1598 he sent an embassy to express his gratitude, and in 1600 a third embassy to obtain the insignia. The investiture was eventually granted by James I in 1603. (Cf. 'Cosen *garmombles*' of IV. v, the *Garter* Inn, and the Garter references in V. v.)
    The Merry Wives was adapted, or rather perverted, by John Dennis in his *The Comicall Gallant*, 1702.

JOHN DENNIS   That this Comedy was not despicable, I guess'd for several
        Reasons: First, I knew very well, that it had pleas'd one of the greatest Queens that ever was in the World, great not only for her Wisdom in the Arts of Government, but for her Knowledge of Polite Learning, and her nice taste of the Drama, for such a taste we may be sure she had, by the relish which she had of the Ancients. This Comedy was written at her Command, and by her direction, and she was so eager to see it Acted, that she commanded it to be finished in fourteen days; and was afterwards, as Tradition tells us, very well pleas'd at the Representation.
                        Epistle to the Comicall Gallant, 1702.

PEPYS After dinner went to the New Theatre [Killigrew's], and there I saw
'The Merry Wives of Windsor' acted—the humours of the country
gentleman and the French doctor very well done, but the rest but very poorly,
and Sir J. Falstaffe as bad as any. (6 *Dec.* 1660.)

To the Theatre, and saw 'The Merry Wives of Windsor' ill done. (25
Sept. 1661.)

To the Duke's house; where a new play. The King and Court there: the
house full, and an act begun. And so we went to the King's, and there saw
'The Merry Wives of Windsor'; which did not please me at all, in no part
of it. (13 *Aug.* 1667.)

DRYDEN In the mechanic beauties of the plot, which are the observation of
the three Unities, Time, Place, and Action, they (Shakespeare and
Fletcher) are both deficient; but Shakespeare most. Ben Jonson reformed
those errors in his comedies, yet one of Shakespeare's was regular before him;
which is, *The Merry Wives of Windsor.*
Preface to Troilus and Cressida, 1679.

CHARLES GILDON The *Fairys* in the fifth Act makes a Handsome Comple-
ment to the Queen, in her Palace of *Windsor,* who had
oblig'd him to write a Play of *Sir John Falstaff* in Love, and which I am
very well assured he perform'd in a Fortnight; a prodigious Thing, when all
is so well contriv'd, and carry'd on without the least Confusion.
Remarks on the Plays of Shakespear, 1710.

RICHARD DAVIES (Shakespeare was) much given to all unluckinesse in
stealing venison & Rabbits particularly from Sr   Lucy
who had him oft whipt & sometimes Imprisoned & at last made Him fly his
Native Country to his great Advancemt. but His reveng was so great that he
is his Justice Clodpate and calls him a great man & yt in allusion to his name
bore three lowses rampant for his Arms.

(Davies was Rector of Sapperton, Glos., 1695–1703.)

WILLIAM OLDYS There was a very aged gentleman living in the neighbourhood of Stratford, (where he died fifty years since,) who
had not only heard, from several old people in that town, of Shakespeare's
transgression, but could remember the first stanza of that bitter ballad,[1]
which, repeating to one of his acquaintance, he preserved it in writing; and

---

[1] 'He had, by a Misfortune common enough to young Fellows, fallen into Ill
Company; and amongst them, some that made a frequent practice of Deer-stealing,
engag'd him with them more than once in robbing a Park that belong'd to Sir
Thomas Lucy of *Cherlecot,* near *Stratford.* For this he was prosecuted by that
Gentleman, as he thought, somewhat too severely; and in order to revenge that ill
Usage, he made a Ballad upon him. And tho' this, probably the first Essay of his
Poetry, be lost, yet it is said to have been so very bitter, that it redoubled the
Prosecution against him to that degree, that he was oblig'd to leave his Business
and Family in *Warwickshire,* for some time, and shelter himself in *London.*'—
Nicholas Rowe, 1709.

here it is, neither better nor worse, but faithfully transcribed from the copy
which his relation very courteously communicated to me.

> A parliemente member, a justice of peace,
> At home a poor scare-crowe, at London an asse,
> If lowsie is Lucy, as some volke miscalle it,
> Then Lucy is lowsie whatever befall it:
> > He thinks himselfe greate,
> > Yet an asse in his state,
> We allowe by his ears but with asses to mate.
> > If Lucy is lowsie, as some volke miscalle it,
> > Sing lowsie Lucy, whatever befall it.

Contemptible as this performance must now appear, at the time when it was
written it might have sufficient power to irritate a vain, weak, and vindictive
magistrate; especially as it was affixed to several of his park-gates, and consequently published among his neighbours.—It may be remarked likewise,
that the jingle on which it turns, occurs in the first scene of *The Merry Wives
of Windsor*.

> Quoted by G. Steevens in his *Works of Shakespeare*,
> from a MS of Oldys (c. 1750).

JOHNSON Of this play there is a tradition preserved by Mr. Rowe, that it was
written at the command of queen Elizabeth, who was so delighted
with the character of Falstaff, that she wished it to be diffused through more
plays; but, suspecting that it might pall by continued uniformity, directed the
poet to diversify his manner, by showing him in love. No task is harder than
that of writing to the ideas of another. Shakespeare knew what the queen, if
the story be true, seems not to have known, that by any real passion of tenderness, the selfish craft, the careless jollity, and the lazy luxury of Falstaff must
have suffered so much abatement, that little of his former cast would have
remained. Falstaff could not love, but by ceasing to be Falstaff. He could
only counterfeit love, and his professions could be prompted, not by the hope
of pleasure, but by money. Thus the poet approached as near as he could to
the work enjoined him; yet having, perhaps, in the former plays, completed
his own idea, seems not to have been able to give Falstaff all his former power
of entertainment.

This comedy is remarkable for the variety and number of the personages,
who exhibit more characters appropriated and discriminated, than, perhaps,
can be found in any other play.

Whether Shakespeare was the first that produced upon the English stage
the effect of language distorted and depraved by provincial or foreign pro-
nunciation, I cannot certainly decide. This mode of forming ridiculous
characters can confer praise only on him who originally discovered it, for it
requires not much of either wit or judgment; its success must be derived
almost wholly from the player, but its power in a skilful mouth even he that
despises it is unable to resist.

The conduct of this drama is deficient; the action begins and ends often before the conclusion, and the different parts might change places without inconvenience; but its general power, that power by which all works of genius shall finally be tried, is such, that, perhaps, it never yet had reader or spectator, who did not think it too soon at an end.

HAZLITT *The Merry Wives of Windsor* is no doubt a very amusing play, with a great deal of humour, character, and nature in it: but we should have liked it much better, if any one else had been the hero of it, instead of Falstaff. We could have been contented if Shakespear had not been 'commanded to show the knight in love'. Wits and philosophers, for the most part, do not shine in that character; and Sir John himself, by no means, comes off with flying colours. Many people complain of the degradation and insults to which Don Quixote is so frequently exposed in his various adventures. But what are the unconscious indignities which he suffers compared with the sensible mortifications which Falstaff is made to bring upon himself? What are the blows and buffetings which the Don receives from the staves of the Yanguesian carriers or from Sancho Panza's more hard-hearted hands, compared with the contamination of the buck-basket, the disguise of the fat woman of Brentford, and the horns of Herne the hunter, which are discovered on Sir John's head? In reading the play, we indeed wish him well through all these discomfitures, but it would have been as well if he had not got into them. Falstaff in the *Merry Wives of Windsor* is not the man he was in the two parts of *Henry IV*. His wit and eloquence have left him. Instead of making a butt of others, he is made a butt of by them. Neither is there a single particle of love in him to excuse his follies: he is merely a designing, bare-faced knave, and an unsuccessful one. The scene with Ford as Master Brook, and that with Simple, Slender's man, who comes to ask after the Wise Woman, are almost the only ones in which his old intellectual ascendancy appears. He is like a person recalled to the stage to perform an unaccustomed and ungracious part; and in which we perceive only 'some faint sparks of those flashes of merriment, that were wont to set the hearers in a roar'. But the single scene with Doll Tearsheet, or Mrs. Quickly's account of his desiring 'to eat some of housewife Keach's prawns', and telling her 'to be no more so familiarity with such people', is worth the whole of the *Merry Wives of Windsor* put together. . . .

Shallow himself has little of his consequence left. But his cousin, Slender, makes up for the deficiency. He is a very potent piece of imbecility. In him the pretensions of the worthy Gloucestershire family are well kept up, and immortalised. He and his friend Sackerson and his book of songs and his love of Anne Page and his having nothing to say to her can never be forgotten. It is the only first-rate character in the play: but it is in that class. Shakespear is the only writer who was as great in describing weakness as strength.

GEORG BRANDES His task was now to entertain a queen and a court 'with their hatred of ideas, their insensibility to beauty, their hard, efficient manners, and their demand for impropriety'. As it amused the London populace to see kings and princes upon the stage, so it entertained the Queen and her court to have a glimpse into the daily life of the middle classes, so remote from their own, to look into their rooms, and hear their chat with the doctor and the parson, to see a picture of the prosperity and contentment which flourished at Windsor right under the windows of the Queen's summer residence, and to witness the downright virtue and merry humour of the red-cheeked, buxom townswomen. Thus was the keynote of the piece determined. Thus it became more prosaic and bourgeois than any other play of Shakespeare's. *The Merry Wives* is indeed the only one of his works which is almost entirely written in prose, and the only one of his comedies in which, the scene being laid in England, he has taken as his subject the contemporary life of the English middle classes. It is not quite unlike the more farcical of Molière's comedies, which also were often written with an eye to royal and courtly audiences. All the more significant is the fact that Shakespeare has found it impossible to content himself with thus dwelling on the common earth, and has introduced at the close a fairy-dance and fairy-song, as though from the *Midsummer Night's Dream* itself, executed, it is true, by children and young girls dressed up as elves, but preserving throughout the air and style of genuine fairy scenes.

William Shakespeare (trans. William Archer), 1898.

LESLIE HOTSON As a result of the investigations detailed in these pages, a number of interesting additions have been made to the sum of our knowledge of Shakespeare's life, of the dates of his works, and of his dramatic methods.

We learn first that by the end of October or the beginning of November 1596 he had moved across the Thames to Southwark. And finding him in close association with Francis Langley, the owner of the Swan in Paris Garden, we conclude that his company was acting in Langley's playhouse. We see the actor Shakespeare and his associate the theatre-owner seriously annoyed by the notoriously unjust local justice, William Gardiner, and that unconsidered trifle, his stepson Wayte: so seriously annoyed, that Wayte swears the gentle Shakespeare put him in terror of his life.

Next we recognize this pair of vexatious interlopers by a series of unmistakable hits in *Henry IV Part Two* and *The Merry Wives of Windsor*. This disclosure gives the *coup de grâce* to the moribund notion that Shakespeare, in drawing the figure of Justice Shallow, was thinking of his worthy neighbour in Warwickshire, Sir Thomas Lucy.

By combining our discoveries with the annals of Queen Elizabeth's Court and with the internal evidence of the comedy itself, we have been enabled to fix the date of first production of the *Merry Wives* on April 23, 1597—a date earlier than recent scholarship has suspected. And since it is generally agreed that *Henry IV Part Two* preceded the *Merry Wives*, the two parts of *Henry IV* must now be pushed back into the season 1596–1597. It is now clear, therefore, that except for the touching account of Falstaff's death in *Henry V*, Shakespeare had completed his portraiture of the fat knight by the spring of 1597.

More important, however, than the fresh light on the external life of

Shakespeare, more significant than the alteration in the dates of his plays, is the ocular demonstration now given us of his dramatic use of some of the life he knew: unique evidence of his use of persons, to quote Ben Jonson,

> . . . such as Comedy would choose
> When she would show an image of the times . . .

When we consider the true history of Justice Gardiner, and the local world's opinion of him, the figure of Justice Shallow appears as a new triumph of the dramatist. Shakespeare is here revealed for the first time as a master of personal satire, taking with devastating humour a satisfactory revenge for himself, his associates of the theatre, and Gardiner's victims in Southwark. A few months after the production of the *Merry Wives*, exit Gardiner from the Elizabethan scene into a well-merited oblivion, carrying with him the bitter sting of the contemporary caricature. As children see nothing more in *Gulliver* than the fascinating story, so the play-going world to-day sees in the Justice Shallow scenes no more than inoffensive folly in a care-free atmosphere of perennial comedy. Shakespeare's magic has transmuted a sordid Southwark into a rural Gloucestershire or an ideal Windsor, set in a pleasant England where knaves are fools, and to live is to laugh them out of countenance. We can forgive Gardiner his crimes; did he not give us Justice Shallow? And as for Wayte, it was an act of sublime inspiration in him to pick a quarrel with Shakespeare; for out of it was born that most exquisite of ninnies, Abraham Slender.

Shakespeare versus Shallow, 1931.

TROILUS AND CRESSIDA

WRITTEN   1601–2. Hotson argues that it is the 'Loue labours wonne' mentioned by Meres in 1598.

PERFORMED   The first registration and the first issue of Q both state that the play had been acted. The second issue of Q omits this record, and the Epistle expressly says that it is 'a new play, never stal'd with the Stage'. There is no record of a production, and it was probably acted privately at one of the Inns of Court.

REGISTERED   1603. '7 februarii. Master Robertes. Entered for his copie in full Court holden this day to print when he hath gotten sufficient aucthority for yt, The booke of Troilus and Cresseda as yt is acted by my lord Chamberlens Men vj^d .'
1609. '28^{uo} Januarii. Richard Bonion Henry Walleys . . . a booke called the history of Troylus and Cressida.'

PUBLISHED   1609 Q. (first issue.) 'The Historie of Troylus and Cresseida. As it was acted by the Kings Maiesties seruants at the Globe. Written by William Shakespeare.'
1609 Q. (second issue.) 'The Famous Historie of Troylus and Cresseid. Written by William Shakespeare.'

An Epistle by the publisher was added to this issue.

1623 F1. Set up from Q (which is a good one) and a MS., possibly Shake-speare's original. It is not mentioned in the Catalogue of plays, but seems to have been inserted at the last moment as the first of the Tragedies.

SOURCES   Chaucer: *Troilus and Criseyde.*
                   Caxton: *The Recuyell of the Historyes of Troye.*
Chapman: translation of the *Iliad.*

Parts of the play have been variously assigned to other authors: to Dekker and Chettle, who wrote a *Troilus and Cressida*, to Chapman, and Marston. But apart from the Epilogue there seems no reason whatever to doubt Shakespeare's authorship, and the authority of the Folio.

Dryden adapted the play in 1679: *Troilus and Cressida, or Truth Found too Late.*

ANON *Kempe*. Few of the vniversity men pen plaies well, they smell too
            much of that writer *Ouid*, and that writer *Metamorphosis*, and talke
too much of *Proserpina & Juppiter*. Why heres our fellow *Shakespeare* puts
them all downe, I and *Ben Iohnson* too. O that *Ben Iohnson* is a pestilent
fellow, he brought vp *Horace* giuing the Poets a pill, but our fellow *Shake-speare* hath giuen him a purge that made him beray his credit.
                                  The Returne from Parnassus, Part II. (1601 ?)
(The 'pill' was Jonson's attack on Marston and Dekker in his *Poetaster*,
1601. Some think the uncomplimentary description of Ajax in *Troilus and
Cressida*, I. ii, is aimed at Jonson, and is the 'purge' referred to in this
anonymous play, *Parnassus*.)

A NEUER WRITER, TO AN EUER READER. NEWES.

Eternall reader, you haue heere a new play, neuer stal'd with the Stage, neuer clapper-clawd with the palmes of the vulger, and yet passing full of the palme comicall; for it is a birth of your braine, that neuer under-tooke any-thing commicall, vainely: And were but the vaine names of commedies changde for the titles of Commodities, or of Playes for Pleas; you should see all those grand censors, that now stile them such vanities, flock to them for the maine grace of their grauities: especially this authors Commedies, that are so fram'd to the life, that they serue for the most common Commentaries, of all the actions of our liues shewing such a dexteritie, and power of witte, that the most displeased with Playes, are pleasd with his Commedies. And all such dull and heauy-witted worldlings, as were neuer capable of the witte of a Commedie, comming by report of them to his representations, haue found that witte there, that they neuer found in them selues, and have parted better wittied than they came: feeling an edge of witte set vpon them, more then ever they dreamd they had braine to grinde it on. So much and such sauored salt of witte is in his Commedies, that they seeme (for their height of pleasure) to be borne in that sea that brought forth *Venus*. Amongst all there is none more witty than this: And had I time I would comment upon it, though I know it needs not, (for so much as will make you thinke your testerne well bestowd) but for so much worth, as euen poore I know to be stuft in it. It deserues such a labour, as well as the best Commedy in *Terence* or *Plautus*. And beleeue this, that when hee is gone, and his Commedies out of sale, you will scramble for them, and set vp a new English Inquisition. Take this for a warning, and at the perrill of your pleasures losse, and Iudgements, refuse not, nor like this the lesse, for not being sullied, with the smoaky breath of the multitude; but thanke fortune for the scape it hath made amongst you. Since by the grand possessors wills I beleeue you should have prayd for them rather than been prayd. And so I leaue all such to bee prayd for (for the states of their wits healths) that will not praise it. Vale.

> *The Publisher's* Epistle *in the second issue of the Quarto,* 1609.

DRYDEN   Yet it must be allowed to the present age, that the tongue in general is so much refined since Shakespeare's time, that many of his words, and more of his phrases, are scarce intelligible. And of those which we understand, some are ungrammatical, others coarse; and his whole style is so pestered with figurative expressions, that it is as affected as it is obscure. 'Tis true, that in his latter plays he had worn off somewhat of the rust; but the tragedy which I have undertaken to correct was in all probability one of his first endeavours on the stage. . . .

Shakespeare (as I hinted), in the apprenticeship of his writing, modelled it into that play, which is now called by the name of *Troilus and Cressida*, but so lamely is it left to us, that it is not divided into acts; which fault I ascribe to the actors who printed it after Shakespeare's death; and that too so carelessly, that a more uncorrect copy I never saw. For the play itself, the author seems to have begun it with some fire; the characters of Pandarus and Thersites are promising enough; but as if he grew weary of his task, after an entrance or two, he lets them fall: and the latter part of the tragedy is nothing but a confusion of drums and trumpets, excursions and alarms. The chief persons, who give name to the tragedy, are left alive; Cressida is false, and is not punished. Yet, after all, because the play was Shakespeare's, and that there appeared in some places of it the admirable genius of the author, I undertook to remove that heap of rubbish under which many excellent thoughts lay wholly buried. Accordingly I new-modelled the plot, threw out many unnecessary persons, improved those characters which were begun and left unfinished, as Hector, Troilus, Pandarus, and Thersites, and added that of Andromache. . . .

I will not wear my reader with the scenes which are added of Pandarus and the lovers in the third act, and those of Thersites, which are wholly altered; but I cannot omit the last scene in it, which is almost half the act, betwixt Troilus and Hector. The occasion of raising it was hinted to me by Mr. Betterton; the contrivance and working of it was my own. They who think to do me an injury by saying that it is an imitation of the scene betwixt Brutus and Cassius, do me an honour by supposing I could imitate the incomparable Shakespeare.

> Preface to *Troilus and Cressida,* 1679.

See, my loved Britons, see your Shakespeare rise,
An awful ghost, confess'd to human eyes!
Unnamed, methinks, distinguish'd I had been
From other shades, by this eternal green,
About whose wreaths the vulgar poets strive,
And with a touch their wither'd bays revive.
Untaught, unpractised in a barbarous age,
I found not, but created first the stage.
And, if I drain'd no Greek or Latin store,
'Twas that my own abundance gave me more.
On foreign trade I needed not rely,
Like fruitful Britain, rich without supply.
In this my rough-drawn play you shall behold
Some master-strokes, so manly and so bold,
That he who meant to alter, found 'em such,
He shook, and thought it sacrilege to touch.

    Prologue to *Troilus and Cressida*. Spoken by Mr. Betterton,
      representing the Ghost of Shakespeare.

JOHNSON This play is more correctly written than most of Shakespeare's
      compositions, but it is not one of those in which either the extent
of his views or elevation of his fancy is fully displayed. As the story abounded
with materials, he has exerted little invention; but he has diversified his
characters with great variety, and preserved them with great exactness. His
vicious characters sometimes disgust, but cannot corrupt, for both Cressida
and Pandarus are detested and contemned. The comic characters seem to
have been the favourites of the writer; they are of the superficial kind, and
exhibit more of manners than nature; but they are copiously filled and powerfully impressed.

COLERIDGE Indeed, there is no one of Shakespeare's plays harder to charac-
      terise. The name and remembrances connected with it, prepare
us for the representation of attachment no less faithful than fervent on the
side of the youth, and of sudden and shameless inconstancy on the part of
the lady. And this is, indeed, as the gold thread on which the scenes are
strung, though often kept out of sight and out of mind by gems of greater
value than itself. But as Shakespeare calls forth nothing from the mausoleum
of history, or the catacombs of tradition, without giving, or eliciting, some
permanent and general interest, and brings forward no subject which he does
not moralise or intellectualise,—so here he has drawn in Cressida the portrait
of a vehement passion, that, having its true origin and proper cause in warmth
of temperament, fastens on, rather than fixes to, some one object by liking
and temporary preference.

    There's language in her eye, her cheek, her lip,
    Nay, her foot speaks: her wanton spirits look out
    At every joint and motive of her body.

This Shakespeare has contrasted with the profound affection represented in Troilus, and alone worthy the name of love; but still having a depth of calmer element in a will stronger than desire, more entire than choice, and which gives permanence to its own act by converting it into faith and duty. Hence with excellent judgment, and with an excellence higher than mere judgment can give, at the close of the play, when Cressida has sunk into infamy below retrieval and beneath hope, the same will, which had been the substance and the basis of his love, while the restless pleasures and passionate longings, like sea-waves, had tossed but on its surface,—this same moral energy is represented as snatching him aloof from all neighbourhood with her dishonour, from all lingering fondness and languishing regrets, whilst it rushes with him into other and nobler duties, and deepens the channel, which his heroic brother's death had left empty for its collected flood. . . .

To all this, however, so little comparative projection is given,—nay, the masterly group of Agamemnon, Nestor, and Ulysses, and, still more in advance, that of Achilles, Ajax, and Thersites, so manifestly occupy the foreground, that the subservience and vassalage of strength and animal courage to intellect and policy seems to be the lesson most often in our poet's view, and which he has taken little pains to connect with the former more interesting moral impersonated in the titular hero and heroine of the drama. . . .

The character of Thersites, in particular, well deserves a more careful examination, as the Caliban of demagogic life;—the admirable portrait of intellectual power deserted by all grace, all moral principle, all not momentary impulse;—just wise enough to detect the weak head, and fool enough to provoke the armed fist of his betters.

HAZLITT This is one of the most loose and desultory of our author's plays: it rambles on just as it happens, but it overtakes, together with some indifferent matter, a prodigious number of fine things in its way. Troilus himself is no character: he is merely a common lover: but Cressida and her uncle Pandarus are hit off with proverbial truth. By the speeches given to the leaders of the Grecian host, Shakespear seems to have known them as well as if he had been a spy sent by the Trojans into the enemy's camp—to say nothing of their affording very lofty examples of didactic eloquence. . . .

It cannot be said of Shakespear, as was said of some one, that he was 'without o'erflowing full'. He was full, even to o'erflowing. He gave heaped measure, running over. This was his greatest fault.

KEATS I throw my whole being into Troilus, and repeating those lines, 'I wander like a lost Soul upon the Stygian Banks staying for waftage', I melt into the air with a voluptuousness so delicate that I am content to be alone.

Letter to George and Georgiana Keats, Oct. 1818.

CAROLINE SPURGEON *Troilus* and *Hamlet* are very closely connected in their imagery. Did we not know it for other reasons we could be sure from the similarity and continuity of symbolism in the two plays that they were written near together, and at a time when the author was suffering from a disillusionment, revulsion, and perturbation of nature, such as we feel nowhere else with the same intensity.

The same two groups of images run through and dominate both plays, disease and food; in *Hamlet* the first is predominant, and in *Troilus* the second.

The main emotional theme in *Troilus*—passionate, idealistic love followed by disillusion and despair—is pictured with overwhelming vividness through physical taste; the exquisite anticipation by a sensitive palate of delicious food and wine, and the sick revolt and disgust on finding on one's tongue only 'greasy relics' or rotting fruit.

The disgust at woman's wantonness seems to express itself instinctively to Shakespeare, especially in these two plays and in *Antony*, in terms of physical appetite and food. 'Heaven and earth' cries Hamlet,

> she would hang on him,
> As if increase of appetite had grown
> By what it fed on: and yet, within a month—
> Let me not think on't.

So lust, says the elder Hamlet, 'though to a radiant angel link'd', will 'prey on garbage'.

Cleopatra, like Cressid, is thought of as a tempting and delicious piece of food, 'a dish for the gods';

> other women cloy
> The appetites they feed, but she makes hungry
> Where most she satisfies:

and in moments of revulsion both alike become a cold and greasy remnant: 'I found you', says Antony,

> 'as a morsel cold upon
> Dead Cæsar's trencher.'

In like manner, before Troilus has been undeceived he thinks of his sweet love as 'food for fortune's tooth', and when the revulsion of disgust follows her treachery, he cries bitterly,

> The fractions of her faith, orts of her love,
> The fragments, scraps, the bits and greasy relics
> Of her o'er-eaten faith, are bound to Diomed.

In that amazing image of the anticipation of her love it is the sense of taste which comes naturally to Troilus's lips as the means of expressing it:

> I am giddy; expectation whirls me round.
> The imaginary relish is so sweet
> That it enchants my sense: what will it be,
> When that the watery palates taste indeed
> Love's thrice repured nectar?

and it is an image drawn from the same sense, as applied to 'the poor creature, small beer', which Cressid uses when Pandarus urges her to moderate her emotion at the thought of parting from Troilus,

> how can I moderate it?
> If I could temporise with my affection,
> Or brew it to a weak and colder palate,
> The like allayment could I give my grief.

Troilus, in the vivid, passionate speeches, the metaphors of which throw so much light on his character (II. ii. 26–32, 37–50, 61–96), twice draws upon food to make his thought more clear. Thus, for instance, when he is fulminating against the prudent counsels of his brothers to let Helen go, based on reason, he uses a curious metaphor from a jugged or stuffed hare, which is clearly an associative one. He scorns their timidity, and in true Shakespearean fashion he expresses the quality by the concrete example of the most timid animal of the fields in England, turning it into an adjective; this, in turn, calls up the memory of the succulent dish still a favourite one with English country folk, and he applies the process of the larding, and cooking of it (which he clearly knows well) to the dulling of men's minds and the sapping of their fiery manhood with overmuch reason and caution:

> Nay, if we talk of reason,
> Let's shut our gates and sleep: manhood and honour
> Should have hare-hearts, would they but fat their thoughts
> With this cramm'd reason.

And a little later, when he is again urging them to stand firm by honour, though it may not be the easiest way or suit them at the moment, he takes an example from ordinary, thrifty household management to illustrate this:

> nor the remainder viands
> We do not throw in unrespective seive,
> Because we now are full.

The force of this dominating symbol is so great that we find that fourteen of the characters make use of images of food, taste, or cooking, and that there are no less than forty-four such images in the play: seething, stewing, mincing, baking, larding, stuffing, broiling, basting, brewing, frying, kneading, boiling, and stirring the ingredients for a pudding, are among the various kinds of cooking described or referred to, sometimes at considerable length, as in the metaphor on grinding the wheat, bolting, leavening, kneading, making the cake, heating the oven, baking, and cooling, carried on with expert knowledge by Pandarus and complete understanding by Troilus in the opening of the play (I. i. 14–26).

A 'crusty batch' (of bread), cheese served for a digestive, or mouse-eaten and dry, an addled egg, mincemeat seasoned with spice and salt and baked in a pie, porridge after meat, a dish of fool (stewed fruit crushed with cream), a fusty nut, a hard sailor's biscuit, fair fruit rotting untasted in an unwholesome dish, and greasy remnants of food are, in addition, all pressed into service; as are also hunger, appetite, ravenous eating, digestion, fasting, feeding, tasting, drinking up the lees and dregs of wine, tossing off a toast, sauce, flavouring, salt, sweet and sour.

Indeed, images of cooking seem so constantly with the speakers that they cannot refrain from using them even in the most far-fetched way; as when Pandarus describes how, when Helen was playing with Troilus, Queen Hecuba laughed so that her eyes ran o'er, and Cassandra laughed, to which Cressida quickly retorts,

> But there was more temperate fire under the pot of her eyes: did her eyes run o'er too?

Or when Ulysses refers to Achilles as the proud lord

> That bastes his arrogance with his own seam (lard),

and declares that if, as had been suggested, Ajax went to him,

> That were to enlard his fat-already pride.

Shakespeare's Imagery, 1935.

O. J. CAMPBELL The finale of *Troilus and Cressida* is a subtle variation of the approved end of the characters derided in dramatic satire. Throughout the play Troilus' infatuation is presented in a way to provoke mingled feelings of revulsion and amusement. This complicated emotion Shakespeare maintained and accentuated in the last scene of the play. Two kinds of denouement had become conventional in the comical satires of Jonson and Marston. The characters chosen as butts of ridicule were either purged and reformed, or scornfully ejected from the comedy. Victims of social folly could be exposed in such a way as to make their amendment and reform seem natural. But moral delinquency was too much a part of the culprit's essential nature to be easily corrected and discarded. It deserved to be pursued to the very last by the scornful laughter of both author and audience.

The formal satirists adopted this last method, ejecting evil men and women from their poems with exclamations of fierce disdain. Jonson, too, had treated vicious characters in just this way. Shakespeare himself at the end of *Twelfth Night* had sent Malvolio running off the stage shouting, 'I'll be revenged on the whole pack of you', and the frantic steward had been pursued by the jeers of the enemies who had exposed him, and by the scorn of the audience.

Troilus and Cressida, too, are dismissed with similar mockery. The critics should then not be troubled that the woman has not been condignly punished for her infidelity or that her lover has not been slain before the eyes of the audience in single combat with Achilles. Such poetic justice would have given each of the lovers the dignity of a tragic figure; and nowhere during the action had they attained such stature. If we insist upon following Troilus beyond the limits of the play, after hearing his hysterical threat to haunt Achilles 'like a wicked conscience still', we may, if we are discerning, anticipate his fate. But, as a victim of uncontrolled passion for a wanton, he did not deserve the dignity of a death on a field of battle. And Cressida deserved a similar moment of nobility still less. Futility, Shakespeare clearly believed, was the proper end for characters designed to fit into the intellectual and structural conventions of dramatic satire.

However, in spite of the fact that Shakespeare employed a firmly established literary convention in fashioning the close of *Troilus and Cressida*, the ending has seldom been understood. The reason seems to be that in the play Shakespeare divested the convention of all its obvious features. Troilus has been caught in no booby trap. His sin and folly have brought him to no obvious disaster. His catastrophe is of a more profound and less tangible sort. In accepting Will instead of Reason for his guide in public affairs as well as in the private life of his emotions, he has disrupted his entire personality and rendered himself distraught and futile. That is the meaning of Troilus' last frantic exit, but no commentator is at hand to interpret it. Pandarus, who might have performed this service for us, instead flings at the audience unsavory jests about the disappointments and disabilities of a pander's trade. Had Shakespeare designed *Troilus and Cressida* for a popular audience, he would never have put the final vile speech into the mouth of Pandarus. But this tirade, perfectly suited to the taste of a crowd of benchers, enhanced for them the meaning and the temper of the play they had just seen.

Nor in all probability would Shakespeare have made so continuous an intellectual demand upon his hearers if he had been writing for a popular audience. . . . The intellectual foundations of the action are laid too deep for the understanding of a cursory reader or an inattentive spectator. . . .

If *Troilus and Cressida* is a kind of satiric play it can be judged by definite artistic standards. It need no longer be regarded as a confused and incomplete tragedy. Nor need it be condemned for the author's failure to adopt all the principles of the new comicall satyre. In *Troilus and Cressida* Shakespeare shows his unfailing independence of his models. He combines his satire of the vices of power politics and of lust with a long philosophical and lyrical debate. In this way he has produced a play filled with a new beauty and new significance. In one sense then the work establishes the standards by which it must be judged. But modern readers can best catch and cherish the magnificent values of *Troilus and Cressida* if they realize that the play is Shakespeare's highly original version of a recently devised form—the comicall satyre of Jonson and Marston.

Shakespeare's Satire, 1943.

ALL'S WELL THAT ENDS WELL

WRITTEN   1603–4.

PERFORMED   The first recorded performance is 1741.

REGISTERED 1623. 8 November. One of the 16 plays registered by Blount
            and Jaggard before publishing F1.

PUBLISHED   1623 F1. Not a very good text: some indications of cutting,
            and of additions by the book-keeper.

SOURCE   Boccaccio's tale of *Giglietta di Nerbona* in the *Decameron*,
            translated in William Painter's *Palace of Pleasure*, 1566.

It has been suggested that *All's Well* is a revised version of 'Loue labours
wonne' mentioned by Meres in his *Palladis Tamia*, 1598. J. M. Robertson
attributes *All's Well* mainly to Chapman; on the other hand Chambers does
'not see that any other assumption helps to make this difficult play more
intelligible than the assumption of Shakespeare working in an abnormal
mood'. Yet it seems quite clear that there are either two hands or two Shakespeares in the play.

JOHNSON This play has many delightful scenes, though not sufficiently
        probable, and some happy characters, though not new, nor pro-
duced by any deep knowledge of human nature. Parolles is a boaster and a
coward, such as has always been the sport of the stage, but, perhaps, never
raised more laughter or contempt than in the hands of Shakespeare.

I cannot reconcile my heart to Bertram; a man noble without generosity,
and young without truth; who marries Helen as a coward, and leaves her as
a profligate: when she is dead by his unkindness, sneaks home to a second
marriage, is accused by a woman whom he has wronged, defends himself by
falsehood, and is dismissed to happiness.

The story of Bertram and Diana had been told before of Mariana and
Angelo, and, to confess the truth, scarcely merited to be heard a second time.

COLERIDGE

        Dia. The Count Rousillon:—know you such a one?
        Hel. But by the ear that hears most nobly of him;
              His face I know not.

Shall we say here, that Shakspeare has unnecessarily made his loveliest
character utter a lie?

HAZLITT *All's Well that Ends Well* is one of the most pleasing of our
        author's comedies. The interest is however more of a serious than
of a comic nature. The character of Helen is one of great sweetness and
delicacy. She is placed in circumstances of the most critical kind, and has to
court her husband both as a virgin and a wife: yet the most scrupulous nicety

of female modesty is not once violated. There is not one thought or action that ought to bring a blush into her cheeks, or that for a moment lessens her in our esteem.

GERVINUS In few plays do we feel, so much as in *All's Well that Ends Well*, what excessive scope the poet leaves open to the actor's art. Few readers, and still fewer female readers, will believe in Helena's womanly nature, even after they have read our explanations and have found them indisputable. The subject has at once repelled them; and so far would we gladly make allowance for this feeling, that we grant that Shakespeare might better have bestowed his psychological art upon more agreeable matter, and that he has often done so. But even he who, by the aid of our remarks, may have overcome his repugnance to the subject, will seldom find himself able by reflection to imagine it possible that such bold and masculine steps could be taken in a thoroughly feminine manner. Only by seeing this work of art and by trusting the eye, can we be sensible of its full and harmonious effect. But that even the eye may be convinced, a great actress is required. Bertram also demands a good actor, if the spectator is to perceive that this is a man capable of rewarding efforts so great on the part of a woman, a man whose painful wooing promises a grateful possession. That this unsentimental youth has a heart, this corrupted libertine a good heart, that this scorner can ever love the scorned, this is indeed *read* in his scanty words, but few readers of the present day are free enough from sentimentality to believe such things on the credit of a few words. The case is entirely different when, in the *acted* Bertram, they *see* the noble nature, the ruin of his character at Florence, and the contrition which his sins and his simplicity call forth; when, from the whole bearing of the brusque man, they perceive what the one word 'pardon' signified in his mouth, when they see his breast heave at the last appearance of Helena bringing ease to his conscience. Credence is then given to his last words; for the great change in his nature—of which now only a forlorn word or two is read and overlooked—would then have been witnessed. Seldom has a task so independent as the character of Bertram been left to the art of the actor; but still more seldom is the actor to be found, who knows how to execute it.

Shakespeare Commentaries, 1850.

W. W. LAWRENCE A solid point of departure, then, for the interpretation of a Shakespearean play founded upon traditional story, is to inquire first of all what its theme would have meant to an Elizabethan audience. The direct source of the play may have been in literary form— Boccaccio or Bandello or an old play—but in spite of all modifications, and, in a sense, irrespective of the direct source, the vital theme emerges, with its old charm and authority, and asserts its power once more. Shakespeare knew that it could be trusted to make its appeal, and unhesitatingly used it for the very foundations of his play. Like story-tellers in all ages, he made changes, introducing new material of his own, altering details of plot and motivation and character, but—and this is the important point—seldom running counter to the fundamental conceptions which his theme involved, not making, for example, a hero out of a villain, or a heroine out of a wanton. He not only retained irrationalities, but he himself sometimes introduced, as in *Measure for Measure*, traditional but irrational elements into a rational situation, where no previous story-teller had done so. . . .

We are now in a position to refute the assertion that Helena is guilty of indelicate persistence in pursuing the man who has rebuffed her. Just such persistence, such single-eyed devotion to a good object, irrespective of all other considerations, was regarded as meritorious. It is one of the most striking features of the Virtue Stories. . . . That a virtue might be carried too far, or that it might transgress the most elementary demands of common-sense and decency in making for its goal, seems to have been little regarded in medieval story. Fantastic exaggerations were common, and due allowance must be made for these exaggerations when we find them woven into the fabric of Shakespeare's plays.

Equally untenable, in the light of early analogues, is the idea that the bed-trick is immodest, unworthy of a refined woman. There is never the least intimation in these analogues that the heroine, in thus proving her devotion, is doing an immodest thing. The answer would have been: she is lying with her husband, as any chaste wife has a right to do. The objection that delicacy would prevent her from doing so under false pretences would have been met by an Elizabethan, partly by the obvious point that she has to do so in order to fulfil her husband's conditions, and partly by the conviction, which we have just noted, that virtue should stick at nothing in pursuing its course. This appears not only in popular but also in aristocratic literature. Would the elegant chronicler of the Count of Artois, writing in the late fifteenth century, in order to compliment the houses of Burgundy and Artois, have attributed this ruse to the elegant and virtuous Countess if it had seemed indelicate? Would Shakespeare, in *Measure for Measure*, have made the ensky'd and sainted Isabella, the gentle forsaken Mariana, and the benevolent Duke use a similar stratagem if it had been felt repugnant to modesty?

What, now, as to the psychological adequacy of the ending of the play? Shall we conclude that 'the triumph of Helena's love will be merely external,' that a union so brought about will never be happy?

To argue thus is to miss the whole point of the Faithful Wife theme, whether in medieval and Renaissance analogues, or in Shakespeare. No matter how harsh the treatment of the woman by the man, no matter how unsuited they may seem to each other, it is a convention of the Virtue Story that they 'live happily ever after'.

> Ful many a yeer in heigh prosperitee
> Liven these two in concord and in reste,

says Chaucer, after the trials of Griselda are over. . . . Would the Prince have really been happy with Cinderella, obviously of a very different social station, just because she happened to have a small foot? The answer is, of course he would; the cold light of reason is no guide in stories.

Shakespeare's Problem Comedies, 1931.

MEASURE FOR MEASURE

WRITTEN   1604–5.

PERFORMED 1604. Dec. 26 at Whitehall. 'By his Maiesties plaiers. On
           St Stiuens night in the Hall A Play Caled Mesur for Mesur.
Shaxberd.' (*Revels Account*.)

REGISTERED 1623. 8 November. One of the 16 plays registered by Blount
           and Jaggard before publishing F1.

PUBLISHED 1623 F1. Not a good text; possibly from a transcript of the
           original MS. There are indications of cutting.

SOURCES   George Whetstone's *Promos and Cassandra* (1578), a play
           based on a story in Giraldi Cinthio's *Hecatommithi* or *Hundred
Tales* (1565).

Davenant wrote an adaptation, *The Law against Lovers*, in which he
combined *Measure for Measure* with Benedick and Beatrice in *Much Ado*.
In 1699 Charles Gildon shortened *Measure for Measure* and introduced a
masque and music.

PEPYS I went to the Opera, and saw 'The Law against Lovers', a good play
       and well performed, especially the little girls, whom I never saw act
before, dancing and singing.

Diary, Feb. 18*th*, 1662.

JOHNSON There is, perhaps, not one of Shakespeare's plays more darkened
        than this, by the peculiarities of its author, and the unskilfulness of
its editors, by distortions of phrase, or negligence of transcription.

The novel of Giraldi Cynthio, from which Shakespeare is supposed to
have borrowed this fable, may be read in Shakespeare Illustrated, elegantly
translated, with remarks, which will assist the inquirer to discover how much
absurdity Shakespeare has admitted or avoided. . . .

Of this play, the light or comic part is very natural and pleasing, but the
grave scenes, if a few passages be excepted, have more labour than elegance.
The plot is rather intricate than artful. The time of the action is indefinite;
some time, we know not how much, must have elapsed between the recess
of the duke and the imprisonment of Claudio; for he must have learned the
story of Mariana in his disguise, or he delegated his power to a man already
known to be corrupted. The unities of action and place are sufficiently
preserved.

COLERIDGE This play, which is Shakspeare's throughout, is to me the most
          painful—say rather, the only painful—part of his genuine
works. The comic and tragic parts equally border on the μισητόν,—the
one being disgusting, the other horrible; and the pardon and marriage of
Angelo not merely baffles the strong indignant claim of justice—(for cruelty,

with lust and damnable baseness, cannot be forgiven, because we cannot conceive them as being morally repented of;) but it is likewise degrading to the character of woman. Beaumont and Fletcher, who can follow Shakspeare in his errors only, have presented a still worse, because more loathsome and contradictory, instance of the same kind in the Night-Walker, in the marriage of Alathe to Algripe. Of the counter-balancing beauties of Measure for Measure, I need say nothing; for I have already remarked that the play is Shakspeare's throughout.

HAZLITT This is a play as full of genius as it is of wisdom. Yet there is an original sin in the nature of the subject, which prevents us from taking a cordial interest in it. 'The height of moral argument' which the author has maintained in the intervals of passion or blended with the more powerful impulses of nature, is hardly surpassed in any of his plays. But there is in general a want of passion; the affections are at a stand; our sympathies are repulsed and defeated in all directions. The only passion which influences the story is that of Angelo; and yet he seems to have a much greater passion for hypocrisy than for his mistress. Neither are we greatly enamoured of Isabella's rigid chastity, though she could not act otherwise than she did. We do not feel the same confidence in the virtue that is 'sublimely good' at another's expense, as if it had been put to some less disinterested trial. As to the Duke, who makes a very imposing and mysterious stage-character, he is more absorbed in his own character than attentive to the feelings and apprehensions of others. Claudio is the only person who feels naturally; and yet he is placed in circumstances of distress which almost preclude the wish for his deliverance. Mariana is also in love with Angelo, whom we hate. In this respect, there may be said to be a general system of cross-purposes between the feelings of the different characters and the sympathy of the reader or the audience. This principle of repugnance seems to have reached its height in the character of Master Barnadine, who not only sets at defiance the opinions of others, but has even thrown off all self-regard,—'one that apprehends death no more dreadfully but as a drunken sleep; careless, reckless, and fearless of what's past, present, and to come'. He is a fine antithesis to the morality and the hypocrisy of the other characters of the play. Barnardine is Caliban transported from Prospero's wizard island to the forests of Bohemia or the prisons of Vienna. He is the creature of bad habits as Caliban is of gross instincts. He has however a strong notion of the natural fitness of things, according to his own sensations—'He has been drinking hard all night, and he will not be hanged that day'—and Shakespear has let him off at last. We do not understand why the philosophical German critic, Schlegel, should be so severe on those pleasant persons, Lucio, Pompey, and Master Froth, as to call them 'wretches'. They appear all mighty comfortable in their occupations, and determined to pursue them, 'as the flesh and fortune should serve'. A very good exposure of the want of self-knowledge and contempt for others, which is so common in the world, is put into the mouth of Abhorson, the jailor, when the Provost proposes to associate Pompey with him in his office—'A bawd, sir? Fie upon him, he will discredit our mystery.' And the same answer will serve in nine instances out of ten to the same kind of remark, 'Go to, sir, you weigh equally; a feather will turn the scale'. Shakespear was in one sense the least moral of all writers; for morality (commonly so called) is made up of antipathies; and his talent consisted in sympathy with human nature, in all its shapes, degrees, depressions, and elevations. The object of the pedantic moralist is to find out the bad in everything: his was to shew that 'there is some soul of goodness in things evil'. Even Master Barnardine is not left to the mercy of what others think of him; but when he comes in, speaks for himself, and pleads his own cause, as well as if counsel had been assigned him. In one sense, Shakespear was no moralist at all: in another, he was the greatest of all moralists. He was a moralist in the same sense in which nature is one. He taught what he had learned from her. He showed the greatest knowledge of humanity with the greatest fellow-feeling for it.

WALTER PATER As Shakespeare in *Measure for Measure* has refashioned, after a nobler pattern, materials already at hand, so that the relics of other men's poetry are incorporated into his perfect work, so traces of the old 'morality', that early form of dramatic composition which had for its function the inculcating of some moral theme, survive in it also, and give it a peculiar ethical interest. This ethical interest, though it can escape no attentive reader, yet, in accordance with that artistic law which demands the predominance of form everywhere over the mere matter or subject handled, is not to be wholly separated from the special circumstances, necessities, embarrassments, of these particular dramatic persons. The old 'moralities' exemplified most often some rough-and-ready lesson. Here the very intricacy and subtlety of the moral world itself, the difficulty of seizing the true relations of so complex a material, the difficulty of just judgment, of judgment that shall not be unjust, are the lessons conveyed. Even in Whetstone's old story this peculiar vein of moralising comes to the surface: even there, we notice the tendency to dwell on mixed motives, the contending issues of action, the presence of virtues and vices alike in unexpected places, on 'the hard choice of two evils', on the 'imprisoning' of men's 'real intents'. *Measure for Measure* is full of expressions drawn from a profound experience of these casuistries, and that ethical interest becomes predominant in it: it is no longer *Promos and Cassandra*, but *Measure for Measure*, its new name expressly suggesting the subject of *poetical justice*. The action of the play, like the action of life itself for the keener observer, develops in us the conception of this poetical justice, and the yearning to realise it, the true justice of which Angelo knows nothing, because it lies for the most part beyond the limits of any acknowledged law. The idea of justice involves the idea of rights. But at bottom rights are equivalent to that which really is, to facts; and the recognition of his rights therefore, the justice he requires of our hands, or our thoughts, is the recognition of that which the person, in his inmost nature, really is; and as sympathy alone can discover that which really is in matters of feeling and thought, true justice is in its essence a finer knowledge through love.

'Tis very pregnant:
The jewel that we find we stoop and take it,
Because we see it; but what we do not see
We tread upon and never think of it.

It is for this finer justice, a justice based on a more delicate appreciation of
the true conditions of men and things, a true respect of persons in our estimate
of actions, that the people in *Measure for Measure* cry out as they pass before
us; and as the poetry of this play is full of the peculiarities of Shakespeare's
poetry, so in its ethics it is an epitome of Shakespeare's moral judgments.
They are the moral judgments of an observer, of one who sits as a spectator,
and knows how the threads in the design before him hold together under the
surface: they are the judgments of the humourist also, who follows with a
half-amused but always pitiful sympathy, the various ways of human disposition, and sees less distance than ordinary men between what are called
respectively great and little things. It is not always that poetry can be the
exponent of morality; but it is this aspect of morals which it represents most
naturally, for this true justice is dependent on just those finer appreciations
which poetry cultivates in us the power of making, those peculiar valuations
of action and its effect which poetry actually requires.

Appreciations, 1889.

HENRI FLUCHÈRE *Measure for Measure* passes for a comedy but it is the
arch-problem play. Its atmosphere is even more oppressive
[than *Troilus and Cressida*]: there is nothing heroic, nothing romantic to
lighten it. Everything in it is fraught with consequences, meticulously con-
certed and arranged. The moral preoccupation is evident from one end of the
play to the other but, serious though it may be, it seems ill defined and gives
rise to divergent interpretations. It was long considered a failure as a play—
as lacking internal unity, expressing the blackest pessimism and showing how
little interest Shakespeare took in his subject. Modern critics take the opposite
view. Wilson Knight has no hesitation in comparing the Duke with Christ.
C. J. Sisson declares that the spirit of the play is 'profoundly Christian'. It is
ardently admired for similar reasons by D. A. Traversi, F. R. Leavis and Miss
M. C. Bradbrook. Finally, Roy W. Battenhouse has gone so far as to base his
interpretation of *Measure for Measure* on the Christian doctrine of the
Atonement. . . .

But it would seem that no repentance can redeem the criminal hypocrisy
of Angelo (whose name is an ironical contradiction of his nature), no docility
in marriage can allay our mistrust of the insensitive Isabella, whose religious
vocation is as questionable as her feeling of outraged virtue. As for Claudio, no
happy ending can make us forget his egoism and physical cowardice in the
presence of death ('Aye, but to die . . .'). These people are either too human
or not human enough; even the wisdom of the philosopher-Duke is a too
conscious attempt to give arbitrary behaviour the guise of benevolence. He
is incapable of true generosity towards Lucio who has offended him personally;
and Lucio is not wholly contemptible: he is at least true to the brotherhood

of sinners, and the ardour with which he defends Claudio at the most dangerous moment is to his credit.

By comparison with these, the disreputable company of pimps and bawds
of whom the play from time to time gives us a glimpse, seems more respectable.
For they at least are sincere to the point of cynicism and do not seek to be
believed. The Duke's decree ruins them and it is not in the name of virtue
that they protest. But the other characters merely fill us with mistrust or repulsion. Shakespeare has made them so equivocal or contemptible, has placed
them in situations so clearly calculated to bring out only their unattractive or
shady sides, that the play's major themes, far from being those of justice, of
honour or love, seem to be those of ugliness, of sin and villainy. The conflict
between instinct and reason, good intentions and the mass of resistance
offered by the complex of vices, touches here the lowest depths if not of
tragedy at least of demoralization. . . .

Or, on reflection, we may be attracted by the mirage of a symbolical interpretation of the play and regard it as a dramatic picture of the story of the
Atonement.[1] The sovereign in disguise mingles with his people, just as God
descended to earth to wage war upon Satan and to deliver Creation from the
bondage of evil. He leaves to his deputy (Angelo) the application of the Law
but at the same time undertakes to moderate its rigours. Thus two great
principles enter into conflict—that of the Law and that of Grace. The Law
will be the instrument whereby Grace can manifest itself, and Grace after a
dramatic struggle will triumph. The pseudo-just are shown to be sinners;
they will be unmasked and punished. The sinners had in them sufficient
Grace to be forgiven and redeemed. Thus the sacrifice of the Prince of Love
will have borne its fruit.

The symbolism of the names (Mariana=Mary+Anne—the Virgin and
her Mother; Angelo=Angel—Satan is a fallen angel; the Duke, Vicentio=
Conqueror, etc.); the numerous biblical images (star of the morning, shepherd, sinner, ransom); the parable themes, notably those of the Miraculous
Draught of Fishes, of the Bridegroom, of the Temptation, of Sin; the
justification of the lie and of disguising for the ends of salvation; the incidents
of the plot (Isabella the saint interceding for the sinner, receiving the proposal
of her spiritual death, rejecting the temptation to do a wicked deed for a good
cause, then agreeing to save her honour and her brother, on the Duke's
advice, by a manœuvre which can be symbolically interpreted as a ruse of the
Divine Spirit fighting the Devil with his own weapons, so as at last to reap
her reward in the form of marriage with the symbolical Bridegroom): all this
points to a supernatural context, which gives the play a richer and higher
meaning. . . .

Thus understood, *Measure for Measure* takes its place in the tradition of the
Mysteries and the Morality plays. On the temporal plane the Duke, full of
indulgence and of loving concern, can act with gentleness by persuasion, and
his keen intelligence guides virtue through the mire of vice; he can also use

[1] As do Wilson Knight (*The Wheel of Fire*) and Roy W. Battenhouse (*P.M.L.A.*,
Dec. 1946, pp. 1029–59: '*Measure for Measure* and the Christian Doctrine of the
Atonement').

his royal authority to ensure for each his due reward. On the supernatural plane, he symbolizes the ideal Prince who strives to put an end to the world's disorder by his spirit of Justice, of Charity, of Wisdom. And Wilson Knight concludes: 'The play should be read not as a picture of normal human affairs but as a parable, like the Parables of Jesus.'

This double interpretation, whether one likes it or not, enlarges the scope of *Measure for Measure* considerably and makes possible at least two conclusions. The first, historical, namely that we should not try to describe too rigidly the moral or 'philosophical curve' of Shakespeare's Works. . . .

And the second conclusion is this: The peculiar characteristic and function of poetic drama is to include not merely words, deeds and structure, but a shifting implication, a margin of uncertainty between the surface meaning and the overriding intention, between matter and spirit. The poet speaks to us in turns by bright or dark signs, and poetic experience, like religious experience, expresses itself through the indirect channels of image, metaphor and symbol. They are all devices for reaching his goal, which is to state a lasting human truth that can be felt through the various aspects of beauty.

Shakespeare (translated by Guy Hamilton), 1953.

OTHELLO

WRITTEN   1604–5.

PERFORMED   1604. 'By the Kings Maiesties plaiers. Hallamas Day being the first of Nouember A Play in the Banketinge house att WhitHall Called The Moor of Venis.' (*Revels Account.*)

1610, April. 'Lundi, 30. S.E. [Prince Frederick of Württemberg] alla au Globe, lieu ordinaire ou l'on joue les Commedies, y fut representé l'histoire du More de Venise.'

1612–13. One of the plays acted at Whitehall at the 'Magnificent Marriage' of Princess Elizabeth.

1629. 'The benefitt of the winters day from the kinges company being brought me [Sir Henry Herbert, Master of the Revels] upon the play of The Moor of Venise, comes, this 22 of Nov. 1629, unto—9^l. 16^s. 0^d.

1635. 'Maij. 6: not farre from home all day att ye bla: ffryers & a play yis day called ye More of Venice.' (*Diary* of Sir Humphrey Mildmay.)

1636. 'Playes acted before the kinge and Queene this present yeare of the lord, 1636 . . . The 8th of December at Hampton Court, the Moore of Venice.'

REGISTERED   1621, by Thomas Walkley.

PUBLISHED   1622 Q1. 'The Tragœdy of Othello, The Moore of Venice. As it hath beene diuerse times acted at the Globe, and at the Black-Friers, by his Maiesties Seruants. Written by William Shakespeare.' A good text; probably printed from a transcript of the original MS.

1623 F1. A good text; probably printed from the original MS.

SOURCE   Giraldi Cinthio's *Hecatommithi.*

Thomas Walkley To set forth a booke without an Epistle, were like to the old English prouerbe, A blew coat without a badge, & the Author being dead, I thought good to take that piece of worke vpon mee: To commend it, I will not, for that which is good, I hope euery man will commend, without intreaty: and I am the bolder, because the Authors name is sufficient to vent his worke. Thus leauing euery one to the liberty of iudgement: I haue ventered to print this Play, and leaue it to the generall censure.

The Stationer to the Reader, Q 1, 1622.

Pepys To the Cockpit to see 'The Moor of Venice', which was well done. Burt acted the Moor: by the same token, a very pretty lady that sat by me called out, to see Desdemona smothered. (*Oct.* 11*th*, 1660.)

  To Deptford by water, reading 'Othello, Moor of Venice', which I ever heretofore esteemed a mighty good play; but, having so lately read 'The Adventures of Five Houres', it seems a mean thing. (*Aug.* 20*th*, 1666.)

Rymer From all the Tragedies acted on our English Stage, *Othello* is said to bear the Bell away. The Subject is more of a piece, and there is indeed something like, there is, as it were, some phantom of a *Fable* . . . Shakespear alters it from the Original in several particulars, but always, unfortunately, for the worse. He bestows a name on his *Moor*; and styles him the Moor of *Venice*: a Note of pre-eminence, which neither History nor Heraldry can allow him. . . .

What ever rubs or difficulties may stick on the Bark, the Moral, sure, of this Fable is very instructive.

1. First, This may be a caution to all Maidens of Quality how, without their Parents consent, they run away with Blackamoors.

Secondly, this may be a warning to all good Wives, that they look well to their Linnen.

Thirdly, This may be a lesson to Husbands, that before their Jealousie be Tragical, the proofs may be Mathematical.

The *Characters* or Manners, which are the second part in a Tragedy, are not less unnatural and improper, than the Fable was improbable and absurd. . . .

But what is most intolerable is *Jago*. He is no Black-amoor Souldier, so we may be sure he should be like other Souldiers of our acquaintance; yet never in Tragedy, nor in Comedy, nor in Nature was a Souldier with his Character. . . .

Shakespear knew his Character of *Jago* was inconsistent. In this very Play he pronounces,

> *If thou dost deliver more or less than Truth,*
> *Thou art no Souldier.*

This he knew, but to entertain the Audience with something new and surprising, against common sense, and Nature, he would pass upon us a close, dissembling, false, insinuating rascal, instead of an open-hearted, frank, plain-dealing Souldier, a character constantly worn by them for some thousands of years in the World. . . .

The third thing to be consider'd is the *Thoughts*. But from such *Characters*, we need not expect many that are either true, or fine, or noble.

And without these, that is, without sense or meaning, the fourth part of Tragedy, which is the *expression* can hardly deserve to be treated on distinctly. The verse rumbling in our Ears are of good use to help off the action.

In the *Neighing* of an Horse, or in the *growling* of a Mastiff, there is a meaning, there is as lively expression, and, may I say, more humanity, than many times in the Tragical flights of *Shakespear*.

Step then amongst the Scenes to observe the Conduct in this Tragedy. . . .

Whence comes it then, that this is the top scene (III. 3), the Scene that raises *Othello* above all other Tragedies on our Theatres? It is purely from the Action; from the Mops and the Mows, the Grimace, the Grins and Gesticulation. Such scenes as this have made all the World run after *Harlequin* and *Scaramuccio*. . . .

So much ado, so much stress, so much passion and repetition about an Handkerchief! Why was not this call'd the *Tragedy of the Handerkchief*? Had it been *Desdemona's* Garter the Sagacious Moor might have smelt a Rat: but the Handkerchief is so remote a trifle, no Booby, on this side *Mauritania*, cou'd make any consequence from it. . . .

What can remain with the Audience to carry home with them from this sort of Poetry, for their use and edification? how can it work, unless (instead of settling the mind, and purging our passions) to delude our senses, disorder our thoughts, addle our brain, pervert our affections, hair our imaginations, corrupt our appetite, and fill our head with vanity, confusion, *Tintamarre*, and Jingle-jangle, beyond what all the Parish Clarks of *London*, with their *old Testament* farces, and interludes, in *Richard* the seconds time cou'd ever pretend to? Our only hopes, for the good of their Souls, can be, that these people go to the Play-house, as they do to Church, to sit still, look on one another, make no reflection, nor mind the Play, more than they would a Sermon.

There is in this Play, some burlesk, some humour, and ramble of Comical Wit, some shew, and some *Mimickry* to divert the spectators: but the tragical part is, plainly none other, than a Bloody Farce, without salt or savour.

A Short View of Tragedy, 1693.

CHARLES GILDON I'm assured from very good hands, that the Person that Acted Jago was in much esteem for a Comœdian, which made *Shakespear* put several words, and expressions into his part (perhaps not so agreeable to his Character) to make the Audience laugh, who had not yet learnt to endure to be serious a whole Play.

Reflections on Rymer's Short View of Tragedy, 1694.

JOHNSON The beauties of this play impress themselves so strongly upon the attention of the reader, that they can draw no aid from critical illustration. The fiery openness of Othaello, magnanimous, artless, and credulous, boundless in his confidence, ardent in his affection, inflexible in his resolution, and obdurate in his revenge; the cool malignity of Iago, silent in his resentment, subtle in his designs, and studious at once of his interest and vengeance; the soft simplicity of Desdemona, confident of merit, and conscious of innocence, her artless perseverance in her suit, and her slowness to suspect that she can be suspected, are such proofs of Shakespeare's skill in human nature, as, I suppose, it is vain to seek in any modern writer. The gradual progress which Iago makes in the Moor's conviction, and the circumstances which he employs to enflame him, are so artfully natural, that, though it will, perhaps, not be said of him as he says of himself, that he is 'a man not easily jealous', yet we cannot but pity him, when at last we find him 'perplexed in the extreme'.

There is always danger, lest wickedness, conjoined with abilities, should steal upon esteem, though it misses of approbation; but the character of Iago is so conducted, that he is, from the first scene to the last, hated and despised. . . .

The scenes, from the beginning to the end, are busy, varied by happy interchanges, and regularly promoting the progression of the story; and the narrative, in the end, though it tells but what is known already, yet is necessary to produce the death of Othello.

Had the scene opened in Cyprus, and the preceding incidents been occasionally related, there had been little wanting to a drama of the most exact and scrupulous regularity.

LAMB Lear is essentially impossible to be represented on a stage. But how many dramatic personages are there in Shakspeare which though more tractable and feasible (if I may so speak) than Lear, yet from some circumstance, some adjunct to their character, are improper to be shown to our bodily eye! Othello for instance. Nothing can be more soothing, more flattering to the nobler parts of our natures, than to read of a young Venetian lady of the highest extraction, through the force of love and from a sense of merit in him whom she loved, laying aside every consideration of kindred, and country, and colour, and wedding with a *coal-black Moor*—(for such he is represented, in the imperfect state of knowledge respecting foreign countries in those days, compared with our own, or in compliance with popular notions, though the Moors are now well enough known to be by many shades less unworthy of a white man's fancy)—it is the perfect triumph of virtue over accidents, of the imagination over the senses. She sees Othello's colour in his mind. But upon the stage, when the imagination is no longer the ruling faculty, but we are left to our poor unassisted senses, I appeal to every one that has seen Othello played, whether he did not, on the contrary, sink Othello's mind in his colour; whether he did not find something extremely revolting in the courtship and wedded caresses of Othello and Desdemona; and whether the actual sight of the thing did not over-weigh all that beautiful compromise which we make in reading;—and the reason it should do so is obvious, because there is just so much reality presented to our senses as to give a perception of disagreement, with not enough of belief in the internal motives,—all that which is unseen,—to overpower and reconcile the first and obvious prejudices.[1] What we see upon a stage is body and bodily action; what we are conscious of in reading is almost exclusively the mind, and its movements; and this I think may sufficiently account for the very different sort of delight with which the same play so often affects us in the reading and the seeing.

On the Tragedies of Shakespeare.

COLERIDGE Roderigo turns off to Othello; and here comes one, if not the only, seeming justification of our blackamoor or negro Othello.

> *Rod.* What a full fortune does the *thick-lips* owe,
> If he can carry't thus.

Even if we supposed this an uninterrupted tradition of the theatre, and that Shakspeare himself, from want of scenes, and the experience that nothing could be made too marked for the senses of his audience, had practically sanctioned it,—would this prove aught concerning his own intention as a poet for all ages? Can we imagine him so utterly ignorant as to make a barbarous negro plead royal birth,—at a time, too, when negroes were not known except as slaves?—As for Iago's language to Brabantio, it implies merely that Othello was a Moor, that is, black. Though I think the rivalry of Roderigo sufficient to account for his wilful confusion of Moor and Negro,—yet, even if compelled to give this up, I should think it only adapted for the acting of the day, and should complain of an enormity built on a single word, in direct contradiction of Iago's 'Barbary horse'. Besides, if we could in good earnest believe Shakspeare ignorant of the distinction, still why should we adopt one disagreeable possibility instead of a ten times greater and more pleasing probability? It is a common error to mistake the epithets applied by the *dramatis personæ* to each other, as truly descriptive of what the audience ought to see or know. No doubt Desdemona saw Othello's visage in his mind; yet, as we are constituted, and most surely as an English audience was disposed in the beginning of the seventeenth century, it would be something monstrous to conceive this beautiful Venetian girl falling in love with a veritable negro. It would argue a disproportionateness, a want of balance, in Desdemona, which Shakspeare does not appear to have in the least contemplated. . . .

Finally, let me repeat that Othello does not kill Desdemona in jealousy, but in a conviction forced upon him by the almost superhuman art of Iago, such a conviction as any man would and must have entertained who had believed Iago's honesty as Othello did. We, the audience, know that Iago is a villain from the beginning; but in considering the essence of the Shakspearian Othello, we must perseveringly place ourselves in his situation, and under his circumstances. Then we shall immediately feel the fundamental difference between the solemn agony of the noble Moor, and the wretched fishing jealousies of Leontes, and the morbid suspiciousness of Leonatus, who

---

[1] In the reading of the play, we see with Desdemona's eyes: in the seeing of it, we are forced to look with our own.

is, in other respects, a fine character. Othello had no life but in Desdemona:—the belief that she, his angel, had fallen from the heaven of her native innocence, wrought a civil war in his heart. She is his counterpart; and, like him, is almost sanctified in our eyes by her absolute unsuspiciousness, and holy entireness of love. As the curtain drops, which do we pity the most?

HAZLITT   Tragedy creates a balance of the affections. It makes us thoughtful spectators in the lists of life. It is the refiner of the species; a discipline of humanity. The habitual study of poetry and works of imagination is one chief part of a well-grounded education. A taste for liberal art is necessary to complete the character of a gentleman. Science alone is hard and mechanical. It exercises the understanding upon things out of ourselves, while it leaves the affections unemployed, or engrossed with our own immediate, narrow interests.—*Othello* furnishes an illustration of these remarks. It excites our sympathy in an extraordinary degree. The moral it conveys has a closer application to the concerns of human life than that of almost any other of Shakespear's plays. 'It comes directly home to the bosoms and business of men.' The pathos in *Lear* is indeed more dreadful and overpowering: but it is less natural, and less of every day's occurrence. We have not the same degree of sympathy with the passions described in *Macbeth*. The interest in *Hamlet* is more remote and reflex. That of *Othello* is at once equally profound and affecting. . . .

The third act of *Othello* is his finest display, not of knowledge or passion separately, but of the two combined, of the knowledge of character with the expression of passion, of consummate art in the keeping up of appearances with the profound workings of nature, and the convulsive movements of uncontrollable agony, of the power of inflicting torture and of suffering it. Not only is the tumult of passion in Othello's mind heaved up from the very bottom of the soul, but every the slightest undulation of feeling is seen on the surface as it arises from the impulses of imagination or the malicious suggestions of Iago. . . .

The character of Iago is one of the supererogations of Shakespear's genius. Some persons, more nice than wise, have thought this whole character unnatural, because his villainy is *without a sufficient motive*. Shakespear, who was as good a philosopher as he was a poet, thought otherwise. He knew that the love of power, which is another name for the love of mischief, is natural to man. He would know this as well or better than if it had been demonstrated to him by a logical diagram, merely from seeing children paddle in the dirt or kill flies for sport. Iago in fact belongs to a class of character, common to Shakspeare and at the same time peculiar to him; whose heads are as acute and active as their hearts are hard and callous. Iago is to be sure an extreme instance of the kind; that is to say, of diseased intellectual activity, with the most perfect indifference to moral good or evil, or rather with a decided preference of the latter, because it falls more readily in with his favourite propensity, gives greater zest to his thoughts and scope to his actions. He is quite or nearly as indifferent to his own fate as to that of others; he runs all risks for a trifling and doubtful advantage; and is himself the dupe and victim of his ruling passion—an insatiable craving after action of the most difficult and dangerous kind. 'Our ancient' is a philosopher, who fancies that a lie that kills has more point in it than an alliteration or an antithesis; who thinks a fatal experiment on the peace of a family a better thing than watching the palpitations in the heart of a flea in a microscope; who plots the ruin of his friends as an exercise for his ingenuity, and stabs men in the dark to prevent *ennui*. His gaiety, such as it is, arises from the success of his treachery; his ease from the torture he has inflicted on others. He is an amateur of tragedy in real life; and instead of employing his invention on imaginary characters, or long-forgotten incidents, he takes the bolder and more desperate course of getting up his plot at home, casts the principal parts among his nearest friends and connections, and rehearses it in downright earnest, with steady nerves and unabated resolution.

A. C. BRADLEY What is the peculiarity of Othello? What is the distinctive impression that it leaves? Of all Shakespeare's tragedies, I would answer, not even excepting *King Lear*, *Othello* is the most painfully exciting and the most terrible. From the moment when the temptation of the hero begins, the reader's heart and mind are held in a vice, experiencing the extremes of pity and fear, sympathy and repulsion, sickening hope and dreadful expectation. Evil is displayed before him, not indeed with the profusion found in *King Lear*, but forming, as it were, the soul of a single character, and united with an intellectual superiority so great that he watches its advance fascinated and appalled. He sees it, in itself almost irresistible, aided at every step by fortunate accidents and the innocent mistakes of its victims. He seems to breathe an atmosphere as fateful as that of *King Lear*, but more confined and oppressive, the darkness not of night but of a close-shut murderous room. His imagination is excited to intense activity, but it is the activity of concentration rather than dilation. . . .

There is a question, which, though of little consequence, is not without dramatic interest, whether Shakespeare imagined Othello as a Negro or as a Moor. Now I will not say that Shakespeare imagined him as a Negro and not as a Moor, for that might imply that he distinguished Negroes and Moors precisely as we do; but what appears to me nearly certain is that he imagined Othello as a black man, and not as a light-brown one.

In the first place, we must remember that the brown or bronze, to which we are now accustomed in the Othellos of our theatres is a recent innovation. Down to Edmund Kean's time, so far as is known, Othello was always quite black. This stage-tradition goes back to the Restoration, and it almost settles our question. For it is impossible that the colour of the original Othello should have been forgotten so soon after Shakespeare's time, and most improbable that it should have been changed from brown to black. . . .

But this is not all. The question whether to Shakespeare Othello was black or brown is not a mere question of isolated fact or historical curiosity; it concerns the character of Desdemona. Coleridge, and still more the American writers, regard her love, in effect, as Brabantio regarded it,[1] and not as

[1] As 'something monstrous to conceive': Coleridge. (See p. 247.)

Shakespeare conceived it. They are simply blurring this glorious conception when they try to lessen the distance between her and Othello, and to smooth away the obstacle which his 'visage' offered to her romantic passion for a hero. Desdemona, the 'eternal womanly' in its most lovely and adorable form, simple and innocent as a child, ardent with the courage and idealism of a saint, radiant with that heavenly purity of heart which men worship the more because nature so rarely permits it to themselves, had no theories about universal brotherhood, and no phrases about 'one blood in the nations of the earth' or 'barbarian, Scythian, bond and free'; but when her soul came in sight of the noblest soul on earth, she made nothing of the shrinking of her senses, but followed her soul until her senses took part with it, and 'loved him with the love which was her doom'. It was not prudent. It even turned out tragically. She met in life with the reward of those who rise too far above our common level; and we continue to allot her the same reward when we consent to forgive her for loving a brown man, but find it monstrous that she should love a black one.

Shakespearean Tragedy, 1904.

F. R. Leavis *Othello*, it will be very generally granted, is of all Shakespeare's great tragedies the simplest: the theme is limited and sharply defined, and the play, everyone agrees, is a brilliantly successful piece of workmanship. The effect is one of a noble, 'classical' clarity—of firm, clear outlines, unblurred and undistracted by cloudy recessions, metaphysical aura, or richly symbolical ambiguities. There would, it seems, be something like a consensus in this sense. And yet it is of *Othello* that one can say bluntly, as of no other of the great tragedies, that it suffers in current appreciation an essential and denaturing falsification.

The generally recognized peculiarity of *Othello* among the tragedies may be indicated by saying that it lends itself as no other of them does to the approach classically associated with Bradley's name: even *Othello* (it will be necessary to insist) is poetic drama, a dramatic poem, and not a psychological novel written in dramatic form and draped in poetry, but relevant discussion of its tragic significance will nevertheless be mainly a matter of character-analysis. It would, that is, have lent itself uniquely well to Bradley's approach if Bradley had made his approach consistently and with moderate intelligence. Actually, however, the section on *Othello* in *Shakespearean Tragedy* is more extravagant in misdirected scrupulosity than any of the others; it is, with a concentration of Bradley's comical solemnity, completely wrong-headed— grossly and palpably false to the evidence it offers to weigh. Grossly and palpably?—yet Bradley's *Othello* is substantially that of common acceptance. And here is the reason for dealing with it, even though not only Bradley but, in its turn, disrespect for Bradley (one gathers) has gone out of fashion (as a matter of fact he is still a very potent and mischievous influence).

According to the version of Othello elaborated by Bradley, the tragedy is the undoing of the noble Moor by the devilish cunning of Iago. Othello we are to see as a nearly faultless hero whose strength and virtue are turned against him. Othello and Desdemona, so far as their fate depended on their characters and untampered-with mutual relations, had every ground for expecting the happiness that romantic courtship had promised. It was external evil, the malice of the demi-devil, that turned a happy story of romantic love— of romantic lovers who were qualified to live happily ever after, so to speak— into a tragedy. This—it is the traditional version of *Othello* and has, moreover, the support of Coleridge—is to sentimentalize Shakespeare's tragedy and to displace its centre. . . . And it is all in the tradition; from Coleridge down, Iago—his motivation or his motivelessness—has commonly been, in commentaries on the play, the main focus of attention.

The plain fact that has to be asserted in the face of this sustained and sanctioned perversity is that in Shakespeare's tragedy of *Othello* Othello is the chief personage—the chief personage in such a sense that the tragedy may fairly be said to be Othello's character in action. Iago is subordinate and merely ancillary. He is not much more than a necessary piece of dramatic mechanism. . . .

It is plain that what we should see in Iago's prompt success is not so much Iago's diabolic intellect as Othello's readiness to respond. Iago's power, in fact, in the temptation-scene is that he represents something that is in Othello —in Othello the husband of Desdemona: the essential traitor is within the gates. For if Shakespeare's Othello too is simple-minded, he is nevertheless more complex than Bradley's. Bradley's Othello is, rather, Othello's; it being an essential datum regarding the Shakespearean Othello that he has an ideal conception of himself. . . .

At this climax of the play, as he sets himself irrevocably in his vindictive resolution, he reassumes formally his heroic self-dramatization—reassumes the Othello of 'the big wars that make ambition virtue'. The part of this conscious nobility, this noble egotism, this self-pride that was justified by experience irrelevant to the present trials and stresses, is thus underlined. Othello's self-idealization, his promptness to jealousy and his blindness are shown in their essential relation. The self-idealization is shown as blindness and the nobility as here no longer something real, but the disguise of an obtuse and brutal egotism. Self-pride becomes stupidity, ferocious stupidity, an insane and self-deceiving passion. The habitual 'nobility' is seen to make self-deception invincible, the egotism it expresses being the drive to catastrophe. Othello's noble lack of self-knowledge is shown as humiliating and disastrous. . . .

The theme of the tragedy is concentrated in it—concentrated in the final speech and action as it could not have been had Othello 'learnt through suffering'. That he should die acting his ideal part is all in the part: the part is manifested here in its rightness and solidity, and the actor as inseparably the man of action. The final blow is as real as the blow it re-enacts, and the histrionic intent symbolically affirms the reality: Othello dies belonging to the world of action in which his true part lay.

The Common Pursuit, 1952.

KING LEAR

WRITTEN   1605–6.

PERFORMED   1606 Dec 26. 'yt was played before the Kinges maiestie at
Whitehall vppon Sainct Stephens night at Christmas Last, by
his maiesties servantes.'

REGISTERED   1607 '26 Novembris. Nathanael Butter John Busby. Entred
for their Copie under thandes of Sir George Buck knight and
Thwardens A booke called. Master William Shakespeare his historye of
Kinge Lear, as yt was played before the Kinges maiestie at Whitehall vppon
Sainct Stephens night at Christmas Last, by his maiesties servantes playing
vsually at the Globe on the Banksyde vj^d.'

PUBLISHED   1608 Q1. 'M. William Shak-speare: His True Chronicle
Historie of the life and death of King Lear and his three
Daughters. With the vnfortunate life of Edgar, sonne and heire to the Earle
of Gloster, and his sullen and assumed humor of Tom of Bedlam: As it was
played before the Kings Maiestie at Whitehall vpon S. Stephans night in
Christmas Hollidayes. By his Maiesties seruants playing vsually at the Globe
on the Bancke-side.' Not a 'bad' Quarto, but there is much mislineation, little
punctuation, and prose printed as verse and verse as prose. It was probably
produced·from shorthand notes. Q1 omits about 100 lines found in F1.
1619 Q2. One of the ten plays printed by Jaggard, many of them with false
dates. This Q is dated 1608.
1623 F1. based on Q1 with alterations possibly from the prompt-copy.
F omits about 300 lines found in Q, including the whole of IV. iii.

SOURCES   Holinshed's *Chronicles.*
The *True Chronicle History of King Leir*, an anonymous play
written about 1594 and published in 1605.
Spenser's *Faerie Queene* II. x.
Sidney's *Arcadia* gives the outline of the Gloucester story.

In 1680 Nahum Tate gave the play a happy ending in which Lear is
restored to his kingdom and Cordelia marries Edgar. This version was
approved by Johnson and acted by Betterton, Garrick, Kemble, Kean. In
1838 Macready returned to Shakespeare's text throughout.

JOHNSON   But though this moral be incidentally enforced [that crimes lead to
crimes, and at last terminate in ruin], Shakespeare has suffered the
virtue of Cordelia to perish in a just cause, contrary to the natural ideas of
justice, to the hope of the reader, and, what is yet more strange, to the faith
of chronicles. Yet his conduct is justified by the Spectator, who blames Tate
for giving Cordelia success and happiness in his alteration, and declares, that,
in his opinion, 'the tragedy has lost half its beauty'. . . . A play in which the
wicked prosper, and the virtuous miscarry, may doubtless be good, because

it is a just representation of the common events of human life: but since all reasonable beings naturally love justice, I cannot easily be persuaded, that the observation of justice makes a play worse; or that, if other excellencies are equal, the audience will not always rise better pleased from the final triumph of persecuted virtue.

In the present case the public has decided. Cordelia, from the time of Tate, has always retired with victory and felicity. And, if my sensations could add anything to the general suffrage, I might relate, I was many years ago so shocked by Cordelia's death, that I know not whether I ever endured to read again the last scenes of the play till I undertook to revise them as an editor.

COLERIDGE Of all Shakespear's plays Macbeth is the most rapid, Hamlet the slowest, in movement. Lear combines length with rapidity,—like the hurricane and the whirlpool, absorbing while it advances. It begins as a stormy day in summer, with brightness; but that brightness is lurid, and anticipates the tempest.

It was not without forethought, nor is it without its due significance, that the division of Lear's kingdom is in the first six lines of the play stated as a thing already determined in all its particulars, previously to the trial of professions, as the relative rewards of which the daughters were to be made to consider their several portions. . . . These facts, these passions, these moral verities, on which the tragedy is founded, are all prepared for, and will to the retrospect be found implied, in these first four or five lines of the play. They let us know that the trial is but a trick; and that the grossness of the old king's rage is in part the natural result of a silly trick suddenly and most unexpectedly baffled and disappointed.

It may here be worthy of notice, that Lear is the only serious performance of Shakespeare, the interest and situations of which are derived from the assumption of a gross improbability. . . .

In Lear old age is itself a character,—its natural imperfections being increased by life-long habits of receiving a prompt obedience. Any addition of individuality would have been unnecessary and painful; for the relations of others to him, of wondrous fidelity and of frightful ingratitude, alone sufficiently distinguish him. Thus Lear becomes the open and ample play-room of nature's passions. . . .

Edgar's assumed madness serves the great purpose of taking off part of the shock which would otherwise be caused by the true madness of Lear, and further displays the profound difference between the two. In every attempt at representing madness throughout the whole range of dramatic literature, with the single exception of Lear, it is mere lightheadedness. In Edgar's ravings Shakespeare all the while lets you see a fixed purpose, a practical end in view; in Lear's, there is only the brooding of the one anguish, an eddy without progression.

LAMB So to see Lear acted,—to see an old man tottering about the stage with a walking-stick, turned out of doors by his daughters in a rainy night, has nothing in it but what is painful and disgusting. We want to take

him into shelter and relieve him. That is all the feeling which the acting of
Lear ever produced in me. But the Lear of Shakespeare cannot be acted. The
contemptible machinery by which they mimic the storm which he goes out
in, is not more inadequate to represent the horrors of the real elements, than
any actor can be to represent Lear: they might more easily propose to personate the Satan of Milton upon a stage, or one of Michael Angelo's terrible
figures. The greatness of Lear is not in corporal dimension, but in intellectual: the explosions of his passion are terrible as a volcano; they are storms
turning up and disclosing to the bottom that sea, his mind, with all its vast
riches. It is his mind which is laid bare. This case of flesh and blood seems
too insignificant to be thought on; even as he himself neglects it. On the stage
we see nothing but corporal infirmities and weakness, the impotence of rage.
While we read it, we see not Lear, but we are Lear: we are in his mind, we
are sustained by a grandeur which baffles the malice of daughters and storms.
In the aberrations of his reason, we discover a mighty irregular power of
reasoning, immethodized from the ordinary purposes of life, but exerting its
powers, as 'the wind bloweth where it listeth', at will upon the corruptions
and abuses of mankind. What have looks, or tones, to do with that sublime
identification of his age with that of the *heavens themselves*, when, in his
reproaches to them for conniving at the injustice of his children, he reminds
them that 'they themselves are old'? What gesture shall we appropriate to
this? What has the voice or the eye to do with such things? But the play is
beyond all art, as the tamperings with it show: it is too hard and stony; it must
have love-scenes, and a happy ending. It is not enough that Cordelia is a
daughter; she must shine as a lover too. Tate has put his hook in the nostrils
of this Leviathan, for Garrick and his followers, the show-men of the scene,
to draw the mighty beast about more easily. A happy ending!—as if the
living martyrdoms that Lear had gone through,—the flaying of his feelings
alive, did not make a fair dismissal from the stage of life the only decorous
thing for him. If he is to live and be happy after, if he could sustain this
world's burden after, why all this pudder and preparation,—why torment us
with all this unnecessary sympathy? As if the childish pleasure of getting his
gilt robes and sceptre again could tempt him to act over again his misused
station!—as if, at his years and with his experience, anything was left but
to die.

On the Tragedies of Shakespeare.

HAZLITT King Lear is then the best of all Shakespeare's plays, for it is the
one in which he was the most in earnest. He was here fairly caught
in the web of his own imagination. The passion which he has taken as his
subject is that which strikes its root deepest into the human heart; of which
the bond is the hardest to be unloosed; and the cancelling and tearing to
pieces of which gives the greatest revulsion to the frame. This depth of nature,
this force of passion, this tug and war of the elements of our being, this firm
faith in filial piety and the giddy anarchy and whirling tumult of the thoughts
at finding this prop failing it, the contrast between the fixed, immoveable
basis of natural affection, and the rapid, irregular starts of imagination, sud-

denly wrenched from all its accustomed holds and resting-places in the soul,
this is what Shakespear has given, and what nobody else but he could give. . . .

That which aggravates the sense of sympathy in the reader, and of uncontrollable anguish in the swoln heart of Lear, is the petrifying indifference, the
cold, calculating, obdurate selfishness of his daughters. His keen passions
seem whetted on their stony hearts. The contrast would be too painful, the
shock too great, but for the intervention of the Fool, whose well-timed levity
comes in to break the continuity of feeling when it can no longer be borne,
and to bring into play again the fibres of the heart just as they are growing
rigid from overstrained excitement.

A. C. BRADLEY The stage is the test of strictly dramatic quality, and *King
             Lear* is too huge for the stage. Of course, I am not denying
that it is a great stage-play. It has scenes immensely effective in the theatre;
three of them—the two between Lear and Goneril and between Lear,
Goneril and Regan, and the ineffably beautiful scene in the fourth act between
Lear and Cordelia—lose in the theatre very little of the spell they have for
the imagination; and the gradual interweaving of the two plots is almost as
masterly as in *Much Ado*. But (not to speak of defects due to mere careless-
ness) that which makes the *peculiar* greatness of *King Lear*,—the immense
scope of the work; the mass and variety of intense experience which it contains; the interpenetration of sublime imagination, piercing pathos, and
humour almost as moving as the pathos; the vastness of the convulsion both
of nature and of human passion; the vagueness of the scene where the action
takes place, and of the movements of the figures which cross this scene; the
strange atmosphere, cold and dark, which strikes on us as we enter this
scene, enfolding these figures and magnifying their dim outlines like a winter
mist; the half-realised suggestions of vast universal powers working in the
world of individual fates and passions,—all this interferes with dramatic
clearness even when the play is read, and in the theatre not only refuses to
reveal itself fully through the senses but seems to be almost in contradiction
with their reports. This is not so with the other great tragedies. No doubt,
as Lamb declared, theatrical representation gives only a part of what we
imagine when we read them; but there is no *conflict* between the representation and the imagination, because these tragedies are, in essentials, perfectly
dramatic. But *King Lear*, as a whole, is imperfectly dramatic, and there is
something in its very essence which is at war with the senses, and demands a
purely imaginative realisation. It is therefore, Shakespeare's greatest work,
but it is not what Hazlitt called it, the best of his plays; and its comparative
unpopularity is due, not merely to the extreme painfulness of the catastrophe,
but in part to its dramatic defects, and in part to a failure in many readers
to catch the peculiar effects to which I have referred,—a failure which is
natural because the appeal is made not so much to dramatic perception as to
a rarer and more strictly poetic kind of imagination. For this reason, too,
even the best attempts at exposition of *King Lear* are disappointing; they
remind us of attempts to reduce to prose the impalpable spirit of the *Tempest*.

Shakespearean Tragedy, 1904.

H. GRANVILLE-BARKER It is here that the scholars' case against the play as a play for the theatre is weak. Lamb's denunciation, indeed, was occasioned not by Shakespeare's play at all, but by Tate's perversion of it. And though he may declare that neither will he have Shakespeare's *King Lear* in the theatre, it is from nothing like Shakespeare's theatre that he bans it. Lamb's was the age of spectacle; he bases his arguments upon it, not upon Shakespeare's. . . . It was the age of 'the beauties of Shakespeare'. That, its beauty beside, this dynamic verse and prose held secrets of stagecraft does not seem to have been considered. . . .

Bradley's objections to the play's staging are more carefully considered than Lamb's, and they are pretty comprehensive. . . . This objection as a whole involves, I fancy, a fallacy about the theatre in general. . . . Dr. Bradley seems to assume that every sort of play, when acted, ought in a single performance to make a clear, complete and final effect on the spectator. But this is surely not so. We need no more expect to receive—lapses of performance and attention apart—the full value of a great drama at a first hearing than we expect it of a complex piece of music. And what preliminary study of the music, with its straiter laws and more homogeneous material, will effect, study of drama will not. A play's interpretation is an unrulier business, and we must face it rather as we face life itself. When we gather up in our minds the total effect made upon us by some past personal experience, we find it to consist of the then immediate emotion, which we can emotionally recall, of our later judgment of the whole matter, and—lodged between these two— of much hybrid sensation and thought, variously recollected. Now, it is the business of the dramatist, doubtless, in turning actuality to art, to clarify all this sort of thing and bring it to terms. But if he aimed only at its clear statement he would produce no illusion of life at all; and this it is his art to do. . . . *King Lear* does perhaps over-abound in sheer power, and will be apt to excite and confuse our emotions unduly. But the corrective of thought is strongly and currently applied. And I believe we may abandon ourselves to the emotions raised by a performance, confident that the complete and final effect produced on us will be fruitful and equable enough, and that, though we may lose at the time in fullness of understanding, we shall gain in conviction. . . .

Lamb rests his condemnation of the play's acting upon the third act and the scenes in the storm. . . .

Lamb states the case, let us admit, about as simply and well as it can be stated, and he fixes upon the supreme moments of dramatic achievement and theatrical difficulty. If we meet the challenge here and make good answer, may not the rest of the play claim a verdict too? Well, Lamb's case, as I suggest, is a bad case because it shows no recognition at all of Elizabethan stagecraft; his case, in fact, is not against Shakespeare the playwright, but against his betrayal. . . .

The chief strength of Elizabethan stagecraft lay in its comprehensive use of poetry. Plot was carried on, character developed and environment created, by the aid of poetry, emotion was sustained by it and illusion held. . . .

What is his exact dramatic need here, and how does he turn to its account this comprehensive use of verse? Be it verse or prose, he has no other resource, we must remember, than the spoken word of the actor, such action as will not mar it, and a negative background to this action. He has no accessories worth mentioning. . . . Lear, Kent and the rest must *act* the storm then; there is no other way. They must not lose themselves in its description; it will not do for us to be interested in the storm at the expense of our interest in them, the loss there would be more than the gain. For the effect of the storm upon Lear is Shakespeare's true objective. So he has to give it magnitude without detracting for one precious moment during the crisis from Lear's own dramatic supremacy. And he solves his problem by making the actor impersonate Lear and the storm together, by identifying Lear's passion with the storm's. Mere association will not serve; there must be no chance left of a rivalry of interest. . . . This is the basis of his stagecraft, to make Lear and the storm as one. And if Lamb saw 'an old man tottering about the stage with a walking-stick' he did not see the Lear of Shakespeare's intention.

Prefaces to Shakespeare, 1927.

MACBETH

WRITTEN 1605–6. J. Dover Wilson suggests 1601–2, and that it was performed at Edinburgh, whither Shakespeare had fled after the Essex rebellion.

PERFORMED 1611 April 20th. There must have been many performances before the one seen by Simon Forman at the Globe.

REGISTERED 1623 8th November. One of the sixteen plays registered by Blount and Jaggard before publishing F1.

PUBLISHED 1623 F1. An unsatisfactory text. There has been cutting—apart from *The Comedy of Errors* and *The Tempest* it is the shortest of the plays—adaptation, and interpolation: the Hecate scenes are probably by Middleton, for the songs indicated in the stage directions of III. v and IV. i, 'Come away' and 'Black spirits', occur in full in his *The Witch*. F was certainly printed from a prompt-copy, for the book-keeper's note, *Ring the Bell* (II. iii), has been printed in the text:

> *Malcolme, Banquo,*
> As from your Graues rise vp, and walke like Sprights,
> To countenance this horror, Ring the Bell.
> *Bell rings. Enter Lady.*

SOURCE Holinshed's *Chronicles*.

Davenant wrote a tidy and refined version of Macbeth which held the stage until Garrick's time. The Porter was dropped, the virtuous Lady Macduff balanced the evil Lady Macbeth, and Shakespeare's

> The devil damn thee black, thou cream-fac'd loon:
> Where got'st thou that goose-look?

became Davenant's

> Now Friend, what means thy change of countenance?

It was Davenant's version of the play that Pepys saw.

SIMON FORMAN In Mackbeth at the Glob, 1610 (1611?), the 20 of Aprill, ther was to be obserued, firste, howe Mackbeth and Bancko, 2 noble men of Scotland, Ridinge thorowe a wod, the stode before them 3 women feiries or Nimphes, And saluted Mackbeth, sayinge, 3 tyms vnto him, haille Mackbeth, king of Codon; for thou shalt be a kinge, but shalt beget No kinges, &c. . . . The next night, beinge at supper with his noble men whom he had bid to a feaste to the which also Banco should have com, he began to speake of Noble Banco, and to wish that he wer ther. And as he thus did, standing up to drincke a Carouse to him, the ghoste of Banco came and sate down in his cheier behind him. And he turninge About to sit down Again sawe the goste of Banco, which fronted him so, that he fell into a great passion of fear and fury, Vtterynge many wordes about his murder, by which, when they hard that Banco was Murdred they Suspected Macbet.

Book of Plaies.

PEPYS To the Duke's house, to see 'Macbeth', a pretty good play, but admirably acted. (5 *Nov.* 1664.)

To the Duke's House, and there saw 'Macbeth' most excellently acted and a most excellent play for variety. (28 *Dec.* 1666.)

To the Duke's House, and saw 'Macbeth', which, though I saw it lately, yet appears a most excellent play in all respects, but especially in divertisement, though it be a deep tragedy; which is a strange perfection in a tragedy, it being most proper here, and suitable. (7 *Jan.* 1667.)

To the play-house, where saw 'Macbeth', which, though I have seen it often, yet it is one of the best plays for a stage, and variety of dancing and musick, that ever I saw. (19 *April* 1667.)

To the Duke of York's house; and I was vexed to see Young, who is but a bad actor at best, act Macbeth, in the room of Betterton, who, poor man! is sick: but, Lord! what a prejudice it wrought in me against the whole play, and everybody else agreed in disliking this fellow. (15 *Oct.* 1667.)

To the Duke of York's house, and saw 'Macbeth', to our great content. (11 *Aug.* 1668.)

To the Duke's playhouse, and saw 'Macbeth'. The King and Court there; and we sat just under them and my Lady Castlemaine. (21 *Dec.* 1668.)

DRYDEN In reading some bombast speeches of Macbeth, which are not to be understood, he (Ben Jonson) used to say that it was horror; and I am much afraid that this is so.

On the Dramatic Poetry of the Last Age, 1672.

JOHNSON When Macbeth is confirming himself in the horrid purpose of
           stabbing his king, he breaks out amidst his emotions into a wish
natural for a murderer:

> Come, thick night!
> And pall thee in the dunnest smoke of hell,
> That my keen knife see not the wound it makes;
> Nor Heaven peep through the blanket of the dark,
> To cry, Hold, hold![1]

In this passage is exerted all the force of poetry; that force which calls new
powers into being, which embodies sentiment, and animates matter; yet,
perhaps, scarce any man now peruses it without some disturbance of his
attention from the counteraction of the words to the ideas. What can be
more dreadful than to implore the presence of night, invested, not in common
obscurity, but in the smoke of hell? Yet the efficacy of this invocation is
destroyed by the insertion of an epithet now seldom heard but in the stable,
and *dun* night may come or go without any other notice than contempt.

If we start into raptures when some hero of the *Iliad* tells us that δόρυ
μαίνεται, his lance rages with eagerness to destroy; if we are alarmed at
the terror of the soldiers commanded by Cæsar to hew down the sacred
grove, who dreaded, says Lucan, lest the axe aimed at the oak should fly
back upon the striker . . . we cannot surely but sympathize with the horrors
of a wretch about to murder his master, his friend, his benefactor, who sus-
pects that the weapon will refuse its office, and start back from the breast
which he is preparing to violate. Yet this sentiment is weakened by the
name of an instrument used by butchers and cooks in the meanest employ-
ments; we do not immediately conceive that any crime of importance is to
be committed with a *knife*; or who does not, at last, from the long habit of
connecting a knife with sordid offices, feel aversion rather than terror?

Macbeth proceeds to wish, in the madness of guilt, that the inspection of
Heaven may be intercepted, and that he may, in the involutions of infernal
darkness, escape the eye of Providence. This is the utmost extravagance of
determined wickedness: yet this is so debased by two unfortunate words, that
while I endeavour to impress on my reader the energy of the sentiment, I
can scarcely check my risibility, when the expression forces itself upon my
mind; for who, without some relaxation of his gravity, can hear of the avengers
of guilt *peeping through a blanket*?

                                                    The Rambler, No. 168.

LAMB Though some resemblance may be traced between the Charms of
        Macbeth and the Incantations in this Play [Thomas Middleton's *The
Witch*], which is supposed to have preceded it, this coincidence will not
detract much from the originality of Shakspeare. His witches are distinguished from the witches of Middleton by essential differences. These are

---

[1] The speech, of course, is really Lady Macbeth's, I. v.

creatures to whom man or woman plotting some dire mischief might resort for occasional consultation. Those originate deeds of blood, and begin bad impulses to men. From the moment that their eyes first meet with Macbeth's, he is spell-bound. That meeting sways his destiny. He can never break the fascination. These witches can hurt the body: those have power over the soul. Hecate in Middleton has a son, a low buffoon: the hags of Shakspeare have neither child of their own, nor seem to be descended from any parent. They are foul Anomalies, of whom we know not whence they are sprung, nor whether they have beginning or ending. As they are without human passions, so they seem to be without human relations. They come with thunder and lightning, and vanish to airy music. This is all we know of them. Except Hecate, they have no names; which heightens their mysteriousness. Their names, and some of the properties, which Middleton has given to his hags, excite smiles. The weird sisters are serious things. Their presence cannot co-exist with mirth. But in a lesser degree, the Witches of Middleton are fine creations. Their power too is, in some measure, over the mind. They raise jars, jealousies, strifes, *like a thick scurf o'er life*.

Specimens of English Dramatic Poets.

HAZLITT *Macbeth* (generally speaking) is done upon a stronger and more systematic principle of contrast than any other of Shakespear's plays. It moves upon the verge of an abyss, and is a constant struggle between life and death. The action is desperate and the reaction is dreadful. It is a huddling together of fierce extremes, a war of opposite natures which of them shall destroy the other. There is nothing but what has a violent end or violent beginnings. The lights and shades are laid on with a determined hand; the transitions from triumph to despair, from the height of terror to the repose of death, are sudden and startling; every passion brings in its fellow-contrary, and the thoughts pitch and jostle against each other as in the dark. The whole play is an unruly chaos of strange and forbidden things, where the ground rocks under our feet. Shakespear's genius here took its full swing, and trod upon the farthest bounds of nature and passion. This circumstance will account for the abruptness and violent antitheses of the style, the throes and labour which run through the expression, and from defects will turn them into beauties. 'So fair and foul a day I have not seen,' etc. 'Such welcome and unwelcome news together.' 'Men's lives are like the flowers in their caps, dying or ere they sicken.' 'Look like the innocent flower, but be the serpent under it.' The scene before the castle-gate follows the appearance of the Witches on the heath, and is followed by a midnight murder. Duncan is cut off betimes by treason leagued with witchcraft, and Macduff is ripped untimely from his mother's womb to avenge his death. Macbeth, after the death of Banquo, wishes for his presence in extravagant terms, 'To him and all we thirst', and when the ghost appears, cries out, 'Avaunt and quit my sight', and being gone, he is 'himself again'. Macbeth resolves to get rid of Macduff, that 'he may sleep in spite of thunder'; and cheers his wife on the doubtful intelligence of Banquo's taking-off with the encouragement—'then be thou jocund; ere the bat has flown his cloistered flight; ere to black Hecate's summons the shard-born beetle has rung night's yawning peal, there shall be done—a deed of dreadful note'. In Lady Macbeth's speech, 'Had he not resembled my father as he slept, I had done't', there is murder and filial piety together; and in urging him to fulfil his vengeance against the defenceless king, her thoughts spare the blood neither of infants nor old age. The description of the Witches is full of the same contradictory principle; they 'rejoice when good things bleed', they are neither of the earth nor the air, but both; they 'should be women but their beards forbid it'; they take all the pains possible to lead Macbeth on to the height of his ambition, only to betray him 'in deeper consequence', and after showing him all the pomp of their art, discover their malignant delight in his disappointed hopes, by that bitter taunt, 'Why stands Macbeth thus amazedly?' We might multiply such instances everywhere.

COLERIDGE Macbeth stands in contrast throughout with Hamlet; in the manner of opening more especially. In the latter, there is a gradual ascent from the simplest forms of conversation to the language of impassioned intellect,—yet the intellect still remaining the seat of passion : in the former, the invocation is at once made to the imagination and the emotions connected therewith. Hence the movement throughout is the most rapid of all Shakespeare's plays; and hence also, with the exception of the disgusting passage of the Porter which I dare pledge myself to demonstrate to be an interpolation of the actors, there is not, to the best of my remembrance, a single pun or play on words in the whole drama. I have previously given an answer to the thousand times repeated charge against Shakspeare upon the subject of his punning, and I here merely mention the fact of the absence of any puns in Macbeth, as justifying a candid doubt at least, whether even in these figures of speech and fanciful modifications of language, Shakspeare may not have followed rules and principles that merit and would stand the test of philosophic examination. And hence, also, there is an entire absence of comedy, nay, even of irony and philosophic contemplation in Macbeth,— the play being wholly and purely tragic. For the same cause, there are no reasonings of equivocal morality, which would have required a more leisurely state and a consequently greater activity of mind;—no sophistry of self-delusion,—except only that previously to the dreadful act, Macbeth mis-translates the recoilings and ominous whispers of conscience into prudential and selfish reasonings, and, after the deed done, the terrors of remorse into fear from external dangers,—like delirious men who run away from the phantoms of their own brains, or, raised by terror to rage, stab the real object that is within their reach :—whilst Lady Macbeth merely endeavours to reconcile his and her own sinkings of heart by anticipations of the worst, and an affected bravado in confronting them. In all the rest, Macbeth's language is the grave utterance of the very heart, conscience-sick, even to the last faintings of moral death. It is the same in all the other characters. The variety arises from rage, caused ever and anon by disruption of anxious thought, and the quick transition of fear into it.

DE QUINCEY For his essay *On the Knocking at the Gate in Macbeth*, see p. 93.

A. C. BRADLEY A Shakespearean tragedy, as a rule, has a special tone or atmosphere of its own, quite perceptible, however difficult to describe. The effect of this atmosphere is marked with unusual strength in *Macbeth*. It is due to a variety of influences which combine with those just noticed, so that, acting and reacting, they form a whole; and the desolation of the blasted heath, the design of the Witches, the guilt in the hero's soul, the darkness of the night, seem to emanate from one and the same source. This effect is strengthened by a multitude of small touches, which at the moment may be little noticed but still leave their mark on the imagination. We may approach the consideration of the characters and the action by distinguishing some of the ingredients of this general effect.

Darkness, we may even say blackness, broods over this tragedy. It is remarkable that almost all the scenes which at once recur to memory take place either at night or in some dark spot. The vision of the dagger, the murder of Duncan, the murder of Banquo, the sleep-walking of Lady Macbeth, all come in night-scenes. The Witches dance in the thick air of a storm, or, 'black and midnight hags', receive Macbeth in a cavern. The blackness of night is to the hero a thing of fear, even of horror; and that which he feels becomes the spirit of the play. . . .

The atmosphere of *Macbeth*, however, is not that of unrelieved blackness. On the contrary, as compared with *King Lear* and its cold, dim gloom, *Macbeth* leaves a decided impression of colour; it is really the impression of a black night broken by flashes of light and colour, sometimes vivid and even glaring. They are the lights and colours of the thunder-storm in the first scene; of the dagger hanging before Macbeth's eyes and glittering alone in the midnight air; of the torch borne by the servant. . . . And, above all, the colour is the colour of blood. It cannot be an accident that the image of blood is forced upon us continually, not merely by the events themselves, but by full descriptions, and even by reiteration of the word in unlikely parts of the dialogue. . . .

Let us observe another point. The vividness, magnitude, and violence of the imagery in some of these passages are characteristic of *Macbeth* almost throughout; and their influence contributes to form its atmosphere. Images like those of the babe torn smiling from the breast and dashed to death; of pouring the sweet milk of concord into hell; of the earth shaking in fever; of the frame of things disjointed; . . . all keep the imagination moving on a 'wild and violent sea', while it is scarcely for a moment permitted to dwell on thoughts of peace and beauty. In its language, as in its action, the drama is full of tumult and storm. . . .

Now all these agencies—darkness, the lights and colours that illuminate it, the storm that rushes through it, the violent and gigantic images—conspire with the appearances of the Witches and the Ghost to awaken horror, and in some degree also a supernatural dread. And to this effect other influences contribute. The pictures called up by the mere words of the Witches stir the same feelings. . . . All this has one effect, to excite supernatural alarm and, even more, a dread of the presence of evil not only in its recognised seat but all through and around our mysterious nature. Perhaps there is no other work equal to *Macbeth* in the production of this effect.

Shakespearean Tragedy, 1904.

EDITH SITWELL In this vast world torn from the universe of night, there are three tragic themes. The first theme is that of the actual guilt, and the separation in damnation of the two characters—the man who, in spite of his guilt, walks the road of the spirit, and who loves the light that has forsaken him—and the woman who, after her invocation to the 'Spirits who tend on mortall thoughts', walks in the material world, and who does not know that light exists, until she is nearing her end and must seek the comfort of one small taper to illumine all the murkiness of Hell.—That small taper is her soul. . . .

The second tragic theme of the play is the man's love for the woman whose damnation is of the earth, who is unable, until death is near, to conceive of the damnation of the spirit, and who in her blindness therefore strays away from him, leaving him for ever in his lonely hell.

The third tragic theme is the woman's despairing love for the man whose vision she cannot see, and whom she has helped to drive into damnation.

The very voices of these two damned souls have therefore a different sound. His voice is like that of some gigantic being in torment—of a lion with a human soul. In her speech invoking darkness [I. v], the actual sound is so murky and thick that the lines seem impervious to light, and, at times, rusty, as though they had lain in the blood that had been spilt, or in some hell-born dew. There is no escape from what we have done. The past will return to confront us. And that is even shown in the verse. In that invocation there are perpetual echoes, sometimes far removed from each other, sometimes placed close together.

For instance, in the line

And fill me from the Crowne to the Toe, top-full

'full' is a darkened dissonance to 'fill'—and these dissonances, put at opposite ends of the line,—together with the particular placing of the alliterative *f*'s of 'fill' and 'full' and the alliterative *t*'s, and the rocking up and down of the dissonantal *o*'s ('Crowne', 'Toe', 'top') show us a mind reeling on the brink of madness, about to topple down into those depths, yet striving to retain its balance. . . .

Sometimes the particular placing of the assonances produces a sound like that of a fevered, uneven pulse,—an example is the effect brought about by the drumming of the dull *un . . . om* sounds in the lines

. . . Duncane
Under my Battlements. Come.

This terrible drumming sound is heard over and over again throughout the passage, and is due not only to the placing of the assonances, but also to the particular placing of double-syllabled and—(this has a still stronger effect)—treble-syllabled words and quick-moving, unaccented one-syllabled words. In the line

> And fill me from the Crowne to the Toe, top-full

'to the' gives an example of the effect of those quick-moving, unaccented one-syllabled words:

> That no compunctious visitings of Nature

is an example of the use of three-syllabled words, disturbing, purposely, the movement of the line.

This march towards Hell is slow. and has a thunderous darkened pomp. It is slow, and yet it has but few pau 3 (for that march is of her own will, she is driven by that will as by a Fury) and these pauses are not long, but deep, like fissures opening down into Hell. . . .

The speeches of Macbeth have a different sound. He, at least, would retreat from the path, if only it were possible. But he is a prisoner, bound for ever to his first hell-born deed, and he must go where his deed drags him.

The dark and terrible voice of Macbeth is not covered by a blood-dewed rust, is not like a black and impenetrable smoke from Hell, or the torch of a Fury—as is the voice of the woman who, to him, is Fate. It is hollow like the depths into which he has fallen, it returns ever (though it, too, has discordances) to one note, dark as the Hell through which he walks with that sleepless soul. The sound is ever 'no more'.

> Cawdor
> Shall sleepe no more, Macbeth shall sleepe no more.

> *A Notebook on William Shakespeare*, 1948.

ANTONY AND CLEOPATRA

WRITTEN　　1606–7.

PERFORMED　　No record of an early performance.

REGISTERED　　1608 '20 Maij. Edward Blount. Entred for his copie under thandes of Sir George Buck knight and Master Warden Seton A booke called. The Booke of Pericles prynce of Tyre. vj^d. Edward Blount. Entred also for his copie by the like Aucthoritie. A booke called Anthony and Cleopatra. vj^d.'
1623 8th November. One of the 16 plays registered by Blount and Jaggard before publishing F1.

PUBLISHED　　1623 F1. A fair text, set up from Shakespeare's MS.

SOURCE　　North's translation of Plutarch's *Life of Antonius*.

Dryden's version of the Antony and Cleopatra story, *All for Love*, was produced at Drury Lane in 1677–8.

DRYDEN In my style, I have professed to imitate the divine Shakespeare; which that I might perform more freely, I have disencumbered myself from rhyme. Not that I condemn my former way, but that this is more proper to my present purpose. I hope I need not to explain myself, that I have not copied my author servilely: words and phrases must of necessity receive a change in succeeding ages; but it is almost a miracle that much of his language remains so pure; and that he who began Dramatic Poetry amongst us, untaught by any, and as Ben Johnson tells us, without learning, should by the force of his own genius perform so much, that in a manner he has left no praise for any who come after him.

Preface to All for Love.

JOHNSON This play keeps curiosity always busy, and the passions always interested. The continual hurry of the action, the variety of incidents, and the quick succession of one personage to another, call the mind forward, without intermission, from the first act to the last. But the power of delighting is derived principally from the frequent changes of the scene; for, except the feminine arts, some of which are too low, which distinguish Cleopatra, no character is very strongly discriminated. Upton, who did not easily miss what he desired to find, has discovered that the language of Antony is, with great skill and learning, made pompous and superb, according to his real practice. But I think his diction not distinguishable from that of others: the most tumid speech in the play is that which Cæsar makes to Octavia.

The events, of which the principal are described according to history, are produced without any art of connexion or care of disposition.

COLERIDGE The highest praise, or rather form of praise, of this play, which I can offer in my own mind, is the doubt which the perusal always occasions in me, whether the Antony and Cleopatra is not, in all exhibitions of a giant power in its strength and vigour of maturity, a formidable rival of Macbeth, Lear, Hamlet, and Othello. *Feliciter audax* is the motto for its style comparatively with that of Shakspeare's other works, even as it is the general motto of all his works compared with those of other poets. Be it remembered, too, that this happy valiancy of style is but the representative and result of all the material excellencies so expressed.

This play should be perused in mental contrast with Romeo and Juliet; as the love of passion and appetite opposed to the love of affection and instinct. But the art displayed in the character of Cleopatra is profound; in this, especially, that the sense of criminality in her passion is lessened by our insight into its depth and energy, at the very moment that we cannot but perceive that the passion itself springs out of the habitual craving of a licentious nature, and that it is supported and reinforced by voluntary stimulus and sought-for associations, instead of blossoming out of spontaneous emotion.

Of all Shakspeare's historical plays, Antony and Cleopatra is by far the most wonderful. There is not one in which he has followed history so minutely, and yet there are few in which he impresses the notion of angelic strength so much; perhaps none in which he impresses it more strongly. This is greatly owing to the manner in which the fiery force is sustained throughout, and to the numerous momentary flashes of nature counteracting the historic abstraction. As a wonderful specimen of the way in which Shakspeare lives up to the very end of this play, read the last part of the concluding scene. And if you would feel the judgment as well as the genius of Shakspeare in your heart's core, compare this astonishing drama with Dryden's All For Love.

HAZLITT This is a very noble play. Though not in the first class of Shake-spear's productions, it stands next to them, and is, we think, the finest of his historical plays, that is, of those in which he made poetry the organ of history, and assumed a certain tone of character and sentiment, in conformity to known facts, instead of trusting to his observations of general nature or to the unlimited indulgence of his own fancy. What he has added to the actual story, is upon a par with it. His genius was, as it were, a match for history as well as nature, and could grapple at will with either. The play is full of that pervading comprehensive power by which the poet could always make himself master of time and circumstances. It presents a fine picture of Roman pride and Eastern magnificence: and in the struggle between the two, the empire of the world seems suspended 'like the swan's down-feather,

> That stands upon the swell at full of tide,
> And neither way inclines'.

The characters breathe, move, and live. Shakespear does not stand reasoning on what his characters would do or say, but at once *becomes* them, and speaks and acts for them. He does not present us with groups of stage-puppets or poetical machines making set speeches on human life, and acting from a calculation of problematical motives, but he brings living men and women on the scene, who speak and act from real feelings, according to the ebbs and flows of passion, without the least tincture of pedantry of logic or rhetoric. Nothing is made out by inference and analogy, by climax and antithesis, but everything takes place just as it would have done in reality, according to the occasion. The character of Cleopatra is a masterpiece. What an extreme contrast it affords to Imogen! One would think it almost impossible for the same person to have drawn both.

J. MIDDLETON MURRY But the greatest mastery of imagery does not lie in the use, however beautiful and revealing, of isolated images, but in the harmonious total impression produced by a succession of subtly related images. In such cases the images appear to grow out of one another and to be fulfilling an independent life of their own. Yet this apparent autonomy is as strictly subordinated to a final impression as the steps of a logical argument are to their conclusion. Such triumphs of imagery are to be conceived as a swift and continuous act of exploration of the world of imagina-tion—though an obvious metaphor is in that phrase. A magnificent example of this peculiar movement of mind on a scale so large that it can be carefully examined is Keats's *Ode to a Nightingale*. The strange combination of imaginative autonomy and profound total harmony in that poem is characteristic of the movement of creative imagery in its highest forms. We can perhaps get a clear glimpse of the nature of this contradictory process of creative imagery—the maximum of independence combined with the most complete and pervasive subordination—in one of the rare moments when we can honestly claim to look over Shakespeare's shoulder. The famous picture of Cleopatra on Cydnus comes substantially from North's Plutarch, of which the following sentence is the original of Shakespeare's first seven lines:

She disdained to set forward otherwise, but to take her barge in the river of Cydnus, the poope whereof was of gold, the sails of purple, and the owers of silver, which kept stroke in rowing after the sound of flutes, howboys, cythern, violls, and such other instruments as they played upon in the barge. . . .

It is often said that Shakespeare followed North as closely as he could, with the minimum of original effort. It is not true. North's sentence would fall quite easily into good blank verse, but it would be nothing like—

> *The barge she sat in, like a burnish'd throne,*
> *Burn'd on the water:* the poop was beaten gold;
> Purple the sails, *and so perfumed that*
> *The winds were love-sick with them;* the oars were silver
> Which to the tune of flutes kept stroke, *and made*
> *The water which they beat to follow faster,*
> *As amorous of their strokes.* . . .

The phrases in italics are Shakespeare's additions: afterwards he keeps more closely to North, until he comes to the climax. North has it:

Others also rann out of the city to see her coming in. So that in the end, there rann such multitudes of people one after another, that *Antonius* was left post alone in the market-place, in his Imperiall seate to give audience.

Which is transformed into:

> The city cast
> Her people out upon her, and Antony,
> Enthron'd in the market-place, did sit alone,
> *Whistling to the air: which, but for vacancy,*
> *Had gone to gaze on Cleopatra too*
> *And made a gap in nature.*

The additions are worth attention. North's somewhat amorphous prose is given a beginning and an end. The additions are all, in spite of formal differences, essentially similes and metaphors; and, after the first, which gathers the vision into one whole which it puts imperishably before the mind's eye, the second and third develop the theme which is clinched in climax by the fourth. In them the successive elements—the winds, the water, the air—are represented all as succumbing to the enchantment of love which breathes from the great Queen and her burning barge; and by this varied return on a single motive North's inconsequential panorama is given an organic unity. It is quite impossible to conceive Shakespeare as dovetailing old and new together. Before his mind's eye as he read North had risen a picture half visible, half spiritual, in short, truly imaginative—the manifestation of Egypt, before whom the elements made obeisance. All of North that was congruous with this enchanted vision he incorporated with a flowing pen into his new creation. And the added imagery, about which he probably took no second thought, grew naturally into harmony with itself and with the whole.

Countries of the Mind, 1931.

CORIOLANUS

WRITTEN   1607–8.

PERFORMED   No record of an early performance.

REGISTERED   1623 Nov. 8th. One of the 16 plays registered by Blount and Jaggard before publishing F1.

PUBLISHED   1623 F1. Not a very satisfactory text: as in *Antony and Cleopatra* there are many mislineations.

SOURCE   North's translation of Plutarch's *Life of Coriolanus*.

Nahum Tate's adaptation of *Coriolanus*, *The Ingratitude of a Commonwealth*, *or*, *The Fall of Caius Martius*, which he vainly hoped would 'turn to money what lay dead before', was produced in 1682. John Dennis's version, *The Invader of his Country*, *or the Fatal Resentment*, was driven from the Drury Lane stage after three performances in 1719.

JOHNSON The tragedy of Coriolanus is one of the most amusing of our author's performances. The old man's merriment in Menenius; the lofty lady's dignity in Volumnia; the bridal modesty in Virgilia; the patrician and military haughtiness in Coriolanus; the plebeian malignity, and tribunitian insolence in Brutus and Sicinius, make a very pleasing and interesting variety: and the various revolutions of the hero's fortune fill the mind with anxious curiosity. There is, perhaps, too much bustle in the first act, and too little in the last.

COLERIDGE This play illustrates the wonderfully philosophic impartiality of Shakspeare's politics. His own country's history furnished him with no matter, but what was too recent to be devoted to patriotism. Besides he knew that the instruction of ancient history would seem more dispassionate.

In Coriolanus and Julius Cæsar, you see Shakspeare's good-natured laugh at mobs. Compare this with Sir Thomas Brown's aristocracy of spirit.

HAZLITT Shakespear has in this play shown himself well versed in history and state-affairs. *Coriolanus* is a store-house of political common-places. Any one who studies it may save himself the trouble of reading Burke's Reflections, or Paine's Rights of Man, or the Debates in both Houses of Parliament since the French Revolution or our own. The arguments for and against aristocracy or democracy, on the privileges of the few and the claims of the many, on liberty and slavery, power and the abuse of it, peace and war, are here very ably handled, with the spirit of a poet and the acuteness of a philosopher. Shakespear himself seems to have had a leaning to the arbitrary side of the question, perhaps from some feeling of contempt for his own origin; and to have spared no occasion of baiting the rabble. What he says of them is very true: what he says of their betters is also very true, though he dwells less upon it.—The cause of the people is indeed but little calculated as a subject for poetry: it admits of rhetoric, which goes into argument and explanation,·but it presents no immediate or distinct images to the mind, 'no jutting frieze, buttress, or coigne of vantage' for poetry 'to make its pendant bed and procreant cradle in'. The language of poetry naturally falls in with the language of power. The imagination is an exaggerating and exclusive faculty: it takes from one thing to add to another: it accumulates circumstances together to give the greatest possible effect to a favourite object. The understanding is a dividing and measuring faculty: it judges of things not according to their immediate impression on the mind, but according to their relations to one another. The one is a monopolising faculty, which seeks the greatest quantity of present excitement by inequality and dispro-portion; the other is a distributive faculty, which seeks the greatest quantity of ultimate good, by justice and proportion. The one is an aristocratical, the other a republican faculty. The principle of poetry is a·very anti-levelling principle. It aims at effect, it exists by contrast. It admits of no medium. It is everything by excess. It rises above the ordinary standard of sufferings and crimes. It presents a dazzling appearance. It shews its head turretted, crowned, and crested. Its front is gilt and blood-stained. Before it 'it carries noise, and behind it leaves tears'. It has its altars and its victims, sacrifices, human sacrifices. Kings, priests, nobles, are its train-bearers, tyrants and slaves its executioners.—'Carnage is its daughter.'—Poetry is right-royal. It puts the individual for the species, the one above the infinite many, might before right. A lion hunting a flock of sheep or a herd of wild asses is a more poetical object than they; and we even take part with the lordly beast, because our vanity or some other feeling makes us disposed to place ourselves in the situation of the strongest party. So we feel some concern for the poor citizens of Rome when they meet together to compare their wants and grievances, till Coriolanus comes in and with blows and big words drives this set of 'poor rats', this rascal scum, to their homes and beggary before him. . . .

The whole dramatic moral of Coriolanus is that those who have little shall have less, and that those who have much shall take all that others have left.

GERVINUS Even if we give up our usual plan of seeking in every one of
          Shakespeare's dramas a fundamental moral view, it is by no means
unimportant, in forming a judgment on this play, whether we take the
political or the psychological idea as the basis for our consideration. If we
take the political struggle between the two orders to be the main point, we
shall readily arrive at wrong conclusions. To instance only one. We see
Coriolanus, as the chief representative of the aristocracy, in strong opposition
to the people and the tribunes; hence we naturally take up the view expressed
by Hazlitt, that Shakespeare had a leaning to the arbitrary side of the question,
to the aristocratical principle, inasmuch as he does not dwell on the truths
he tells of the nobles in the same proportion as he does on those of the people.
Hazlitt has added excellent grounds for proving even the naturalness and
need of this inclination in the poet. He showed that the poetic imagination
is an exaggerating, exclusive, aristocratic faculty, that the principle of poetry
is everywhere an anti-levelling principle, that the lion which attacks a flock
of sheep is a far more poetical object than the flock, that we feel more admiration for the proud, arbitrary man than for the humble crowd that bow
before him, for the oppressor rather than for the oppressed. All this is very
true, and seems to gain more force by its application to Coriolanus. But
Shakespeare's poetry is always so closely connected with morality, his imaginative power is so linked with sound reason, his ideal is so full of actual truth,
that his poetry seemed to us always distinguished from all other poetry
exactly by this: that there is nothing exclusive in it, that candour and impartiality are the most prominent marks of the poet and his poetry, that if
imagination even with him strives sometimes after effect, exists by contrasts,
and admits no middle course, yet in the very placing, describing, and colouring of the very highest poetical contrasts, there appears ever for the moral
judgment that golden mean of impartiality which is the precious prerogative
of the truly wise. Shakespeare has depicted the man of freedom, Brutus, nay,
even the harder master-spirit of the revolution, Cassius, far nobler and with
much more love than the man of the aristocracy, Coriolanus. It will be
allowed that, from the example of Brutus, many more would be won over
to the cause of the people than would be won over to aristocratic principles
by Coriolanus. If we regard Coriolanus not merely in reference to the many,
but if we weigh its character in itself and with itself, we must confess, after
the closest consideration, that personified aristocracy is here represented in
its noblest and in its worst side, with that impartiality which Shakespeare's
nature could scarcely avoid. It may be replied, the people are not so depicted.
Yet even on the nobles as a body our poet has just as little thrown a favourable
light at last; for it lies in the nature of things that a multitude can never be
compared with one man who is to be the subject of poetical representation,
and who, on that very account, must stand alone, one single man distinguished
from the many. But it may be said, the representatives of the people, the
tribunes also, are not thus impartially depicted. Yet where would have been
the poetic harmony, if Shakespeare had made these prominent? where the
truth, if he had given dignity and energy to a new power created in a tumult?
where our sympathy in his hero, if he had placed a Marcus Brutus in oppo-

sition to him in the tribunate? In proportion as he had raised our interest in the tribunes, he would have withdrawn it from Coriolanus, who had already enough to do to bear his own burden of declension.

Shakespeare Commentaries, 1850.

CAROLINE SPURGEON *Coriolanus*, however, has a central symbol and a very definite one, but it is significant that this has not been born out of the creator's feeling of the tragedy, but has just been taken over by him wholesale, with much else, from North's *Plutarch*.

It is the old tale, with which the play opens, expounded by Menenius, of the rebellion of the various members of the body—the citizens—against the belly—the senate—which they accuse of being idle while they do all the work, and the belly's answer, somewhat developed by Shakespeare, that, on the contrary, it is the 'storehouse and the shop of the whole body', sending out, through rivers of blood, sustenance to all.

The images arising out of this central theme from the body and sickness are many, nearly one-fifth of the whole; and by means of them this idea is played upon throughout, though in a somewhat languid and artificial way.

The king, statesman, soldier, horse, and trumpeter are compared to the head, eye and heart, arm, leg, and tongue, and Menenius laughingly taunts one of the basest of the citizens with being the great toe of the rebellion. The people are the hands, the tribunes are the 'tongue o' the common mouth', or they are the mouths themselves, as when Coriolanus, turning on them, asks

You being their mouths, why rule you not their teeth? . . .

The condition of the time is a 'violent fit' that craves physic, a sore which needs a physician, for it cannot be cured by self-probing, and so on; it is wearisome to pursue it further for it is very obvious, and a rather laboured and overworked metaphor at best.

It obtrudes itself throughout the play; any one on a first reading will notice and remember it, whereas it might be possible to know *Lear* or *Macbeth* very well without consciously realizing the dominating symbolic 'motives' in these plays. That is because in them the symbols are the outcome of the imagination at white heat, and thus become one with the movement and characters and could be no other than they are.

So one feels, for example, that Coriolanus is called a diseased limb or a gangrened foot because it fits in with a preconceived design, but Kent, in his agonized grief, sees the death of Lear as the release of a tortured body from the rack, not because bodily struggle and torture has been the dominating symbol throughout, but because, after the experience of burning through

the fierce dispute
Betwixt damnation and impassioned clay,

there was no other way possible to see it.

Shakespeare's Imagery, 1935.

TIMON OF ATHENS

WRITTEN   1607–8?

PERFORMED   No record of any early performance. Shadwell's refined version
           was produced in 1671.

REGISTERED   1623 8th November. One of the 16 plays registered byBlount
            and Jaggard before publishing F1.

PUBLISHED   1623 F1. *Timon* is printed between *Romeo and Juliet* and
           Julius Cæsar where *Troilus and Cressida* was originally to have
gone. There is much mislineation in the text.

SOURCES   Plutarch's *Lives of Antonius* and *Alcibiades*; Paynter's *Palace
          of Pleasure*; Lucian's dialogue *Timon, or the Misanthrope*.

It may be that the play is unfinished. Possibly Shakespeare abandoned the
story of Timon in favour of that of Lear, the theme of which—ingratitude—
is the same. If so it would justify Professor Dover Wilson's claim that *Timon*
is the 'still-born twin' of *Lear*. In any event, it was probably written before
Coriolanus and *Antony and Cleopatra*.

JOHNSON The play of Timon is a domestic tragedy, and, therefore, strongly
         fastens on the attention of the reader. In the plan there is not
much art, but the incidents are natural, and the characters various and
exact. The catastrophe affords a very powerful warning against that osten-
tatious liberality, which scatters bounty, but confers no benefits, and buys
flattery, but not friendship.
    In this tragedy are many passages perplexed, obscure, and probably
corrupt. . . .

COLERIDGE But where shall we class the Timon of Athens? Perhaps im-
           mediately below Lear. It is a Lear of the satirical drama; a
Lear of domestic or ordinary life;—a local eddy of passion on the high road
of society, while all around is the week-day goings on of wind and weather;
a Lear, therefore, without its soul-searching flashes, its ear-cleaving thunder-
claps, its meteoric splendours,—without the contagion and the fearful
sympathies of nature, the fates, the furies, the frenzied elements, dancing in
and out, now breaking through, and scattering,—now hand in hand with,—
the fierce or fantastic group of human passions, crimes, and anguishes, reeling
on the unsteady ground, in a wild harmony to the shock and the swell of an
earthquake.

HAZLITT *Timon of Athens* always appeared to us to be written with as intense
         a feeling of his subject as any one play of Shakespeare. It is one
of the few in which he seems to be in earnest throughout, never to trifle nor
go out of his way. He does not relax in his efforts, nor lose sight of the unity

of his design. It is the only play of our author in which spleen is the predominant feeling of the mind. It is as much a satire as a play: and contains some of the finest pieces of invective possible to be conceived, both in the snarling, captious answers of the cynic Apemantus, and in the impassioned and more terrible imprecations of Timon. The latter remind the classical reader of the force and swelling impetuosity of the moral declamations in *Juvenal*, while the former have all the keenness and caustic severity of the old Stoic philosophers. The soul of Diogenes appears to have been seated on the lips of Apemantus. The churlish profession of misanthropy in the cynic is contrasted with the profound feeling of it in Timon, and also with the soldier-like and determined resentment of Alcibiades against his countrymen, who have banished him, though this forms only an incidental episode in the tragedy. . . .

The moral sententiousness of this play equals that of Lord Bacon's Treatise on the Wisdom of the Ancients, and is indeed seasoned with greater variety. Every topic of contempt or indignation is here exhausted; but while the sordid licentiousness of Apemantus, which turns everything to gall and bitterness, shews only the natural virulence of his temper and antipathy to good or evil alike, Timon does not utter an imprecation, without betraying the extravagant workings of disappointed passion, of love altered to hate. Apemantus sees nothing good in any object, and exaggerates whatever is disgusting: Timon is tormented with the perpetual contrast between things and appearances, between the fresh, tempting outside and the rottenness within, and invokes mischiefs on the heads of mankind proportioned to the sense of his wrongs and of their treacheries.

ULRICI In spite of the censured defects of the play, it is, in my opinion, wonderful with what skill Shakspeare has contrived to form so unmanageable a subject, as is offered by the story of Timon, into a living and drastic action. This he has accomplished partly by the relations he has established between the life and fortunes of the individual persons and the whole nation and state; particularly, however, by the triple contrast in which he has placed the character of Timon as regards the other chief persons of the piece. In the first place in its contrast to the worthless flatterers and parasites who affect the same friendship, devotion and philanthropy towards Timon, merely in order to prey upon him. These personages are certainly but little individualised, they are in reality as like as peas, and yet the poet has with striking irony contrived to give each his peculiar shade of colour, as is especially indicated in the different ways in which they accept and reject Timon's entreaties for assistance. Opposed to this friendship of semblance and falsehood, stands the true and warm affection of Timon's household, especially that of his steward Flavius, whom Timon declares the only honest man. . . .

A very contrast to Timon, in his self-made misanthropy and in his sincere hatred of mankind, is found in the cynic Apemantus. . . . He moves about like a ridiculous phantom, useless to himself and a burden to others, the warning example of a view of life quite similar to that of Timon's, only that it is the perverted, reverse side. In the end he is far surpassed in his department by Timon, and we may assume that he was affected by this humiliation, or got better of his own accord. Alcibiades, lastly, on the one hand, connects the relations between the personal life of the hero and the general life of the state and people, on the other, he too forms a certain contrast to Timon. Thus he, like all the other characters, is a necessary member of the organism of the whole, in so far as he essentially co-operates in the development of the character of the hero, as well as in the progress of the action, which again is the result of the development of the hero's character. For he exhibits in his person the *right* way in which *such* people, *such* men ought to be treated. He repels injustice by injustice, force by force, and preaches sense and morality sword in hand. But his *right* manner of ordering life is suitable only for such a *wrong* sort of men, such a law*less* people, and thus, in reality, it is in and of itself simply a *wrong* way.

Now, it is the very fact of Alcibiades being, or at least appearing in the end to be in the right, that constitutes the defect of the drama. It too is wanting in the elevating, conciliatory element of the tragic pathos, and this especially marks its affinity to 'Titus Andronicus'. If Alcibiades is right, then life is not worth the living; there would, in reality, be no history, because there is no ethical progress in humanity.

Shakspeare's Dramatic Art, 1839.

G. Wilson Knight Timon, in love or hate, bears truly a heart of gold. He
              is a thing apart, a choice soul crucified. He has a mind
'unmatched' (IV. iii. 523). He is one

Whose star-like nobleness gave life and influence (V. i. 66)

to the world that has driven him without its walls. Sun-like he used to 'shine' on men (III. iv. 10). And the issues for which a Timon contends are the issues not of Athens but humanity. He is a principle of the human soul, a possibility, a symbol of mankind's aspiration. His servants know that his loss is as the loss of a golden age. A bright spirit has been on earth, spirit of infinite and rich love and bounty, and its wings have been soiled by mortality. Timon, who 'flashed a phœnix' (II. i. 32), is left a 'naked gull'. The elected of the heavens has been scorned of man. So the poetry of this play is large and deep, immeasurably grand, and pregnant of human fate. When Timon lifts his voice to heaven proclaiming 'one honest man' (IV. iii. 504), his words hold an echo no less universal than Abraham's prayer to Jehovah to spare the iniquitous city, if ten men be found therein; when Timon's servants part to wander abroad separated, they are as disciples of the Christ meeting after the Crucifixion. Of these thoughts the poetry is indeed most worthy. It is loaded with a massive, compulsive emotion, in comparison with which the words of Hamlet, Troilus, Othello, and even Lear, are as the plaintive accents of children. A mighty rhythm of a race's longing, of human destiny unalterable and uncomplained, sounds through the whole play, and wakes an unearthly majesty of words in the symphonic harmonies of the final acts. There is no turning aside, no regret in all the passion of Timon, but it

holds an eagle's course, bold and forth on,
Leaving no tract behind—

until, in the poetry of the latter half of the play, the mind is a-voyage on
unfathomed and uncharted seas, whose solid deeps of passion but wanly and
waveringly reflect the vastest images that man can dream. In this recurrent
solemnity of utterance more grand for its massive and fathomless simplicity,
we joy in that we listen not to the accents of mortality but to those of the
spirit of a race. Therefore, though Flavius saves mankind from utter condemnation by one act of faith, we know that the organ notes of implacable
hatred cannot so be stilled, since by them alone the soul of Timon pursues its
course: he is no 'idle votarist' (IV. iii. 27):

> Hate all, curse all, show charity to none. (IV. iii. 534)

The profoundest problems of racial destiny are here symbolized and fought
out. In no other play is a more forceful, a more irresistible, mastery of technique—almost crude in its massive, architectural effects—employed. But then
no play is so massive, so rough-hewn into Atlantean shapes from the mountain
rock of the poet's mind or soul, as this of Timon. 'I have in this rough work
shap'd out a man . . .' It is true. No technical scaffolding in Shakespeare has
to stand so weighty and shattering a stress. For this play is *Hamlet*, *Troilus*,
Othello, *Lear*, become self-conscious and universal; it includes and transcends
them all; it is the recurrent and tormenting Hate-theme of Shakespeare,
developed, raised to an infinite power, presented in all its tyrannic strength
and profundity, and—killed. Three acts form the prologue. Our vision thus
with infinite care and every possible device focused, we await the onrush of a
passion which sums in its torrential energy all the lesser passions of those
protagonists foregone. Timon is the totality of all, his love more rich and
oceanic than all of theirs—all lift their lonely voices in his universal curse;
Christ-like, he suffers that their pain may cease, and leaves the Shakespearian
universe redeemed that Cleopatra may win her Antony in death, and Thaisa
be restored to Pericles.

The Wheel of Fire, 1930.

CYMBELINE

WRITTEN 1609–10.

PERFORMED 1611. Dr. Simon Forman, the astrologer, saw a performance
        probably at the Globe in April, at any rate before his death on
Sept. 12th.
1634. 'On Wensday night the first of January, Cymbeline was acted at
Court by the Kings players. Well likte by the kinge.' (*Office Book* of Sir
Henry Herbert.)

REGISTERED 1623 November 8th. One of the 16 plays registered by Blount
        and Jaggard before the publication of F1.

PUBLISHED   1623 F 1. The last play in the Folio. A fair text.

SOURCES   The wager theme: from Boccaccio's *Decameron* (the story of
             Bernabo of Genoa).

The historical parts: from Holinshed's *Chronicles*.

There are resemblances to Beaumont and Fletcher's *Philaster*, but it is impossible to say whether *Cymbeline* or *Philaster* came first.

In 1682 a melodramatic adaptation of *Cymbeline* by Thomas D'Urfey, *The Injur'd Princess*, was performed at Drury Lane. Garrick returned largely to Shakespeare's text, Posthumus being one of his best parts.

SIMON FORMAN Remember also the storri of Cymbalin king of England, in Lucius tyme, howe Lucius Cam from Octauus Cesar for Tribut, and being denied, after sent Lucius with a greate Arme of Souldiars who landed at Milford hauen, and Affter wer vanquished by Cimbalin, and Lucius taken prisoner, and all by means of 3 outlawes, of the which 2 of them were the sonns of Cimbalin, stolen from him when they were but 2 yers old by an old man whom Cymbalin banished, and he kept them as his own sonns 20 yers with him in A cave. And howe (one) of them slewe Clotan, that was the quens sonn, goinge to Milford hauen to sek the loue of Innogen the kinges daughter, whom he had banished also for louinge his daughter, and howe the Italian that cam from her loue conveied him selfe into A Cheste, and said yt was a chest of plate sent from her loue & others, to be presented to the kinge. And in the depest of the night, she being aslepe, he opened the cheste, & cam forth of yt, And vewed her in her bed, and the markes of her body, & toke awai her braslet, & after Accused her of adultery to her loue, &c. And in thend howe he came with the Romains into England & was taken prisoner, and after Reueled to Innogen, Who had turned her self into mans apparell & fled to mete her loue at Milford hauen, & chanchsed to fall on the Caue in the wodes wher her 2 brothers were, & howe by eating a sleping Dram they thought she had bin deed, & laid her in the wodes, & the body of Cloten by her, in her loues apparell that he left behind him, & howe she was found by Lucius, &c.

Booke of Plaies, 1611.

JOHNSON This play has many just sentiments, some natural dialogues, and some pleasing scenes, but they are obtained at the expense of much incongruity. To remark the folly of the fiction, the absurdity of the conduct, the confusion of the names and manners of different times, and the impossibility of the events in any system of life, were to waste criticism upon unresisting imbecility, upon faults too evident for detection, and too gross for aggravation.

HAZLITT *Cymbeline* is one of the most delightful of Shakespear's historical plays. It may be considered as a dramatic romance, in which the most striking parts of the story are thrown into the form of a dialogue, and the intermediate circumstances are explained by the different speakers, as occasion renders it necessary. The action is less concentrated in consequence; but the interest becomes more aerial and refined from the principle of perspective introduced into the subject by the imaginary changes of scene, as well as by the length of time it occupies. The reading of this play is like going a journey with some uncertain object at the end of it, and in which the suspense is kept up and heightened by the long intervals between each action. Though the events are scattered over such an extent of surface, and relate to such a variety of characters, yet the links which bind the different interests of the story together are never entirely broken. The most straggling and seemingly casual incidents are contrived in such a manner as to lead at last to the most complete development of the catastrophe. The ease and conscious unconcern with which this is effected only makes the skill more wonderful. The business of the plot evidently thickens in the last act: the story moves forward with increasing rapidity at every step; its various ramifications are drawn from the most distant points to the same centre; the principal characters are brought together, and placed in very critical situations; and the fate of almost every person in the drama is made to depend on the solution of a single circumstance—the answer of Iachimo to the question of Imogen respecting the obtaining of the ring from Posthumus. Dr. Johnson is of opinion that Shakspear was generally inattentive to the winding-up of his plots. We think the contrary is true. . . .

Posthumus is the ostensible hero of the piece, but its greatest charm is the character of Imogen. Posthumus is only interesting from the interest she takes in him; and she is only interesting herself from her tenderness and constancy to her husband. It is the peculiar excellence of Shakespear's heroines, that they seem to exist only in their attachment to others. They are pure abstractions of the affections. We think as little of their persons as they do themselves, because we are let into the secrets of their hearts, which are more important. . . .

We have almost as great an affection for Imogen as she had for Posthumus; and she deserves it better. Of all Shakespear's women she is perhaps the most tender and the most artless. . . .

The striking and powerful contrasts in which Shakespear abounds could not escape observation; but the use he makes of the principle of analogy to reconcile the greatest diversities of character and to maintain a continuity of feeling throughout, has not been sufficiently attended to. In *Cymbeline*, for instance, the principal interest arises out of the unalterable fidelity of Imogen to her husband under the most trying circumstances. Now the other parts of the picture are filled up with subordinate examples of the same feeling, variously modified by different situations, and applied to the purposes of virtue or vice. The plot is aided by the amorous importunities of Cloten, by the persevering determination of Iachimo to conceal the defeat of his project by a daring imposture: the faithful attachment of Pisanio to his mistress is an affecting accompaniment to the whole; the obstinate adherence to his purpose in Bellarius, who keeps the fate of the young princes so long a secret in resentment for the ungrateful return to his former services, the incorrigible wickedness of the Queen, and even the blind uxorious confidence of Cymbeline, are all so many lines of the same story, tending to the same point. The effect of this coincidence is rather felt than observe●, and as the impression exists unconsciously in the mind of the reader, so it probably arose in the same manner in the mind of the author, not from design, but from the force of natural association, a particular train of thought suggesting different inflections of the same predominant feeling, melting into, and strengthening one another, like chords in music.

SWINBURNE The time is wellnigh come now for me to consecrate in this book my good will if not good work to the threefold and thrice happy memory of the three who have written of Shakespeare as never man wrote, nor ever man may write again; to the everlasting praise and honour and glory of Charles Lamb, Samuel Taylor Coleridge, and Walter Savage Landor; 'wishing', I hardly dare to say, 'what I write may be read by their light'. The play of plays, which is *Cymbeline*, remains alone to receive the last salute of all my love.

I think, as far as I can tell, I may say I have always loved this one beyond all other children of Shakespeare. The too literal egoism of this profession will not be attributed by any candid or even commonly honest reader to the violence of vanity so much more than comical as to make me suppose that such a record or assurance could in itself be matter of interest to any man: but simply to the real and simple reason, that I wish to show cause for my choice of this work to wind up with, beyond the mere chance of its position at the close of the chaotically inconsequent catalogue of contents affixed to the first edition. In this casualty—for no good thing can reasonably be ascribed to design on the part of the first editors—there would seem to be something more than usual of what we may call, if it so please us, a happy providence. It is certain that no studious arrangement could possibly have brought the book to a happier end. Here is depth enough with height enough of tragic beauty and passion, terror and love and pity, to approve the presence of the most tragic Master's hand; subtlety enough of sweet and bitter truth to attest the passage of the mightiest and wisest scholar or teacher in the school of the human spirit; beauty with delight enough and glory of life and grace of nature to proclaim the advent of the one omnipotent Maker among all who bear that name. Here above all is the most heavenly triad of human figures that ever even Shakespeare brought together; a diviner three, as it were a living god-garland of the noblest earth-born brothers and loveworthiest heaven-born sister, than the very givers of all grace and happiness to their Grecian worshippers of old time over long before. The passion of Posthumus is noble, and potent the poison of Iachimo; Cymbeline has enough for Shakespeare's present purpose of 'the king-becoming graces'; but we think first and last of her who was 'truest speaker' and those who 'called her brother, when she was but their sister; she them brothers, when they were so indeed'. The very crown and flower of all her father's daughters,—I do not speak here of her human father, but her divine—the woman above all Shakespeare's women is Imogen. As in Cleopatra we found the incarnate sex, the woman everlasting, so in Imogen we find half glorified already the immortal godhead of womanhood. I would fain have some honey in my words at parting—with Shakespeare never, but for ever with these notes on Shakespeare; and I am therefore something more than fain to close my book upon the name of the woman best beloved in all the world of song and all the tide of time; upon the name of Shakespeare's Imogen.

A Study of Shakespeare, 1880.

BERNARD SHAW Cymbeline, though one of the finest of Shakespear's later plays now on the stage, goes to pieces in the last act. In fact I mooted the point myself by thoughtlessly saying that the revival would be all right if I wrote a last act for it. To my surprise this blasphemy was received with acclamation; and as the applause, like the proposal, was not wholly jocular, the fancy began to haunt me, and persisted until I exorcised it by writing the pages which ensue.

I had a second surprise when I began reading the authentic last act carefully through. I had not done so for many years, and had the common impression about it that it was a cobbled-up affair by several hands, including a vision in prison accompanied by scraps of quite ridiculous doggerel.

For this estimate I found absolutely no justification nor excuse. I must have got it from the last revival of the play at the old Lyceum theatre, when Irving, as Iachimo, a statue of romantic melancholy, stood dumb on the stage for hours (as it seemed) whilst the others toiled through a series of *dénouements* of crushing tedium, in which the characters lost all their vitality and individuality, and had nothing to do but identify themselves by moles on their necks, or explain why they were not dead. The vision and the verses were cut out as a matter of course; and I ignorantly thanked Heaven for it.

When I read the act as aforesaid I found that my notion that it is a cobbled-up *pasticcio* by other hands was an unpardonable stupidity. The act is genuine Shakespear to the last full stop, and late phase Shakespear in point of verbal workmanship.

The doggerel is not doggerel: it is a versified masque, in Shakespear's careless woodnotes wild, complete with Jupiter as *deus ex machina*, eagle and all, introduced, like the Ceres scene in The Tempest, to please King Jamie, or else because an irresistible fashion had set in, just as at all the great continental opera houses a ballet used to be *de rigeur*. . . . So, I take it, Shakespear had to stick a masque into Cymbeline. Performed as such, with suitable music and enough pictorial splendor, it is not only entertaining on the stage, but, with the very Shakespearean feature of a comic jailor which precedes it, just the thing to save the last act.

Without it the act is a tedious string of unsurprising *dénouements* sugared with insincere sentimentality after a ludicrous stage battle. With one exception the characters have vanished and left nothing but dolls being moved about like the glass balls in the game of solitaire until they are all got rid of but one. The exception is the hero, or rather the husband of the heroine, Leonatus Posthumus. . . . One may say that he is the only character left really alive in the last act; and as I cannot change him for the better I have left most of his part untouched. I make no apology for my attempt to bring the others back to dramatic activity and individuality.

I should like to have retained Cornelius as the exponent of Shakespear's sensible and scientific detestation of vivisection. But as he has nothing to say except that the Queen is dead, and nobody can possibly care a rap whether she is alive or dead, I have left him with her in the box of puppets that are done with.

I have ruthlessly cut out the surprises that no longer surprise anybody. I really could not keep my countenance over the identification of Guiderius by the mole on his neck. That device was killed by Maddison Morton, once a famous farce writer, now forgotten by everyone save Mr. Gordon Craig and myself. In Morton's masterpiece, Box and Cox, Box asks Cox whether he has a strawberry mark on his left arm. 'No', says Cox. 'Then you are my long lost brother', says Box as they fall into one another's arms and end the farce happily. One could wish that Guiderius had anticipated Cox.

Plot has always been the curse of serious drama, and indeed of serious literature of any kind. It is so out-of-place there that Shakespear never could invent one. Unfortunately, instead of taking Nature's hint and discarding plots, he borrowed them all over the place and got into trouble through having to unravel them in the last act, especially in The Two Gentlemen of Verona and Cymbeline. The more childish spectators may find some delight in the revelation that Polydore and Cadwal are Imogen's long lost brothers and Cymbeline's long lost sons; that Iachimo is now an occupant of the penitent form and very unlike his old self; and that Imogen is so dutiful that she accepts her husband's attempt to have her murdered with affectionate docility. I cannot share these infantile joys. Having become interested in Iachimo, in Imogen, and even in the two long lost princes, I wanted to know how their characters would react to the *éclaircissement* which follows the battle. The only way to satisfy this curiosity was to rewrite the act as Shakespear might have written it if he had been post-Ibsen and post-Shaw instead of post-Marlowe. . . .

I shall not press my version on managers producing Cymbeline if they have the courage and good sense to present the original word-for-word as Shakespear left it, and the means to do justice to the masque. But if they are half-hearted about it, and inclined to compromise by leaving out the masque and the comic jailor and mutilating the rest, as their manner is, I unhesitatingly recommend my version. The audience will not know the difference; and the few critics who have read Cymbeline will be too grateful for my shortening of the last act to complain.

Cymbeline Refinished, 1945.

THE WINTER'S TALE

WRITTEN   1610–11.

PERFORMED   1611 May 15, seen by Simon Forman at the Globe.
            1611. 'The Kings players: The 5th of nouember A play Called
ye winters nightes Tayle.' (*Revels Account.*)
1613. One of the plays performed at Whitehall at the marriage festivities of
Elizabeth and the Count Palatine.
1618 April 7, at Court.
1624. 'To the Duchess of Richmond, in the King's absence, was given The
Winters Tale, by the K. company, the 18 Janu. 1623. Att Whitehall.'
(*Office Book of Sir Henry Herbert.*)
1634 Jan. 16. 'The Winters Tale was acted on Thursday night at Court, by
the K. players. and likt.' (*Office Book.*)

REGISTERED   1623, 8th November. One of the 16 plays registered by Blount
            and Jaggard before publishing F 1.

PUBLISHED   1623 F 1. A good text.

SOURCES   Robert Greene's romance *Pandosto or The Triumph of Time*
          (1588), reprinted as *Dorastus and Fawnia* (1607).

In 1756 Garrick produced a version of *The Winter's Tale* called *Florizel
and Perdita*. By cutting two acts, 'sliding o'er sixteen years' by means of a
confidant, and shipwrecking Leontes in Bohemia, he achieved unity of time
and place and 'an elegant form to a monstrous composition'. The version
met with 'very good success'. So did 'a very compleat and entertaining farce,
called "The Sheepshearing",' by M. Morgan.
    For Kean's production in 1856 see p. 24.

SIMON FORMAN In the Winters Talle at the glob 1611 the 15 of maye. Obserue
            ther howe Lyontes the kinge of Cicillia was overcom with
Jelosy of his wife with the kinge of Bohemia his frind that came to see him,
and howe he contriued his death and wold haue had his cup berer to haue
poisoned, who gaue the king of Bohemia warning therof & fled with him
to Bohemia. . . .
    Remember also the Rog that cam in all tottered like coll pixci and howe he
feyned him sicke & to haue bin Robbed of all that he had and howe he cosened
the por man of all his money, and after cam to the shep sher with a pedlers
packe & ther cosened them Again of all their money And how he changed
apparrell with the kinge of Bomia his sonn, and then howe he turned Courtier
&c. Beware of trustinge feined beggars or fawninge fellouss.

                                        Booke of Plaies, 1611.

BEN JONSON Sheakspear in a play brought in a number of men saying they
                had suffered Shipwrack in Bohemia, wher ther is no Sea neer
by some 100 Miles.

Conversations with William Drummond, 1619.

For the king's players. An olde playe called Winter's Tale, formerly
allowed of by Sir George Bucke, and likewyse by mee on Mr Hemmings
his worde that there was nothing profane added or reformed, thogh the
allowed booke was missinge; and therefore I returned it without a fee, this
19 of August, 1623.

Office Book of Sir Henry Herbert.[1]

JOHNSON This play, as Dr. Warburton justly observes, is, with all its ab-
            surdities, very entertaining. The character of Autolycus is very
naturally conceived, and strongly represented.

COLERIDGE The idea of this delightful drama is a genuine jealousy of dis-
              position, and it should be immediately followed by the perusal of
Othello, which is the direct contrast of it in every particular. For jealousy is a
vice of the mind, a culpable tendency of the temper, having certain well known
and well defined effects and concomitants, all of which are visible in Leontes,
and, I boldly say, not one of which marks its presence in Othello;—such as,
first, an excitability by the most inadequate causes, and an eagerness to snatch
at proofs; secondly, a grossness of conception, and a disposition to degrade the
object of the passion by sensual fancies and images ; thirdly, a sense of shame
of his own feelings exhibited in a solitary moodiness of humour, and yet from
the violence of the passion forced to utter itself, and therefore catching occasions to ease the mind by ambiguities, equivoques, by talking to those who
cannot, and who are known not to be able to understand what is said to them,
—in short by soliloquy in the form of dialogue, and hence a confused, broken,
and fragmentary, manner ; fourthly, a dread of vulgar ridicule, as distinct
from a high sense of honour, or a mistaken sense of duty ; and lastly, and immediately, consequent on this, a spirit of selfish vindictiveness.

HAZLITT We wonder that Mr. Pope should have entertained doubts of the
            genuineness of this play. He was, we suppose, shocked (as a
certain critic suggests) at the Chorus, Time, leaping over sixteen years with
his crutch between the third and fourth act, and at Antigonus's landing with
the infant Perdita on the sea-coast of Bohemia. These slips or blemishes
however do not prove it not to be Shakespear's; for he was as likely to fall
into them as any body; but we do not know any body but himself who could
produce the beauties. The *stuff* of which the tragic passion is composed, the
romantic sweetness, the comic humour, are evidently his. Even the crabbed

---

[1] Sir Henry Herbert was Master of the Revels and *ex officio* censor and licenser
for the printing of plays. Sir G. Buck was his predecessor. The Office Book is
now lost. Perhaps the 'allowed book' (*i.e.* authorised MS.) had been mislaid during
the printing of F1.

and tortuous style of the speeches of Leontes, reasoning on his own jealousy, beset with doubts and fears, and entangled more and more in the thorny labyrinth, bears every mark of Shakespear's peculiar manner of conveying the painful struggle of different thoughts and feelings, labouring for utterance, and almost strangled in the birth. . . .

The Winter's Tale is one of the best-acting of our author's plays. We remember seeing it with great pleasure many years ago. It was on the night that King took leave of the stage, when he and Mrs. Jordan played together in the after-piece of the Wedding-day. Nothing could go off with more éclat, with more spirit, and grandeur of effect. Mrs. Siddons played Hermione, and in the last scene acted the painted statue to the life—with true monumental dignity and noble passion; Mr. Kemble, in Leontes, worked himself up into a very fine classical phrensy; and Bannister, as Autolycus, roared as loud for pity as a sturdy beggar could do who felt none of the pain he counterfeited, and was sound of wind and limb. We shall never see these parts so acted again; or if we did, it would be in vain. Actors grow old, or no longer surprise us by their novelty. But true poetry, like nature, is always young; and we still read the courtship of Florizel and Perdita, as we welcome the return of spring, with the same feelings as ever.

James Agate Why is The Winter's Tale so little popular? Some people have alleged the gap in time between the third and fourth acts. On the theory, shall we say, that devouring Time blunts more things than lions' paws—to wit, theatrical interest. It was Shakespeare's failure to live up to the dramatic principles laid down by Mr. Curdle which led the commentator Pope to entertain doubts of the play's genuineness. Hazlitt quickly disposed of Pope by saying that what slips or blunders there were in the play did not prove it not to be Shakespeare, 'for he was as like to fall into them as anybody; but we do not know anybody but himself who could produce the beauties'. . . .

I think the reason The Winter's Tale is unpopular is that Hermione talks too much.

The Contemporary Theatre, 1944.

W. H. Clemen Of Shakespeare's romances The Winter's Tale shows the widest range of imagery. It embraces romantic and poetical imagery (as becoming to a 'romance') as well as drastic and realistic imagery of the workaday world. The more intellectual types of imagery by which passion and thought express themselves are also represented, as well as the subtle and complex images that derive their effect from condensation and ambiguity. Mr. Bethell has made the acute observation . . . that in *The Winter's Tale* we find a use of imagery and conceit more Jacobean than Elizabethan. Thus Shakespeare's imagery does not only develop along the lines of Shakespeare's artistic evolution, but it also reflects the changes which we can trace in the transition of poetic style from the Elizabethan to the Jacobean period.

The Winter's Tale reveals in several respects an essentially Shakespearian tendency which we can trace throughout his whole dramatic career and which becomes more and more conspicuous towards its end: the endeavour to establish a balance between opposites, never to give only one colour without supplementing it by a complementary colour, never to yield to one specific mood without contrasting it by other entirely different moods and spheres. This desire always to create a complex, round and full picture partly accounts for Shakespeare's masterly faculty to blend various genres, sources and elements into a new organic whole. It is not only brought out by his maturer technique of characterization but becomes evident in almost all aspects and features of his art. Imagery, in this connection, is a considerable help in securing this balance and complexity of which *The Winter's Tale* is a good example.

The imagery in the first three acts of the play which so much resemble a tragedy is set off distinctly from the imagery in the 'romance' of the fourth act, where we again can trace various contrasting patterns. Compared to the fourth act, the images in that first part are shorter and more thinly spread all over the text. We have more single metaphors than in the fourth act, in which the images appear more in clusters, are more compact, stand out from the context more colourfully and strikingly and (in a longer passage) often crowd so closely that the effect and the impression of this passage seems to lie solely in the imagery. In the first part, on the other hand, the imagery, being more subsidiary, has rather the function of being an expression for thought and passion, whereas in the fourth part the imagery seems largely to have been introduced for its own sake.

It could also be said that in the first acts, the imagery is more 'subterranean' and subordinate; every now and then, from this hidden stream, images rise up to the surface and tinge the language, sometimes only by way of metaphor. This subterranean flow of imagery not only finds its expression in a chain of iterative imagery, but also in the associative interrelation of images. Leontes' aside, for example, in I. ii. 180, 'I am angling now, . . .' gives rise, fourteen lines later, to 'And his pond fish'd . . .', which may have also been suggested by 'sluic'd' in the preceding line. . . .

And then we discover that there is more in the details of imagery than we had at first anticipated. This holds good of *The Winter's Tale*, too. The contrasting and blending of the ideal romance-world with the realistically and drastically represented village life is more than a mere collocation of different atmospheres, and contains a deeper meaning which in fact leads us a little nearer to the play's central problem. Shakespeare evidently wanted to show that the renewal and regeneration of a decaying world as symbolized by the Perdita-Florizel episode in the fourth act must have roots in the firm reality and simplicity of the country-life as well as in the more refined court-world. 'Country and court are necessary to each other, Shakespeare seems to imply, the sober virtues of the one and the graces of the other compounding a perfect whole', as Mr. Bethell has put it. And this necessary union is again indicated by the imagery.

The Development of Shakespeare's Imagery, 1936, translated 1951.

THE TEMPEST

Written   1611–12.

Performed   1611 Nov. 1. 'By the Kings players: Hallowmas nyght was
          presented att Whithall before ye kinges Maiestie a play Called
the Tempest.' (*Revels Account*.)
1613. 'Item paid to John Heminges upon the Cowncells warrant dated att
Whitehall xx° die Maij 1613, for presentinge before the Princes Highnes the
Lady Elizabeth and the Prince Pallatyne Elector fowerteene severall playes,
viz: . . . The Tempest . . .' (*Chamber Account*.)

Registered   1623. 8th November. One of the 16 plays registered by
          Blount and Jaggard before publishing F 1.

Published   1623 F 1. A good text with more detailed stage-directions than
          any other play. The first play in the Folio.

Sources   For the Island: Narratives of the wreck of Sir George Somers,
          Sir Thomas Gates, William Strachey, Sylvester Jourdan, and
others on the Bermudas in 1609:—
Jourdan's *A Discovery of the Barmudas* (1610).
A True Declaration of the Estate of the Colonie in Virginia (1610). An
official report.
Strachey's *A True Reportory of the Wracke and Redemption of Sir Thomas
Gates*.
For the plot: possibly *Die Schöne Sidea*, by Jacob Ayrer of Nuremberg who
died 1605.

Davenant's and Dryden's adaptation was seen by Pepys in 1667. They
achieve a nice classical symmetry by introducing Dorinda, a younger sister
of Miranda, and Hippolito, a young man who had never seen a woman.
Caliban is balanced by the female monster Sycorax, and Ariel by the female
spirit Milcha. This version was acted by Garrick and was the basis of
Kemble's two versions, the second of which so infuriated Hazlitt when he
saw it in 1815. 'The common place sentiments, and all the heavy tinsel and
affected formality which Dryden had borrowed from the French school'
made him 'almost come to the resolution of never going to another representation of a play of Shakespeare's as long as we lived; and we certainly did
come to this determination, that we would never go *by choice*'.
Macready returned to Shakespeare's play, slightly altered, in 1838, as did
Phelps in 1847 and Charles Kean in 1857.
In 1673 the Davenant-Dryden play was turned into an opera with music
by Purcell, and in 1756 Garrick produced 'a new opera, called The Tempest,
altered from Shakespeare', with music by J. C. Smith.

Pepys   At noon resolved with Sir W. Pen to go to see 'The Tempest', an
        old play of Shakespeare's, acted, I hear, the first day; and so my wife,

and girl, and W. Hewer by themselves, and Sir W. Pen and I afterwards by ourselves: and forced to sit in the side balcony over against the musique-room at the Duke's house, close by my Lady Dorset and a great many great ones. The house mighty full; the King and Court there: and the most innocent play that ever I saw; and a curious piece of musick in an echo of half sentences, the echo repeating the former half, while the man goes on to the latter; which is mighty pretty.[1] The play has no great wit, but yet good, above ordinary plays. (7 *Nov.* 1667.)

To the Duke of York's house, and there saw the Tempest again, which is very pleasant, and full of so good variety that I cannot be more pleased almost in a comedy, only the seaman's part a little too tedious. (13 *Nov.* 1667.)

To the Duke of York's house, and saw 'The Tempest', and the house very full. (12 *Dec.* 1667.)

DRYDEN
> As when a tree's cut down, the secret root
> Lives under ground, and thence new branches shoot;
> So from old Shakespear's honour'd dust, this day
> Springs up and buds a new reviving play:
> Shakespear, who (taught by none) did first impart
> To Fletcher wit, to labouring Jonson art.
> He, monarch like, gave those, his subjects, law;
> And is that nature which they paint and draw.
> Fletcher reach'd that which on his heights did grow,
> While Jonson crept, and gather'd all below.
> This did his love, and this his mirth digest:
> One imitates him most, the other best.
> If they have since outwrit all other men,
> 'Tis with the drops which fell from Shakespear's pen.
> The storm, which vanish'd on the neighbouring shore,
> Was taught by Shakespear's Tempest first to roar.
> That innocence and beauty, which did smile
> In Fletcher, grew on this enchanted isle.
> But Shakespear's magic could not copied be;
> Within that circle none durst walk but he.
> I must confess 'twas bold, nor would you now
> That liberty to vulgar wits allow,
> Which works by magic supernatural things:
> But Shakespear's power is sacred as a king's.
> Those legends from old priesthood were received,
> And he then writ, as people then believed.
> > *Prologue to The Tempest.*

To return once more to Shakespear; no man ever drew so many characters, or generally distinguished 'em better from one another, excepting only

[1] Ferdinand's song in which Ariel echoes 'Go thy way'. This is, of course, the Davenant-Dryden adaptation with music by Banister.

Jonson. I will instance but in one, to show the copiousness of his invention; it is that of Caliban, or the monster, in the *Tempest*. He seems there to have created a person which was not in nature, a boldness which, at first sight, would appear intolerable; for he makes him a species of himself, begotten by an incubus on a witch; but this, as I have elsewhere proved, is not wholly beyond the bounds of credibility, at least the vulgar still believe it. We have the separated notions of spirit, and of a witch (and spirits, according to Plato, are vested with a subtle body; according to some of his followers, have different sexes); therefore, as from the distinct apprehensions of a horse, and of a man, imagination has formed a centaur; so, from those of an incubus and a sorceress, Shakespear has produced his monster. Whether or no his generation can be defended, I leave to philosophy; but of this I am certain, that the poet has most judiciously furnished him with a person, a language, and a character, which will suit him, both by father's and mother's side: he has all the discontents and malice of a witch, and of a devil, besides a convenient proportion of the deadly sins; gluttony, sloth, and lust, are manifest; the dejectedness of a slave is likewise given him, and the ignorance of one bred up in a desert island. His person is monstrous, and he is the product of un-natural lust; and his language is as hobgoblin as his person; in all things he is distinguished from other mortals. The characters of Fletcher are poor and narrow, in comparison of Shakespear's; I remember not one which is not borrowed from him; unless you will accept that strange mixture of a man in the *King and no King*; so that in this part Shakespear is generally worth our imitation; and to imitate Fletcher is but to copy after him who was a copyer.

Preface to Troilus and Cressida.

JOHNSON It is observed of The Tempest, that its plan is regular; this the author of The Revisal thinks, what I think too, an accidental effect of the story, not intended or regarded by our author. But whatever might be Shakespeare's intention in forming or adopting the plot, he has made it instrumental to the production of many characters, diversified with boundless invention, and preserved with profound skill in nature, extensive knowledge of opinions, and accurate observation of life. In a single drama are here exhibited princes, courtiers, and sailors, all speaking in their real characters. There is the agency of airy spirits, and of an earthly goblin; the operations of magick, the tumults of a storm, the adventures of a desert island, the native effusion of untaught affection, the punishment of guilt, and the final happiness of the pair for whom our passions and reason are equally interested.

COLERIDGE The Tempest is a specimen of the purely romantic drama, in which the interest is not historical, or dependent upon fidelity of portraiture, or the natural connexion of events,—but is a birth of the imagination, and rests only on the coaptation and union of the elements granted to, or assumed by the poet. It is a species of drama which owes no allegiance to time or space, and in which, therefore, errors of chronology and geography —no mortal sins in any species—are venial faults, and count for nothing. It addresses itself entirely to the imaginative faculty; and although the illusion may be assisted by the effect on the senses of the complicated machinery and decorations of modern times, yet this sort of assistance is dangerous. For the principal and only genuine excitement ought to come from within,—from the moved and sympathetic imagination; whereas, where so much is addressed to the mere external senses of seeing and hearing, the spiritual vision is apt to languish, and the attraction from without will withdraw the mind from the proper and only legitimate interest which is intended to spring from within.

The romance opens with a busy scene admirably appropriate to the kind of drama, and giving, as it were, the keynote to the whole harmony. It prepares and initiates the excitement required for the entire piece, and yet does not demand any thing from the spectators, which their previous habits had not fitted them to understand. It is the bustle of a tempest, from which the real horrors are abstracted;—therefore it is poetical, though not in strictness natural—(the distinction to which I have so often alluded)—and is purposely restrained from concentering the interest on itself, but used merely as an induction or tuning for what is to follow.

In the second scene, Prospero's speeches, till the entrance of Ariel, contain the finest example, I remember, of retrospective narration for the purpose of exciting immediate interest, and putting the audience in possession of all the information necessary for the understanding of the plot. Observe, too, the perfect probability of the moment chosen by Prospero (the very Shakspeare himself, as it were, of the tempest) to open out the truth to his daughter, his own romantic bearing, and how completely any thing that might have been disagreeable to us in the magician, is reconciled and shaded in the humanity and natural feelings of the father. In the very first speech of Miranda the simplicity and tenderness of her character are at once laid open;—it would have been lost in direct contact with the agitation of the first scene. . . .

The appearance and characters of the super or ultra-natural servants are finely contrasted. Ariel has in every thing the airy tint which gives the name; and it is worthy of remark that Miranda is never directly brought into comparison with Ariel, lest the natural and human of the one and the supernatural of the other should tend to neutralize each other; Caliban, on the other hand, is all earth, all condensed and gross in feelings and images; he has the dawnings of understanding without reason or the moral sense, and in him, as in some brute animals, this advance to the intellectual faculties, without the moral sense, is marked by the appearance of vice.

HAZLITT *The Tempest* is one of the most original and perfect of Shakespear's productions, and he has shewn in it all the variety of his powers. It is full of grace and grandeur. The human and imaginary characters, the dramatic and the grotesque, are blended together with the greatest art, and without any appearance of it. Though he has here given 'to airy nothing a local habitation and a name', yet that part which is only the fantastic creation of his mind, has the same palpable texture, and coheres 'semblably' with the rest. As the preternatural part has the air of reality, and almost haunts the imagination with a sense of truth, the real characters and events partake of the

wildness of a dream. The stately magician, Prospero, driven from his duke-
dom, but around whom (so potent is his art) airy spirits throng numberless
to do his bidding; his daughter Miranda ('worthy of that name') to whom
all the power of his art points, and who seems the goddess of the isle; the
princely Ferdinand, cast by fate upon the heaven of his happiness in this idol
of his love; the delicate Ariel; the savage Caliban, half brute, half demon; the
drunken ship's crew—are all connected parts of the story, and can hardly be
spared from the place they fill. Even the local scenery is of a piece and
character with the subject. Prospero's enchanted island seems to have risen
up out of the sea; the airy music, the tempest-tost vessel, the turbulent waves,
all have the effect of the landscape background of some fine picture. Shakespear's pencil is (to use an allusion of his own) 'like the dyer's hand, subdued
to what it works in'. Everything in him, though it partakes of 'the liberty
of wit', is also subjected to 'the law' of the understanding. For instance, even
the drunken sailors, who are made reeling-ripe, share, in the disorder of their
minds and bodies, in the tumult of the elements, and seem on shore to be as
much at the mercy of chance as they were before at the mercy of the winds
and waves. These fellows with their sea-wit are the least to our taste of any
part of the play: but they are as like drunken sailors as they can be, and are
an indirect foil to Caliban, whose figure acquires a classical dignity in the
comparison.

Sir A. Quiller-Couch And I conclude by asseverating that were a greater
                        than Ariel to wing down from Heaven and stand
and offer me to choose which, of all the books written in the world, should
be mine, I should choose—not the *Odyssey*, not the *Æneid*, not the *Divine
Comedy*, not *Paradise Lost*; not *Othello*, nor *Hamlet*, nor *Lear*; but this little
matter of 2,000 odd lines—*The Tempest*. 'What?—rather than *Othello* or
than *Lear*?' 'Yes: for I can just imagine a future age of men, in which their
characterisation has passed into a curiosity, a pale thing of antiquity; as I can
barely imagine, yet can just imagine, a world in which the murder of Desdemona, the fate of Cordelia, will be considered curiously, as brute happenings
proper to a time outlived; and again, while I reverence the artist who in
Othello or in *Lear* purges our passion, forcing us to weep for present human
woe, *The Tempest*, as I see it, forces diviner tears, tears for sheer beauty; with
a royal sense of this world and how it passes away, with a catch at the heart
of what is to come. And still the sense is royal: it is the majesty of art: we
feel that we are greater than we know. So on the surge of our emotion, as on
the surges ringing Prospero's island, is blown a spray, a mist. Actually it
dwells in our eyes, bedimming them: and as involuntarily we would brush
it away, there rides in it a rainbow; and its colours are wisdom and charity,
with forgiveness, tender ruth for all men and women growing older, and
perennial trust in young love.

Shakespeare's Workmanship, 1918.

F. E. Halliday It is true that simile and metaphor are things inessential to
                poetry, but it is equally true that spontaneous and illumina-

ting imagery is one of the most potent forces in poetry. Aristotle even goes so far as to say, 'The greatest thing of all by far is to be a master of metaphor. It is the one thing that cannot be learned from others: and it is also a sign of original genius, since a good metaphor implies the intuitive perception of the similarity in dissimilars'. Here then is a third form of the contrapuntal, or at least harmonic, principle in poetry. As the words are an image of the experience, and the imposed rhythm a reflection of the emotion and an echo of the basic metre, so metaphor is an image of the thing described; and as the reader recognises with a shock of delight the equivalence of the experience and the words, of the emotion and the rhythm, so does he recognise the equivalence, the essential harmony, of the thing described and the secondary image of the metaphor. For we take a natural delight in this recognition of a real unity in apparent diversity, and the revelation of this fundamental harmony is the preoccupation of the artist. . . .

The same unifying and harmonising principle is often found within the smaller unit of a speech that is of sufficient length and dramatic importance: a restatement of an earlier image, which resolves the intermediate images and brings them within its pattern, as when Ophelia describes Hamlet as 'The expectancy and rose of the fair state', that is, to put it into another Shakespearean idiom, as the promised beauty of the unblown rose, then after the intervening images of mirror and model, bells and discord, returns with infinite pathos to the initial image, 'That unmatched form and feature of blown youth blasted with ecstasy'. Then, consider Prospero's speech when he dismisses the spirits that have performed the Masque of the Three Goddesses:

> Our revels now are ended. These our actors,
> As I foretold you, were all spirits, and
> Are melted into air, into thin air;
> And like the baseless fabric of this vision,
> The cloud-capp'd towers, the gorgeous palaces,
> The solemn temples, the great globe itself,
> Yea, all which it inherit, shall dissolve,
> And, like this insubstantial pageant faded,
> Leave not a rack behind. We are such stuff
> As dreams are made on, and our little life
> Is rounded with a sleep.

In these lines, perhaps the most beautiful that Shakespeare ever wrote, the triple counterpoint of imagery, phrase and rhythm reaches its final perfection. Though metrically almost regular, much of their beauty lies in the counter-rhythm induced by the assonantal sequence of false trochees and related words—*revels, temples; actors, fabric, pageant, baseless*—sequences that are linked by that of the verbs, *ended, melted, faded,* with their remote connotations and fading cadences. The verse must be slowly and deliberately spoken, and full emphasis given to its imposed and falling rhythm, though there are perhaps no other three words so difficult to speak, because of their sheer beauty, as 'insubstantial pageant faded'.

The speech begins with a simple statement, introducing three lines which, by the disproportionate number of words that begin with a vowel, by the fragility of these words and by the slight pause necessitated before speaking them, express something of the heartache for what time has taken away. Then begins the deeper and more solemn music of the development: what time will take away. The theme of finality and dissolution is announced by *ended*, and developed with variations by the other three verbs, *ended* being linked to *rounded* by its rhyming consonants, while the rhythm of 'Are melted into air' is exactly repeated in 'Is rounded with a sleep', so that air and sleep are imaginatively identified with one another and with an enveloping forgetfulness. Then, the central image of the dissolution of the great globe itself, Lear's 'thick rotundity o' the world', is restated, or recalled by the final image, with its antithesis, of the oblivion that lies beyond life's dream, 'our *little* life is *rounded* with a sleep.'

It is such poetry as this, which, by its perfection of phrase, its musical sequences of words, its imposed and varying rhythms, its illuminating and harmonising imagery, conveys more than has ever been communicated by any other poet, of the experience, the vision that inspired the writing; it is such poetry—not the learning, not the philosophy, not even the characters, for they are themselves the poetry—that makes the plays of Shakespeare so incomparably the greatest achievement of man's genius.

The Poetry of Shakespeare's Plays, 1954.

HENRY THE EIGHTH

WRITTEN   1612–13.

PERFORMED 1613 June 29 at the Globe, when it was burned down.
           1628 July 29 at the Globe.

REGISTERED 1623 8th November. One of the 16 plays registered by Blount and Jaggard before publishing F1.

PUBLISHED 1623 F1. A good text.

SOURCES   Holinshed's *Chronicles*; Foxe's *Book of Martyrs*.

Scholars are generally agreed that there are two authors in this play. As early as 1850 James Spedding asked '*Who wrote Henry VIII?*' and, basing his opinion on a study of the verse, attributed to Shakespeare only I. i, ii: II. iii, iv; III. ii, 1–203; V. i; and the rest to Fletcher. Perhaps, before leaving London, Shakespeare wrote a draft of the play which was worked up and mostly rewritten by Fletcher in 1612–13. It is not certain that Fletcher was the other author, but he is supposed to have collaborated with Shakespeare in *The Two Noble Kinsmen*, and in the lost play *Cardenio*, and the surfeit of feminine endings, the exhausted and monotonous rhythms, and the exploitation of the pathetic all sound like Fletcher.

Davenant produced a spectacular version of *Henry VIII* which was seen by Pepys.

The Famous Hiſtory of the Life of
King HENRY the Eight.

THE PROLOGVE.

Come no more to make you laugh, Things now,
That beare a Weighty, and a Serious Brow,
Sad, high, and working, full of State and Woe:
Such Noble Scænes, as draw the Eye to flow
We now present. Those that can Pitty, heere
May (if they thinke it well) let fall a Teare,
The Subiect will deserue it. Such as giue
Their Money out of hope they may beleeue,
May heere finde Truth too. Those that come to see
Onely a show or two, and so agree,
The Play may passe: If they be still, and willing,
Ile vndertake may see away their shilling
Richly in two short houres. Onely they
That come to heare a Merry, Bawdy Play,
A noyse of Targets: Or to see a Fellow
In a long Motley Coate, garded with Yellow,

Will be deceyu'd. For gentle Hearer's, know
To ranke our chosen Truth with such a show
As Foole, and Fight is, beside forfeyting
Our owne Braines, and the Opinion that we bring
To make that onely true, we now intend,
Will leaue vs neuer an vnderstanding Friend.
Therefore, for Goodnesse sake, and as you are knowne
The First and Happiest Hearers of the Towne,
Be sad, as we would make ye. Thinke ye see
The very Persons of our Noble Story,
As they were Liuing: Thinke you see them Great,
And follow'd with the generall throng, and sweat
Of thousand Friends: Then, in a moment, see
How soone this Mightinesse, meets Misery:
And if you can be merry then, Ile say,
A Man may weepe vpon his Wedding day.

Actus Primus. Scœna Prima.

Enter the Duke of Norfolke at one doore. At the other,
the Duke of Buckingham, and the Lord
Aburgauenny.

Buckingham.

Good morrow, and well met. How haue ye done
Since last we saw in France?
  Norf. I thanke your Grace:
Healthfull, and euer since a fresh Admirer
Of what I saw there.
  Buck. An vntimely Ague
Staid me a Prisoner in my Chamber, when
Those Sunnes of Glory, those two Lights of Men
Met in the vale of Andren.
  Nor. Twixt Guynes and Arde,
I was then present, saw them salute on Horsebacke,
Beheld them when they lighted, how they clung
In their Embracement, as they grew together,
Which had they,
What foure Thron'd ones could haue weigh'd
Such a compounded one?
  Buck. All the whole time
I was my Chambers Prisoner.

  Nor. Then you lost
The view of earthly glory: Men might say
Till this time Pompe was single, but now married
To one aboue it selfe. Each following day
Became the next dayes master, till the last
Made former Wonders, it's. To day the French,
All Clinquant all in Gold, like Heathen Gods
Shone downe the English; and to morrow, they
Made Britaine, India: Euery man that stood,
Shew'd like a Mine. Their Dwarfish Pages were
As Cherubins, all gilt: the Madams too,
Not vs'd to toyle, did almost sweat to beare
The Pride vpon them, that their very labour
Was to them, as a Painting. Now this Maske
Was cry'de incomparable; and th'ensuing night
Made it a Foole, and Begger. The two Kings
Equall in lustre, were now best, now worst
As presence did present them: Him in eye,
Still him in praise, and being present both,
Twas said they saw but one, and no Discerner
Durst wagge his Tongue in censure, when these Sunnes
(For so they phrase 'em) by their Heralds challeng'd
The Noble Spirits to Armes, they did performe
                                         Beyond

 t 3

Sir Henry Wotton Now, to let matters of state sleep, I will entertain you at the present with what has happened this week at the Bank's side. The King's players had a new play, called *All is True*, representing some principal pieces of the reign of Henry VIII, which was set forth with many extraordinary circumstances of pomp and majesty, even to the matting of the stage; the Knights of the Order with their Georges and garters, the Guards with their embroidered coats, and the like: sufficient in truth within a while to make greatness very familiar, if not ridiculous. Now, King Henry making a masque at the Cardinal Wolsey's house, and certain chambers being shot off at his entry, some of the paper, or other stuff, where with one of them was stopped, did light on the thatch, where being thought at first but an idle smoke, and their eyes more attentive to the show, it kindled inwardly, and ran round like a train, consuming within less than an hour the whole house to the very grounds. This was the fatal period to that virtuous fabric, wherein yet nothing did perish but wood and straw, and a few forsaken cloaks; only one man had his breeches set on fire, that would perhaps have broiled him, if he had not by the benefit of a provident wit put it out with bottle ale.

Letter to Sir Edmund Bacon, 2 July 1613.

Robert Gell On Teusday his Grace (the Duke of Buckingham) was present at ye acting of K. Hen. 8 at ye Globe, a play bespoken of purpose by himself; whereat he stayd till ye Duke of Buckingham was beheaded, & then departed. Some say, he should rather have seen ye fall of Cardinall Woolsey, who was a more lively type of himself, having governed this kingdom 18 yeares, as he hath done 14.

Letter to Sir Martyn Stuteville, 9 Aug. 1628.

Pepys Calling at Wotton's, my shoemaker's to-day, he tells me that Harris is come to the Duke's house again; and of a rare play to be acted this week of Sir William Davenant's: the story of Henry the Eighth, with all his wives. (10 *Dec.* 1663.)

Went to the Duke's house, the first play I have been at these six months, according to my last vowe, and here saw the so much cried-up play of 'Henry the Eighth', which, though I went with resolution to like it, is so simple a thing, made up of a great many patches, that, besides the shows and processions in it, there is nothing in the world good or well done. (1 *Jan.* 1664.)

The street full of coaches at the new play, at 'The Indian Queene'; which for show, they say, exceeds 'Henry the Eighth'. (27 *Jan.* 1664.)

After dinner, my wife and I to the Duke's playhouse, and there did see 'King Harry the Eighth'; and was mightily pleased, better than I ever expected, with the history and shows of it. (30 *Dec.* 1668.)

John Downes King *Henry* the 8*th.* . . . The part of the King was so right and justly done by Mr *Betterton*, he being instructed in it by Sir *William*, who had it from old Mr *Lowen*, that had his Instructions from

Mr *Shakespear* himself, that I dare and will aver, none can, or will come near him in this Age, in the performance of that part.

Roscius Anglicanus, 1708.

JOHNSON The play of Henry VIII is one of those which still keeps possession of the stage by the splendour of its pageantry. The coronation, about forty years ago, drew the people together in multitudes for a great part of the winter. Yet pomp is not the only merit of this play. The meek sorrows and virtuous distress of Catharine have furnished some scenes which may be justly numbered among the greatest efforts of tragedy. But the genius of Shakespeare comes in and goes out with Catharine. Every other part may be easily conceived, and easily written.

The historical dramas are now concluded, of which the two parts of Henry IV and Henry V are among the happiest of our author's compositions; and King John, Richard III and Henry VIII deservedly stand in the second class. Those whose curiosity would refer the historical scenes to their original may consult Holinshed, and sometimes Hall: from Holinshed, Shakespeare has often inserted whole speeches, with no more alteration than was necessary to the numbers of his verse. . . .

To play histories, or to exhibit a succession of events by action and dialogue, was a common entertainment among our rude ancestors upon great festivities. The parish clerks once performed at Clerkenwell a play, which lasted three days, containing the History of the World.

BOSWELL Having placed himself by her [Mrs. Siddons], he [Johnson] with great good humour entered upon a consideration of the English drama; and, among other enquiries, particularly asked her which of Shakespeare's characters she was most pleased with. Upon her answering that she thought the character of Queen Catharine, in Henry the Eighth, the most natural:—'I think so too, Madam, (said he;) and whenever you perform it I will once more hobble out to the theatre myself.' Mrs. Siddons promised she would do herself the honour of acting his favourite part for him; but many circumstances happened to prevent the representation of King Henry the Eighth during the Doctor's life.

Life of Johnson, 1791.

HAZLITT This play contains little action or violence of passion, yet it has considerable interest of a more mild and thoughtful cast, and some of the most striking passages in the author's works. The character of Queen Katherine is the most perfect delineation of matronly dignity, sweetness, and resignation, that can be conceived. Her appeals to the protection of the king, her remonstrances to the cardinals, her conversations with her women, shew a noble and generous spirit accompanied with the utmost gentleness of nature. . . .

Dr. Johnson observes of this play, that 'the meek sorrows and virtuous distress of Katherine have furnished some scenes, which may be justly numbered among the greatest efforts of tragedy. But the genius of Shakespear

comes in and goes out with Katherine. Every other part may be easily conceived and easily written.' This is easily said; but with all due deference to
so great a reputed authority as that of Johnson, it is not true. For instance,
the scene of Buckingham led to execution is one of the most affecting and
natural in Shakespear, and one to which there is hardly an approach in any
other author. Again, the character of Wolsey, the description of his pride
and of his fall, are inimitable, and have, besides their gorgeousness of effect, a
pathos, which only the genius of Shakespear could lend to the distresses of a
proud, bad man, like Wolsey. There is a sort of child-like simplicity in the
very helplessness of his situation, arising from the recollection of his past over-
bearing ambition. After the cutting sarcasms of his enemies on his disgrace,
against which he bears up with a spirit conscious of his own superiority, he
breaks out into that fine apostrophe—

Farewell, a long farewell, to all my greatness! . . .

There is in this passage, as well as in the well-known dialogue with Cromwell which follows, something which stretches beyond commonplace; nor is
the account which Griffiths gives of Wolsey's death less Shakespearian; and
the candour with which Queen Katherine listens to the praise of 'him whom
of all men while living she hated most' adds the last graceful finishing to her
character. . . .

No reader of history can be a lover of kings. We have often wondered that
Henry VIII as he is drawn by Shakespear, and as we have seen him represented in all the bloated deformity of mind and person, is not hooted from
the English stage.

G. Wilson Knight *The Tempest* would scarcely have been quite satisfying
                                as Shakespeare's last play, since despite its many subtle
recapitulations, it might yet seem to dissolve the stern political and national
interest of earlier works into a haze of esoteric mysticism. One expects, from
such a poet, a less visionary and enigmatic conclusion.

Shakespeare seems continually to have been forced backwards as his
historical interest developed and plots became exhausted. . . . There is
profound examination throughout the Tragedies and Final Plays of such
ever-vital and contemporary matters as state-order, warrior honour, kingship
and tyranny; many of which are worked, as we have seen, into *The Tempest*.
Finally the poet, copying his analogue Prospero, returns deliberately to a
national and contemporary theme, and writes *Henry VIII*. He may, indeed,
have originally purposed such a conclusion, holding it in reserve for his
crowning work. . . .

This [the last scene, V. v], our culminating ceremonial, is of all the most
richly conceived. Too often commentators have dismissed the greater part of
Henry VIII as 'pageantry': it is that, but the mistake lies in ranking it among
Hamlet's 'inexplicable dumb shows' instead of observing the great architecture of sequent pageants and their deeper meanings. . . .

Cranmer is the centre of a vast stage, composed of nobles, ecclesiastics, crowds, the King himself, a glittering and packed assembly. . . . His speech moves with a massive, swaying movement, accumulating greater and yet greater mass and, when seeming exhausted, rising to a new self-begotten life, new energy and expansive grasp. No words in Shakespeare are more potently placed, none so deeply loaded with a life's wisdom rolled within the volumes of a single, yet for ever unfurling, speech. Nor does anything in our literature demand a subtler understanding in tone, emphasis, pause, and variation of speed and local colour:

> *Cranmer.*   Let me speak, sir,
> For heaven now bids me; and the words I utter
> Let none think flattery, for they'll find 'em truth . . .

This, then, is the crowning act for which the Ariel of Shakespeare's art has been steadily, from play to play, disciplined and matured. Therefore the prophecy cannot be confined to the two sovereigns to whom it is directly offered. Shakespeare thinks poet-wise, drama-wise, through persons or, failing that, ritual and symbol, and has little truck with the abstractions normally current as powers of thought, so here he says nothing of England as a 'nation', still less of a national 'destiny', nothing of the 'community'; and yet, in working his story, with all its tragic, historic and theological undertones, all its humanity and humour, and all its ritual and crowds, to the culminating ceremonial from which the prophecy flowers—as prophecy should flower from poetry—so, in making Cranmer voice for the reigns of two successive sovereigns, he has not only defined the indwelling spirit of his nation, but also outlined that greater peace, those 'olives of endless age', whose cause that nation was, and is, to serve; has thus pushed his art up to a proclamation and a heralding, lifting his whole lifework to this point, with cumulative force and authority.

The Crown of Life, 1947.

THE SHAKESPEAREAN APOCRYPHA

I

The Seven Additional Plays of the Third Folio, 1664

The Third Folio was printed in 1663 for Philip Chetwinde who, to a second issue of 1664, added seven plays that had already been attributed either to W.S. or to William Shakespeare. According to the title-page of 1664:

> Unto this impression is added seven Playes, never before Printed in Folio. viz.: Pericles, Prince of Tyre. The London Prodigall. The History of Thomas Ld. Cromwell. Sir John Oldcastle, Lord Cobham. The Puritan Widow. A Yorkshire Tragedy. The Tragedy of Locrine.

Of these *Pericles* is the only one that can seriously be considered as being, at least in part, by Shakespeare.

PERICLES

WRITTEN   1608–9.

PERFORMED   According to evidence given at a trial in Venice in 1617 Zorzi Giustinian 'went with the French ambassador and his wife to a play called *Percicles*', sometime between 5 Jan. 1606 and 23 Nov. 1608, when he was Venetian ambassador in England.
1619 May at Whitehall.[1]
1631 June, at the Globe.[2]
1660. *Pericles* appears to have been the first Shakespearean play produced after the Restoration.

[1] The Marquise Trenell on Thursday last tooke leaue of the Kinge: that night was feasted at Whitehall, by the Duke of Lennox in the Queenes greate chamber. . . . In the kinges greate Chamber they went to see the play of Pirrocles, Prince of Tyre, which lasted till 2 aclocke. After two actes, the players ceased till the French all refreshed them with sweetmeates brought on Chinay voiders, & wyne & ale in bottells, after the players begann anewe.
Letter of Sir Gerrard Herbert to Sir Dudley Carleton, 20th May, 1619.
[2] Received of Mr. Benfielde, in the name of the kings company, for a gratuity for ther liberty gaind unto them of playinge, upon the cessation of the plague, this 10 of June, 1631,—£3. 10. 0. This was taken upon Pericles at the Globe.—*Office Book.*

REGISTERED 1608. '20 Maij. Edward Blount. Entred for his copie . . . A booke called. the booke of Pericles prynce of Tyre.'

PUBLISHED 1609 Q1. 'The Late, And much admired Play, Called Pericles, Prince of Tyre. With the true Relation of the whole Historie, aduentures, and fortunes of the said Prince: As also, The no lesse strange, and worthy accidents, in the Birth and Life, of his Daughter Mariana. As it hath been diuers and sundry times acted by his Maiesties Seruants, at the Globe on the Banck-side. By William Shakespeare. Imprinted at London for Henry Gosson.' The text, the basis of later editions, is corrupt, and possibly a shortened report.

1609 Q2, 1611 Q3, 1619 Q4, 1630 Q5, 1635 Q6.

1664 F3, second issue. 'And unto this Impression is added seven Playes, never before Printed in Folio. viz. Pericles, Prince of Tyre. . . . The much admired Play, called Pericles, Prince of Tyre. With the true Relation of the whole History, Adventures, and Fortunes of the said Prince. Written by W. Shakespeare, and published in his life time.' Set up from Q6.

SOURCES The story of Apollonius of Tyre in Gower's *Confessio Amantis* (1393). Laurence Twine's *The Patterne of Paynfull Adventures*, a prose version of the story, registered 1576, reprinted 1607.

It is not clear why Blount failed to publish a Quarto after his registration in 1608. The play was not included in F1, presumably because Heminge and Condell knew that it was not all Shakespeare's work.

Acts III, IV, V are unmistakably the work of Shakespeare and contain some of his very finest poetry. There is no reason to doubt the authenticity of the three finely written brothel scenes in Act IV.

Acts I and II are clearly by another author, competent but undistinguished, who may also have written the choruses spoken by Gower—they are certainly not by Shakespeare. In 1608 George Wilkins published his prose novel, *The Painfull Aduentures of Pericles Prince of Tyre. Being the true History of the Play of Pericles, as it was lately presented by the worthy and ancient Poet Iohn Gower*, apparently based on performances of the play.

BEN JONSON
>   No doubt some mouldy tale,
>   Like Pericles, and stale
>   As the shrieve's crusts, and nasty as his fish—
>   Scraps, out of every dish
>   Thrown forth, and raked into the common tub,
>   May keep up the Play-club:
>   There, sweepings do as well
>   As the best-order'd meal;
>   For who the relish of these guests will fit,
>   Needs set them but the alms-basket of wit.

Ode to Himself written after the failure of his play, *The New Inn* (1629).

Owen Feltham   Jug, Pierce, Peck, Fly,[1] and all
       Your jests so nominal,
  Are things so far beneath an able brain,
       As they do throw a stain
  Through all th'unlikely plot, and do displease
       As deep as Pericles,
      Where, yet, there is not laid
      Before a chambermaid
  Discourse so weigh'd as might have serv'd of old
  For schools, when they of love and valour told.

An Answer to Jonson's Ode.

Anon   Amazde I stood, to see a Crowd
  Of *Ciuill Throats* stretchd out so lowd;
  (As at a *New-play*) all the Roomes
  Did swarme with *Gentiles* mix'd with *Groomes*,
  So that I truly thought all These
  Came to see *Shore* or *Pericles*.

Pimlyco or Runne Red-Cap (1609).

Dryden   Your *Ben* and *Fletcher* in their first young flight
  Did no Volpone, no Arbaces write.
  But hopp'd about, and short excursions made
  From Bough to Bough, as if they were afraid,
  And each were guilty of some *slighted Maid*.
  Shakespear's own Muse her *Pericles* first bore,
  The Prince of *Tyre* was elder than the *Moore*:
  'Tis miracle to see a first good Play,
  All Hawthorns do not bloom on *Christmas-day*.
  A slender Poet must have time to grow,
  And spread and burnish as his brothers do.
  Who still looks lean, sure with some pox is curst,
  But no Man can be *Falstaff* fat at first.

An Epilogue in *Miscellany Poems* (1684).

Rowe Mr. *Dryden* seems to think that *Pericles* is one of his first Plays; but
there is no judgment to be form'd on that, since there is good Reason
to believe that the greatest part of that Play was not written by him; tho' it
is own'd, some part of it certainly was, particularly the last Act.

Life of Shakespeare, 1709.

A. W. Schlegel *Pericles* was acknowledged by Dryden, but as a youthful
work of Shakespear. It is most undoubtedly his, and it
has been admitted into several of the late editions. The supposed imperfections originate in the circumstance, that Shakespear here handled a childish

[1] Characters in *The New Inn*.

and extravagant romance of the old poet Gower, and was unwilling to drag the subject out of its proper sphere. Hence he even introduces Gower himself, and makes him deliver a prologue entirely in his antiquated language and versification. This power of assuming so foreign a manner is at least no proof of helplessness.

Lectures on Dramatic Art, 1808.

HAZLITT The circumstance which inclines us to reject the external evidence in favour of this play [*Titus Andronicus*] being Shakespear's is, that the grammatical construction is constantly false and mixed up with vulgar abbreviations, a fault that never occurs in any of his genuine plays. A similar defect, and the halting measure of the verse are the chief objections to *Pericles of Tyre*, if we accept the far-fetched and complicated absurdity of the story. The movement of the thoughts and passions has something in it not unlike Shakespear, and several of the descriptions are either the original hints of passages which Shakespear has ingrafted on his other plays, or are imitations of them by some contemporary poet. The most memorable idea in it is in Marina's speech, where she compares the world to 'a lasting storm, hurrying her from her friends'.

COLERIDGE I think Shakspeare's earliest dramatic attempt—perhaps even prior to the Venus and Adonis and planned before he left Stratford—was Love's Labour's Lost. Shortly afterwards I suppose Pericles and certain scenes in Jeronymo to have been produced; and in the same epoch, I place the Winter's Tale and Cymbeline, differing from the Pericles by the entire *rifacimento* of it, when Shakspeare's celebrity as poet, and his interest, no less than his influence as manager, enabled him to bring forward the laid by labours of his youth.

SWINBURNE When the storm breaks upon us with the opening of the third act we know where we are. We are in the very heaven of heavens to which none can be admitted save by the grace of the greatest among poets. We are at sea, συντετάρακται δ' αἰθὴρ πόντω. Æschylus the father and Shakespeare the son are revealed as one God in the sight of all men not too impotent to perceive and too abject to adore: for the divine humanity of Shakespeare is as great as even the superhuman sublimity of Æschylus. The matchless loveliness of lightning and the matchless music of thunder give here the signal, not of war with a deathless and a more than godlike enemy of an evil and omnipotent God, but of war against a woman in travail and her newborn child. The pity of it is as great and as terrible as the terror. Every verse rings and clings in the ear for ever. 'These surges that wash both heaven and hell' give such immortal echo to the transitory harmonies of an actual storm at sea as no man but one could have translated or transfigured into articulate utterance. There is no more splendid poetry in 'Othello' or 'King Lear' than Shakespeare's magnificent prodigality has lavished on the lament of Pericles over Thaisa; on a passage in a play which he cannot have taken as seriously as all readers may see that he must have taken such masterpieces of his own creation as those which he remoulded and rewrote from end to end. . . .

That any doubt should ever have been cast upon the authorship of the scenes in which the heroic purity of Marina is tried and tested as by fire is a memorable piece of evidence that the Shakespearean criticism of the nineteenth century was by no means always superior or never inferior to that of the eighteenth. The unsavoury atmosphere is not denser in the Mytilene of 'Pericles' than the air we breathe in the Vienna of 'Measure for Measure'. Pompey and his mistress, whose very names are unclean, are certainly no decenter creatures than Boult and his employers. In 'Troilus and Cressida' there are far loathsomer passages, far noisomer allusions and expressions, than can be found anywhere in Shakespeare outside the marvellously horrible and magnificently hideous part of Thersites. The author of these two canonical plays was certainly not too prudish or squeamish to have written the certainly not more offensive passages which have offended modern readers in the apocryphal play of 'Pericles'. And who else could have written them?

Introduction to Pericles, c. 1900.

J. W. MACKAIL No thrill in the whole of Shakespeare is greater than that felt when after ploughing through Acts I and II and the chorus-prologue of Act III, the full swell of the incomparable Shakespearian verse bursts on us with: 'Thou God of this great vast, rebuke these surges.' From this point onwards, some patches of the original are left—and they are poor and flat enough—but the whole movement is Shakespearianized. Even in the scenes in the brothel at Mytilene, the supple elastic prose shows the master-hand: one has only to think of how Fletcher, for instance, would have handled them to be sure of this. The recognition scene in Act V is unsurpassed—one sometimes is inclined to say, unequalled—for sheer perfection of beauty in the whole of Shakespeare's work. . . . Speech has become music. In the printed texts you will find a stage-direction just before this passage, 'Marina sings'. It is not authentic. From the Quarto and Folio texts it is clear that the 'song' indicated is sung while Marina approaches, and not by her. It has not been preserved; and we do not miss it. 'When she speaks, she seems to sing.' The resurgence, but now with richer harmonies, of the lyrical quality which in tragedy was necessarily suppressed, is very marked throughout the Shakespearian scenes of *Pericles*, and here it culminates. At the end of this scene, after Pericles' wild cry of joy,

> Mine own, Helicanus!
>
> She is not dead!

it melts and etherealizes into that supreme lyric utterance in which a few of the simplest, shortest, most ordinary words are transfigured and become pure air and fire:

> But what music?
> My lord, I hear none.
>   None?
> The music of the spheres: list, my Marina!

In virtue of this single scene, Marina takes rank as a fourth in the triple garland
of the world, beside Miranda, Perdita, Imogen.

The Approach to Shakespeare, 1930.

THE LONDON PRODIGAL

1605 Q   'The London Prodigall. As it was plaide by the Kings Maiestie
seruants. By William Shakespeare.'

A most un-Shakespearean comedy of the reformation of the prodigal
Matthew Flowerdale by his faithful wife.

THOMAS LORD CROMWELL

1602   Registered.

1602 Q 1   'The True Chronicle Historie of the whole life and death of
Thomas Lord Cromwell. As it hath beene sundrie times pub-
likely Acted by the Right Honorable the Lord Chamberlaine his Seruants.
Written by W.S.'

1613 Q 2   Schlegel thought it one of Shakespeare's 'best and maturest works',
but nobody to-day would ascribe it to Shakespeare.

SIR JOHN OLDCASTLE

1600   Registered.

1600 Q 1   Anonymous.

1619 Q 2   'The first part Of the true & honorable history, of the Life of
Sir Iohn Old-Castle, the good Lord Cobham. As it hath bene
lately acted by the Right honorable the Earle of Notingham Lord High
Admirall of England, his Seruants. Written by William Shakespeare.'

This is one of the ten plays printed by Jaggard in 1619, some of them with
false dates. This one is dated 1600.

The play was written by Drayton, Hathaway, Wilson, and Munday, and no
doubt an attempt to profit from the popularity of Shakespeare's *Henry IV*
which had just been published.

THE PURITAN WIDOW

1607 Registered.

1607 Q 'The Puritaine Or The Widdow of Watling-streete. Acted by the Children of Paules. Written by W.S.'

A play of contemporary life, dealing with the tricks of George Pyeboard to win the widow.

A YORKSHIRE TRAGEDY

1608 Registered as 'A booke Called A Yorkshire Tragedy written by Wylliam Shakespere.'

1608 Q1 'A Yorkshire Tragedy. Not so New as Lamentable and true. Acted by his Maiesties Players at the Globe. Written by W. Shakspeare.'

1619 Q2 Another of the ten plays reprinted by Jaggard, some with false dates.

The crude story of the murder by 'Walter Calverly, of Calverly in Yorkshire Esquire' of his two young children.

LOCRINE

1594 Registered.

1595 Q 'The Lamentable Tragedie of Locrine, the eldest sonne of King Brutus, discoursing the warres of the Britaines, and Hunnes, with their discomfiture: The Britaines victorie with their Accidents, and the death of Albanact. No lesse pleasant than profitable. Newly set foorth, ouerseene and corrected, By W.S.'

Fustian stuff in the manner of Pistol.

II

Other Plays Ascribed to Shakespeare

THE TWO NOBLE KINSMEN

WRITTEN   1612–13.

PERFORMED   1619, at Court?

REGISTERED   1634 '8° Aprilis Master John Waterson Entred for his Copy
. . . a Tragi Comedy called the two noble kinsmen by John
ffletcher and William Shakespeare. vj^d.'
1646 'The 31st of October 1646. Master Moseley. Assigned over unto him
. . . all the Estate, right, title & interest which the said Mr Waterson hath in
these Playes following (viz)

> The Elder Brother, his parte.⎫ by Mr
> Mounsieur Thomas.   ⎬ Flesher.'
> The Noble kinsman.   ⎭

PUBLISHED   1634 Q. 'The Two Noble Kinsmen: Presented at the Black-
friers by the Kings Maiesties servants, with great applause:
Written by the memorable Worthies of their time;

> ⎧ Mr. John Fletcher, and ⎫ Gent.'
> ⎩ Mr. William Shakspeare. ⎭

SOURCE   Chaucer's *Knight's Tale*.

According to the title-page of Q the play was written by Fletcher and
Shakespeare, and certainly there are two authors. Fletcher's work is easily
detected by his flaccid and enervated verse and pretty pathos, and even more
easily by the tainted atmosphere that he creates. Like the Restoration wits
with whom his work was so popular, Fletcher has the vicious virtue of cor-
rupting everything that he touches. The Tilburina-like sub-plot of the gaoler's
daughter is at once laughable and revolting, and seems to be entirely the fruit
of Fletcher's fertile and perverse invention; nothing could be more unlike
Chaucer and Shakespeare. There is fine, and occasionally great verse in
Acts III and V, and Shakespeare must have been mainly responsible for
I. i. ii.; III. i.; V. i. iii.; especially for the magnificent invocations to Mars,
Venus, and Diana in V. i.

This is Shakespeare:

> Thou mighty one, that with thy power hast turn'd
> Green Neptune into purple; whose approach
> Comets prewarn; whose havoc in vast field
> Unearthed skulls proclaim; whose breath blows down
> The teeming Ceres' foison; who dost pluck
> With hand armipotent from forth blue clouds

The mason'd turrets; that both mak'st and break'st
The stony girths of cities; me thy pupil,
Young'st follower of thy drum, instruct this day
With military skill, that to thy laud
I may advance my streamer, and by thee
Be styl'd the lord o' the day;—give me, great Mars,
Some token of thy pleasure.
O great corrector of enormous times,
Shaker of o'er-rank states, thou grand decider
Of dusty old titles, that heal'st with blood
The earth when it is sick, and cur'st the world
O' the plurisy of people; I do take
Thy signs auspiciously, and in thy name
To my design march boldly.

This Fletcher:

His shackles will betray him, he'll be taken;
And what shall I do then? I'll bring a bevy,
A hundred black-ey'd maids that love as I do,
With chaplets on their heads of daffodillies,
With cherry lips, and cheeks of damask roses,
And all we'll dance an antic 'fore the duke,
And beg his pardon.

DRYDEN For what remains, the excellency of that poet [Shakespeare] was, as I have said, in the more manly passions; Fletcher's in the softer: Shakespeare writ better betwixt man and man; Fletcher, betwixt man and woman: consequently, the one described friendship better; the other love: yet Shakespeare taught Fletcher to write love: and Juliet and Desdemona are originals. 'Tis true, the scholar had the softer soul; but the master had the kinder. Friendship is both a virtue and a passion essentially; love is a passion only in its nature, and is not a virtue but by accident: good nature makes friendship; but effeminacy love. Shakespeare had an universal mind, which comprehended all characters and passions; Fletcher a more confined and limited: for though he treated love in perfection, yet honour, ambition, revenge, and generally all the stronger passions, he either touched not, or not masterly. To conclude all, he was a limb of Shakespeare.

Preface to Troilus and Cressida, 1679.

COLERIDGE On comparing the prison scene of Palamon and Arcite, Act ii. sc. 2, with the dialogue between the same speakers, Act i. sc. 2, I can scarcely retain a doubt as to the first act's having been written by Shakspeare. Assuredly it was not written by B. and F. I hold Jonson more probable than either of these two.

The main presumption, however, for Shakspeare's share in this play rests on a point, to which the sturdy critics of this edition (and indeed all before them) were blind,—that is, the construction of the blank verse, which proves beyond all doubt an intentional imitation, if not the proper hand of Shakspeare. Now, whatever improbability there is in the former, (which supposes

Fletcher conscious of the inferiority, the too poematic *minus*-dramatic nature, of his versification, and of which there is neither proof, nor likelihood), adds so much to the probability of the latter. On the other hand, the harshness of many of these very passages, a harshness unrelieved by any lyrical inter-breathings, and still more the want of profundity in the thoughts, keeps me from an absolute decision. . . .

It would be worth while to note how many of these plays (by Beaumont and Fletcher) are founded on rapes,—how many on incestuous passions, and how many on mere lunacies. Then their virtuous women are either crazy superstitions of a merely bodily negation of having been acted on, or strumpets in their imaginations and wishes, or, as in this Maid in the Mill, both at the same time. In the men, the love is merely lust in one direction,—exclusive preference of one object. The tyrant's speeches are mostly taken from the mouths of indignant denouncers of the tyrant's character, with the substitution of 'I' for 'he', and the omission of the prefatory 'he acts as if he thought' so and so. The only feelings they can possibly excite are disgust at the Æciuses, if regarded as sane loyalists, or compassion, if considered as Bedlamites. So much for their tragedies. But even their comedies are, most of them, disturbed by the fantasticalness, or gross caricature, of the persons or incidents. There are few characters that you can really like,—(even though you should have erased from your mind all the filth which bespatters the most likeable of them, as Piniero in The Island Princess for instance,)—scarcely one whom you can love. How different this from Shakespeare, who makes one have a sort of sneaking affection even for his Barnardines;—whose very Iagos and Richards are awful, and, by the counteracting power of profound intellects, rendered fearful rather than hateful;—and even the exceptions, as Goneril and Regan, are proofs of superlative judgment and the finest moral tact, in being left utter monsters, *nulla virtute redemptæ*, and in being kept out of sight as much as possible,—they being, indeed, only means for the excitement and deepening of noblest emotions towards the Lear, Cordelia, &c. and employed with the severest economy! But even Shakspeare's grossness—that which is really so, independently of the increase in modern times of vicious associations with things indifferent—(for there is a state of manners conceivable so pure, that the language of Hamlet at Ophelia's feet might be a harmless rallying, or playful teazing, of a shame that would exist in Paradise)—at the worst, how diverse in kind is it from Beaumont and Fletcher's! In Shakespeare it is the mere generalities of sex, mere words for the most part, seldom or never distinct images, all head-work, and fancy-drolleries; there is no sensation supposed in the speaker. I need not proceed to contrast this with B. and F.

Notes on Beaumont and Fletcher.

CARDENIO

1613 'Item paid to John Heminges vppon lyke warrant, dated att White-
     hall ix° die Julij 1613 for himself and the rest of his fellowes his
Majesties servauntes and Players for presentinge a playe before the Duke of
Savoyes Embassadour on the viij^th daye of June, 1613, called Cardenna, the
some of vj^li, xiij^s iiij^d.'

1653 Sept. 9. Humphrey Moseley, a stationer and collector of play-manu-
     scripts, registered
'The History of Cardennio, by Mr. Fletcher. & Shakespeare.'

1727 Dec. 13. *Double Falsehood*, a play by Lewis Theobald, was produced
     at Drury Lane.

1728 *Double Falsehood* published with the title-page:
     'Double Falshood; Or, The Distrest Lovers. A Play, as it is Acted at
the Theatre-Royal in Drury-Lane. Written originally by W. Shakespeare;
and now Revised and Adapted to the Stage By Mr. Theobald, the Author of
Shakespeare Restor'd.'

Theobald's play is based on the story of Cardenio and Lucinda in *Don
Quixote*, Thomas Shelton's translation of which had appeared in 1612, and
was probably the source of the original play, *Cardenna*. In his preface to
Double Falsehood Theobald wrote:

'It has been alledg'd as incredible, that such a Curiosity should be stifled
and lost to the World for above a Century. To This my Answer is short;
that tho' it never till now made its Appearance on the Stage, yet one of the
Manuscript Copies, which I have, is of above Sixty Years Standing, in the
Handwriting of Mr. *Downes*, the famous Old Prompter; and, as I am
credibly inform'd, was early in the Possession of the celebrated Mr. *Betterton*,
and by Him design'd to have been usher'd into the World. What Accident
prevented This Purpose of his, I do not pretend to know: Or thro' what
hands it had successively pass'd before that Period of Time. There is a
Tradition (which I have from the Noble Person, who supply'd me with One
of my Copies) that it was given by our Author, as a Present of Value, to a
Natural Daughter of his, for whose Sake he wrote it, in the Time of his
Retirement from the Stage. Two other Copies I have (one of which I was
glad to purchase at a very good Rate), which may not, perhaps, be quite so
old as the Former; but One of Them is much more perfect, and has fewer
Flaws and Interruptions in the Sense . . . Others again, to depreciate the
Affair, as they thought, have been pleased to urge, that tho' the Play may
have some resemblances of *Shakespeare*, yet the *Colouring*, *Diction*, and
Characters come nearer to the Style and Manner of *Fletcher*. This, I think,
is far from deserving any Answer.'

There is nothing Shakespearean about Theobald's play. The manuscripts that he claimed to possess have never been found, nor did he in his edition of Shakespeare (1733), although he ascribed the original play to Shakespeare, make any attempt to publish it. On the other hand, a play on the same subject was acted by Shakespeare's company in 1613; it is unlikely that Theobald knew of this record; and at about this date Fletcher was almost certainly collaborating with Shakespeare in *Henry VIII* and *The Two Noble Kinsmen*.

SIR THOMAS MORE

1844 The play of *Sir Thomas More* is in manuscript, and was first printed in 1844 in an edition prepared by the Rev. Alexander Dyce for the Shakespeare Society. There are no divisions in the original text, but it falls naturally into three sections, making seventeen scenes in all.

1871 Richard Simpson, basing his conclusions both on style and handwriting, claimed that part of the play was in Shakespeare's autograph: 'The way in which the letters are formed is absolutely the same as the way in which they are formed in the signatures of Shakespeare.'

1872 James Spedding reduced to three the pages that he thought could be assigned to Shakespeare, and wrote: 'If there is in the British Museum an entire dramatic scene filling three pages of fifty lines each, composed by Shakespeare when he was about twenty-five years old,[1] and *written out with his own hand*, it is a "new fact" of much more value than all the new facts put together which have caused so much hot controversy of late years. As a curiosity it would command a high price; but it is better than a curiosity. To know what kind of hand Shakespeare wrote would often help to discover what words he wrote.'

1911 Sir Walter Greg edited the play and showed that there were thirteen leaves in a main hand, which he called S, seven leaves of Additions in five different hands, called A-E, and notes by the Master of the Revels and censor, Edmund Tilney. Greg identified the hand of S, the writer of the original thirteen leaves, as that of Anthony Munday, and that of the Addition E as Thomas Dekker's.

1916 Sir Edward Maunde Thompson, the palæographer, after an exhaustive study of the manuscript and comparison with the six signatures of Shakespeare, pronounced that one of the additions, that of hand D, was in Shakespeare's handwriting, but added that the case for Shakespeare's authorship must rest on 'the convergence of a number of independent lines of argument—palæographic, orthographic, linguistic, stylistic, psychological— and not on any one alone'.

Addition D is three pages, making 147 lines, of Scene vi in which More pacifies the anti-alien riot of 1517.

[1] Dyce had dated the play about 1590. It is now thought to be five to ten years later than this.

1923 *Shakespeare's Hand in the Play of Sir Thomas More* was published, containing papers by A. W. Pollard, W. W. Greg, E. M. Thompson, J. D. Wilson, and R. W. Chambers.

From a study of the 'good' Quartos of Shakespeare Professor Dover Wilson was able to show that misprints must often have been the result of certain peculiarities in Shakespeare's handwriting: for instance, he must have made dangerously alike the letters *c* and *i*, *r* and *w*, *e* and *d*, *e* and *o*. He was also an old-fashioned speller for, in spite of the printers' attempts to bring his orthography up to date, old-fashioned forms have slipped into the Quartos. The author of the three pages, D, formed his letters in a way that would have led to similar misprints; he was also an old-fashioned speller.

Professor R. W. Chambers showed that the author of Addition D had a political philosophy similar to that of Shakespeare, a respect for order and rank, a sympathetic understanding of the mob, and a belief that it is susceptible to oratory.

1935 The imagery of the D Addition is typical of Shakespeare's as analysed by Dr. Caroline Spurgeon in her *Shakespeare's Imagery*.

Compare Sir Thomas More's political philosophy and imagery:

> Grant . . . that you sit as kings in your desires,
> Authority quite silenced by your brawl,
> And you in ruff of your opinions clothed,
> What had you got? I'll tell you: you had taught
> How insolence and strong hand should prevail,
> How order should be quelled; and by this pattern
> Not one of you should live an aged man.
> For other ruffians, as their fancies wrought
> With self same hand, self reasons, and self right,
> Would shark on you, and men like ravenous fishes
> *Would feed on one another,*

with that of Coriolanus:

> What's the matter,
> That in these several places of the city
> You cry against the noble senate, who,
> Under the gods, keep you in awe, which else
> *Would feed on one another?*

and with that of Ulysses in *Troilus and Cressida*:

> Take but degree away, untune that string,
> And hark, what discord follows! . . .
> Then everything includes itself in power,
> Power into will, will into appetite;
> And appetite, an universal wolf,
> So doubly seconded with will and power,
> Must make perforce an universal prey,
> *And last eat up himself.*

Professor A. W. Pollard puts the date of *Sir Thomas More* with its Additions about 1596, and writes: 'In fact Shakespeare had a technique of his own for crowd scenes, and a technique of his own in developing the argument for order and authority, and this technique, in which the same phrases and ideas tend to recur, is so peculiar to himself that when, between 2 *Henry VI* at one end of the nineties and *Julius Cæsar* and *Troilus* at the other, it is found in 1596 or a little earlier, in three autograph pages contributed to the play of *Sir Thomas More*, in a handwriting admittedly of the same kind as Shakespeare's, and unlike that of any of his known contemporaries, and with slightly archaic spellings, all of which occur sporadically in good texts of his plays, it seems pedantic to refuse to acknowledge that the contributor must have been Shakespeare himself.'

If the three pages of *Sir Thomas More* really are by Shakespeare, it is clear that a knowledge of his handwriting and spelling is an invaluable aid to the elucidation of Shakespeare's text; that, in the words of Spedding, 'to know what kind of hand Shakespeare wrote would often help to discover what words he wrote'. It is with the aid of this knowledge that Professor Dover Wilson is editing the *New Shakespeare*. (See also *Shakespeare Survey 2*, 1949.)

EDWARD THE THIRD

1595   Registered by Cuthbert Burby.

1596 Q1   'The Raigne of King Edward the third: As it hath bin sundrie times plaied about the Citie of London.'

1599 Q2

There is no external evidence of Shakespeare's authorship save its ascription to Shakespeare in the play-list of Richard Rogers and William Ley (1656). Capell reprinted it in his *Prolusions* in 1760, and described it as 'thought to be writ by Shakespeare', on the grounds that he was the only man who could have written so well in 1595. Tennyson agreed with Capell, and Swinburne disagreed.

Vocabulary and imagery tests suggest that at least part of the play may be Shakespeare's, and there are echoes in *Henry V* and *Measure for Measure*. (See the article by Kenneth Muir in *Shakespeare Survey 6*, 1953.)

THE TROUBLESOME REIGN OF KING JOHN

1591 Q1   'The Troublesome Raigne of Iohn King of England, with the discouerie of King Richard Cordelions Base sonne (vulgarly named, The Bastard Fawconbridge): also the death of King Iohn at Swinstead Abbey. As it was (sundry times) publikely acted by the Queenes Maiesties Players, in the honourable Citie of London.'

1591   'The Second part of the troublesome Raigne of King Iohn, con-
            teining the death of Arthur Plantaginet. the landing of Lewes,
and the poysning of King Iohn at Swinstead Abbey.'

1611 Q2   'The First and second Part of the troublesome Raigne of John
            King of England . . . Written by W. Sh.'

1622 Q3   'The First and second Part of the troublesome Raigne of John
            King of England . . . Written by W. Shakespeare.'

The Troublesome Reign is the source of Shakespeare's *King John*, but they
have only one line in common. Pope suggested Shakespeare and William
Rowley as joint authors (cf. *The Birth of Merlin*), Malone suggested Marlowe,
and H. D. Sykes ascribes it to Peele. Tillyard suggests that it may be a 'bad'
Quarto of an early version of *King John*.

THE BIRTH OF MERLIN

1662 Q   'The Birth of Merlin: Or, The Childe hath Found his Father.
            As it hath been several times Acted with great Applause. Written
by William Shakespear, and William Rowley.'

Rowley is generally taken to be the author or reviser. The play is certainly
not Shakespearean.

The following plays have been attributed wholly or in part to Shakespeare,
though there is neither external nor internal evidence to support their claims:

Arden of Faversham. 1592. 'The lamentable and true Tragedie of M. Arden
of Feversham in Kent. Who was most wickedlye murdered, by the meanes
of his disloyall and wanton wyfe, who for the love she bare to one Mosbie,
hyred two desperat ruffins, Blackwill and Shakbag, to kill him.' The play
has some merit, and was reprinted in 1599 and 1633, and first assigned to
Shakespeare in the edition of 1770 which was printed by Edward Jacob who
lived at Faversham.

*The Pleasant Comedie of Faire Em, The Millers Daughter of Manchester:
With the loue of William the Conqueror*. Published in 1631, but acted 'by
the right Honourable the Lord Strange his seruants' as early as 1591 when
it was ridiculed by Robert Greene.

The Merry Devil of Edmonton. Performed before 1600; registered in 1607;
published anonymously in 1608.

The Comedy of Mucedorus. Published anonymously in 1598. *Mucedorus, Fair
Em*, and *The Merry Devil of Edmonton* were bound together in Charles II's
library and labelled 'Shakespeare Vol. 1'.

Humphrey Moseley, the collector of play-manuscripts, who registered *Cardenio* in 1653, also registered:

'*Henry ye first, & Hen: ye 2d.* by Shakespeare, & Dauenport'. Robert Davenport's *History of Henry the First* was licensed for performance by the King's Men in 1624.

The History of King Stephen.
Duke Humphrey, a Tragedy.   by Will:
Iphis and Iantha, or a marriage   Shakespeare.
without a man, a Comedy.

Nothing more is known of these last three plays, though if they ever existed they may have perished when some manuscripts were 'unluckely burnd or put under Pye bottoms'.

In the play-lists of the booksellers Richard Rogers and William Ley (1656), Edward Archer (1656), and Francis Kirkman (1661, 1671) the following plays were ascribed to Shakespeare:

Anonymous: *Edward III, Edward IV,* 1 *Jeronimo, Leir, Merry Devil of Edmonton, Mucedorus.*
Beaumont and Fletcher: *Chances.*
Chettle: *Hoffman.*
Kyd: *Spanish Tragedy.*
Marlowe: *Edward II.*
Massinger: *The Roman Actor.*
Middleton: *A Trick to Catch the Old One.*
Peele: *The Arraignment of Paris.*

NOTE ON THE ORDER OF THE PLAYS

The following is an extract from Malone's *Attempt to ascertain the Order in which the Plays attributed to Shakspeare were Written*, published in Steevens's edition of Shakespeare, 1778. Malone was acquainted with Mere's *Palladis Tamia*, the early Quartos, and with 'the entries in the books of the Stationers' company, extracted and now first published by Mr. Steevens'; then, to his observations on *Love's Labour's Lost*, he adds the note:

'It is not, therefore, merely the use of rhymes, mingled with blank verse, but their *frequency*, that is here urged, as a circumstance which seems to characterize and distinguish our poet's earliest performances. In the whole number of pieces which were written antecedent to the year 1600, and which for the sake of perspicuity, have been called his *early* compositions, more rhyming couplets are found, than in all the plays composed subsequently to that year; which have been named his *late productions*. Whether in process of time, Shakespeare grew weary of the bondage of rhyme, or whether he became convinced of its impropriety in a dramatick dialogue, his neglect of rhyming (for he never wholly disused it) seems to have been *gradual*. As, therefore, most of his early productions are characterized by the multitude of similar terminations which they exhibit, whenever, of two early pieces it is doubtful which preceded the other, I am disposed to believe (other proofs being wanting) that play in which the greater number of rhymes is found, to have been first composed.'

'It is probable', he concludes, 'that the plays attributed to our author were written nearly in the following succession.'

1.	*Titus Andronicus*	1589
2.	Love's Labour's Lost	1591
3.	First Part of King Henry VI	1591
4.	Second Part of King Henry VI	1592
5.	Third Part of King Henry VI	1592
6.	*Pericles*	1592
7.	*Locrine*	1593
8.	The Two Gentlemen of Verona	1593
9.	The Winter's Tale	1594
10.	A Midsummer Night's Dream	1595
11.	Romeo and Juliet	1595
12.	The Comedy of Errors	1596
13.	Hamlet	1596
14.	King John	1596
15.	King Richard II	1597
16.	King Richard III	1597
17.	First Part of King Henry IV	1597
18.	The Merchant of Venice	1598
19.	All's Well that Ends Well	1598
20.	*Sir John Oldcastle*	1598
21.	Second Part of King Henry IV	1598
22.	King Henry V	1599
23.	*The Puritan*	1600
24.	Much Ado about Nothing	1600
25.	As You Like It	1600
26.	Merry Wives of Windsor	1601
27.	King Henry VIII	1601
28.	*Life and Death of Lord Cromwell*	1602
29.	Troilus and Cressida	1602
30.	Measure for Measure	1603
31.	Cymbeline	1604
32.	*The London Prodigal*	1605
33.	King Lear	1605
34.	Macbeth	1606
35.	The Taming of the Shrew	1606

36. Julius Cæsar	1607
37. *A Yorkshire Tragedy*	1608
38. Antony and Cleopatra	1608
39. Coriolanus	1609
40. Timon of Athens	1610
41. Othello	1611
42. The Tempest	1612
43. Twelfth Night	1614

The table opposite is based on the researches of scholars, English and German, who followed Malone. It illustrates the development of Shakespeare's verse from the comparative monotony and inflexibility of *Henry VI* to the variety and plasticity of *The Winter's Tale* and *The Tempest*, the high proportion of rhyme in the 'lyrical' period of *Love's Labour's Lost* and *A Midsummer Night's Dream*, and of prose in the histories and comedies from *Henry IV* to *Twelfth Night*. With a few interesting exceptions, the development is fairly steady, the most spectacular change being the sudden leap in the number of light and weak endings in *Antony and Cleopatra*. It should be added that the evidence of verse-tests as a means of dating the plays is accepted with caution to-day.

	Total Lines	Proportion (%) of					Number of	
		Prose to Total	Rhyme to Verse	Femin-ine Endings	Run-on Lines	Mid-line Speech Endings	Light Endings	Weak Endings
2 H. VI	3162	18	3	14	11	1	2	1
3 H. VI	2904	0·1	3	14	10	1	3	0
1 H. VI	2677	0	10	8	10	1	3	1
R. III	3619	2	4	20	13	3	4	0
C.E.	1778	14	19	17	13	1	0	0
Tit. An.	2523	2	4	9	12	3	5	0
T. Sh.¹	2649	23	4	18	8	4	1	1
T.G.V.	2294	29	7	18	12	6	0	0
L.L.L.	2789	39	62	8	18	10	3	0
R.J.	3052	15	17	8	14	15	6	1
R. II	2756	0	19	11	20	7	4	0
M.N.D.	2174	22	43	7	13	17	0	1
John	2570	0	5	6	18	13	7	0
M.V.	2660	24	5	18	22	22	6	1
1 H. IV	3176	47	3	5	23	14	5	2
2 H. IV	3446	53	3	16	21	17	1	0
M. Ado	2826	75	5	23	19	21	1	1
Hen. V	3380	42	3	21	22	18	2	0
J.C.	2478	7	1	20	19	20	10	0
A.Y.L.I.	2857	57	6	26	17	22	2	0
T.N.	2690	64	14	26	15	36	3	1
Hamlet	3931	31	3	23	23	52	8	0
M.W.W.	3018	88	6	27	20	21	1	0
T.C.	3496	34	9	24	27	31	6	0
A. Well	2966	50	19	29	28	74	11	2
M.M.	2821	41	4	26	23	51	7	0
Oth.	3316	20	3	28	20	54³	2	0
Lear	3334	20	3	29	29	61	5	1
Mac.	2108	7	6	26	37	77	21	2
A.C.	3063	9	1	27	43	78	71	28
Cor.	3410	24	1	28	46	79	60	44
Timon	2373	29	9	22	33	63	16	5
Per.²	(1140)	30	3	22	25	71³	15	5
Cym.	3339	16	3	31	46	85	78	52
W.T.	3075	28	0	33	38	88	57	43
Tem.	2064	22	0·1	35	42	85	42	25
H. VIII²	(1167)	0·6	0·5	32	39	72	45	37
T.N.K.²	(1131)	5	2	30	30	92⁴	50	34

¹ Whole play.   ² Shakespeare's part (Chambers's figures).   ³ Bradley's figure.
⁴ My figure.

Weak endings are lines ending with a monosyllabic preposition or conjunction, light endings those with other lightly stressed monosyllables.

CHAPTER IV

THE POEMS AND THEIR CRITICS

VENUS AND ADONIS

WRITTEN   1592. Mentioned by Meres, 1598.

REGISTERED 1593. April 18th, by Richard Field.

PUBLISHED   Q1. 1593. 'Venus and Adonis. Vilia miretur vulgus: mihi
flauus Apollo Pocula Castalia plena ministret aqua. London
Imprinted by Richard Field.'
It was reprinted fifteen times before 1640.

SOURCE   *Venus and Adonis* is written in the *sesta rima*, a quatrain followed by a couplet, used by Spenser in his *Astrophel*, and by
Thomas Lodge in his *Scillaes Metamorphosis*. Lodge's poem and Ovid's
Metamorphoses gave Shakespeare his theme and also suggestions for its
treatment.

DEDICATION To the Right Honorable Henrie Wriothesley, Earle of Southampton, and Baron of Titchfield

Right Honourable, I know not how I shall offend in dedicating my
vnpolisht lines to your Lordship, nor how the worlde will censure mee for
choosing so strong a proppe to support so weake a burthen: onelye if your
Honour seeme but pleased, I account my selfe highly praised, and vowe to
take aduantage of all idle houres till I haue honoured you with some grauer
labour. But if the first heire of my inuention proue deformed, I shall be sorie
it had so noble a god-father, & neuer after eare so barren a land, for feare it
yeeld me still so bad a haruest, I leaue it to your Honourable suruey, and your
Honor to your hearts content which I wish may alwaies answere your owne
wish, and the worlds hopefull expectation.

Your Honors in all dutie,
WILLIAM SHAKESPEARE.

COLERIDGE But Shakespeare had shown himself a poet, previously to his
appearance as a dramatic poet; and had no Lear, no Othello, no
Henry IV, no Twelfth Night ever appeared, we must have admitted that
Shakespeare possessed the chief, if not every, requisite of a poet,—deep
feeling and exquisite sense of beauty, both as exhibited to the eye in the
combinations of form, and to the ear in sweet and appropriate melody; that
these feelings were under the command of his own will; that in his very first
productions he projected his mind out of his own particular being, and felt,
and made others feel, on subjects no way connected with himself, except by

VENVS
AND ADONIS

Vilia miretur vulgus: mihi flauus Apollo
Pocula Castalia plena ministret aqua.

LONDON
Imprinted by Richard Field, and are to be sold at
the signe of the white Greyhound in
Paules Church-yard.
1593.

TITLE-PAGE OF THE FIRST QUARTO

force of contemplation and that sublime faculty by which a great mind becomes that on which it meditates. To this must be added that affectionate love of nature and natural objects, without which no man could have observed so steadily, or painted so truly and passionately, the very minutest beauties of the external world.

Moreover Shakespeare had shown that he possessed fancy, considered as the faculty of bringing together images dissimilar in the main by some one point or more of likeness, as in such a passage as this:—

> Full gently now she takes him by the hand,
> A lily prisoned in a jail of snow,
> Or ivory in an alabaster band:
> So white a friend ingirts so white a foe.

And still mounting the intellectual ladder, he had as unequivocally proved the indwelling in his mind of imagination, or the power by which one image or feeling is made to modify many others, and by a sort of fusion to force many into one, . . . and which, combining many circumstances into one moment of consciousness, tends to produce that ultimate end of all human thought and human feeling, unity, and thereby the reduction of the spirit to its principle and fountain, who is alone truly one.

Various are the workings of this, the greatest faculty of the human mind, both passionate and tranquil. In its tranquil and purely pleasurable operation, it acts chiefly by creating out of many things, as they would have appeared in the description of an ordinary mind, detailed in unimpassioned succession, a oneness, even as nature, the greatest of poets, acts upon us, when we open our eyes upon an extended prospect. Thus the flight of Adonis in the dusk of the evening:—

> Look! how a bright star shooteth from the sky;
> So glides he in the night from Venus' eye.

How many images and feelings are here brought together without effort and without discord, in the beauty of Adonis, the rapidity of his flight, the yearning, yet hopelessness, of the enamoured gazer, while a shadowy ideal character is thrown over the whole!

Or this power acts by impressing the stamp of humanity, and of human feelings, on inanimate or mere natural objects:—

> Lo! here the gentle lark, weary of rest,
> From his moist cabinet mounts up on high,
> And wakes the morning, from whose silver breast
> The sun ariseth in his majesty,
> Who doth the world so gloriously behold,
> The cedar-tops and hills seem burnished gold.

Or again, it acts by so carrying on the eye of the reader as to make him almost lose the consciousness of words,—to make him see everything flashed, as Wordsworth has grandly and appropriately said,—

Flashed upon that inward eye
Which is the bliss of solitude:—

and this without exciting any painful or laborious attention, without any anatomy of description, but with the sweetness and easy movement of nature. This energy is an absolute essential of poetry, and of itself would constitute a poet, though not one of the highest class;—it is, however, a most hopeful symptom, and the Venus and Adonis is one continued specimen of it.

In this beautiful poem there is an endless activity of thought in all the possible associations of thought with thought, thought with feeling, or with words, of feelings with feelings, and of words with words. . . .

> Over one arm the lusty courser's rein,
> Under the other was the tender boy,
> Who blushed and pouted in a dull disdain,
> With leaden appetite, unapt to toy;
> She red and hot, as coals of glowing fire,
> He red for shame, but frosty to desire.

This stanza and the two following afford good instances of that poetic power, which I mentioned above, of making every thing present to the imagination—both the forms, and the passions which modify those forms, either actually, as in the representations of love, or anger, or other human affections; or imaginatively, by the different manner in which inanimate objects, or objects unimpassioned themselves, are caused to be seen by the mind in moments of strong excitement, and according to the kind of the excitement,—whether of jealousy, or rage, or love, in the only appropriate sense of the word, or of the lower impulses of our nature, or finally of the poetic feeling itself. It is, perhaps, chiefly in the power of producing and reproducing the latter that the poet stands distinct.

The subject of the Venus and Adonis is unpleasing; but the poem itself is for that very reason the more illustrative of Shakespeare. There are many who can write passages of deepest pathos and even sublimity on circumstances peculiar to themselves and stimulative of their own passions; but they are not, therefore, on this account poets. Read that magnificent burst of woman's patriotism and exultation, Deborah's song of victory; it is glorious, but nature is the poet there. It is quite another matter to become all things and yet remain the same,—to make the changeful god be felt in the river, the lion and the flame;—this it is, that is the true imagination. Shakespeare writes in this poem, as if he were of another planet, charming you to gaze on the movements of Venus and Adonis, as you would on the twinkling dance of two butterflies.

Finally, in this poem and the Rape of Lucrece, Shakespeare gave ample proof of his possession of a most profound, energetic, and philosophical mind, without which he might have pleased, but could not have been a great dramatic poet.

HAZLITT Our idolatry of Shakespear (not to say our admiration) ceases with his plays. In his other productions, he was a mere author, though not a common author. It was only by representing others, that he became himself. He could go out of himself, and express the soul of Cleopatra; but in his own person, he appeared to be always waiting for the prompter's cue. In expressing the thoughts of others, he seemed inspired; in expressing his own he was a mechanic. The licence of an assumed character was necessary to restore his genius to the privileges of nature, and to give him courage to break through the tyranny of fashion, the trammels of custom. In his plays, he was 'as broad and casing as the general air': in his poems, on the contrary, he appears to be 'cooped, and cabined in' by all the technicalities of art, by all the petty intricacies of thought and language, which poetry had learned from the controversial jargon of the schools, where words had been made a substitute for things.

THE RAPE OF LUCRECE

WRITTEN   1593–4. Mentioned by Meres, 1598.

REGISTERED   1594. '9 Maij, a booke intituled the Ravyshement of Lucrece.'

PUBLISHED   1594 Q. 'Lucrece. London. Printed by Richard Field.'
             It was reprinted seven times before 1640.

SOURCES   Ovid: *Fasti II*. Chaucer: *The Legend of Good Women*. The poem is written in *rhyme-royal*, a seven-line stanza.

DEDICATION   To the Right Honourable, Henry Wriothesley, Earle of Southampton, and Baron of Titchfield.

The loue I dedicate to your Lordship is without end; whereof this Pamphlet without beginning is but a superfluous Moity. The warrant I haue of your honourable disposition, not the worth of my vntutored Lines makes it assured of acceptance. What I haue done is yours, what I hauve to doe is yours, being part in all I haue, deuoted yours. Were my worth greater, my duety would shew greater, meane time, as it is, it is bound to your Lordship; To whom I wish long life still lengthned with all happinesse.

Your Lordships in all duety.
WILLIAM SHAKESPEARE.

HAZLITT   In a word, we do not like Shakespear's poems, because we like his plays: the one, in all their excellencies, are just the reverse of the other. It has been the fashion of late to cry up our author's poems as equal to his plays: this is the desperate cant of modern criticism. We would ask, was there the slightest comparison between Shakespear, and either Chaucer or Spenser, as mere poets? Not any.—The two poems of Venus and Adonis and of Tarquin and Lucrece appear to us like a couple of ice houses. They are about as hard, as glittering, and as cold. The author seem all the time to be thinking of his verses, and not of his subject,—not of what his characters would feel, but of what he shall say; and as it must happen in all such cases, he always puts into their mouths those things which they would be the last to think of, and which it shews the greatest ingenuity in him to find out. The whole is laboured up-hill work. The poet is perpetually singing out the difficulties of the art to make an exhibition of his strength and skill in wrestling with them. He is making perpetual trials of them as if his mastery over them were doubted. The images, which are often striking, are generally applied to things which they are the least like: so that they do not blend with the poem, but seem stuck upon it, like splendid patch-work, or remain quite distinct from it, like detached substances, painted and varnished over. A beautiful thought is sure to be lost in an endless commentary upon it. The speakers are like persons who have both leisure and inclination to make riddles on their own situation, and to twist and turn every object or incident into acrostics and anagrams. Everything is spun out into allegory; and a digression is always preferred to the main story. Sentiment is built up upon plays of words; the hero or heroine feels, not from the impulse of passion, but from the force of dialectics. There is besides a strange attempt to substitute the language of painting for that of poetry, to make us *see* their feelings in the faces of the persons; and again, consistently with this, in the description of the picture in Tarquin and Lucrece, those circumstances are chiefly insisted on, which it would be impossible to convey except by words. The invocation to Opportunity in the Tarquin and Lucrece is full of thoughts and images, but at the same time it is over-loaded by them. The concluding stanza expresses all our objections to this kind of poetry:—

> Oh! idle words, servants to shallow fools;
> Unprofitable sounds, weak arbitrators;
> Busy yourselves in skill-contending schools;
> Debate when leisure serves with dull debaters;
> To trembling clients be their mediators:
> For me I force not argument a straw,
> Since that my case is past all help of law.

LOGAN PEARSALL SMITH The two long poems, composed when he was nearly thirty—that 'couple of ice-houses', as Hazlitt called them, are pedantic studies of lust, without the least evidence of a dramatic gift—they are samples of good, sound, but uninspired Elizabethan verse. Yet two signs of power they do reveal: first of all that rich sensuousness and, indeed, sensuality which is almost a necessary part of great artistic endowment and with which no art, as Goethe said, can afford to dispense;—and with this, and due, no doubt, to a richness and concreteness of imagery and sense-impressions. A sensuous love of words they also show, and a meticulous care in the choice of phrases, a love of literary polish, and a laborious effort to acquire that mastery of language, which, to the artist whose medium of expression it is, must be the first and most essential endowment—or acquirement—of all.

On Reading Shakespeare, 1933.

THE SONNETS

WRITTEN   1593–1600? Meres mentions Shakespeare's 'sugred Sonnets among his priuate friends', 1598.

REGISTERED 1609. '20 Maij Thomas Thorpe Entred for his copie vnder thandes of master Wilson and master Lownes Warden a Booke called Shakespeares sonnettes.'

PUBLISHED Q. 1609. 'Shake-speares Sonnets. Neuer before Imprinted. At London By G. Eld for T.T.'
Thorpe dedicated the volume as follows:

TO.THE.ONLIE.BEGETTER.OF.
THESE.INSVING.SONNETS.
Mr.W.H.ALL.HAPPINESSE.
AND.THAT.ETERNITIE.
PROMISED.
BY.
OVR.EVER-LIVING.POET.
WISHETH.
THE.WELL-WISHING.
ADVENTURER.IN.
SETTING.
FORTH.

T.T.

1640. 'Poems: Written by Wil. Shake-speare. Gent. Printed at London by Tho. Cotes, and are to be sold by Iohn Benson.' This edition seems to be printed from the Quarto, though six sonnets are omitted, the rest re-arranged, and so altered that the poems addressed to a man appear to be written to a woman.

Many interpretations have been put upon these *Sonnets*: among others that they are allegorical; that they are dramatic and not personal; that Shakespeare wrote them merely as exercises in the fashionable sonnet-form. Some doubt the authenticity of the order of the *Sonnets*, but assuming Thorpe's order to be approximately Shakespeare's, the main problems are the following:

Their date.
In *Shakespeare's Sonnets Dated* (1949) Leslie Hotson argues that Sonnets 107, 123, 124 were written by 1589 and, on the assumption that the group 1–126 is chronological, that 'Shakespeare completed this main group of his sonnets by 1589'. If so, neither Southampton nor Pembroke, then aged 16 and 9, can well be Mr. W. H., for if 104 is autobiographical, Shakespeare met his friend three years before writing that sonnet. In 1899 Samuel Butler dated the series 1–126 between April 1585 and December 1st, 1588.

SHAKE-SPEARES

SONNETS

Neuer before Imprinted.

AT LONDON
By *G. Eld* for *T. T.* and are
to be folde by *william Aƒpley.*
1609.

TITLE-PAGE OF THE QUARTO

Mr. W. H.

One theory is that Thorpe's dedication is addressed to the man who procured ('the only begetter') the *Sonnets* for him to publish. Sir Sidney Lee identified him with William Hall, a printer, who however did not print the *Sonnets*.

More probably the 'begetter' of the *Sonnets* means the inspirer of them. One candidate is Henry Wriothesley, Earl of Southampton, to whom Shakespeare dedicated *Venus and Adonis* and *Lucrece*.

Another is William Herbert, Earl of Pembroke. It was to him and his brother, Philip Herbert, Earl of Montgomery, that Heminge and Condell dedicated the First Folio of 1623. This, so far as we know, is the only connection between William Herbert and Shakespeare, and in any event as Herbert was not born until 1580 he was scarcely old enough to be the 'begetter' of the *Sonnets*.

Henry Willobie has been identified by some with Mr. W.H. In 1594 he published a collection of poems in dialogue called *Willobie his Avisa*, in which he tells how H.W. falls in love with the virtuous Avisa, and confides his unrequited love to his 'familiar friend W.S.' who has just recovered from a similar passion. W.S. 'determined to see whether it would sort to a happier end for this new actor, than it did for the old player'. It is just possible that Shakespeare is W.S., 'the old player', and if so that Henry Willobie is Mr. W.H.

The Rival Poet.

There are various candidates, George Chapman being the general favourite, though as far as we know he dedicated nothing in Elizabeth's reign to Southampton, to Herbert, or to any Mr. W.H.

The Dark Lady.

There have been many guesses, but nobody really knows who she was. Thomas Tyler first suggested Mary Fitton, Pembroke's mistress.

JOHN BENSON I Here presume (under favour) to present to your view, some excellent and sweetely composed Poems, of Master William Shakespeare. Which in themselves appeare of the same purity, the Authour himselfe then living avouched; they had not the fortune by reason of their Infancie in his death, to have the due accomodation of proportionable glory, with the rest of his everliving Workes, yet the lines of themselves will afford you a more authentick approbation than my assurance any way can, to invite your allowance, in your perusall you shall finde them *Seren*, cleere and eligantly plaine, such gentle straines as shall recreate and not perplexe your braine, no intricate or cloudy stuffe to puzzell intellect, but perfect eloquence; such as will raise your admiration to his praise: this assurance I know will not differ from your acknowledgement. And certaine I am, my opinion will be seconded by the sufficiency of these ensuing Lines; I have beene somewhat solicitus to bring this forth to the perfect view of all men; and in so doing, glad to be serviceable for the continuance of glory to the deserved Author in these his poems.

Epistle To the Reader, Poems, 1640.

GEORGE STEEVENS We have not reprinted the Sonnets, &c. of Shakspeare, because the strongest act of parliament that could be framed would fail to compel readers into their service; notwithstanding these miscellaneous poems have derived every possible advantage from the literature and judgment of their only intelligent editor, Mr. Malone, whose implements of criticism, like the ivory rake and golden spade in Prudentius, are on this occasion disgraced by the objects of their culture. Had Shakspeare produced no other works than these, his name would have reached us with as little celebrity as time has conferred on that of Thomas Watson, an older and much more elegant sonnetteer.

Advertisement to his edition of Shakespeare, 1793.

KEATS One of the three books I have with me is Shakspeare's Poems: I never found so many beauties in the sonnets—they seem to be full of fine things said unintentionally—in the intensity of working out conceits. Is this to be borne? Hark ye!

> When lofty trees I see barren of leaves,
> Which erst from heat did canopy the herd,
> And summer's green all girded up in sheaves.
> Borne on the bier with white and bristly beard.

He has left nothing to say about nothing or anything: for look at snails—you know what he says about Snails—you know when he talks about 'cockled Snails'—well, in one of these sonnets, he says—the chap slips into—no! I lie! this is the Venus and Adonis: the simile brought it to my mind.

> As the snail, whose tender horns being hit,
> Shrinks back into his shelly cave with pain,
> And there all smothered up in shade doth sit,
> Long after fearing to put forth again;
>   So at his bloody view her eyes are fled
>   Into the deep-dark Cabins of her head.

He overwhelms a genuine Lover of poesy with all manner of abuse, talking about—

> a poet's rage
> And stretched metre of an antique song.

Which, by the bye, will be a capital motto for my poem, won't it? He speaks too of 'Time's antique pen'—and 'April's first-born flowers'—and 'Death's eternal cold'.—By the Whim-King!

Letter to John Hamilton Reynolds, 22 Nov. 1817.

MARK VAN DOREN The poems of Shakespeare are seldom perfect. The songs
                that shoot like stars across his plays are brightest at the
beginning, and often burn out before the end. Few of his sonnets are powerful
at the finish. And neither of his narrative poems has mastered its stanza. He
seems to have been without interest in the relatively unimportant matter of
mechanical form. Perhaps he was without skill, but his possession of all other
skills renders this doubtful. It is more likely that the duty of a poem in his
mind was to be as good as possible whenever possible; once the thing had
been said, the impulse satisfied, the target hit, he could walk indifferently
away, for conclusions were arbitrary. . . .

The mechanical imperfection of the sonnets has more than mechanical
importance. It is an imperfection with respect to the virtue of evenness, if
evenness is a virtue; the sequence is radically uneven, and so is the average
sonnet within the series. Only the 71st maintains its music to the ending
syllable. The others die as poetry at the couplet; or cease somewhat less
suddenly at the close of a quatrain. Again it is as if Shakespeare had recognized that once his burden had been discharged the remainder of the journey
could be made by a substitute. Or he may not have recognized this; he may
have labored every line. What he was conscious of matters less than what he
did and what he did not do. He wrote some of the finest poetry in the language, and he did not write perfect poems. . . .

What, then, is the great poet of the sonnets writing about—unmistakably,
whether he knows it or not? He is writing about the world, the largeness of
which he has perhaps only recently discovered, and his power to release
which in a line he may be only now discovering. The sonnets are not, finally,
love poems. They are poems. Their subject is the greatest possible subject,
existence: beautiful or ugly, near or remote, celestial or domestic, and sometimes so awesome that its force can be no more than hinted at.

On a certain level Shakespeare would seem to be entertained by a variety
of subjects satisfactory in themselves. He is clearly in love with the word
'golden'. He ranges after faraway images: the lion's paws, the fierce tiger's
jaws, the long-liv'd phœnix (19). He considers the stars in their secret
influence on the shows of men (15), and he looks forward to the crooked
eclipses that foreshadow death (60). Music, the theater, the law, the state of
the times—these hold him here and there. And human life has caught his
eye: the painful warrior (25), the decrepit father who takes delight in his
active child (37), the rider of a tired horse (50, 51), the fancier of hawks and
hounds (91), the dyer's hand (111), the misery of lust (129), the transparent
deceptions of lovers (138), sick men (140, 147), the careful housewife
with her babe (143), and conscience that is born of love (151). The multi-
plicity of the world has become enormously interesting to the poet of the
sonnets.

But on another level there is a single subject. The great single subject of
the sonnets is Time, swift-footed, terrible Time that writes death on faces,
roots out the work of masonry, fades roses, brings winter after spring, and
makes in general the music to which all the world marches groaning to its
end. Under the wing of this bloody tyrant (16) Shakespeare has composed the

sonnets which the world knows best; in so far as the sequence has unity it is organized about the theme of Time's decay. . . .

By so much does the caliber of the sonnets at their best surpass in interest the crux of their occasion. At their poorest they are perhaps quite personal in the biographer's sense of that term. At their richest, when the volume of their sound suggests a deep, an almost subterranean hum of energy coming from the dark center of all the power there is, they may be personal too; but they are personal at such times rather to the artist than to the man. Shakespeare had found his subject. It was the universe, pulsing under change.

Shakespeare, 1939.

A LOVER'S COMPLAINT

WRITTEN   ?

PUBLISHED   1609 at the end of the Quarto edition of the *Sonnets*.
            1640, included in John Benson's edition of Shakespeare's *Poems*.
Shakespeare's authorship of *A Lover's Complaint* is questioned: J. W. Mackail suggests that the author was the rival poet of the *Sonnets*; J. M. Robertson that he was Chapman.

MORTON LUCE Of Shakespeare's music and painting A Lover's Complaint
            has little indeed; but of words not elsewhere used by Shakespeare it has an extraordinary proportion—quite one to each stanza, Nevertheless it has some Shakespearean elements, mostly of the unlovelier kind. I regard it as an exercise of much earlier date than any other of Shakespeare's extant poetical work; we have nothing elsewhere so utterly crude as:

> Which fortified her visage from the sun,
> Whereon the thought might think sometime it saw.

On the other hand, while these crudities and poetical imbecilities are everywhere abundant, passages—if any—that rise above the lowest Shakespearean flight are incredibly scarce; we have plenty of immature and absolutely bad work in the 'Venus' and the Sonnets; but we have also plenty of what is good, and not a little of what is excellent.

Handbook to Shakespeare's Works, 1906.

GEORGE RYLANDS The style of that little-appreciated Elizabethan masterpiece *A Lover's Complaint* shows an advance on the lyrical *Venus and Adonis* and the rhetorical *Lucrece*. As in the *Sonnets* the intelligence has more play and the climax, although it at once diverges into Elizabethanism, surpasses any effect in the other two narrative poems.

O father, what a hell of witchcraft lies
In the small orb of one particular tear!

It surpasses Donne's *Witchcraft by a Picture*.
Shakespeare the Poet (*A Companion to*
Shakespeare Studies, 1934).

THE PASSIONATE PILGRIM

PUBLISHED   1599. 'The Passionate ⁿilgrime. By W. Shakespeare. At London
            Printed for W. Iaggaɪ.... 1599.'
   Of the 21 poems in *The Passionate Pilgrim* only 5 are certainly by Shakespeare:
   1. A version of Shakespeare's Sonnet 138.
   2. A version of Shakespeare's Sonnet 144.
   3. A version of Longaville's Sonnet in *Love's Labour's Lost*, IV. iii.
   5. A version of Biron's sonnet in *Love's Labour's Lost*, IV. ii.
  17. Dumain's address to 'most divine Kate' in *Love's Labour's Lost*, IV. iii.

1612. 'The Passionate Pilgrime Or Certaine Amorous Sonnets, betweene
Venus and Adonis, newly corrected and augmented. By W. Shakespeare.
The third Edition. Whereunto is newly added two Loue-Epistles, the first
from Paris to Hellen, and Hellens answere backe again to Paris. Printed by
W. Iaggard.'

In his *Epistle* to the printer after *An Apology for Actors* (1612) Thomas
Heywood protested against Jaggard's incorporation of the two 'Loue-
Epistles' from his *Troia Britanica*, which Jaggard himself had printed in
1609:
   'Here likewise, I must necessarily insert a manifest injury done me in that
worke, by taking the two Epistles of *Paris* to *Helen*, and *Helen* to *Paris*, and
printing them in a lesse volume, vnder the name of another, which may put
the world in opinion I might steale from him; and hee to doe himselfe right,
hath since published them in his owne name: but as I must acknowledge my
lines not worthy his patronage, vnder whom he hath publisht them, so the
Author I know much offended with M. *Jaggard* that (altogether vnknowne
to him) presumed to make so bold with his name.'

THE PHŒNIX AND TURTLE

WRITTEN   1601?

PUBLISHED   1601 Q1. 'Loves Martyr: Or, Rosalins Complaint. Allegori-
            cally shadowing the truth of Loue, in the constant Fate of the
Phœnix and Turtle. A Poeme . . . By Robert Chester. . . .

Hereafter Follow Diuerse Poeticall Essaies on the former Subject; viz:
the Turtle and Phœnix. Done by the best and chiefest of our moderne
writers, with their names subscribed to their particular works: neuer before
extant. And (now first) consecrated by them all generally, to the loue and
merite of the true-noble Knight, Sir Iohn Salisburie.'
1611 Q2.

One of the fourteen 'Diuerse Poeticall Essaies' on the Turtle and Phœnix
appended to Chester's poems is attributed to Shakespeare, others to Marston,
Chapman, Jonson, and the rest are anonymous or pseudonymous.

Love's Martyr is a collection of poems by Robert Chester celebrating,
under the symbols of the Phœnix (Love) and the Turtle-dove (Constancy),
the love of his patron Sir John Salisbury and his wife Ursula, and its consummation in their daughter Jane. The poem attributed to Shakespeare,
however, is a celebration of the spiritual love of the Phœnix and the Turtle.

SIR SIDNEY LEE The poet describes in enigmatic language the obsequies of
            the Phœnix and the Turtle-dove, who had been united in
life by the ties of a purely spiritual love. The poem may be a mere play of
fancy without recondite intention, or it may be of allegorical import; but
whether it bear relation to pending ecclesiastical, political, or metaphysical
controversy, or whether it interpret popular grief for the death of some
leaders of contemporary society, is not easily determined. Happily Shakespeare wrote nothing else of like character.
                                    A Life of William Shakespeare, 1898.

JOHN MASEFIELD This strange, very beautiful poem was published in 1601.
            . . . In dark and noble verse it describes a spiritual mar-
riage, suddenly ended by death. It is too strange to be the fruit of a human
sorrow. It is the work of a great mind trying to express in unusual symbols
a thought too subtle and too intense to be expressed in any other way. Spiritual
ecstasy is the only key to work of this kind. To the reader without that key
it can only be so many strange words set in a noble rhythm for no apparent
cause.
                                    William Shakespeare, 1911.

A SELECT BIBLIOGRAPHY

Seventeenth-century Criticism
Dryden, J. *Critical Essays* (ed. W. P. Ker, 2 vols. 1900).
Rymer, T. *A Short View of Tragedy* (1693).

Eighteenth-century Criticism
Johnson, S. *Johnson on Shakespeare* (ed. W. Raleigh 1908).
Montagu, E. *On the Genius and Writings of Shakespear* (1769).
Morgann, M. *An Essay on the Dramatic Character of Sir John Falstaff* (1777).
Pope, A. *Preface to Shakespear's Works* (1725).
Richardson, W. *A Philosophical Analysis and Illustration of some of Shakspeare's Remarkable Characters* (1774).
Whately, T. *Remarks on some of the Characters of Shakspeare* (1785).
Whiter, W. *A Specimen of a Commentary on Shakspeare* (1794).

Nineteenth-century Criticism
Abbott, E. A. *A Shakespearian Grammar* (1869).
Brandes, G. *William Shakespeare* (tr. 2 vols. 1898).
Coleridge, S. T. *Coleridge's Shakespearean Criticism* (ed. T. M. Raysor, 2 vols. 1930).
De Quincey, T. *On the Knocking at the Gate in 'Macbeth'* (1823).
Dowden, E. *Shakspere: A Critical Study of his Mind and Art* (1875).
Gervinus, G. G. *Shakespeare Commentaries* (tr. 1863).
Hazlitt, W. *Characters of Shakespear's Plays* (1817). *Lectures on the English Poets* (1818).
Keats, J. *Letters* (ed. M. B. Forman, 2 vols. 1935).
Lamb, C. *On the Tragedies of Shakspeare* (1811).
Moulton, R. G. *Shakespeare as a Dramatic Artist* (1885).
Pater, W. H. *Appreciations* (1889).
Rümelin, G. *Shakespeare Studies by a Realist* (tr. 1864).
Schlegel, A. W. *Lectures on Dramatic Art and Literature* (tr. 1846).
Swinburne, A. C. *A Study of Shakespeare* (1880).
Ulrici, H. *Shakespeare's Dramatic Art* (2 vols. tr. 1876).

Twentieth-century Criticism
Abercrombie, L. *A Plea for the Liberty of Interpreting Shakespeare* (1930).
Adams, J. Q. *A Life of William Shakespeare* (1923).
Alexander, P. *Shakespeare's Life and Art* (1939).
Armstrong, E. A. *Shakespeare's Imagination* (1946).
Bailey, J. *Shakespeare* (1929).
Baker, G. P. *The Development of Shakespeare as a Dramatist* (1907).
Bethell, G. P. *Shakespeare and the Popular Dramatic Tradition* (1944).
Blunden, E. *Shakespeare's Significances* (1929).
Bradbrook, M. C. *Themes and Conventions of Elizabethan Tragedy* (1935). *Shakespeare and Elizabethan Poetry* (1951).
Bradley, A. C. *Shakespearean Tragedy* (1904). *Oxford Lectures on Poetry* (1909).

Brown, I. *Shakespeare* (1949).
Campbell, L. B. *Shakespeare's 'Histories'* (1947).
Campbell, O. J. *Shakespeare's Satire* (1943).
Chambers, E. K. *Shakespeare: A Survey* (1925).
Charlton, H. B. *Shakespearian Comedy* (1938). *Shakespearian Tragedy* (1948).
Clemen, W. H. *The Development of Shakespeare's Imagery* (tr. 1951).
Craig, H. *An Interpretation of Shakespeare* (1948).
Croce, B. *Shakespeare* (new ed. 1948).
Curry, W. C. *Shakespeare's Philosophical Patterns* (1937).
Danby, F. J. *Shakespeare's Doctrine of Nature: A Study of 'King Lear'* (1949).
Doren, M. van. *Shakespeare* (1939).
Duthie, G. I. *Shakespeare* (1951).
Eliot, T. S. *Selected Essays* (1932).
Ellis-Fermor, U. *The Frontiers of Drama* (1945).
Evans, B. I. *The Language of Shakespeare's Plays* (1952).
Fluchère, H. *Shakespeare* (tr. 1953).
Ford, B. (ed.) *The Age of Shakespeare* (1955).
Fripp, E. I. *Shakespeare, Man and Artist* (2 vols. 1938).
Gordon, G. *Shakespearian Comedy* (1944).
Granville-Barker, H. *Prefaces to Shakespeare* (5 vols. 1927–47).
Greg, W. W. *The Editorial Problem in Shakespeare* (1942; revised 1951).
Halliday, F. E. *The Poetry of Shakespeare's Plays* (1954).
Harbage, A. *As They Liked It: An Essay on Shakespeare and Morality* (1941).
Heilman, R. B. *This Great Stage: Image and Structure in 'King Lear'* (1948).
Hotson, L. *Shakespeare versus Shallow* (1931).
 The First Night of 'Twelfth Night' (1954).
Jones, E. *Hamlet and Œdipus* (1949).
Knight, G. W. *The Wheel of Fire* (1930).
 The Imperial Theme (1931).
 The Shakespearian Tempest (1932).
 The Crown of Life (1947).
 The Mutual Flame (1955).
Knights, L. C. *Explorations* (1946).
Lawrence, W. W. *Shakespeare's Problem Comedies* (1931).
Leavis, F. R. *The Common Pursuit* (1952).
Mackail, J. W. *The Approach to Shakespeare* (1930).
Madariaga, S. de. *On 'Hamlet'* (1948).
Mahood, M. M. *Shakespeare's Wordplay* (1957).
Masefield, J. *William Shakespeare* (1911; revised 1956).
Muir, K. *Shakespeare's Sources: I, Comedies and Tragedies* (1957).
Murry, J. M. *Shakespeare* (1936).
Nicoll, A. *Shakespeare* (1952).
Palmer, J. *Political Characters of Shakespeare* (1945).
 Comic Characters of Shakespeare (1946).
Parrott, T. M. *Shakespearean Comedy* (1949).
Partridge, E. *Shakespeare's Bawdy* (1947).
Pettet, E. C. *Shakespeare and the Romance Tradition* (1949).
Quiller-Couch, A. T. *Shakespeare's Workmanship* (1918).
Raleigh, W. *Shakespeare* (1907).
Rylands, G. H. W. *Words and Poetry* (1928).
Schücking, L. L. *Character Problems in Shakespeare's Plays* (tr. 1922).
Sewell, A. *Character and Society in Shakespeare* (1951).

Shaw, G. B. *Dramatic Opinions and Essays* (2 vols. 1907).

Sisson, C. J. *Shakespeare* (1955).

Sitwell, E. *A Notebook on William Shakespeare* (1948).

Smith, L. P. *On Reading Shakespeare* (1933).

Spencer, H. *The Art and Life of William Shakespeare* (1940).

Spencer, T. *Shakespeare and the Nature of Man* (1942).

Spurgeon, C. F. E. *Shakespeare's Imagery and What It Tells Us* (1935).

Stewart, J. I. M. *Character and Motive in Shakespeare* (1949).

Still, C. *Shakespeare's Mystery Play* (1921).

Stoll, E. E. *Art and Artifice in Shakespeare* (1933).
   Shakespeare and Other Masters (1940).

Strachey, L. '*Shakespeare's Final Period*' (1906) in *Books and Characters* (1922).

Tillyard, E. M. W. *Shakespeare's Last Plays* (1938).
   Shakespeare's History Plays (1944).
   Shakespeare's Problem Plays (1949).

Tolstoy, L. N. *Shakespeare and the Drama* (tr. 1906).

Wilson, F. P. *Marlowe and the Early Shakespeare* (1953).

Wilson, J. D. *The Essential Shakespeare* (1932).
   What Happens in 'Hamlet' (1935).
   The Fortunes of Falstaff (1943).

Anthologies

Ingleby, C. M. (ed.) *Shakespeare's Centurie of Prayse* (1875). Revised by J. Munro in 1909 as *The Shakespeare Allusion Book, 1591–1700*, and again revised by E. K. Chambers (2 vols. 1932).

Smith, D. N. (ed.) *Shakespeare Criticism, 1623–1846* (1916).

Boswell-Malone. *The Third Variorum Edition of Shakespeare* (21 vols. 1821) gives most of the important 18th-century essays.

Ridler, A. *Shakespeare Criticism, 1919–1935* (1936).

Current Periodicals

Shakespeare Jahrbuch (Heidelberg).

Shakespeare Quarterly (New York).

Shakespeare Survey (Cambridge), 'an Annual Survey of Shakespearian Study and Production', edited by Allardyce Nicoll, and first published in 1948.

INDEX OF CRITICS QUOTED IN
CHAPTERS II, III, AND IV

GENERAL INDEX